Infinite Divergence

Eric Pauker

For my beautiful wife Laurie.
Without your love and support this book
would never have been possible.

Contents

Introduction

This book is the first of a series that will follow Jack Campbell and his friends on their adventures into the unknown. I had been unknowingly writing small parts of this book when I was writing short stories for myself over the last couple decades. One day when reading through them all, I realized they were all part of a much larger story, thus began my work on this series. The first few books will focus on Jack and his friends as they try to resolve all the questions and problems that arise in this book. But there are many stories in this books universe besides the ones involving Jack . Many of the characters he will encounter throughout this book will be the focus of adventures in future books.

Chapter 1

The smell of barbeque would soon be all throughout the small town of Brentwood as people prepared for a town wide festival. Normally most of the town folk would be in bed this early on a Saturday morning since there wasn't much to do other than hiking, hunting and camping, but thanks to Jack Campbell that had changed, for at least one day. Brentwood was only a few hundred kilometers east of Vancouver, but being in a valley between two mountains with no highways nearby made it quite an isolated place. Being remote, the town had not changed much since it was founded in the early part of the twenty first century. Most townsfolk preferred a simpler life with minimal technology, making Jack somewhat unique since he bought every new gadget available. Jack grew up in Brentwood and still lived there, working for the search and rescue based in Chilliwack. He worked with his neighbor Fred Anderson, a helicopter pilot, to help people throughout south western British Columbia. On his time off Jack was usually helping the people of Brentwood with various community projects, such as his latest idea for the day long festival.

Being the first day of Jack's annual vacation, he had been awake since dawn, working in his garage packing some gear for a fishing trip he was going to take with his friends on the following weekend. Checking his phone he realized it was almost eight thirty in the morning. There was only half an hour before the festival would officially begin, so he quickly left to help get everything started at the town hall. Jack noticed Fred was not outside and all the curtains in his house were closed. Jack had hoped Fred would participate in the festival to maybe shake off his reputation in the neighborhood as 'that grumpy old guy' which he had built up over the last few years.

Jack walked over to his car, which was described as a 'bright red jelly bean' by Fred. The car had the latest gadgets available, including off road self driving as well as seats which reclined into beds for long trips. "Take me to the Brentwood town hall, back parking lot," said Jack as the car turned on, strapping him into the seat. On the way, he saw a few people decorating their yards with balloons and ribbons, or barbequing food for breakfast, but most homes appeared locked up. He had hoped a few more people would be participating, but since this was the first time for the festival he was not expecting everyone to be interested. As the car arrived at the town hall it pulled into the first empty spot in the parking lot before releasing Jack from the seat.

As Jack walked into the hall, he saw his friend Bob Jackson, who ran the RCMP detachment in Brentwood, talking with a group of shop owners. "Hey Jack, come here a minute!" said Bob.

"Hi Bob is there a problem?" asked Jack.

"Huh? Oh, no, no problems. I just wanted to let you know something. I know we discussed blocking the road just outside the town square, so the shop owners and their customers could still drive right up to the stores. But they've all been telling me they would rather have me block it off at the edge of town so they can use the street in front of the shops for their festival setups and avoid having sidewalks overcrowded with people."

"OK, sounds good. Do you really think that many people are going to show up? Most of the houses on the way here looked locked up. I think most people are still asleep."

"Jack old pal, you're underestimating how much the people here have been looking forward to this. I'd say at least half the people in town are helping the shop owners set up right now. That's why you didn't see much going on in the houses."

"They are? I thought we wanted to spread this all around the town," said Jack sounding confused.

"Yeah, we do. But last night when the shop owners decided they wanted to use the street for their displays and games, they organized a bunch of people to help them set up before they started at their homes."

"Well this is a nice surprise. I was only expecting people to do things in their yards. I never expected the shops to participate too."

"They wanted to add something to the festival too. They didn't think it was right not giving back to the town that keeps their businesses going. Apparently they've been planning this for the last couple weeks as a surprise."

"I don't know what to say guys. This is great."

"Think nothing of it Jack. You and the people of this town have given a lot to us. It's only right that we give something back. So I had to organize something. I knew you would think it was too much of a burden and that's why you didn't ask for anything from us," said Owen, the elderly owner of the town's grocery store.

"You are right, with all the time you spend running your shops, I would never feel right asking you to give up more of your time to help the festival."

"Ha! Give up? That's not the way I see it. We've had more fun the last couple weeks preparing for this than we have in years."

"The festival's set to start soon, what do you say we help finish with the decorations on the hall?" asked Bob.

"Yes, let's get this thing going," said Jack as they all walked outside.

Sitting outside the main entrance was a large open box with a folded banner inside. "This is the only big decoration that still needs to be put up," said Bob, "Everything else is almost done."

"It shouldn't be too hard to hang it with you, me, and a couple of your officers doing the job."

"Exactly what we were thinking," said Bob while opening a storage crate containing various sizes and lengths of rope, "A couple of my officers have already gone to get the ladders."

"You ready for the trip this weekend? I have all my gear packed up and ready to go," said Jack as he and Bob started threading ropes through the grommets on the top and bottom of the banner

"You bet! It's been over a month since we've done any camping or fishing. All this great weather's been wasted on yard work and house painting," said Bob with a chuckle, "Is Fred still coming with us? I haven't heard from him in at least a week."

"As far as I know he is. I think he's been hiding from all this festival stuff. His place was locked up tight when I left earlier"

"Aw, that's too bad. He really needs to spend some time with other people besides the two of us."

"Yeah, I know, he just doesn't seem to care about much anymore. I've run out of ideas of how to help him."

"It's been what, five years? I don't think there's anything we can do, especially since a therapist couldn't even help."

"That's because he refused to talk to them. He went to three sessions and said nothing. He thinks they're going to lock him up if he says the wrong thing."

"I didn't know that. Why didn't you tell me before?"

"He asked me not to talk about it with anyone. But I'm getting tired of him not willing to even try. Maybe we could talk to him about it during the trip."

"Let's wait until the last day when we are heading back. I suspect he won't be very happy with us and I wouldn't want to ruin the whole trip for him. After all, the trips we take are the only activity he does anymore outside of yard work."

"You're probably right. Here come your men with the ladders. Time to hang this thing up," said Jack as the officers placed the ladders against the building. Jack and Bob climbed the ladders, tying the top rope to decorating hooks under the gutters, while the officers tied the bottom rope to hooks above the windows. Once everything was securely tied they walked to the street to get a better view of the banner which read 'First Annual Brentwood Town Festival' in bright red letters on a white background with small red maple leafs scattered randomly.

"Looks real nice, the kids at the school did a great job with the design!" said Bob.

"I think it is about time to start, judging by all the people the banner is attracting," said Jack as he watched a large crowd gathering around the hall.

"All ready for your big speech? The microphone on the podium is wired into the sound system they set up last night, so everyone in town will be able to hear you."

"Ha! No one wants to hear me blabber on. I will keep it short and simple," said Jack as he headed towards the podium, pausing, "Wait, the whole town?"

"Yeah, we didn't want the people who stayed at home to miss the start, so we set up some speakers on all the street corners. Didn't cost anything extra since the system we rented is usually used in a stadium and has more speakers than we would ever need."

After stepping up to the podium Jack turned on the microphone. "Hello everyone Welcome to the first annual Brentwood Town Festival," said Jack as everyone cheered. "First I would like to thank everyone for taking the time to participate, whether at home or here downtown with the shops. Second, I would like to thank the shop owners for setting up all the displays and activities outside their shops. That was a very unexpected and pleasant surprise. Remember that this festival is happening everywhere. There will be barbeques and activities on all the streets, and I have been told that there is a street hockey game being organized at the school for later this afternoon. Well, that's enough from me, so let's get this started!" said Jack stepping down.

"Good job, nice and short. Maybe you could teach the mayor how to speak like that," said Bob.

"I am pretty sure that politicians are hardwired to talk nonstop, so it is probably a lost cause. Right now I want to check out what they set up down the street. I could see a little of it from here and it looked very interesting."

"Ok, my men and I will be stationed here for most of the day, so I'll see you later then."

Jack followed the crowd moving out of the town square towards the shops, catching up to Owen who was at the back moving slowly, "You are going to have a busy day I think. Sure you and Rose are up to it?"

"Huh, oh, hi Jack, you bet we are. Our bodies may not move as fast as they did forty years ago, but we still have the same stamina. I think you'll like what we've done. We didn't want to detract from all the work everyone is doing at their homes to feed everyone, or with the entertainment they will be providing. So we decided to set up some simple games and other things to raise money for various charities. At my shop, for example, I set up a dart board with prizes in each spot. For a donation to the monks that run the foster home a person gets one dart to throw and I match the donation amount."

"That's very generous of you, but I really hadn't intended for the shop owners to be giving away their hard earned money."

"We wouldn't stay in business very long if we did that, now would we? No, everything that we are doing won't cost us anything in the long run, and if we get enough outside visitors today it may even help draw more people here once they find out about everything there is to do in the area."

Jack and Owen wandered around the area where the shops had set up their games. Jack tried out each one, giving a five dollar donation to the charity they were supporting, saving Owen's store for last. "Well, I have not had any luck yet. Let's see how I do here," said Jack carefully throwing a dart which landed on the piece of paper on the outer edge of the board.

"Very good, looks like all those nights in the pub have paid off. Let's see what you get," said Owen as he examined the paper closely, "Ah! Something for a camping trip I think. It's a can a refried beans."

"Hah, just what I needed," said Jack with a chuckle, "I think this can go in with the donations you are collecting for the monks."

"Thanks Jack. They can always use more food."

"I think I am going to head back home now. I'll check out how everyone is doing along the way. I won't be starting my barbeque until late in the afternoon, so if you have time, drop by for some food."

"I will definitely do that. Most of the activity will have moved back up into people's homes by then."

Jack started walking back home, waving to Bob as he passed the town hall. The smell of breakfast barbequing was everywhere, making him realize he forgot to eat something before leaving home. Luckily many of the homes had food ready to eat, so by the time he arrived at his street he had eaten twice the amount of food he would have normally. Two months earlier when he had proposed the festival at a city council meeting, he had no idea so many others would be interested in participating. With everyone in town taking part either cooking, entertaining or going from house to house to see what was being offered, it was turning out better than he had hoped. Upon arriving home, much to Jack's delight, he saw Fred on his front lawn barbequing and having a great time.

"Fred! I thought you had have left the town and avoided all this 'noise and mayhem' as I seem to remember you describing it," said Jack.

Fred gave Jack a slight scowl while chuckling, "I was going to do just that! But I stayed for you. You are one of the few people who put up with me over the last few years and the least I could do is help you with your festival, but I didn't plan on enjoying myself!" Fred flipped a few breakfast sausages and chuckled again. "By the way, thanks for ruining my reputation as the grumpy guy to stay away from. Every kid in the area likes my cooking, just look at this line up!" said Fred pointing to fifteen smiling children waiting in his yard for some burgers.

"You love the attention and you know it. By the way, are you ready for the trip this weekend?" asked Jack.

"You forget who you're talking to? Have we ever gone on a camping trip where you and Bob weren't helping me to find all my stuff the morning we leave?"

"No, but I was hoping. There is always a first time."

The sound system speaker at the end of the street started humming, slowly turning into a loud buzzing noise. "Uh oh, sounds like someone shorted out something back at the town hall," said Jack. The entertainment system one of his neighbors was using to play music also started making a loud buzzing noise.

"Almost sounds like the affect of a lightning storm, but there isn't a cloud in the sky," said Fred sounding confused.

"Could be something wrong with the power grid, we might want to turn off everything until it clears up. We wouldn't want everything to burn out if there is a power surge," said Jack noticing someone down the street pointing up. He looked to where they were pointing to see a very bright object moving across the sky towards the mountains to the North.

"What the hell is that," said Jack as Fred looked up.

"A meteor?" asked Fred.

"It looks like a rocket!" said one of the children.

"There's no smoke behind it," said another child.

"I think it's going to crash in the mountains," said a third child.

Three more objects appeared near where the first one did, all heading south. The first object disappeared behind the northern mountains, followed a few seconds later by a blinding flash of light with a loud blast and shockwave. A buzzing noise similar to a swarm of bees was heard everywhere as the ground started to shake slightly. The other three objects eventually disappeared behind the mountains to the south.

"I'll call Bob and see if he knows what's happening," said Jack as grabbed his phone from his pocket, but quickly dropped it. "AHHH! Damn thing burned my hand!"

Fred looked over at his phone that was lying on a nearby table with smoke coming out the side, "Looks like mine is ruined too."

"It is times like this I am glad I kept my old land line," said Jack as he headed towards his home. Entering his home he noticed everything electrical was off. He tried turning on a few things but there was no power. He picked up the old land line but it was dead too. Anything with batteries was too hot to touch except for a radio which he took. When he went outside everyone was talking of similar problems with burnt out phones and no power.

"No power in the house. It looks like the whole area is out. Everything with a battery is ruined except this old radio," said Jack. He fiddled with the radio but it wasn't picking up anything. "Bob is working at the town hall today taking care of crowd control. I'm going to head down there and see if he can help."

"You may have a bit of a walk," said Fred as he pointed to various cars parked on the street with smoke coming from under their hoods, "Looks like they were damaged too."

"I left my car at the hall anyway, but I don't plan on walking," said Jack as he walked to the storage shed in his back yard, took out an old bicycle and started pedaling. The trip took half an hour but would have been faster if everyone had not stopped him to ask what was happening. During the ride dozens more objects appeared in the same area in the sky, flying off in various directions. All of them disappeared on the horizon without any flashes of light.

Jack found Bob standing at the podium telling the worried crowd to remain calm.

"Bob! What's happening?" asked Jack.

"We don't know yet. But when we do I will let everyone know."

"We? You have been able to talk with someone outside the town?"

Bob showed Jack his handheld CB radio while smiling. "Yup, whatever that blast was, it didn't affect this old hunk of junk. The batteries got extremely hot though, hot enough to make the cover soften. Look!" He turned the radio around to show an indentation from his thumb on the battery cover. "Right now we are asking everyone to treat this as a power outage and continue enjoying the festival while we wait for the power to come back on."

"Let's go into the station for a minute, I could use your help," said Bob, walking to the police station next to the hall. Bob closed the door as they entered. "OK, enough with the BS, I didn't want to panic anyone out there but you and I know this is not just a power outage cause by some meteors like most of the people out there believe.

"Have we been attacked by someone? Are we at war? This all looks like the same effect as the EMP from a nuclear blast," said Jack.

"The truth really is that we don't know what is happening. If it was a nuke then the blast north of here should have leveled the town. All police stations have these old hand held radios to use in emergencies like this. We have been able to communicate with most stations in the region and they are all experiencing the same effects. Whatever this is, it has happened in Canada and the U.S."

"Have many people been hurt or killed? How many cities have been hit by these things?" asked Jack sounding worried.

"None! So far every one of these things has landed far outside of any populated areas. From what we can tell the one that landed north of here is about ten kilometers away."

"Has anyone gone to check it out?"

"Yeah," said Bob with a sigh, "We had some old dirt bikes we seized a few years ago that still worked, no complicated electronics to burn out on those things. I had a couple officers ride them to the logging road since it passes near the area. But their radios cut out when they got close to the road. That was twenty minutes ago and we haven't heard from them again."

"What can I do to help?"

"Go back to your neighborhood and try to keep everyone calm. Everyone in town looks up to you and if you keep calm and cool, hopefully no one will panic and cause more problems. If we need you for more, I will come and get you."

"Sure thing," said Jack as he headed back outside.

On the ride back Jack reassured everyone who wanted to talk about what is going on. He convinced them it was just a power outage, telling them to relax and continue enjoying the festival. When he arrived at his house he was pleasantly surprised to see that Fred was keeping the children calm with entertaining stories while barbequing more food.

"Jack!" said Fred, "I was just telling everyone about the time I had to rescue you from..." Before he could finish the sentence the ground started shaking again, followed shortly by a noise from the north sounding like a cross between a swarm of bees and static electricity. "What in the world!"

"Probably the two officers that went north taking care of whatever is causing the power problems. Bob told me he sent them up there when this all started," said Jack changing to a whisper, "Just play along, we don't want to panic anyone."

Fred gave Jack a brief worried look, quickly changing to a smile as he turned to the children, "Alight then! Who is ready for another burger?"

After getting burgers for everyone, Fred and Jack walked out of earshot of the children. "Alright Jack, what's really happening?"

"No one knows," said Jack, telling Fred everything he has learned.

"You think those two cops are dead?" asked Fred.

"I just don't know. But let's not assume the worst. For all we know that noise was the result of them destroying whatever caused this."

"Or the other way around"

"Come on Fred, we need to stay confident and calm. No need to make everyone else panic"

"Yeah, I know. It's just that this day was going so well. First time since Joan died that I've felt useful or needed by anyone outside of work."

"You are still needed old buddy. You were keeping those kids over there calm with your stories, and that put their parents at ease because their children were not frightened. You may have tried to be 'a grumpy old man' the past couple years, but no one around here believed it. We've known you too long."

"Yeah, you're right. I was just letting my own fears get the better of me."

As the ground continued shaking, the buzzing noise started getting louder. A glow appeared from behind the mountain to the North as a wall of flickering light appeared at the top of the mountain. It slowly moved down towards the edge of town, causing the trees to sway as though a strong wind was blowing.

"Oh shit," said Fred, "This is definitely not good."

"We need to keep it together and make sure everyone keeps calm. A town full of panicked people is the last thing we want."

"Good luck with that," said Fred pointing to the north at the lower slopes of the mountain where the town starts, "Look at the people running down the streets! When everyone here notices they are going to go nuts too."

"Crap! They should be getting inside their homes not running. Damn, everyone has noticed!" said Jack, "People, please listen! Panicking and running will only get everyone hurt. Please go into your homes and wait for whatever this is to pass over us."

"Screw that! I'm not waiting around for whatever that is to kill me," said someone in the street.

"People please! There's no reason to believe it will hurt us. Look at the mountain; it isn't doing any damage to the trees," said Jack.

A few people started running south towards the town center, followed shortly by almost everyone else.

"People, please stay, you are only going to get hurt if you panic!" said Jack, but everyone ignored him.

"I'm with you Jack. You've always had the cool head in an emergency. Those people can't run forever and whatever that light is, it doesn't look like it is slowing down or fading so it will eventually catch up to them." said Fred.

"Let's get in my house and wait for it to pass over us."

Jack and Fred entered the house noticing everything that ran on electricity was turning back on.

"Hmmm, maybe those cops did fix something," said Fred.

"I wouldn't be too sure of that. Look at the phone," said Jack.

They watched Jack's old landline phone as it started buzzing and sparking. "Let's get into the garage, the only thing in there is my fishing and camping gear, nothing to electrocute us," said Jack.

As they walked briskly to the garage, sparks started shooting out of all the electronics in the house. The buzzing noise from outside combined with the noise coming from in the house was deafening, making them cover their ears. After a few minutes the light wall started to pass through the house.

"Awe crap!" said Fred.

"Stay calm buddy! We'll make it through this. Run through it."

The light slowly moved through the garage, looking like a sheet of glowing threads blowing in a light breeze. The threads moved independently of each other with little lights moving down each one towards the ground. As Jack and Fred ran through it, the hairs on their heads and arms stood on end when the little lights hit them.

"I feel like there are ants crawling all over me!" said Fred.

"Me too, I think it's a big static charge."

"That was horrible. I still feel something crawling on my skin," said Fred, flopping against the garage wall.

"It's just a really large static charge," said Jack while looking at the hair on his arms which was now standing on end.

Since the light was moving slowly through the garage, Jack decided to get a closer look.

"Careful! Don't get too close."

"Don't worry I'm not going to touch it. I just want a closer look."

As Jack got close to an electrical outlet on the wall, an arc of electricity jumped from his arm to the outlet, followed by an arc between his back and Fred's leg. Both men yelled out in pain, dropping to the ground.

"Still think it was better to not run after being electrocuted?" said Fred with a groan as he sat up.

"Better than being trampled by a mob of panicking people. Look, it has passed through the wall, it's probably in the kitchen now," said Jack also groaning.

Jack got up and walked towards the door to the house.

"I don't think that's a good idea"

Jack opened the door, letting a little black smoke billow into the garage along with the smell of burning plastic. "I don't see any flames."

As the two men slowly entered the house they saw the plastic case on the phone had melted and was smoking. In the kitchen they saw the light near the back wall.

"Looks like it's almost passed through," said Jack.

"Look at your entertainment center. Don't think you'll be watching any movies on that again."

They stared at the entertainment center for a moment. The plastic casings on the electronics had warped and partially melted. Some of the circuit boards were exposed with extensive charring. Anything than ran on electricity in the house was in a similar state.

"Looks like everything's been fried, let's check out your place," said Jack.

Exited through the kitchen door they walked over to Fred's house, entering through the door to his kitchen.

"Not as bad over here, I don't collect as much electronic crap as you do," said Fred.

"It got all your lights though," said Jack, picking up a small lamp. What remained of the socket and bulb disintegrated, causing the shade to fall off.

"I think for the cost of your entertainment center I could replace every lamp in here twenty times over," said Fred.

"Let's go back outside and see if everyone that stayed is OK. The smell of burning plastic is starting to make me sick."

As they left the house through the front door, they saw three other families outside their houses. All appeared frightened, but no one looked hurt.

"Are you two OK?" asked one of the neighbors, Bill James.

Jack and Fred walked over to Bill with the other neighbors following.

"A little shaken, but none the worse for wear, are all of you OK?" asked Jack.

"A little sore from whatever that light was, but I think we're fine," said Bill.

"Good, all of you should stay near your homes and wait for help. Open the windows to let out the smoke. Take anything that is still smoking or hot and put it in your yards in case it starts burning. Some of you should also check the rest of the homes on the block to make sure there is no one hurt and nothing is burning. I am going back to Bob, he's going to need some help right now," said Jack.

Jack turned, heading back towards his house to get his bike.

"I'm going with you," said Fred sternly.

"Are you just going to jog behind me?"

"Not when you have three old bikes in your shed I won't."

"Forgot about those," said Jack as they walked to the shed, "Take your pick."

Fred examined the bikes, choosing the one that didn't have a seat missing. "Other ones might be a tad uncomfortable," said Fred while checking the tires. One tire was a little flat so he grabbed a tire pump, adding air before they left.

The trip only took a few minutes since no one was around to stop them for a talk. Everyone who stayed in town had gathered in front of the police station.

As Jack and Fred approached they were greeted by Bob who was standing outside with everyone.

"Jack, Fred!" said Bob "Am I glad to see you two. My men and I have our hands full trying to keep everyone calm and bandaging up some minor injuries, so I need your help."

"What can we do?" asked Jack.

"I need someone to go up to the woods and try to find my two officers. We need them back here now. I still haven't heard from them and I doubt I will after what that... that... whatever it was did to all out equipment. Your bikes will have to do for transport. As I told you earlier, the last thing I heard from them was they were near the logging road."

"We're on it," said Jack.

"We'll find them," said Fred.

"We'll need to pick up a few supplies from my place," said Jack as they got on their bikes.

They stopped at Jack's garage to take his camping backpack. "All loaded up for the trip next weekend. We might need these too," said Jack picking up a couple hunting knives and a rifle, strapped one knife to his leg. "Here, you take the rifle and a knife. I'll carry the backpack. If any bears attack I'll just lie face down while you take care of them."

"Them!" said Fred, "Gee, thanks. I'll have to return the favor."

They took the main road that went to the north part of the town, eventually turning into a logging road. Everything looked overgrown in the northern area of the town with the lawns looking like they had not been tended to in a long time.

"Wow, I haven't been through this area in a few years, it sure has gone downhill. Look at the overgrown lawns, and all the weeds growing in the cracks in the pavement," said Jack.

"I was here a couple months ago. It wasn't like this. Too many people going camping and ignoring their yards if you ask me."

"Can you blame them? This has been a great summer so far and after having five in a row where it rained most of the time I think anyone would take advantage of it."

"True, but they could have at least hired some kids to mow their lawns every week. Maybe that way they wouldn't be spending all day running around our neighborhood making noise."

"Don't know where you got that grumpy old man reputation from," mumbled Jack.

"What was that?" asked Fred.

"I said we're almost at the logging road."

The gravel logging road was quite rough, bumpy and overgrown, appearing to have not been used in quite a while.

"I thought Bob told you he sent a couple cops up here. The road doesn't look like anyone has used it for a long time," said Fred.

"He did. He told them to use this road. He was sure they went this way, but I don't see any signs of dirt bikes around here. The hiking trails to the east would have been much harder to maneuver, and they don't run as close to the area as this road does," said Jack, looking around the area, feeling confused and pausing to think. "He did say their radios cut out when they got close to the logging road, maybe they had bikes problems too. But I don't see the bikes anywhere around here. Let's keep going, even if they had problems they would not have stopped, they must be somewhere up ahead."

Chapter 2

The old logging road was filled with pot holes overgrown with weeds, making the ride slow and bumpy since they were difficult to see. The buzzing noise from the light wall slowly faded away as Fred Jack moved north, being replaced by a quiet low frequency hum. Other than a few trees with some small broken branches, there was no visible damage from the earlier shock wave.

"I don't know how much longer I can take these potholes, I must have hit every one so far," said Fred.

"I don't think we need to ride any further, look up ahead," said Jack, stopping his bike.

Fred saw part of a dirt bike sticking out of the bushes ahead on the side of the road, "How did they get them up here without kicking up gravel? Our bikes have made an obvious path through the weeds. Theirs should have done the same."

"Not sure," said Jack, walking towards the dirt bikes, "What the heck! Looks like weeds have grown around the spokes and handle bars. These can't be the bikes they took up here. These ones have been here a while."

"I don't know about that," said Fred, picking up a damaged CB radio, "Isn't this the same kind of radio that you said Bob was using?"

"It sure looks like it," said Jack as he examined the radio, "Yeah, it is. Look, there is an ID plate riveted to the side, just like the others used by the police. But if these are their bikes, why are they overgrown with weeds? They've been gone for a couple hours and this looks like a couple weeks of growth."

"I don't like this, something feels very wrong here"

"I know, it doesn't feel right to me either, but our job is to help people in need, and I have a feeling those two officers need help."

"I feel much safer when I am in a helicopter and can go get extra help quickly," said Fred.

"Yeah, me too," said Jack as he looked around, "Let's head up this way to the top of this hill and see if we can locate where the officers went and where that object crashed," he said while pointing to a bare hilltop to the east of the road.

Fred took out the rifle as they started towards the hill. "I don't hear any animals just that damn hum," said Fred when they were halfway up the hill.

"Hmm, me neither. I don't recall hearing or seeing any animals for a while. There was one squirrel near the dirt bikes when we approached, but that was it... Looks like we're about half way up, the sooner we find those officers the better. I am starting to feel real uneasy in this area."

Reaching the top of the hill, looking down the other side they were confused and unsettled by what they saw.

"My god, what the hell is that?" asked Fred, "What is it doing?"

Jack was initially speechless but eventually said, "I... I'm not. My binoculars! They're in the left side pouch. Could you get them for me?"

"Sure," said Fred, fumbling for them while trying to watch the scene below, "Here they are."

Below the two men a very bright object was hovering about twenty meters above the ground, looking like a large ball of light, too bright to make out any shape. Everything within one hundred meters of it was gone, only bare rock and dirt remained. Six cylindrical stone pillars roughly three meters tall and one meter wide surrounded it with newly dug tunnels behind each one. Strings that appeared to be made of light were moving around the pillars then travelling through the tunnels as well as between the tops of the pillars and object. To the north east there was a large bare area which might have once been a small lake.

"I don't see anyone down there," said Jack as he scanned the area, "There is a cabin up the side of that hill to the east, maybe the officers went... wait, there's something moving down there... three large wolves. They are wandering around the outskirts of the area. They appear to be staying in the area between the northern pillar and tunnel. If we head down the south-east slope of this hill and stay in the bushes we should be able to go around the cleared area and get to the cabin without them noticing us."

"How do you know that thing won't see us and zap us into dust? It looks like it didn't have any problems clearing the forest below."

"If it didn't want anyone around it, the cabin would have been destroyed just in case there was someone in it, and it left those wolves untouched. It also appears to be digging tunnels, leading me to believe it cleared the forest for some reason other than just killing everything."

"Like what?" asked Fred.

"Don't know. But that doesn't mean I think it's safe to get close to it. We need to stay in the bushes and out of that cleared area, so we can get to the cabin and help anyone who may be in there."

16

"I hope you're right, let's get this over with and get out of here," said Fred.

"You'll get no argument from me on that."

The two men moved as quietly as possible down the side of the hill staying out sight of the object as much as possible. When they reached the bottom they stayed amongst the trees whenever they could, crawling through the underbrush when there were no trees to cover their movement. As they passed near the pillar on the south edge of the cleared area, they paused for a moment.

"Look at that," said Jack in amazement, "It's not stone, it looks some sort of concrete. Look in the tunnel over there, the strings of light are digging out the material and bringing it back to the pillars."

"Amazing, they are separating all the materials too, look there," said Fred pointing to the area in front of the tunnel, "piles of dirt and clay."

"The object must be supplying what can't be found in the ground."

Jack noticed the wolves he saw earlier appear from behind the pillar. "Those wolves are behind the pillar," he whispered while pushing Fred to the ground.

"I thought there were three?" asked Fred peering through the shrubs.

"There are, these may be two of them, or there may be more than the three I saw. Let's get to that cabin; I'll feel a lot safe with a closed door between us and those wolves."

They crawled through the brush towards some trees then to the cabin. The main door of the cabin was cracked with its top hinge broken off and a window on the second floor was broken. While Fred watched for the wolves, Jack carefully pushed the door open.

"What a mess," said Jack who now saw most of the furniture was smashed. Moving inside, he saw two bullet holes in the wall near the door. "Over there," said Jack , pointing to a pile of broken furniture.

"What is it?" asked Fred.

"Part of a shirt sleeve from a police uniform," said Jack while pulling out a piece of bloodied cloth from the mess.

"Awe shit! Let me block up the door then we can check the rest of the cabin."

"I'll help," said Jack as they both push the door closed, piling broken furniture in front of it.

They searched through the remaining rubble on the ground floor finding a few blood stains. The only damage in the kitchen was a broken chair. Jack took a quick look out the back door, which was already open, but saw no sign of the officers so he closed it. He decided to take off the backpack, leaving it on the kitchen table, while they checked the rest of the cabin. As they walked quietly up the stairs in the back, the sound of glass shattering outside was heard. They paused a moment, listening, but heard nothing else so continued on. Entering the master bedroom at the top of the stairs they found a similar mess to the one downstairs. Jack began looking through broken furniture while Fred checked the master bathroom. Fred took a quick look around but found no damage or anything unusual.

"Found something," said Jack, picking up an old gun from under the rubble. "Has some bullets in it. Looks really old. Hope it works."

The floor in the hall outside the bedroom creaked, causing both men to look towards the doorway. They saw a large limping wolf which didn't notice them until it turned its head towards the room. The wolf growled loudly while jumping across the rubble towards Jack, who fell sideways trying to avoid it while aiming his gun. The wolf managed to bite down on Jack's leg before he took a shot at its head. The bullet hit one of the wolf's eyes resulting in a shower of sparks shooting from the eye socket with the wolf being knocked backwards into the wall. The two men noticed the leg that it was limping on had a large gash, exposing what looked like a metal post instead of a bone. Fred aimed his rifle at the wolf's head, pulled the trigger, but the bullet ricocheted off the head leaving a large dent in a now exposed metal plate. The wolfs growled again, this time with a mechanical undertone to the sound, then began lunging at random spots on the wall.

"What. The. Hell," said Fred extremely confused.

Jack and Fred were stunned motionless until they heard the other wolves growling while trying to break through the front door. They ran out of the room, heading downstairs towards the back door. Jack grabbed the backpack as they ran through the kitchen but didn't put it on.

"Quick, up the hill into the denser bush behind the cabin!" said Jack.

When they had run far enough into the bush to no longer see the cabin, Jack collapsed on the ground. Fred looked around, listening for anything that might have followed them, but sensed nothing.

"What the hell was that thing? Your leg OK?" asked Fred.

"It's not broken, but I'm bleeding quite a bit," said Jack as he searched through the backpack for his first aid kit. Using a pair of scissors to cut open the blood soaked pant leg they could see quite a few gouges on his lower leg, but nothing deep enough to need stitches.

"Looks like you'll live. Another second and it probably would have torn your leg off. I'll clean it up and bandage it for you," said Fred.

"We didn't get a chance to look through the whole cabin for the officers"

"If those other wolves are the same as the one in the cabin they would probably kill us before we could take one of them out."

"You got that right," said a voice somewhere in the bushes.

They both look in the direction the voice came from while Fred grabbed the rifle.

"You won't need that," said the voice as one of the missing police officers emerged from the bush. "Jim Franklin. I assume you have been sent to find me and my partner."

"Yes, I'm Jack Campbell and this is Fred Anderson. Where's your partner?"

"Those things got him! George never had a chance," said Jim angrily.

"George Johnson? I know him. Did those wolves kill him?" asked Jack.

"I don't know what they did to him." said Jim sounding unsettled, "We got here shortly after the blast and walked down to the clearing to get a better look at that ball of light. As soon as we entered the cleared area two of those things came after us. We ran to the cabin and locked the door but they smashed through it quite easily. George shoved me out of the way as one grabbed him by the arm, dragging him underneath the ball of light. Then a bunch of those light things wrapped around him and he was gone. I managed to shoot the second one in the leg before it saw where I was but that only seemed to slow it down a little. I got upstairs to the bedroom before it caught up. I kept shooting at the thing but it dodged so fast I couldn't hit it again. The only reason it didn't get me was because I managed to push a bookshelf on top of it. That gave me enough time to run out the back door. I ran for what seemed an eternity before I collapsed. I guess it didn't see which way I went because I never saw it again."

"I don't know what we can do here. This is way beyond us to handle. We need to get back to Bob and figure out a way to get some military help," said Jack.

"Shouldn't be too hard, they have the same kind of handheld radios we do," said Jim.

"He doesn't know," said Fred.

"Know what? Did something happen to Bob?"

"No, Bob's fine, it's what that wall of light did," said Jack.

"What wall of light?"

"You didn't see it? It must have happened after you took off into the woods," said Jack as he explained everything that happened after the wall of light swept through the town.

"Did we do that? Did we cause it to happen?" asked Jim.

"I don't know the answer to that, but don't blame yourself. If it happened because you came up here then there was no way to stop it, because someone needed to come up here and find out what was going on," said Jack.

"We better get going Jack. We only have a few more hours of daylight and I don't want to be stuck out here at night with those things running around. If we cut across that dried out lake we saw earlier we can avoid the wolves and that light," said Fred.

"I don't think it will be easy to cross. When George and I got up here there was still water in it. That ball of light appeared to be draining it. So the lake bed will probably be a thick layer of mud right now," said Jim.

"What did it do with all the water?" asked Jack.

"No idea. Those light things were strung out from it to the lake and the water was draining up into the ball."

"Holy crap!" said Jack and Fred in unison.

"OK then, we'll have to go back the way we came. But we'll go farther into the woods this time to completely avoid being seen by anything," said Jack.

The three men headed back towards the cabin. As they got closer they could hear growling and crashing noises coming from inside.

"There's someone else in trouble in there," said Jim.

"No, it's just that wolf you shot in the leg. I shot out one of its eyes out and Fred got it in the side of the head. Probably broke whatever makes it run because it's just jumping at the walls now," said Jack.

They travelled in a wide arc around the cleared area, slowly making their way to towards the logging road, with Fred complaining about the thick brush all the way. When they got back to the bikes they stood stunned for a moment at what they saw. The weeds on the road had doubled in size and the bikes were now completely entangled.

"What happened here?" asked Jim, "This road was clear when we came up here."

"It was overgrown when we got here," said Jack.

"Just not this much," said Fred.

"We'll have to walk. Even if we had three bikes they would be slower than walking in this mess," said Jack while checking the bikes.

They started walking back to the town, slowly picking up the pace as they went. As they approached they saw that the plants in town had also grown, but not doubled in size like they did further up the road. About half an hour before sunset they reached the town center, where Bob was tending to the remaining townsfolk.

"You found them! Wait, where's George?" asked Bob as they approached.

"We need to talk," said Jack as he walked to towards the police station. They entered and he explained everything that had happened up to the point when they found Jim, who explained everything that happened to him and George while Bob's face slowly paled

"We... we gotta get everyone out of this town. It's not safe here anymore, but I don't know where half the people are. The ones that ran out of the town earlier never came back," said Bob.

"We have to think about the people that stayed. The others could have run anywhere and we don't have the people needed to track them down right now," said Jack.

"I know. I'm just rambling, too much happening too quickly. I took this job because it this supposed to be a nice quiet, out of the way place where nothing happens." Bob sighed as he thought for a moment, "Some of the people that didn't run went back to their homes, but most wanted to stay here so we have set up the town hall as a temporary shelter. My men are going to build a few camp fires to light up the town center tonight and we have enough food from the festival to feed everyone for a while. Tomorrow morning I'll get some of my officers to round up the people who went home then we can head to Chilliwack. It's a one hour drive by car, so we will probably spend most of the day walking there. We will need to gather up enough bicycles for the children and everyone else if possible, that would speed up the trip considerably. There are a few injured and elderly who won't be able to ride a bike, so we will need to get the horses and carts from my brother in laws ranch just outside town. He is in Mexico and left the keys to all his buildings with me."

"Those horses know me and Fred, so we can go get them at first light."

"Sounds good to me," said Bob tossing the keys to Jack, "Jim, I'll put you in charge of rounding up the people that went home. There are only five families that left, but there may be more who didn't run in the first place."

"There were three on my street and we didn't see any up the main road earlier."

"Good, that eliminates checking at least half the houses."

"I'm willing to check all the houses tonight. I can make torches using drop cloths, paint sticks and linseed oil from the hardware store," said Jim.

"Only if you take a couple other officers with you and at the first sign of anything unusual you head back here on the double."

"Understood," said Jim as he got up to leave.

"Well, if we're staying the night, let's get outside and help build the fires. I don't relish spending the night here, but it sounds a lot better than walking through the middle of nowhere in total darkness," said Jack.

"The fires have already been set up. But I could use your help gathering supplies. Owen has offered the canned and dry food from his store for the trip. He already gave us all the food in his coolers to cook after the power went out, but it will only be good for another day at most. He and his wife are too old to gather it all by themselves, so if you two could help them I am sure they would be grateful."

"We'll get right on it," said Jack and Fred in unison. They glare at each other, "Stop that!" they said in unison again.

"Ok," said Bob with a chuckle, "I'll be outside planning tomorrow's trip with my officers."

The sun had set behind the mountains to the west but the sky was still clear and bright. Jack and Fred walked quickly to the store, finding Owen trying to push a shopping cart filled taller than him over a bump in the sidewalk outside the stores entrance.

"Here, let us help," said Jack as he lifted up the front of the cart pulling it over the bump.

"Thank you so much. Rose and I are not used to moving this many goods at one time," said Owen.

"No need to worry Owen. We will help you get everything over to the town hall so it's ready to load up in the morning."

"That is great news. There are only five shelves to unload, and everything else in the back is still packed in boxes on three palettes. I have two palette movers so this won't take long with you two helping," said Owen.

With Jack and Fred's help they were able to finish moving all the supplies before the twilight ended, so they joined some townsfolk gathered around one of the camp fires.

Jack, Fred and Bob spent the next hour discussing the next day's trip, how much food to bring, and who would be responsible for what. Since Jack and Fred had already volunteered to get the horses they decided to also take care of them. Bob and Jim would scout ahead of the convoy to clear any vehicles that might have blocked the road, while the rest of the officers would be interspersed with the group to help anyone in need. There was only one road out of the town which eventually met up with two other roads at a gas station outside the town of Hope. One road led directly to the Trans Canada highway, but Bob had talked to officers from Chilliwack earlier, finding out the highway was blocked with cars that were damaged by the shockwave. The other road, which they decided to take, was also a highway but in reality it was just a wide country road that wound through the mountains and farmland to a town north of Chilliwack. From there they would take various roads that passed through more farmland then to the city.

Jack leaned back stretching his arms while looking up, developing a worried look on his face.

"What?" asked Bob as he looked up.

They saw streams of barely visibly pulsating light stretching across the dark sky in various directions. They all originated from the area where the object landed earlier in the day, where a bright glow was now pulsating.

"Do you think they were in the sky earlier but we didn't notice them because of the daylight?" asked Fred.

"Maybe, but we were pretty damn close to that thing and I didn't see anything like those coming out of it," said Jack.

While discussing what the streams could be, they saw Jim coming down the main street with many of the families that went home.

"Good work Jim. Is this everyone?" asked Bob as Jim arrived.

"No, three families refused to leave their houses. Insisted it was safer staying here even after I told them about that thing. I told them our plans and asked that they rethink how they will survive without any food, electricity or water and..." Before Jim could finish, a loud crackling noise came from the sky as the streams lit up like the sun. Pulses of light were seen moving down the streams away from where the object was located.

"This is definitely not good," said Fred.

"Everyone into the town hall! Any officers near a fire, put it out now!" said Bob.

One of the officers who had a shovel started digging the lawn in front of the town hall and tossing the dirt on the fires while the rest pushed the dirt with their boots to smother the burning wood. Once everyone was in, Bob locked the entrance to the hall. "Check all the doors and windows! Make sure they are all locked!"

While the officers checked the doors and windows, everyone else was looking out the large pane glass doors, which gave them a clear view up the main street running into the town. They could see one of the families running down the street towards the town center. Behind them in the mountains there were thousands of light strings moving quickly through the trees and over each house. Before anyone had a chance to say anything the strings caught up with the family enveloping them, quickly pulling them to the woods. Some of the children started crying, while the adults were too stunned to say anything.

"Everyone to the center of the hall! All officers form a circle around these people! If those things get in here keep them off the townsfolk!" said Bob.

Jack and Fred moved to join the circle.

"No! If anything happens to us you two need to take care of these people. Get behind us and stay with them," said Bob.

Jack thought about arguing for a moment, but he decided to do as Bob ordered.

The strings moved extremely fast through the town center, covering all the buildings, entering the ones with open doors or windows. As they covered the town hall the light coming through the windows was blinding. The doors and Windows all shuddered, but nothing was getting into the building. They started to move off the buildings heading out of the town, but before anyone could breathe a sigh of relief, a string was spotted moving out of a back room into the main hall.

"Shit, the old fireplace in the mayor's office!" said Bob, "They're getting in through the chimney!"

Jim and two other officers shot at the string, missing as it quickly dodged the bullets. Jim grabbed one end of the string with two others grabbing the second end. The string contracted and coiled itself, throwing the officers around, eventually throwing Jim across the room. Three more strings entered the room, moved towards the two officers trying to hold the string, wrapping around them. A few of the townsfolk got up and ran to the entrance. Jack and Fred try to keep everyone in the hall, but too many were trying to run away for them to control.

24

"No! Don't!" yelled Bob as they opened the door and ran outside. Bob and the remaining officers tried to grab the strings on the two officers but were whipped across the room. The strings quickly dragged the two out the door, heading up the street towards the woods. A few strings that were still winding around some of the buildings moved towards the people that ran into the street. They were surrounded by the strings which pulled them towards the woods.

"No one else leave the building! Shut all the doors leading out of this room!" said Bob as he ran over to shut the main doors while the others ran to the doors leading to other parts of the hall to shut them. Everyone stood motionless for a moment listening. The only sound heard was the crackling coming from the sky. Bob looked out the windows on both sides of the hall and the main door. He could see the remaining strings continuing to move out of the town and back to the woods where they came from.

"I don't think those things are smart enough to know how to open doors or windows. They also didn't try to break any windows to get in the hall so they probably didn't notice us in here," said Bob as he walked to the center of the hall.

"They could have some sort of infrared vision, like the goggles we use during night searches," said Jack.

"Makes sense, the stone on the building will still be hot from the sun during the day, throwing off enough heat to block their vision. They just swarmed all the buildings but didn't notice us in here until some of them actually got in," said Fred.

"What about the people they took? Aren't you going to go help them?" asked one of the men angrily.

"You saw what a few of those things did to Bob and his officers! They swatted them away like flies, what chance would they have out there with thousands of them?" asked one of the women.

"Right now I am only concerned with keeping those things out of this building and keeping the rest of you safe. If the others had not opened the door we might have had a chance to get those things off my men. They are extremely strong but all of us together could have removed them," said Bob.

"Then what? Ask them politely to leave?" asked the man again.

"I don't know. But at least we would have had a chance to try something. If we panic then we have no chance of getting out of here," said Bob exasperatedly.

The man sat down on the ground in a huff, glaring at Bob.

"Jack, Fred, we need to get out of the town tonight. I hate to ask you but..." said Bob.

"Yes, I agree. We'll go get the horses and cart now," said Jack as Fred nodded his approval.

"Thank you, I knew I could count on you two."

They walked to the main doors, checking for any movement outside before opening it. "We'll run up and ride back. Shouldn't be more than an hour"

"Keep safe, and get inside if you see any of those things," said Bob as he closed the doors.

The ranch was to the east at the end of the only road that passed through the town. The trip was all downhill to the ranch, making the run easy and uneventful. They noticed the weeds had doubled in size again with new vegetation breaking through the pavement. When they arrived at the ranch the horses were running around, panicked, in the enclosure outside the stables. Jack approached the fence whistling loudly to get their attention. The horses ran over to him, still very agitated but obviously happy to see him. Jack tried to calm them down as he climbed over the fence to lead them back to the stables.

"Fred, could you prep the cart while I get them a bit more calmed down?"

"Sure thing," said Fred as he started gathering up saddles and other equipment for the cart.

Jack filled a couple feed bags giving them to the horses.

"Hey Jack, what about the cows?"

"I didn't even think about them. We better open up the barn so they can get out, or they will starve. I hope there is enough grass in the fields to keep them going before someone gets a chance to come back for them."

"I'll let them out while you hitch up the horses." After opening the barn doors, Fred opened the gates to the cow pens but most of the cows stayed inside. He grabbed a couple axes and shovels on the way back to the cart, attaching them to the utility racks on the side.

"Looks like we are almost ready. Help me get a few sacks of oats on the cart then we can leave," said Jack as he hitched the horses to the cart.

They got on the cart with Jack taking the reins. The ride back was quick but bumpy since the pavement was starting to buckle with the weeds growing through it. As they approached the town center they were horrified to see the main doors of the town hall smashed off their hinges with no sign of anyone around. They slowed the cart, stopping near the hall. They could see streaks of blood on the ground leading out of the hall, down the road. Fred readied his rifle as they slowly approached the hall.

"Looks like the wolves have been here. They got someone too. That thing must have sent them down here to get everyone who survived the first attack," said Fred fearful and angry.

They checked all the rooms in the hall but found no one.

"What are we going to do? They've got everyone and we're next," said Fred desperately.

"We've got to get out of here fast before they come again. Help me throw a few supplies on the cart and then let's move."

"OK," said Fred sounding defeated.

"Don't give up Fred. We've made it this far. We have to keep going. Someone in the city has to be able to help us."

As they were loading the cart, the crackling noise stopped with the streams in the sky dimming back to their previous brightness.

"I can't see a damn thing now," said Fred.

"Wait for your eyes to adjust." After a few minutes they could see enough to continue loading the cart. "We need to keep everything dark. I don't want that thing to know we are still out here."

"You think the horses can see enough to make their way down the road?" asked Fred.

"Definitely, I've ridden horses at night on camping trips before. They can see things better than most animals at night."

Chapter 3

Jack and Fred rode down the road for about an hour with Jack at the reins and Fred watching the road behind them. Fred looked up at the streams of light, taking notice of the one closest to them. "That one there is going in the general direction of Chilliwack or maybe Vancouver" said Fred while pointing at the stream.

"I noticed earlier, but I didn't want to cause you more stress. No point in worrying about them right now since we don't know where they go or what they do. I think we've travelled enough for tonight, let's make camp by the runaway lane up ahead."

"Sure, no chance of any logging trucks coming by."

After hitching the horses to the posts on the runaway lane sign they spent the night trying, mostly unsuccessfully, to sleep in the back of the cart. Jack was not getting any rest despite being asleep. His dreams were filled with images of the people he knew, calling out to him for help while being attacked by wolves and strangled by the light strings.

"Get off them!" said Jack while he flailed his arms hitting Fred across the chest.

Fred jumped up in a daze looking for the rifle. "Are they back? Are we being attacked?" asked Fred.

They both looked around, confused for a moment as Jack slowly realized he had been dreaming.

"Just a dream," said Jack.

"Don't do that anymore, you almost gave me a heart attack!" said Fred while giving Jack a relieved look.

"Sorry, I haven't been able to sleep much. I keep thinking there must have been something I could have done."

"If we had stayed behind then we would be gone too. You and I both saw how those things treated Bob and his men like rag dolls."

"I know. I just can't stop thinking about it." Jack looked up at the sky while rubbing his leg. "Getting light, the sun will be up soon. Let's eat something then get moving."

"Your leg OK?" asked Fred, "We never had a chance to get it checked out by a doctor."

"Probably just needs new bandages," said Jack taking the first aid kit from his backpack. As he took the old bandages off both men were shocked to see

28

the gouges were mostly healed. Under his skin there were little threads of light moving around.

"What did that thing do to you?"

"I don't know but I'm not leaving those in my leg," said Jack while looking for a knife. He found a small pocket knife, which he tried to use to make a cut over one of the light threads. As soon as the knife touched his leg there was a shower of sparks with a loud zapping noise, the knife was knocked out of his hand as he yelped in pain. "Ah! Damn, that hurt."

"Look, the tip of the knife has been burnt off. And the cut you made is healing over!"

They watch as one of the threads wiggled around while the skin above it quickly healed.

"This doesn't make any sense. Why would that wolf try to bite my leg off then leave something behind that fixes it?"

"Maybe whoever is controlling those things doesn't want you dead."

"That is an even scarier thought than them wanting to kill me. Oh God, do you think they were coming after me in the town? If I hadn't gone back do you think everyone would still be OK?" asked Jack in a worried tone.

"I doubt it, remember, that light wave came through the town long before we went up there."

"But maybe that's all that would have happened. I could be the reason everyone is dead!"

"Jack, stop blaming yourself for what happened. Neither of us knows who they are or why they are doing this. Your lack of sleep is making you crazy. Why don't I drive the cart for a few hours and you try your best to get some real sleep. Look, take some of the pain pills from the first aid kit, they will make you drowsy and maybe you will sleep."

"But what if..."

"You're no good to either of us in this state," said Fred glaring at Jack.

"OK... but only one pill, I don't want to be out of it all day."

Jack took a pill while Fred opened up a couple cans of brown beans. "Here, lots of protein. It'll keep us going for hours. Hmmm, bad choice of words but you know what I mean."

Jack smiled a little as Fred started eating. He took a spoonful with a drink from his water bottle. "Bottoms up," said Jack causing Fred to nearly choke on his food.

Fred fed the horses while getting the cart ready as Jack leaned against one of the sacks of oats trying to fall asleep. Once the cart was moving and it started rocking on the uneven pavement he fell asleep quickly.

Jack dreamt of his first day working search and rescue ten years ago, the same day he met Fred who would become his trainer and eventually best friend.

"You must be the new kid. Fred Anderson, I'll be showing you the tricks of the trade," said a younger, happier Fred.

"Good to meet ya, I'm Jack. I don't know if there will be much for you to show me, I've just finished six months of training."

"You might be good at pulling a dummy up a cliff in sunny weather, but have you ever done it with a half dozen seriously injured people in a snow storm?" said Fred chuckling loudly.

Jack went slightly pale and asked, "Does that happen a lot?"

"More than I would like."

The dream then faded to the day Fred told him the house next door was for sale and convinced him to buy it, but something was different. There was a buzzing noise in the air that wasn't there that day.

"The house is small, but it's perfect for a bachelor."

"I don't know. I was planning on buying a place closer to the city. I've been here all my life and there isn't much to do," said Jack, rubbing his ears trying to make the buzzing go away.

"Well, this town has become a central gathering spot for people who want to go camping, hunting, and fishing in the mountains. People are always looking for a guide or someone to show them the ropes. We could make some extra cash doing what we do in our free time and all we have to do is show some greenhorns how to do it."

The dream then faded to the day he moved. Fred and his wife Joan were helping him unload his furniture.

"How did a bachelor who is never home gather up so much crap?" asked Fred with a chuckle while helping to move a very large TV into the house.

"Fred! That's not very nice!" said Joan.

"That's OK Joan, my back is killing me and I'm starting to think Fred is probably right."

Fred started to speak but the dream world changed before anything was said. The sky darkened, the buzzing came back, louder this time, and Fred's eyes were replaced by glowing balls of light.

"You are the one they are looking for," said Fred.

The dream quickly shifted to the day he met Bob at a town meeting. Everyone was in the town hall to debate whether or not to allow logging trucks to use the town roads again. Almost everyone except the mayor and council were against it.

"Is there anyone else who wishes to say something?" asked the mayor.

A man stood and walked towards the speaker's podium to say something. The buzzing started again as his eyes turned to glowing balls of light while he turned to Jack. "They must find you before the others do," said the man.

A wolf crashed through a window, grabbing Bob by the arm. As it dragged him out of the hall his eyes also started to glow. "Don't let the others find you," said Bob.

The dream shifted again, to the previous day at the cabin in the woods. The buzzing was extremely loud. Fred was looking through the rubble, but he was covered in the light strings and his eyes were glowing. He stood, turning to Jack. "The others will extinguish your light," said Fred. The door flew open and Fred was pulled into the ball of light in the clearing which gave off a bright flash of light.

Thousands of light strings were now extending from the ball of light towards Jack as he stood in place unable to move. "They must find you first," said a loud booming voice coming from the ball of light.

Jack was jolted awake and kicked some of the supplies, he was sweating and breathing fast.

Fred heard the supplies being knocked around and looked back at Jack, "You OK? You look pale."

"I think so, I just had a very weird dream," said Jack, as he began describing the dream to Fred. "What do you think all that means?"

"I think it means you are too stressed out from everything that has happened and you are worried that those light things are going to kill you too. The ones in your leg might also be causing you to hallucinate for all I know."

Jack moved his cut up pant leg out of the way and they were shocked to see his leg was perfectly healed with no sign of the light threads.

"My leg doesn't look like it has ever been injured. Even the old scar I got back in high school is gone."

"I just hope those things are really gone, not just hiding somewhere in your leg."

"You sure know how to put someone at ease!"

"Sorry, thinking out loud again. We're almost to the gas station."

"Why didn't they kill me?" asked Jack confused.

"Probably not their job. You remember at the cabin? There were hundreds of those things and not one came after us. Some were digging tunnels, others were building. I'll bet those ones in your leg were supposed to fix the wolf that attacked us, but got into you when it bit you and you shot it."

"Maybe. I hope your right."

"When we get to Chilliwack we'll head for the hospital and find someone to check you out... There's the gas station up ahead. I don't see anyone outside."

Fred slowed down the cart as they approached. "Hang on to the cart, if I see anything suspicious I'm kicking these horses into high gear and the ride will get bumpy."

The gas station was empty, the garage bay door was up with a car was still on the lift. There were a couple cars with their hoods up near the pumps. The displays on the pumps looked burnt. The weeds had grown through every crack in the cement and started growing inside the building.

"Looks like they were hit too. Everyone's gone. The plants have really gone nuts here, much worse than back in town," said Jack.

"Let's see if there's anything left inside the store to drink. I'll stop the cart next to that lamp post and we can hitch the horses to it." After Fred stopped the cart, Jack scanned the area with his binoculars before getting out. As they walked to the store they noticed burn marks on the cars batteries. All the electronic parts in the cars were destroyed. The plastic covers on the gas pump displays had melted, running down the front of the pumps.

"Damn lucky no one was pumping gas. This place probably wouldn't be here if they had," said Fred.

"This place looks like no one has been here for months, not half a day," said Jack.

"Look at that," said Fred pointing to one of the shelves near the door. They both stared a while at a packet of raw unshelled sunflower seeds that had sprouted and started growing, the roots breaking through the packaging and growing towards the ground.

"How can they do that? There's no water or soil in the packets."

"Let's grab some water and get out of here. This place is starting to creep me out."

"I can see some jugs of filtered water in the cooler over there."

"I'll grab them."

While Fred got the water, Jack took out his wallet and stuffed twenty dollars into the burnt out cash register.

"I don't think anyone is going to come back for that," said Fred.

"Probably not, but I don't feel right just taking the water."

As they left the store and walked back to the cart, Jack noticed a flash of light far up the road from where they came.

"Get down!" yelled Jack.

"What is it," said Fred as they crouched beside one of the cars.

"A light up the road, I think we're being followed."

They both looked under the car, up the road and saw more flashes of light.

"It doesn't look like those strings, there's only one light and it's flashing intermittently," said Fred

After a few minutes had passed they could make out that it was someone on a bike. The flashes of light were just the sun reflecting off the handlebars.

"They are going to be exhausted if they rode all the way from town," said Jack as they stood up and started running towards the bike. As they got closer they could see the rider was Bob and he was covered in dried blood. As soon as Bob noticed them he stopped the bike and collapsed in the road.

"Bob! Don't give up now! You'll be OK!" yelled Jack.

"Come on Bob, you didn't ride all this way to die on us did you?" yelled Fred.

When they got to Bob, Jack sat him up and could see he was covered is scrapes and scratches. "What happened to you? What happened to everyone in the hall?" asked Jack.

"So tired and sore," said Bob out of breath, "They're all gone... all of them... just gone..."

"He's dehydrated and in shock, help me get him to the cart," said Jack, "Bob, can you get back on the bike? We can push you to the cart quicker that way."

"I... I think so..." said Bob.

Fred held the bike steady while Jack helped Bob back on the bike. They quickly pushed him to the cart, lifted him in and gave him some water.

"Drink a little, not too much at first though," said Jack.

Bob took a large drink and sputtered most of it out.

"Slower, your body can't handle that much right now. Take small sips and wait for your mouth to dry out a little between sips," said Jack.

Bob sipped the water slowly, managing to keep it down, so Jack and Fred start cleaning up his wounds.

"What happened to you?" asked Jack, "There are splinters in your head."

"We decided to... we knew the lights would come back. So the people... we had to... they needed someplace better to hide. We were going to hide them in the old cellar under the hall. There is only one way in, a hatch in the floor of the mayor's office." He paused for a moment staring up the road. "We were going to hide them in there with Jim so they had someone to help them if the lights came back before you." He took another sip of water before continuing. "I had just started opening the hatch when someone saw the lights coming back and before I could prop it open everyone rushed into the office. Jim was pushed into me and knocked me head first into the hatch. I fell into the cellar and the hatch slammed shut."

"Ah, that explains the splinters. Did all the rest happen from the fall?" asked Jack.

"No, I landed on the empty boxes the towns computers came in. If they hadn't been there I would have hit the gravel floor." He took another sip. "I couldn't see anything, but I could hear a lot of screaming, some gunshots, then... nothing. By the time I managed to find the ladder and get out all I could see were the lights up the hill near the edge of the woods. I wasn't going to wait around for them to come back for me, and I figured if they didn't get you two, you would eventually catch up so I grabbed a bike and took off."

"But we saw no sign of you on the road," said Fred.

"That's because when the sky went back to being dark I could no longer see. Before I could stop the bike I hit a large bump, lost control, rode off the road and was knocked off the bike. I fell into the ravine and got knocked out when I hit a tree. I woke up when it started getting light out. I could see the road in the distance where it meets up with the ravine, so I walked out then rode the bike until I found you."

"Well, sit back and rest now. We're heading for the hospital in the city, we'll get you checked out there," said Jack.

"Oh, I forgot about your leg, has it gotten worse?" asked Bob.

Jack lifted his pant leg and Bob got a confused look on his face. "I'll explain on the way there."

As they progressed down the weed covered highway the ride began to feel more and more like a ride across a farm field than a paved road. Fred drove the cart, Jack scanned the distance with his binoculars for any trouble, while Bob got some sleep. The amount of plants growing through the pavement continued to increase as they got closer to the city. The grass in the fields where the cows and horses grazed had grown so tall the animals could no longer be seen. The vegetable fields and fruit groves looked like they were ready for harvest weeks ago. They encountered no other people along the road and passed only two abandoned cars. As they approached the point where the highway forked, one leading to Vancouver and one to Chilliwack, Jack could see a problem with the overpass which was part of the road they wanted to take.

"Crap, looks like the overpass has collapsed," said Jack.

"What, the whole thing?" asked Fred a little panicked.

"Yeah, sure looks like it from here."

"Well, we'll just have to try to navigate through the town. With any luck the streets won't be jammed up with dead cars."

"That may be the least of our problems."

"Why, what else is there."

"Chilliwack is on the other side of the river, if we stay on this side there are dozens of bridges and overpasses before the new bridge that crosses over to the city, but the bridge near here that crosses the river is older than any of them."

"Shit, never thought about that. But none of the small bridges and overpasses the way we came collapsed, so maybe there was structural flaw with this overpass."

"I hope so. I don't think we could get the cart across the river, even at the shallow points, because of the depth of the mud."

They continued along the road and as they got closer to the overpass they saw that one support wall had partially crumbled, causing one of the deck support spans to collapse on one end. The rest of the wall was cracked, looking ready to collapse. There were a few abandoned cars near the overpass, but no signs that anyone was on or under the overpass when it collapsed.

"This makes me want to try crossing the mud, but the old bridge is probably the best bet" said Fred.

"I agree, through the town it is," said Jack.

"Looks like a lot more abandoned cars up ahead."

"The road is probably going to be packed with cars with the lake a few minutes away. I think they had some sort of festival happening this weekend as well."

The number of dead cars at the side of the road continued to increase as they got further into the town, but nothing was blocking the road. The cart hit a large pothole, jarring Bob awake.

"Wa, huh!" said Bob groggily.

"Just a pothole. Feeling better?" asked Jack.

"Yeah, still really sore, but the sleep helped a lot. Where are we? I thought we were going to Chilliwack."

"Slight route change, the overpass back there has collapsed so we are going to go through the town and backtrack to the other side."

"There's a police station up ahead. I know a few of the officers there. We should stop and see if they know anything more than we do."

"Sounds good to me"

"Me too, time to stop to eat anyway," said Fred.

"It's that brown building two blocks ahead," said Bob.

"Don't see anyone outside. We haven't seen a single person all day," said Jack, scanning ahead through his binoculars.

"No one?" asked Bob.

"Nope, they're either hiding or have all headed to Chilliwack like we are."

At the station everything was covered in plants with the main doorway covered in vines. Parts of the siding had been pushed off by the weeds and a tree branch had grown through a window.

"I don't think anyone's home. I'll wait out here with the horses and get some food ready while you two check out the station," said Fred.

Jack and Bob walked towards the main doors while scanning around for possible danger. Bob started pulling the vines off the door while Jack looked through the broken window.

"Don't see anyone in the main office," said Jack.

"There, door's all clear. Let's check it out," said Bob as he pulled the last vine out of the way.

"Wow, look at this place. There are plants growing out of everything."

"I thought this was only happening outside."

"Fred and I saw it at the gas station just before you showed up, but it wasn't anywhere near as bad as this."

"Let me check their logs to see what happened after we lost contact," Bob read for a while then said, "Hmm, same as us, wall of light, everything electrical burning out. Apparently the wall of light came from the north end of the lake, must be another ball of light up there."

"Anything else?"

"Just a lot of entries about various people wanting help. The last entry says they planned on sending someone to Chilliwack in the morning to get some help."

"Maybe they all decided to go there?"

"I couldn't see them all leaving unless the entire town was convinced to go also, which is doubtful. I have a sinking feeling that what happened in Brentwood happened here too."

"I sure hope not. What about Chilliwack, you don't think they were attacked too do you? There are over one million people living there!"

"I'm trying not to think about that, because if Chilliwack is gone what chance do we have?"

"I think whoever is attacking doesn't realize that we got away. If they did then they would have sent out those light strings again. Is that book the only place they keep the written log?"

"Each officer would keep their own log, but they keep it with them while on duty. I'll do a quick check of all the desks but I doubt anyone was not on duty last night."

Bob checked the desks but found nothing of interest. They did find the keys to the stations weapons locker, the plants had not gotten into it yet and it still contained a couple guns and three boxes of bullets.

"Better than nothing I guess. Would have preferred a rocket launcher," said Jack.

"I'm pretty sure those aren't standard issue in Canada."

"Let's go back outside and eat something, this place is starting to depress me."

They walked back to the cart to see that Fred had set up a small camp fire in the stations parking lot to cook some chili.

"Where did you get all this?" asked Jack

Fred pointed across the street to a small restaurant. "The food in there was going to be worthless soon and there were some cooked beef strips in the fridge that were still cool, so I figure it is still safe to eat. You two find anything useful?"

Jack explained what they found while Fred looked increasingly worried and depressed. "Well, at least Joan doesn't have to live through this. Who would want to do this to us? I thought we had no enemies," said Fred.

"The bigger question for me is how they are doing this. I've never heard of anyone having something that could do what we have seen," said Bob.

"Wouldn't be the first time a country had a powerful weapon that no one knew about," said Fred.

"Maybe we're just caught in the cross fire, so to speak, being only twenty kilometers from the U.S. Maybe they are being attacked."

"Could be. Half the planet hates them, but doing something like this won't bring the rest of the world to their side." Fred stirred the chili, "Food should be hot enough now, let eat and get moving again."

The men ate quickly in silence before packing up. They took the road towards the residential area of town where it connected to the road on the other side of the overpass. Many of the cars had their hoods up exposing their burnt out electrical systems. As they approached one of the bigger intersections they saw five cars had collided and were blocking their path. There was no sign of the people who were driving the cars.

"Looks like we're going to have to go through the subdivisions to get through here," said Fred, "We'll have to unhitch the horses then spin the cart around ourselves. Not enough room to do it with them hooked up."

"Let's try moving some of the parked cars near the intersection out of the way first. If we move those two over there and then that one on the other side we should have enough room to get by on the sidewalk and yards," said Jack.

Jack and Bob jumped off the cart and walked to the nearest car.

"Unlocked!" said Bob happily as he opened the door and released the parking brake, "Let's push it into that driveway over there."

The other two cars were also unlocked and easily moved. Once they were done they helped guide the horses and cart around the intersection and through the yards before getting back on the cart.

"Much quicker than trying to turn this thing around," said Jack.

"Good work. Didn't think you had enough room to move the cars out of the way," said Fred.

They continued through the subdivisions without encountering any more blocked roads, eventually arriving at the other side of the overpass to head towards the bridge leading to the outskirts of Chilliwack. The road to the bridge was slightly elevated above the farmland giving them all a much farther, disturbing view of everything. The fields were not filled with just various grains, which would be expected during the summer, but instead they were being smothered by weeds and vines. The road was heavily covered in plant life with much of the pavement broken up. In the distance towards the city Jack noticed three areas where there was a bright glow appearing behind the large trees along the river.

"Guys look," said Jack.

"I hope that isn't what I think it is," said Fred.

"This is not good," said Bob.

"The bridge might be high enough to let us see what is causing the glow," said Jack.

"Speaking of the bridge, take a look at it!" said Fred in a worried tone.

The other two men turned to look at what now looked more like a vine covered pergola than a bridge. Most of the support structure was covered with the deck looked like an overgrown field more than a road.

"You think we can make it across without falling through?" asked Fred stopping the cart just before the start of the bridge deck.

"I'll go check it out," said Jack as he jumped off the cart. He could see through the broken pavement in spots, so he kicked some of it away to reveal that the underlying metal deck structure wasn't damaged. He stamped his foot on the metal deck a few times to check for weak spots, but found none. While he walked back to the cart he examined the main support structure of the bridge to find it had not been damaged by the vines. "We should be OK if we go slowly, but it's going to be a very bumpy ride with the broken up pavement, I'll walk ahead and look out for any trouble spots."

Fred kept the cart moving as slowly as possible across the bridge, steering around a couple spots where Jack found the metal deck was loose. Even at the tallest spot on the bridge they still could not see what was causing the glow behind the trees. The road on the other side looked like an overgrown strip of land with large chunks of rubble in it, with the abandoned cars completely covered in vines looking like large bumps in the land.

"Do you really think we are going to find anything in Chilliwack? This just keeps getting worse!"said Fred sounding depressed.

"Yes it does, but all these plants seem to be doing is crumbling cement and pavement right now. The station back there was covered in plants, but it was still standing. They appear to be growing into the wood, so even though they are weakening the structure, the vines are holding it all together, at least for a while," said Jack.

"But for how long?"

"Don't know. Weeks. Days. But we need to keep moving towards the city. There is a greater chance of someone still being there than out here. If there is no one there, we can still head for Vancouver. Short of a nuke, a city that size would not be destroyed by a few thousand of those light strings and a bunch of over achieving plants. I for one don't want to just sit around here waiting for whoever did this to come and get me."

"He's right. When we had working radios the police in Vancouver told me that only one of those light balls landed in the mountains north of the city. Assuming it could do what the one in Brentwood did, there would be more than enough people to fight off a few thousand light strings. If my men and I had known their strength before we tried to grab one we would have easily controlled it," said Bob.

"You think so?" asked Fred sounding hopeful.

"Definitely. They might be able to get a few people, but with over three million people they wouldn't last long. I'm sure an axe or sledge hammer could destroy them if they were held steady long enough," said Bob.

"OK, let's keep going then. The next side road winds through the farmland and should have been relatively unused except for farm vehicles. It will be a longer ride, but less chance of a blocked road that way."

"We'll be alright. We're trained to survive. That's what we do," said Jack patting Fred on the back.

The ride continued to get rougher as the road became increasingly crumbled. The only way they could tell if they were still on the road was to keep the cart between the lamp posts, which now looked like tall skinny trees with one branch at the top. The buildings near the first intersection were no longer visible because they had been completely covered in plants, with the roads near them looking like a seldom used path through a forest. The power lines that ran down one side of the road crossing over to each building were also covered in vines making the area feel like a jungle. Once they passed through to the farms the closed in feeling started to go away, even though the crops have grown too high to see over. The quiet was broken by a loud rumbling noise with the ground shaking for a few seconds.

"What the hell was that!" said Fred.

"Look over there," said Jack.

In the sky towards the city they saw a large cloud of white smoke billowing into the air, but because of the plants they could not see what was causing it.

"I don't think we should go into the city tonight. If we run into trouble we'll want lots of daylight to find our way out quickly," said Bob

"Agreed," said Jack and Fred in unison. They glared at each other but said nothing.

"I'll stop at the next farm," said Fred.

After a few more minutes they approached what looked like an overgrown path through the fields off the side of the road. The only indication it was really a driveway were the ornate brick pillars with a wrought iron gate barely visible under the vines. As they passed through the gate they could see a few milk tanker trucks covered in vines in a large clear area.

"Looks like a dairy farm. Going to be a lot of unhappy cows here," said Fred.

"Why, you think they are going to be starving after less than a day?" asked Bob.

"That's the least of their problems, on a farm this size they are probably using hormones to make the cows produce a lot of milk, so they need to be milked at least once a day."

"Oh, what happens if they don't get milked?"

"Imagine drinking six liters of water and then not being able to go to the bathroom for a week."

"Ouch!"

"I'll stop next to what I am assuming is the house," said Fred pointing to what looked like a two storey tall pile of plants.

"I'll see if I can do anything for the cows and look for some feed," said Jack.

"I'll unhitch the cart and feed the horses," said Fred.

"I guess that leaves the house to me. I'll see if it is safe to stay inside," said Bob.

There were three buildings aside from the house on the farm, so Jack decided to check them from smallest to largest. The first building appeared to be a workshop containing nothing but tools and farm vehicle parts. The second contained some milk storage tanks, tractors and a meat cooler. The third was where the cows and feed were kept. Since the doors to the field were open, all the cows along with some calves were wandering outside. The bags of feed had been split open by various plants that had spread inside the building. A few appear to have also been ripped open, probably by a hungry animal. Jack walked out to the field to one of the cows. It appeared to be OK with no signs of needing to be milked. A quick check of the other cows revealed the same so he walked back to the cart.

"Lucky cows," said Jack.

"No need to milk?" asked Fred.

"Nope, looks like they were raising beef cows, the milk is just a bonus. The sacks of feed are worthless though. They're all ripped open, feed spread all over the place."

Bob walked to the cart after emerging from the house, "Looks mostly safe in there. The east side of the house is sinking into the ground, but I don't think any of it will collapse any time soon. I took a look out the windows on the top floor, but there are still too many trees to see what exactly is causing the glowing in the city."

Jack looked around and stared in the distance with a concerned look on his face.

"What's wrong?" asked Fred.

"Where are the dogs?" asked Jack.

"Maybe this farm didn't have any."

"No, I mean all the dogs, where are they. We haven't seen or heard any dogs anywhere since yesterday. We've seen a couple cats, a lot of horses and cows, but no dogs."

"That is weird, did either of you notice any dogs after the light wall? I think I saw one with the people that were running out of town," said Bob.

"Maybe they all went with their owners, I don't remember seeing any after that," said Jack.

"Maybe, but what are the chances every dog from here to Brentwood was with their owners, or even outside yesterday?" asked Fred.

"Well, missing dogs are the least of our problems right now," said Bob.

"Bah! There's too much happening. Let's eat something and decide what to do tomorrow," said Fred.

"Probably a good idea, anyone up for a can of beans?" asked Jack.

"Ah! I've got a better idea," said Bob.

"I am not eating the horse feed!" said Fred with a smile.

"No, something much better. I saw a small garden behind the house. Lots of fresh vegetables," said Bob.

"We can load up the cart with those veggies and some of the corn from the fields for the horses, we should be good for a few days," said Jack.

They spent the next couple hours picking food from the garden, loading it into the cart. Once everything was ready for the next day Jack fed the horses before everyone filled up on canned beans and vegetables. As the sun set they could now see a glowing light in the sky coming from the three areas they had noticed earlier. There also appeared to be a large amount of light dust or smoke in the sky over those areas.

"You think the city is on fire?" asked Fred, "Looks like a lot of smoke."

"It would have to be a lot of very clean dry wood to make light smoke like that," said Jack.

"Yeah, if the city were burning I would expect a lot of black smoke from all the plastics and other crap," said Bob.

"Look, the streams of light are still up there," said Jack.

"And a bunch of them look like they go to one of those glowing spots in the city! I'm really not sure about going there tomorrow," said Fred anxiously.

"Neither are we, but there is no other place to go, even if we decide to go to Vancouver we need to pass through Chilliwack first," said Jack.

"Maybe we should have stayed on the other side of the river," said Bob.

"Too many bridges and overpasses," said Fred.

"Looks like we need to go through hell to get to..." said Jack.

"More hell?" said Fred.

Everyone was silent for a few seconds.

"Sorry guys, ever since Joan died I haven't found much to keep me in a good mood. The last two days have done nothing to help that. I need some sleep," said Fred.

"We'll get through this buddy. One way or another we will get through it," said Jack.

Fred stared into the sky at one of the glowing areas.

"I don't think we should sleep in the house. We will be in complete darkness and if we have to get out in a hurry tonight someone will get hurt. I'm just going to sleep in the cart," said Jack.

"Sounds good," said Bob.

Fred was silent as prepared to sleep.

Other than an occasional flare up on one of the streams in the sky followed by a crackling noise, everything was fairly normal with the sounds of crickets and frogs all around. Once the sun had completely set an owl started hooting somewhere in the distance as everyone quickly fell asleep.

In the middle of the night the ground started shaking again along with a loud scraping metal noise, followed by an even louder crashing noise.

All three men were startled awake.

"What's happening? Are we being attacked?" yelled Fred while jumping out of the cart.

Jack and Bob also jumped out as one of the three glowing lights coming from the city got brighter, lighting up the sky like a full moon.

"We might be able to see what's happening from the second floor in the house!" said Bob.

The three of them ran towards the house. Bob ran upstairs, followed by the other two, to a window facing the glow. The trees still blocked whatever was causing the glow but it appeared to be moving closer to them. Towards the direction of the noise, somewhere behind the trees, a large dust cloud could be seen billowing up. As the glow got close they caught a glimpse of a light string through the trees.

"Ah shit! We're screwed," said Fred.

"Only if a bunch of them are heading this way and only if they are looking for us," said Bob.

"The glow seems to have stopped moving, looks like it could be somewhere near that dust cloud," said Jack.

Glancing at Fred, Jack was sure his eyes were glowing. He shook his head and stared at Fred but could no longer see a glow.

"What?" asked Fred noticing him staring.

"Nothing, just the light doing strange things," said Jack.

There was a loud boom as the ground shook a little more. The dust cloud continued to get bigger.

"What the hell are they doing?"

"I don't know, but they don't seem to be noticing us. The road we were on doesn't go near that area does it?"

"From what I remember it heads north-west from here and then connects up with a residential area. We might be able to see that area from the road though."

"And whatever is there might see us too," said Bob.

"I doubt anything is going to be seen with the way the plants are growing," said Jack.

"Maybe, assuming there is anything left growing in the city."

"I don't know about you two, but I don't think I am going to be able to fall asleep again."

"I am just going to sit here and wait for daylight so we can go."

Fred looked down towards the cart then sat back letting out a sigh of relief. "Good, the horses are OK. I was worried they might have hurt themselves trying to break free but they don't seem to care about all the noise."

"Probably used to it after being part of so many parades. They've had fire crackers thrown at them more times than I care to remember," said Jack.

They spent the next couple hours watching the area where the dust cloud appeared, catching a glimpse of a light string through the trees every once in a while. Shortly before dawn the glow moved back to where it came from as the dust cloud dissipated.

"Looks like they've finished whatever they were doing," said Jack.

"Let's eat something and get out of here," said Fred.

After walking quickly back to the cart, Jack and Fred hitched the horses back to the cart preparing to move towards the main part of the city while Bob took out some food to eat on the way.

Chapter 4

The road curved then ran north-west for a few kilometers, eventually bringing the men past the rows of trees planted at the edge of the farms that had been blocking their view. Now they could see the top of a ball of light poking up above the overgrown fields. There was a large bright stream of light emanating from the top of the ball towards the sky, eventually breaking into smaller, dimmer streams which curved off in various directions eventually fading out of view in the bright daylight.

"Well, I guess that settles that question. Those light balls are connected to each other by the streams," said Fred.

"I wonder what they do?" asked Bob rhetorically.

Jack stared up in the sky, mesmerized by the streams, forgetting about everything else around him, but was startled back to alertness by a sudden blinding flash coming from the closest one. He held his hand up to block the light while looking down, only to see Fred and Bob's eyes glowing brightly. "What the hell?" yelled Jack as he jumped backwards out of the cart landing on his back.

Fred quickly stopped the cart then he and Bob jumped out to help Jack.

"Why did you jump out?" asked Fred.

Jack looked up to see their eyes were no longer glowing. "After that flash of light, I would have sworn on my life your eyes were glowing."

"What flash of light?" asked Fred sounding concerned.

"Fred's eyes were glowing?" asked Bob.

"Yours too," said Jack, "That bright flash just a couple seconds ago."

"I didn't see any flash Jack," said Fred sounding more concerned.

"Me neither," said Bob.

"What is happening to me? I keep seeing your eyes glowing, and that damn dream!" said Jack in a worried tone.

"You had the dream again?" asked Fred.

"Last night. Exactly the same. Seemed more real this time. Those things must have screwed up my mind," said Jack sounding panicked.

"Calm down, nothing is screwing up your mind. You probably just saw a flash of light out of the corner of your eye and when you looked at us you were just seeing the after effects of it making us look like we were glowing," said Fred.

"No! It was a bright flash, directly in from of me, and just your eyes were glowing!" yelled Jack definitely panicking now.

"Ok, ok, calm down, other than seeing lights and glowing eyes, have you been seeing anything else?" asked Fred in his calmest voice.

"No. just that," said Jack a little less panicky.

"Ok, so maybe those things that were in your leg also caused your eyes to become oversensitive to light," said Fred.

Jack began to speak but Fred interrupted. "No, I don't know how, it's just an idea. But it makes more sense than them screwing up your mind. Why would they fix your leg only to drive you insane? Seems kind of pointless to me."

Jack thought for a while, looking back and forth between Fred and Bob. "I must look like an idiot, you're probably right. Every time I've seen your eyes glow I have been looking at something really bright. But that still doesn't explain the dream," said Jack.

"Hmm, if Joan were here she would have a lot to say about that. Probably something like: Your mind is trying to resolve unsettled conflicts from the events of previous days, and is manifesting an attempt at those resolutions in your dreams," said Fred.

"Where the heck did you get that from?" asked Bob.

"Joan. That's what she told me when I kept having nightmares after that group of hikers died before we could get to them a few years ago. It basically means you are mentally kicking yourself for not being able to help anyone even though there was no way for you to help," said Fred.

"How did you make the dream go away?" asked Jack.

"I didn't. I just learned to live with it. People like us can never let go of something that we think we could have done better or prevented from happening in the first place, even if there is no way we could have helped."

"So I am going to be having this nightmare for the rest of my life."

"Only if you let it be a nightmare. Try recreating the dream in your mind before you fall asleep and controlling it yourself. You may eventually be able to control the actual dream when it happens and change the outcome."

"Can you do that with yours?"

"Sometime, but every scenario with a good outcome is very unrealistic. Still, it helps though."

Jack stared at the ground and thought for a while before standing up, "I'm sorry about all this guys. I'll try not to be so panicky from now on."

"Nothing to be sorry about Jack," said Bob.

"Yeah, most people would have gone nuts the first time it happened to them. I'd say you're doing OK. Let's get moving again," said Fred.

"That ball of light doesn't look too far away. If it is anything like the one we saw in the mountains I'd say it's less than one kilometer away," said Jack.

"The first thing after this farmland should be a subdivision then some shops and some high rises before the hospital. They should all give us about the same amount of cover as these overgrown fields," said Fred as he jumped back into the cart.

The road continued on straight for a couple more kilometers then curved towards the main part of the city. Once around the curve they were shocked by what they saw in the distance. The eastern side of the city that started at the edge of the farm land was gone, replaced with bare land and piles of rubble. Some of the high rise apartment buildings near the city center had fallen. Most of the other buildings, including the hospital, were gone. The buildings that were still standing were completely covered in plants. Another ball of light was visible off in the distance between two of the remaining apartment buildings.

"Is there another way in?" asked Jack.

"Don't think so. Other than the road on the dyke along the river, but that's a couple hundred meters north of here on the other side of the fields," said Fred.

"Let's keep going and stop the cart just before the end of the farmland. Then we can go on foot to scout out the first part of the..." said Jack.

"Warzone? Forget about your idea of being caught in the cross fire Bob. It's pretty obvious to me that we have been attacked," said Fred in an angry tone.

Bob continued staring in disbelief at what was left of the city, not hearing what Fred was saying.

As they approached the end of the farm land, Fred stopped the cart next to a very overgrown power pole. "Look at this thing. The vines have grown thicker than my leg! Help me clear off a spot so I can hitch the horses."

Jack took out his hunting knife to start slicing the vines while Fred pulled them off. The pole underneath was extremely damaged from all the roots that had grown into it.

"Hmmm, don't think this will hold them. It would probably split in two if they tried to pull away. Not sure the power lines could still hold it up if it broke," said Fred.

"I think we are going to have to leave them here and hope they don't get spooked by anything and take off," said Jack.

"Yeah, but let's unhitch them from the cart, so if they do we will at least still have our supplies"

"Good idea."

Bob was still sitting in the cart staring. "Unbelievable".

Jack shook Bob's arm to snap him out of his daze.

"What's happening?" asked Bob.

"We're going to scout the area just past the farm land, are you up to it?" asked Jack.

"Huh? ...Yeah... Let's go."

"You OK?"

"Not really. I grew up in this city. I lived here until I was twelve. I thought I had prepared myself for whatever we found."

"Oh, I didn't realize. You can wait here if you want, we shouldn't be too long."

"No... No, I'll be OK. I need to see what happened, let's get this over with."

They walked along the edge of the corn in the field to the south to shield their movement from the light ball they saw earlier. As they approached the rubble they saw everything up to the river was gone. The rubble itself was not just piles of debris from the city, but neatly piled dirt, metal, rocks and other sorted materials. There were no plants anywhere in the areas that had been cleared. When they got to the edge of the field they peered around the crops, seeing more bleakness along with another shocking sight to the south.

The ball of light they had seen earlier was much farther away than they had estimated. This one was also much larger than the one seen in the mountains, roughly ten times the size. It was hovering slightly above what was once the Trans Canada highway, but there were no pillars near it. Further to the south another light ball could be seen, this one looked like the one from the mountains, also surrounded by six pillars. Two of the thousands of streamers coming out of the large ball were connected to the two smaller balls. Slightly to the east was a large group of light strings which were breaking up the highway, creating new piles of rubble from it.

"How can we ever hope to fight something like that?" asked Fred while the other two stared in disbelief.

"Vancouver. We have to get to Vancouver," said Jack.

"You plan on casually walking across this wasteland and hoping they don't notice you?" asked Fred incredulously.

Before Jack could respond there was a sudden very loud sound of creaking and cracking metal coming from the west where one of the apartment buildings was staring to lean. There were loud snapping sounds as the building slowly fell on its side causing the ground to shake violently.

"This must be what happened last night," said Jack.

They all looked towards the large ball to see how it reacted but nothing happened. The light strings that were dismantling the road also continued their work.

"Do you hear buzzing?" asked Jack.

The other two listened carefully eventually noticing the noise as it exponentially increased in volume. A swarm of light strings exited the field about thirty meters away from them heading towards the collapsed building. A few of the strings broke out of the swarm, moving towards the men.

"We're not getting out of this one guys. Let's try to take some of these bastards out before they get us!" said Bob sounding defeated but preparing to fight.

The strings were moving at a tremendous speed getting to them in less than one second. They circled the men for a few seconds then moved back to the swarm which was now at the building.

"What the hell just happened?" asked Bob.

"I think Fred was right, that's what happened," said Jack.

"OK, I'm lost. Want to fill me in?"

"Oh right, you had not found us yet. Fred came up with the idea that those strings all have different jobs. That's why the ones we first saw didn't attack, but the other ones that came to the town did. These strings are probably just mean to be destroying buildings."

"OK, but what if the strings that saw us and tell someone we are here and they send out the strings that want to kill us?"

"Good point. We should probably get moving then, just in case that happens."

"What... you mean into the city?" asked Fred shocked.

"Yes, if we stay here this would be the first place they look. If we stay far away from the areas that are being cleared we should be able to avoid the strings seeing us again. Let's travel north along the edge of the corn fields to the dyke and follow it into the untouched areas. We will be less noticeable against the fields and side of the dyke than we would be out in the open. With any luck we will get to the other side of the city by noon," said Jack.

"We'll need to go slow enough to not kick up a lot of dust, but we still might make it by noon," said Fred.

"Whatever you two decide is OK by me. You guys have had more luck avoiding getting killed by these things than anyone else has," said Bob.

They walked quickly to the cart to find the horses were a little agitated. Jack quickly calmed them down allowing Fred to hitch them to the cart. Once they got off the road and into the wasteland the ride became unexpectedly smooth. The ground was very flat, looking as though it had been compacted by a steam roller. There were no signs that this area was a city two days ago, not a single piece of pavement or part of a building remained.

The men sat silently in the cart during the ride, trying to comprehend what had happened. Every once in a while Jack looked at the larger ball of light then at Fred and Bob trying to make their eyes glow, but was unsuccessful. The strings dismantling the building that collapsed were making new piles of material from it, while the strings on the remains of the highway began dismantling an overpass.

As they got closer to the untouched part of the city Jack used his binoculars to look for any signs of other strings. Other than being completely covered in plants he could not see anything unusual. He then scanned the area around the larger buildings noticing some of the strings on the lower floors of several apartment buildings.

"They are all by the apartments. Everything up ahead is as overgrown as the farm area with no signs of the strings," said Jack.

"If we follow the main road on the north side of the city we will avoid getting too close to that smaller light ball on the west side of the city. We will eventually meet up with the road that runs alongside the highway," said Fred.

"We should keep moving as long as possible. If this growth continues we will eventually not be able to see where the roads are or where we are going"

"I can easily stay up all night, but I don't think the horses would be as willing"

"As long as we give them enough food and water and some breaks they will be able to pull us for about twelve hours a day, for a couple days anyway. My brother in law used them for pulling log sleds out of the woods, so this cart is quite easy for them, even on the crumbling roads," said Bob.

"There are a lot of farms between here and Abbotsford but after that everything is city. There won't be any more corn fields, so we should load up the cart at the next field," said Jack.

"We'll need water too. I doubt we are going to find anymore abandoned stores with usable supplies along the way," said Fred.

"Looks like we have about eight liters left, the horses will need a lot more than that."

"There are quite a few small rivers and streams that cross under the highway. I'll stop at the first one that looks clean enough to drink."

The roads and smaller buildings in the city were no longer visible because of the plant cover. Anyone who had never been there before would have thought it was an odd looking forest. Many of the lamp posts had bent over under the weight of the vines. The abandoned vehicles were not visible because the amount of vines that had grown between them and the buildings.

"We're not getting through that. Someone would have to clear out all the vines before the horses could pull us through," said Fred as they approached the main road.

"I hate to say it, but I think we are going to have to ride along the road on the dyke," said Jack.

"We'll have no cover up there. But it's probably better than trying to get to the highway with all those things over there. If I remember correctly, there is a park that borders the dyke all the way to the other side of the city a few blocks west of here, so we won't need to stay up there too long."

"Perfect! No cars to block our path, at least for a while anyway."

Fred drove the horses towards a gently sloped area of the dyke that was once an access road. When they got part way to the top it was clear that the dyke was not as tall they originally thought. The grass on the sides had grown extremely tall extending above the sides of the cart.

"Think you can steer this thing from the back of the cart?" asked Jack.

"What did you have in mind?" asked Fred.

"Right now we are mostly covered from the view of that thing, other than the horse's heads and the two of us. If we sit back there it might just look like a couple of horses on the dyke."

"Least I can do is try," said Fred as he tied the reins to the sides of his seat. Once they were in the back, he grabbed the reins and guided the horses on to the dyke heading towards the park. "A little awkward, but I should be able to pull it off."

They were successful at not attracting any attention, arriving at the park in only a few minutes. Other than being very overgrown the park was still quite beautiful. The grass fields looked like wheat fields and the cherry trees were laden with fruit. Once Fred had maneuvered the cart into the park he got back into his seat while Jack stood up to survey the area with his binoculars.

"The only thing I can see to worry about is that ball to the south west of us. Other than that this area looks clear," said Jack.

"Hey guys, there's a pond over there. We should get some water for the horses," said Bob.

"Good idea, they would probably also be happy to graze in this field for a while. It's a little early, but we can eat now too. No telling when or if we will find a place this nice to stop again."

"I'm going to pick a load of cherries while we're here. They will last a few days and be a nice break from canned food."

"That's assuming they don't start growing into trees," said Fred.

"OK, maybe they'll just last a day, but it's still a nice break. I think I'll eat some of them for lunch."

Once the horses were unhitched they trotted over to the pond. After drinking for a few minutes, they wandered into the overgrown field to eat some grass. Taking one of the empty oat sacks, Bob headed to a cherry tree. They were extremely full of fruit with the lower branches at Bob's eye level. Jack and Fred walked over to help, but Jack stopped, staring at the oat sack.

"What?" asked Bob.

"Everything's growing out of control, even seeds that are not in soil or water have sprouted," said Jack.

"I think we've all noticed that," said Bob a little confused.

"Yes, but why haven't these oats or the others on the cart sprouted?" asked Jack.

"Not sure, maybe they're treated with something that stops them from growing?" asked Bob.

"No, they are just raw oats, no processing and nothing added"

"Let's just be glad they aren't sprouting and hope the cherries do the same. We can try to figure out why later." Bob looked at the sack, back at Jack, shrugging before going back to picking cherries.

They spent more time in the park than initially planned after finding a couple apple trees and picking all the apples they could reach. There was also a drink vending machine under a covered picnic area that had bottled fruit juice. After emptying the vending machine they continued through the park towards the west side of the city. Some of the picnic tables still had dishes of food from the day the attack started. A few birds were on one of the tables eating the abandoned food.

The road at the end of the park had fewer cars on it than it did near the city center with the vines staying mainly on the lamp posts and buildings. The nearest light ball was now to the south east with very little blocking it from view.

When not surveying the distance for trouble, Jack wondered about not seeing any dogs for the last two days: Where did they go, had they been scared away? Had they been killed too? Why had the oats not started to grow? Was it because they were moving? Maybe they were too old? He also worried about what the threads in his leg were doing to him.

Bob studied the ball, trying to figure out what it was and how it worked. He had spent his early years in the armed forces, allowing him to see quite a few classified energy weapons, but nothing on this scale with this capability. He didn't wonder about who could have made it since he knew it had to have been one of the super powers, but instead wondered about why they would attack Canada but he could not come up with any reasons.

Fred thought only about Joan and ignored everything else. Since the attack started he had missed her more than he had in quite a while. But he was relieved, in a strange way, that she was not there to see everything he had seen.

The cart started passing a side street that had a direct view of the area where the nearest light ball was located. "Stop the cart!" said Jack, causing Fred to pull back hard on the reins, stopping the horses abruptly which sent Bob flying to the front of the cart, smashing his shoulder against a sack of oats.

"Sorry! You startled me, what's wrong?" asked Fred.

"Don't be sorry, my fault for yelling. It's just that I have a clear view down this street," said Jack.

"Anything besides that light up there?" asked Bob as he sat up, rubbing his shoulder.

"Yes, a lot of those light strings and... not sure... it went behind one of the pillars... no, there it is, another wolf!" said Jack.

"Awe crap, the last thing we need is more of those," said Fred.

"Two... Three... Four... Shit! There are a lot of them up there. Let's get moving again before anything sees us."

Fred got the cart moving again as Jack put down the binoculars.

"I wonder if they are at all the light balls?" asked Bob.

"Could be, maybe they're guarding whatever is being built," said Fred.

54

"I don't care to find out. The sooner we are away from this place the better," said Jack.

"We'll be at the highway in an hour at this rate. Then it should be faster travelling since the side road is used mainly by transports during the weekdays and should be mostly empty."

Getting closer to the highway the number of cars on the road had increased, but not so much as to block their path. The road that ran alongside the highway was mostly hidden since it had no power lines or lamp posts. Fred was unsure of where it started since there were no vehicles near the intersection, so Jack decided to walk around the area looking for broken up pavement in the overgrowth. Once he found the start of the road a short distance away, he helped guide the horses on to it. The highway, only ten meters away from the side road, was clogged with abandoned vehicles. After riding for a couple kilometers they started encountering abandoned trucks every few hundred meters. When they passed a warehouse complex the number of trucks dropped significantly. The area didn't have as many vines growing as the city or farm land before it did, but that was made up for by the amount of weeds growing everywhere. The rest of the day was uneventful with only one more abandoned car on the road. Just before sunset they approached a point where the road curved south.

"Uh oh, I forgot about this," said Fred.

"Doesn't the road go all the way to Abbotsford?" asked Jack.

"Kind of. There is a river up ahead and there is a road on the other side, but there is no bridge connecting it to this one"

"Where does this road end up?"

"Somewhere in the farms south of the highway, but I don't know if it ever crosses the river. The only times I have been in this area I was on the highway."

"There has to be a road that crosses somewhere or else all the farm vehicles would have to use the highway to get to the other side," said Bob

"Good point, but let's make camp up ahead by the river. I'd rather travel through unfamiliar territory during full daylight, especially with all this overgrowth blocking our view most of the time. Hmm, the grass doesn't look as tall up ahead. I'll try to maneuver the horses down to the river."

The plants were much shorter between the river and where the road curved because of a cement boat launch, allowing Fred to drive the horses right up to the river.

After eating some of the fruit they had picked earlier Jack watched the reflection of the sunset in the river until it faded away, when he noticed a faint glowing light in the water. "Guys look, what's that?" asked Jack.

"Can't tell from here," said Fred.

Jack grabbed his binoculars to get a better look at the glow. "Holy crap, it's a fish! It has glowing lights moving around it skin!"

"Does it look anything like..."

"My leg did? Yes. I can't see any threads, but the glowing looks the same"

"Why would those things be in a fish?" asked Bob.

"Don't know and don't care. Let's move back up to the road, I don't feel comfortable down here anymore," said Fred, preparing to move the cart.

"Did you guy notice that the only glowing in the sky is coming from the east, in Chilliwack, and nothing in the west?" asked Jack.

"Hey yeah, your right, maybe they haven't attacked anything west of here yet," said Bob scanning the sky.

"Or they're already done... Sorry for being the downer here, but I've seen nothing in the last two days that gives me any hope for a good outcome to all this. I just want a shot at whoever did this before they kill me too," said Fred angrily.

"You're not alone on that, if we can get near them I want a shot too, then another, and another, and..." said Bob.

"OK guys, we should get some sleep so we can get going early tomorrow. No point in working ourselves up over something we cannot do right now anyway," said Jack.

They sat in silence for a while. Fred flopped against the side of the cart trying to sleep while Jack and Bob watched the glowing sky to the east.

"You think he's right?" asked Bob in a whisper.

"Maybe, maybe not. I can't blame him for his outlook though. The accident broke his spirit and left him with a huge hole in his life. A lot of people in his situation would have completely given up long ago, but I still see the old Fred once in a while and refuse to give up on him... I think I'll try to sleep now."

Falling asleep wasn't easy for anyone to do with everything they had seen during the day. Thoughts of what happened in Chilliwack and what might have happened in every other city kept everybody's mind racing. Jack thought about the dream he had two nights ago, deciding if it happens again he will try to control the outcome. The night was very quiet other than the sound of water flowing in the river. Eventually they all fell asleep, more from exhaustion than sleepiness.

Jack's dream started again with everything unfolding the same way as before, only this time it felt completely real and nothing like a dream. This time when Fred's eyes first started glowing Jack grabbed his arm. "Who are they? Where are they?" demanded Jack, but the dream continued as it did before. When the dream got to the point just before Bob was attacked by a wolf, Jack jumped in front of him before the wolf appeared, but this time the wolf crashed through a different window. Once again the dream continued as it did before, moving along to the point where Jack was standing in front of the ball of light. "Who are they? Where are they?" demanded Jack again. This time instead of being jolted awake the dream continued. The voice coming from the ball of light said, "Your time is over. Your time must begin. The others will end your time. He must find you now." Jack tried to speak again, but could not. He stared at the ball of light because was sure he could make out the faint image of gigantic stone towers on a cliff. The dream faded away as he entered a dreamless sleep, until the sound of Fred knocking over some cans woke him.

Chapter 5

Jack sat up slowly while rubbing his eyes. The sun was almost up but he felt like he had not slept at all.

"You look like crap. Couldn't sleep?" asked Fred.

"I did, but I don't feel like I did."

"Maybe Fred's snoring kept you awake. Sure didn't help me sleep," said Bob as he sat up.

"No, it's something else," said Jack as he described how he managed to change his dream.

"That's strange; you added to your dream. Mine has always ended at the same spot," said Fred.

"Does it mean anything that he added to it like that?" asked Bob.

"Dunno. Joan talked a lot about dreams and how to control them. She never mentioned anything about adding to them. She would have a lot of fun trying to figure out that 'your time is over' mumbo jumbo I bet."

"It didn't feel like I was asleep though. It was as real as sitting here talking to you two is, and I swear that someone was watching me," said Jack.

Fred pointed to a couple cows standing next to the cart behind Jack . "Maybe it was them, they wandered over here sometime during the night. I'm impressed and a little jealous though. It took me over a week to get the slightest control over my dream."

"Maybe after a couple more nights you'll figure out who did this and how we can go kick their asses," said Bob.

"I'll try to remember that tonight," said Jack with a chuckle.

Fred opened a can of beans and started eating, with the other two doing the same. After breakfast they continued south, deciding to take the first road they found that crossed the river. Once across the river they would travel southwest to the road that ran along the border, following it to avoid the major roads which would be clogged with abandoned vehicles. Their main concern was that as they got closer to Vancouver the number of vehicles would increase, most certainly blocking them from taking the cart into the city.

They travelled a short distance south before finding a road crossing the river. For the rest of the morning the trip was uneventful. No buildings could be seen because of the plants covering them, but their locations were still easy to spot due to their shapes. Near noon they approached an industrial area at the bottom of a hill that looked more like a cubist painting of a jungle than a place where warehouses would be located. They decided to stop near one of the larger buildings to let the horses rest. After giving the horses something to eat and drink they decided to check out a few of the buildings. Every once in a while something could be heard crashing to the ground inside a building.

"Looks like the roofs have caved in on most of these, and the rest don't look like they are going to last much longer," said Fred.

"Yeah, don't think it's to safe going in any of these buildings, the ones still standing are falling apart fast," said Bob.

"I doubt we will find any buildings that are safe. A couple more days and everything is going to be rubble, either from those strings tearing them apart or the weight of the plants causing them to collapse," said Jack.

"We better cut the amount of rest and sleep time we take in half. If we don't get to Vancouver quick there may be nothing left to get to," said Fred.

"Might not be much left now... If we continue up this road we will eventually get to the airport, right?"

"Yeah, but I wouldn't count on finding any working aircraft if that's what you had in mind."

"No, but the control tower is made from reinforced concrete so if the strings haven't gotten to it yet..."

"It should still be standing and we can use it to survey the region!" said Fred excitedly.

"Yes, that tower is the highest point in the area. We should be able to see at least fifty kilometers in all directions."

"I need to start thinking more clearly. I should have thought of that myself. I've flown us in and out of that airport hundreds of times," said Fred, slightly angry with himself.

"I hate to be the one to bring this up guys, but what do we do if things look worse towards Vancouver?" asked Bob.

"When you used your radio back in Brentwood, what was the farthest station that you talked with?" asked Jack.

"Portland to the south. They had talked with Salem which had not been hit. Kelowna to the east and Walla Walla to the south east, neither place had been able to contact anyone further east."

"Well then, if there is nothing left here we should head south since there may be a chance these attacks ended at Salem. Even if they didn't, living through winter up here would be much more difficult than it would the farther south we go."

They walked quickly back to the cart without checking more buildings so they would arrive at the airport before dark. The road went up the hill for a short distance then into a forested area. Once the cart reached the top of the hill they could see in the distance, past the trees, there was nothing but empty land.

"Shouldn't there be some subdivisions up ahead?" asked Jack.

"Yes, and some stores too. Looks like they've been here too," said Fred losing the small bit of excitement he had earlier.

When they reached the end of the forested area, there was no longer any indication a city had been there. As far as they could see, the rolling hills were now covered in nothing but grass. Off in the distance they could see the tops of a few towers similar to the pillars they had seen near the balls of light.

"Why destroy a city to turn it into a field of grass? This doesn't make any sense, it's like they are trying to erase everything we have ever made," said Fred.

"Succeeding I'd say. I don't think there is any point trying to get to..." said Bob

"Put your hands where I can see them and don't move, do anything else and I will kill you!" yelled a voice from the woods behind them.

They slowly held their hands in the air. "Who are you? Where are you from?" asked the voice.

"I'm Jack Campbell from Brentwood," said Jack.

"Fred Anderson from the same place," said Fred.

"Inspector Bob Jackson, Brentwood RCMP," said Bob.

"You three are the first survivors we have seen since the lights came! Eddie, come on out, they are Canadian! Sorry men, you can relax now, I didn't realize others had survived," said the voice.

The three men put down their hands while turning around to see an armed forces captain with an automatic rifle standing behind them and a corporal emerging from the woods.

"Captain George Ellis, that is Corporal Eddie Vern," said the Captain as he walked towards the cart.

"How did you survive the attack? Is there anyone else? Who is doing this?" asked Bob.

"Those are the same questions we had for you. Where did you manage to find all this fruit?" asked Captain Ellis looking in the back of the cart.

Jack, Fred and Bob started telling the two soldiers everything that had happened to them since the attack started. When they told them about the light threads in Jack's leg Captain Ellis got a concerned look on his face while gripped his rifle.

"Whoa, calm down Captain, they're gone now! Jack, show him your leg," said Bob.

Jack moved his tattered pant leg out of the way, showing where the gouge was.

"We can't see them, so what, how do I know they are gone and not controlling you right now?" asked Captain Ellis.

"Look at his arms and leg, they're all scratched up from when he jumping out of the cart yesterday. If those things were in him, the scratches would be healed up by now," said Bob.

"That just proves they are no longer healing him, for all I know they are hiding somewhere in his body waiting for the right moment to turn him into God knows what! Or maybe they transferred themselves to one of you two!"

"What would be the point Captain? To make a few of us think we are going to survive for a few days until suddenly BAM! They kill us all? I've seen nothing in the last couple days that indicates whoever is doing this want to do anything but wipe out any trace of us as quickly as possible. Let us finish telling everything that has happened than you can decide if we are dangerous or not, OK?"

"OK, but do it fast"

They continued telling the soldiers about their experiences as well as Fred's theory of how there were different strings for different jobs. They all silently decided not to say anything about Jack's dreams to avoid any more confrontations. After they were finished the soldiers looked a little less concerned but were still gripping their guns tightly.

"So you think they came from the wolf that bit you? Then why did they just disappear after fixing your leg" asked Captain Ellis.

"I am not one hundred percent sure they did disappear. They might only do something if I am seriously hurt," said Jack.

"Then why should I trust any of you? For all I know, you were sent here to infect us with those things." said Captain Ellis.

"OK Captain, how about this: you can take my hunting knife and gouge my leg. I'll tell you how to do it so you won't cause any permanent damage if those things aren't in me anymore. Fred please get some rubbing alcohol from the first aid kit to clean the knife"

"Jack this is not a good idea," said Fred.

"The captain is right to worry. I have been worrying about it myself and I need to know if they are really gone. Don't worry Fred, I will help him to only cut through my skin and not damage anything else."

"This is just plain stupid" grumbled Fred as he got the alcohol.

The captain cleaned the knife then with Jack's guidance cut into in his leg.

Jack yelped in pain, "AHHH! That knife isn't as sharp as I had thought. It feels like my leg has been ripped apart. It's bleeding much worse than before."

They all watch the leg bleed for a while before Fred bandaged it up.

"Well, they are either gone or hiding," said Captain Ellis.

"Listen Captain, if you are that worried about it then there is going to be no way for us to convince you that it is safe to be around us, so maybe you would feel safer travelling on your own again," said Bob.

"No, you misunderstand. I'm just not ruling out that they might still be in him somewhere. You are correct that it would not follow the enemy's pattern to toy with a few random people before killing them, but that doesn't make me believe those things are completely harmless," said Captain Ellis.

"That's the same way I have felt since discovering them in my leg, but there isn't much I can do other than hope they are really gone." said Jack.

"So now that you know everything that happened to us, how did you two survive the attacks?" asked Fred.

"Just in the right place when it all happened. We were in a convoy of transports on the highway when one of those light went shooting across the sky north towards the mountains and a little while later the shockwave hit. Every vehicle skidded to a stop, there were quite a few injuries from the larger vehicles ramming into smaller ones. The Major in charge of the convoy had the other men carry the injured while guiding everyone else to the hotels just south of here. The airport was sending out requests for help treating a large number people who were injured when a plane rammed into the terminal after losing power. So the corporal and I were sent to the airport with some first aid gear. We got as far as the university just off the highway when the second attack happened. A lot of people ran away but most just went indoors. Quite a few people were burnt when the electronic devices they were near blew apart. We did what we could to help them, but mainly showed others what to do so we could continue to the airport. When we finally arrived at the airport in the late afternoon we patched up everyone the best we could, luckily there were no serious injuries. It was getting too dark to walk back so I decided that the corporal and I would share watch duty in the tower since it had the best view of the area. Shortly after dark we saw the same event you did in the sky followed by strings... millions of them coming from the north... covering everything as far as we could see. When they hit the airport we could see everyone being dragged away. We jammed the doors shut with some chairs but they never came up the stairwell as far as we could tell. When they started climbing the outside of the tower we hid out of sight under the desks and stayed there until they left. They swarmed over the city for a while then went back to the mountains. When it started getting light we headed back to the convoy, this time taking the road that you took up here. Before we got to the woods over there, one of those lights came in from the north and hovered in front of the airport. We ran into the woods and watched as it sent out those strings to very quickly dismantle the entire structure. It was gone in under an hour. We continued hiding in the woods, since they didn't seem interested in them, only the city. By the end of the day there was nothing left but bare dirt. A total of five lights had shown up to build those towers off in the distance. When we woke up today there were grass fields instead of dirt and the lights were gone. We surveyed the area to find everything north of the highway was gone as well. The only area they didn't destroy is between these woods and the warehouse area east of here, but we have no idea why they left it."

"Sounds like what we saw in Chilliwack only they worked a lot faster here," said Jack.

"Did either of you see or hear any planes crash?" asked Fred.

"No, and we've wondered about that too. If everything lost power why aren't there crash sites all over the valley? There are... were planes landing and taking off here every five to ten minutes," said Captain Ellis.

"Well, it looks like going to Vancouver will be pointless now. Our other option was to head south until we found someplace that wasn't attacked. Could take months, you two are welcome to come with us," said Jack.

"Thank you for the offer, but we have other plans. For all we know Canada has been wiped out, but it is still our duty to protect what is left and drive out the enemy."

"I seriously doubt your guns will have much effect on them Captain."

"I agree. We have no plans to get ourselves killed trying to shoot those lights. Our first action will to be scout out those towers they built. See if they have any obvious weaknesses, or if we are lucky they might contain something we can use against them. We could always use more people if you three are interested in helping."

"We're not soldiers, but I would love a chance at giving these bastards some payback," said Fred.

"That makes two of us," said Bob.

"I've never been much of a fighter, but I am willing to help scout the towers to look for anything that might be useful to you," said Jack.

"Thank you, I know you two would prefer a fight, but that would only get you killed, "said Captain Ellis to Fred and Bob. "We need to find their weak spots and hit them hard, but we need to do it in a way that won't lead them to us. I doubt the towers are for decoration, so I am assuming they have some sort of military purpose, therefore there will be some sort of weaponry in them."

"What sort of weapons would they have? All they have used on us are those light strings," said Jack.

"That's exactly what I am hoping is in those towers. If they are storing some there, I want to figure out how to reconfigure them to attack the balls."

"That seems very risky Captain. Are you just going to walk in there and take them?" asked Fred.

"I haven't planned that far yet, I am just giving you my best case scenario. That's why we scout first then decide the next step. Keeping your mind on the best case outcome will help to remove any doubt or fear and let you overcome great odds and survive. If you always think about what could go wrong or why it won't work you could get yourself or any one of us killed."

Fred started to speak but Jack interrupted, "Sorry captain, but we haven't had much to be positive about. Fred and I work for search and rescue and the first thing on our mind is always survival."

"Good to know, I don't want to put anyone in a situation where the only outcome would be to get themselves killed. If you are all ready we should prepare to scout those towers. Our main problem is to remain unseen. As long as we are in or near these woods we should be safe, but out in those open fields they will notice us without even trying."

"So we'll need to wait for it to get dark out again then," said Jack.

"Yes, that's exactly what we planned to do. We counted seven in all. Found a nice large Oak to climb in the Northern part of these woods, which made it easy. They closest is about seven kilometers away and the furthest about ten. The central tower is slightly taller and wider than the outer ones. Here, look at this old map of Abbotsford we used to show roughly where they are."

"How did you get those distances with no streets or buildings for reference?"

"I live here, or lived I guess. I know the rough distances down the highway between each hill, so I made a best guess by figuring out which hills lines up with which tower. It was a little difficult with nothing but fields out here now, but I can still picture in my mind where everything was on these hills," said Corporal Vern.

"Lucky you have someone from the area in your unit, eh Captain," said Fred.

"The luck is that we have Eddie here. I grew up in Abbotsford also, but I don't have the knack for working with distances and landmarks like he does... You three can scout the three towers on the south while we scout the three on the north then we can meet up just west of the one in the middle and scout it together before coming back here," said Captain Ellis.

"Hey Jack, I just noticed the layout of those towers," said Fred.

"Yeah me too, I wonder why they build them like that?" said Jack

"You've seen this before?" asked Captain Ellis.

"Yes, light balls we have seen were always hovering in the air surrounded by six pillars in this hexagon pattern. The only exception was that giant one that was all by itself"

"Since the balls you have seen seemed to be some sort of central gathering spot for the strings that could mean this central tower is some sort of gathering spot also"

"But for what?"

"Nothing good I suspect. Let's meet between the two towers on the west instead, a little further away from the central tower than the original spot. If anything prevents any of us from getting there we will meet back here in the woods. I don't suppose any of you have a mechanical watch?" asked Captain Ellis.

"I have a stopwatch in my survival gear."

"That will do. Can you prevent it from being stopped accidentally?"

"Yes, there is a lockout switch on the side which disengages the buttons."

"OK this should work then. When my watch hits eight pm you will start your stopwatch then lock it out. An hour later it will be dark enough to head out, you three south and us two north. Giving about four hours to scout the towers and rendezvous, we will meet up at when my watch is at one am and your stopwatch is at the five hour mark. I will give a one hour buffer to make up for any unforeseen circumstances. So if one of our groups isn't there by two a.m. then we will fall back to meeting here. There is a partial moon tonight for a while after sunset, so keep anything metal out of sight. I don't want anyone to be noticed due to a glint of light. Take this face paint and blackout anything metal on you that cannot be hidden. We have quite a few hours before sunset, so let's hide the horses and cart deeper in the woods then rest."

They maneuvered the cart behind the trees lining the remains of the road and tied the horses to one of the trees. Jack was uneasy leaving the horses tied up since there was no guarantee they would be able to come back, so they decided to untie the horses before leaving. By late afternoon they had finished preparations, so everyone except Captain Ellis decided to get a bit of sleep.

Jack started having the same dream again, feeling more real than the last time. This time when Fred's eye's first started to glow he grabbed Jack by the shoulders. "You must stay away from them! They will extinguish your light! Your time must begin!" said Fred in a panicked tone.

"Who are they, what do you mean, who you are?" asked Jack very confused.

"They are him; he is them! Do not go to them!"

"I don't understand who they are. How can I avoid them if I don't understand?"

"They are force, he is thought."

As Fred let go of Jack the dream world swirled into a ball of light before fading to black.

Jack woke up feeling very confused and decided not to tell anyone about his latest dream. Sunset was still about an hour away so he took some time to feed the horses a little extra food in case they didn't make it back when planned. When the horses were no longer interested in eating, he decided to study what could be seen of the towers through his binoculars.

"Here, try mine," said Captain Ellis, handing Jack his binoculars.

"These look more like two short telescopes welded together," said Jack with a slight laugh.

"Might be. You can certainly see as far with them, take a look at the central tower."

There were two figures moving around the top of the central tower which had a short wall around it, blocking what they were working on. They were completely covered in a smooth dull black material which didn't appear to have any openings. The tower itself was made from the same material as all the pillars he had seen in the last couple days. The smaller towers, also made from the same material, did not have anyone moving on top. All the towers were very plain looking with no apparent openings on them.

"Wow, wish search and rescue had these binoculars... I can see people moving on the top, but what are they wearing?"

"Near as I can tell it's some sort of full body armor. It appears to cover them one hundred percent. I couldn't see any gaps in it. I am guessing the surface of the headpiece has audio and video sensors with a display on the inside. It would also be filtering the air for them. Only seen stuff like that on a drawing board. Had no idea someone had actually made it."

"Who would have the ability to make something like this? Wouldn't the military have known about it?"

"Anyone, hell half the universities on the planet were designing suits like that for space exploration."

"So anyone could have made the light balls and strings then?"

"No, those are different. I've never heard of anyone working on stuff like that. Those would have come from a very well off country with a lot of money for research and the ability to keep it secret. But any country like that is supposed to be our friend, which means someone has turned on us."

Jack studied the tower until sunset, he and the captain then synchronized the watch and stopwatch before everyone checked their weapons. The faint light from the streamers started to appear as the two groups set off to their scouting targets. The ground was quite flat with short grass, making the walk very easy. The first thing they all noticed after getting about one kilometer from the woods was the lack of sound. There were no crickets, frogs or anything else that would be expected to be making noise at night. The only sounds were coming from their breathing, their boots walking on the grass, and a low hum from the towers in the distance.

"This is damn creepy, feels like that area we walked through after that huge forest fire," said Fred.

As they reached the top of the first hill on their path they stopped for a moment since they could now see the entire first tower they would be scouting. There were no lights coming from the tower, only a very faint streamer emerging from the top then connected with the rest in the sky. The larger tower in the distance had a slight glow coming from the top.

"Doesn't look like it has any windows, let's keep moving. I want to stay at least one hundred meters away from it," said Jack in a low voice as they all started walking again.

"No argument from me on that. Even with the lack of light I still feel like I'm being watched," said Fred.

They decided to walk to a hill south of the tower which would give them a better view as well as provide some cover. Once at the hill, they each took a turn examining the tower through the binoculars.

"I don't know what we expected to see by getting closer, just looks like a solid stone tower to me. No doors, no windows, nothing but tower," said Bob.

"I didn't see anything moving on or around the tower. I want to get a closer look," said Jack.

"Have you gone crazy? What if there is a door on the other side with a platoon of soldiers waiting inside?" asked Fred.

"I don't want to walk right up to it. We can circle around until we can see the other side then slowly get closer."

"Still doesn't sound safe"

"Well, we won't learn much about the tower or whoever built it if we don't take some risks. It will be easy to approach quietly with only grass under our feet. If we see a door we won't get too close."

"Let's go for it. I'm tired of running away from all this," said Bob.

"Yeah, you're right. I'm just feeling really nervous tonight, I still feel like someone is watching us. Let's go," said Fred.

They circled around the tower, moving closer with each step. When they got to the other side they could see an opening at the base of the tower facing the large central tower. There was a very faint glow inside, but no sign of movement. They took turns using the binoculars to examine the opening but decided not to get any closer. They moved on to the next two towers which looked identical to the first one, each with an opening facing the large tower. When they arrived at the rendezvous point Jack checked the stopwatch which was at four hours forty five minutes.

"Looks like we are early," said Jack.

"Well, knowing military types, If the other towers are like the ones we saw the captain probably will have gone in one to check it out so we are going to have a bit of a wait," said Bob.

They watched the large tower for a while then Jack decided to tell his friends about the dream he had earlier asking for their opinions of what it meant.

"I think those strings are still in you somewhere, that's what I think. They're screwing with your mind," said Fred.

"Maybe, or they could actually be trying to help him. Maybe someone is trying to help us get out of this," said Bob.

"Why would anyone do that?" asked Fred.

"Well, in Jack's dream you said 'they are force, he is thought '. Thought could mean some sort of spy and force could mean the military. Maybe our country has a double agent working with whoever is doing this. Those threads in Jack may be letting them communicate through dreams."

"Well if that's true maybe they are trying to keep us away from the big tower. But who can do that? There is nothing that can let you talk to people in their dreams."

"That's not actually true. When I was in the forces I worked at a site where messages were sent to our agents using microwaves. Someone with a brain much bigger than mine discovered a way to modulate the microwaves so they interacted with someone's brain to create images and sounds. Damn dangerous though, it could literally cook someone's brain if used too much. Please don't mention this to the soldiers, they would probably shoot me for treason if they found out I told you."

"Wow, so I'm not going insane," said Jack with a sigh of relief.

"No and I apologize for not saying anything sooner. Until this last dream I thought you were just having nightmares."

"We should probably not mention anything we have been talking about to the soldiers. They would not only shoot Bob for treason, they would probably think Fred and me are spies and shoot us too."

"Agreed, speaking of the soldiers, I think I see something moving in the distance," said Fred.

Jack used his binoculars to see what it was, "I think it's them. Two soldier shaped silhouettes."

After a short wait the soldiers arrived explaining what they saw. The captain had decided to examine the inside of one of the towers, where they discovered a glowing spiral ramp which appeared to run all the way to the top. They had also gone closer to the large tower, but since there were a few dozen figures moving around it they decide not to approach.

"So the towers all appear to be the same, each about fifteen meters in diameter, except the middle one which appears to be at least double the width with soldiers guarding it. I want to go to the top of one of these smaller towers but I won't ask anyone else to come unless they are up for the risk. I couldn't see anything inside but that doesn't mean it is safe," said Captain Ellis.

"You can count me in," said Jack and Fred in unison.

"Me too sir," said Corporal Vern.

"No way I'm going to be the only human left alive if this goes bad. I'm going too," said Bob.

"Good, let head out then," said Captain Ellis.

They all walked to the nearest tower with the two soldiers leading the way. When they got to the opening Captain Ellis took a quick look inside up the ramp, "Nothing as far as I can see. Corporal, you stay down here. Alert us if anything unusual happens."

"I'll go halfway up with you so if Corporal Vern does have to call us he won't have to yell very loud and possibly alert the enemy," said Bob.

"Good, then the three of us will scout out the top half."

Corporal Vern walked a few meters in front of the tower scanning the surrounding area while the other four entered the tower. Up close the tower looked and felt smooth but not slick, like ground unpolished stone. The ramp had small sparks of light moving randomly around the surface but flowing up towards the top of the tower. Captain Ellis touched the ramp with the tip of his boot but nothing happened, so he stepped onto it to start walking up. There were no features or windows anywhere in the tower. Everything was just a plain stone surface. Halfway up Bob stopped to sit down while the others continued on. At the top they discovered a short wall which was blocking the view of a small metal sphere about one meter in diameter sitting in the middle of the tower. The lights flowed off the ramp, towards the sphere, over its surface, converging into a single stream that ran into the sky.

"So this must be what those streamers are made up from, but what are they?" asked Jack.

"Maybe some sort of communications system," said Captain Ellis.

"The surface of this sphere is very interesting. It looks polished, but there are no reflections."

"These little lights remind me of sparks from a fire, only they are much whiter," said Fred.

"We've got trouble!" yelled Bob from inside the tower.

They looked over the edge to see Corporal Vern running inside the tower and a large number of silhouettes approaching fast from the direction of the large tower.

"Shit, get ready for a fight men!" yelled Captain Ellis.

The streamer coming from the sphere started to get brighter, as did the one going to the large tower. As Bob arrived at the top of the tower a loud crackling noise came from the sky with pulses of light flowing to the sphere which was starting to hum loudly.

"What the hell is that?" asked Bob, stopping at the top of the ramp as soon as he saw the sphere.

Jack saw a bright flash of light come from the sphere. "Use it now!" said a booming voice in Jack's mind as the light disappeared. He shook his head, unsure of what just happened. In the distance towards Chilliwack he could see a light ball moving quickly towards them.

"This is it, let try to take some of them out before they get us!" yelled Fred.

"I have an idea," said Jack as he moved to the sphere touching it.

"What the hell are you doing!" yelled Captain Ellis.

Jack could feel something move out of his palm as the sphere started vibrating. The surface of the sphere started rippling like a liquid then broke free of the tower. He pushed it on to the ramp causing it to accelerate down. The streamer broke off, pulling up into the sky as the humming stopped.

"Why the hell did you do that?" asked Captain Ellis.

"I'm not sure, I just had an overwhelming feeling I should do it," said Jack.

"Uh guys, look," said Fred pointing to the field below them where the figures were now moving quickly away from the tower.

Before anyone could say or do anything else the sphere reached the bottom of the ramp, slamming into the wall of the tower then exploding, sending a shockwave of light out in all directions which destroyed the base of the tower. The tower started to collapse as everyone tried desperately to hang on to the wall. The shockwave appeared to vaporize the figures in the field as well as the base of the other towers. A loud metallic groan came from the large tower which was followed by a bright flash of light with a crackling noise as it was reduced to rubble. The top of the tower Jack was on stopped falling with a sharp jolt only to start tipping over, eventually landing on its side covering everyone in debris as it crumbled from the impact. Jack was unable to move, blood was trickling down his face. All he could see was a swarm of light strings coming out of the ball approaching them, but before anything happened everything faded to darkness as he lost consciousness.

Chapter 6

Jack was floating weightless in front of a ball of light. Is this a dream? I feel awake. The world around him was nothing but swirling lights with a constant low hum. He touched his head where he had felt the blood, but there was no blood or wound. I must be dreaming. The ball of light was also different this time, having some patches which were not as bright as the rest of it.

A voice came from the ball of light, this time it was Jack's own voice. "He apologizes. You are safe."

"I don't understand. Who is he? Where am I? If I am safe, why apologize?" asked Jack.

The world faded to black once more, but instead of losing consciousness Jack began to feel a throbbing in his head with an aching in his entire body. As a feeling of weight returned he realized he was lying on the ground, but there was no rubble covering him. He opened his eyes slowly seeing he was surrounded by a dense forest, or was it a jungle. The sun was now up. The trees looked like huge cedars, but there was also gigantic bamboo and ferns everywhere. As he sat up looking around, he realized he was sitting in the middle of a dirt path. He touched his head again but there was still no wound or any blood. There was a rustling in the ferns before a light string quickly emerged. It circled him a few times before moving back into the woods.

Jack felt extremely confused. What the hell is going on? Where am I? It's daytime, how long have I been out of it? Why am I not hurt? He decided to see where the path led so he got up. After walking a while he could hear some noises, maybe voices, in the distance. As he approached the sounds he moved into the foliage to keep out of sight. A short distance away he could see the top of a wall that looked like it had been built from the bamboo. Eventually he could see an opening in the wall with two figures standing on each side. They were wearing the same kind of body armor he saw earlier. Why is this structure built from bamboo instead of the stone used everywhere else? Maybe there isn't enough rock here?

Jack watched the figures near the opening for a while when he heard something moving up the path. Eventually two men came into view, approaching the opening. They were wearing dirty, torn clothing looking like they had not washed for many weeks. When they passed through the opening one of the men waved to the armored figure closest to him as it waved back. What the... they know each other. Are these men the ones who attacked us?

Jack started moving as quietly as possible away from the wall. He decided to avoid any paths, staying in the dense foliage. Moving through the woods was difficult at times because of the amount of bamboo, but eventually he emerged on the shore of a small pond. From there he could see that the trees were each at least seventy meters tall and the bamboo at least twenty meters tall. The sky was clear, the sun was overhead, but the air was cooler than it should be for a mid-summer day.

Walking around the pond Jack eventually saw an opening in the trees with the remains of many high rise towers in the distance. I must be near a city! Many of the towers had fallen against other towers, some had partially collapsed. He quickened his pace in an attempt to get to the other side of the pond but was startled by a woman's voice coming from a trail that he had not noticed.

"Depressing, isn't it?" asked the woman.

Jack turned around to see two women walking up the trail, both in worn, dirt covered clothes.

"I haven't seen you before, are you new? I'm Valerie and this is Jill."

"Where am I, who are you, how did I get here?" asked Jack very confused.

"You don't know where you are, how did you get here?" asked Valerie.

"I woke up way back over there," said Jack pointing in the direction he came from.

"He might have a head injury if he doesn't remember how he got here. Let's get you to Doc," said Jill.

"I'm not going anywhere until I know where I am and who you are," said Jack stubbornly.

"You are in Vancouver, in what was Stanley Park. If you came from over there you were very close to our settlement," said Valerie.

"The only settlement I saw had enemies guarding the entrance," said Jack.

"Enemies... Oh! The guys in the armor. Don't worry, they're with us. Come with us, Doc will explain everything," said Valerie.

"You have their armor?"

"Yes, Doc can explain it all. She's heard the stories first hand."

Jack cautiously followed the two women back to the wall he found earlier.

"Found another wanderer did you? That's the second one this week!" said one of the figures as they approach.

"This week" thinks Jack, "Have I been out of it for a week?"

As they passed through the opening Jack could see they were in a large fort like structure. The walls were lined with small rooms also built from bamboo. A few dozen people were spread out in the open central area, some talking, others sleeping. There was a ledge near the top of the wall with a three more figures in armor walking between three towers. He was led to a large room near the back which appeared to be some sort of doctor's office. Sitting on a stool next to a bed was an older woman who was examining a child's ankle.

"Found another one Doc, he doesn't know how he got here so we thought you should check him out," said Valerie.

"He's not very dirty. He didn't swim in the pond did he? That's our only supply of clean water" said Doc.

"I don't think so, did you?" Valerie asked Jack.

"No, I was more interested in getting to the city. I assume you are a doctor. Can you tell me why I don't remember what happened to me?" asked Jack.

"Yes, Doctor Nancy Blake, but everyone just calls me Doc. What is the last thing you remember?"

Jack explains the scouting mission he was on, destroying the towers, and the ball of light he saw before becoming unconscious.

Doc's face went pale as thought she had seen a ghost. "What is your name?"

"Jack Campbell."

Valerie and Jill both gasped.

"You are one lucky son of a bitch. Everyone thought the only survivors were a couple of soldiers, and from what they described you should be dead," said Doc.

"Wait, you've talked to Captain Ellis and Corporal Vern?"

"Yes, they were in the city a few weeks ago and told a few of us what happened."

"Weeks! How long ago did everything happen?"

"Well, the first attack happened five and a half weeks ago"

"First! Five and a half weeks! Why don't I remember anything since then, and how did I end up here?" asked Jack.

"Calm down dear, we will figure it all out soon enough. Let's get you checked out first though, OK." said Doc in a soothing voice.

Jack thought for a second then started to calm down a little, "OK, I'm just very confused, and worried about my friends. What do you want me to do?"

74

"Lie down on the examining bench over there while I get my equipment. Why don't you two wait outside and give him a little privacy."

Valerie and Jill left the makeshift doctors office. Soon afterwards Jack heard many whispered conversations starting up outside.

"There… all ready to start," said Doc as she opened metal box. Inside there were various devices which look like nothing Jack had seen before.

"I thought all the electronics were destroyed," said Jack.

"They were. These were taken from the enemy, as were the armored suits you saw the guards wearing."

"How…"

"All in good time my dear, now lay back and let me examine you… Oh my, now I see why you survived," said Doc while scanning Jack's body with one of the devices.

"What is it?"

"You have some power threads in your body. They power the suits, but also have the side effect of healing wounds."

"The light threads are still in me?"

"Yes. You know about them and knew they were in you? Did you inject them yourself?"

"No, my friends and I think they came from a robotic wolf that bit me."

"You were attacked by one of those things and are still around to talk about it! How?"

"It was damaged, I managed to shoot its eye out and Fred got it in the side if the head."

"Your luck seems to be endless. I would keep this to myself for now if I were you."

"You don't think everyone out there will trust me if they know about them?"

"No, quite the opposite. You see, as the story about how you destroyed the towers spread, you and your friends became heroes to everyone. I'm afraid if they know you have a bunch of those things in your body some of them will start thinking you are invincible. They may insist or even try to force you to attack the enemy again."

"Oh… that wouldn't be good… What happened to my friends? You keep mentioning the soldiers, but not Fred or Bob."

"Until today we all thought the three of you were dead. The soldiers saw those strings take your friends into the ball of light that showed up after your attack. The strings had just picked you up out of the rubble when one of the metal spheres from another tower exploded, blasting some rubble into the ball, sending it flying off towards the mountains."

"Fred and Bob are gone?"

"They assumed so, but the ball hadn't got you yet so they figured you were vaporized by the blast, since no body was found."

"How did the captain and corporal survive the second blast?"

"Seems they have luck too. They ended up on top of the pile of rubble of the tower. Apparently the shockwave those spheres make when they explode stays close to the ground so it passed right underneath them and vaporized some of the rubble."

"Where are they now?"

"No clue, they didn't stay long. Some soldiers they met up with on their journey here told them about us as well as something far south of here. After they unload the equipment they recovered they went to investigate without telling us anything about it."

"Others have survived?"

"Yes yes, and all due to you and your friends. After your attack the enemy stopped advancing on the city for a while, giving us enough time to fortify this camp and the headquarters then go out looking for survivors. You see, that large tower you destroyed was loaded with all sorts of useful stuff."

"Like that medical instrument and the armor."

"Yes, but we can talk about that later. Let me finish the examination first." Doc continued scanning Jack with the device then took a couple blood samples. "Well I hate to do this to you, but the examination is done, time for you to go outside and meet everyone."

"I am not looking forward to this. I've had people treat me like I'm some sort of hero before because of my work in the search and rescue, and it makes me very uncomfortable. I don't think I can handle a large group of people like that."

"Tell ya what, tell me a bit about yourself and then rest here for a while. I'll go outside and talk to everyone first. Maybe they will be a little less star struck once they know you are just a regular person like them."

"Thank you, I don't know how to repay you for this, but if you every need help with anything just let me know." Jack continued by telling Doc about the work he did with search and rescue, his life in Brentwood, and his friendship with Fred and Bob.

"That should be enough to keep me talking for a while. If you're tired you can use the table for a nap, or there are some books on the shelf over there if you prefer. You can stay in here until we eat if you want, but feel free to come out earlier if you are ready to be swamped by more questions," said Doc with a laugh as she walked towards the door.

Jack did not feel tired, in fact he felt like he already had a full night's sleep, so he decided to check out the books. On top of the book shelf he saw what looked like a sheet of glass, but when he picked it up the surface glowed where his fingers touched it. He ran his index finger over the surface and the glow followed his finger tip. When he lifted his finger the glow faded slowly. So he tried moving it around the surface quickly, managing to create a glowing line following behind the movement. He decided to press his palm on the surface to make a bigger glow, but instead the sheet lit up as a holographic image of earth rose out of it, causing Jack to jerk his hand away. Surprised by the detail on the globe, he stared at it for a while before trying to touch it. Where his finger touched the surface of the globe a small glow appeared. When he moved his hand the globe rotated to follow. He noticed a tiny green glow coming from the location of every large city in Canada and the US. He touched the glow where Vancouver would be, causing the hologram to rapidly zoom in keeping the city centered on his finger while cutting off any of the globe that was more than one meter away from the glass. Jack moved his finger away when he noticed that every place where he had seen a ball of light or a tower there was a small red glow. When he rotated the globe he could see red glows in various spots in Vancouver and the surrounding mountains.

"How did you do that? I thought it was just a sheet of glass," said Doc as she came back into the building.

"I touched the surface with my hand and a globe appeared."

"Amazing. Those threads in you must be powering it."

"I thought they were dead or burnt out since none of the scrapes and scratches I've gotten lately have instantly healed up."

"We have only seen them activate their healing abilities when someone gets seriously hurt."

"Do you have many of them?"

"Yes, some, they found them in one of the scanners. There weren't many so they were given to anyone who was going to fight, one per person until we ran out. One seems to be enough though; one of the guards stepped into a rabbit hole one night and broke his ankle. A couple hours later he was up and walking again."

"How many do I have in me?"

"Seven."

"OK, now I understand why you said to not mention them."

"Is that Vancouver?" asked Doc.

"Looks like it, but look at the red spots. The ones out in the valley and in the mountains are in locations where the enemy built something."

"You're right, some of the ones in Vancouver are where they built towers, but most of them don't mark anything... This thing must contain their plans! That could be why they stopped, they're afraid we will be waiting for them at the spots they haven't built anything yet. We need to get you and this thing to the major right now."

"Is he here in the camp?"

"No he's at the headquarters they set up in the Hotel Vancouver. It's one of the few buildings that weren't destroyed. There is a group that was going to return after we eat, but I think they should go now and take you with them."

"Returning?"

"Yes, oh I haven't told you have I? This camp is where the injured are sent to recover. It's much safer being hidden in the forest than in what's left of the city. No telling when they will attack it again, but so far they have left the park alone."

"Are you the only doctor they have here to help these people?"

"I am the only doctor anywhere as far as we know. They haven't found any others that made it through the attacks. So far only a few hundred people have been found."

"I had been hoping everyone somehow managed to run away and hide, but I guess I was just being delusional."

"That's a perfectly normal reaction in an extreme situation like this. Our minds aren't conditioned to accept tens of millions of people just disappearing in an instant and will do their best to come up with explanations for where they went. Now that you have started to accept the reality of what happened the hard part starts: you now have to deal with the fact that they are not coming back."

"All my friends..." said Jack as he put the glass back on the shelf, causing the globe to fade away. The reality of what had happened started to sink in. He felt a little shaky so he sat on a stool.

"Yes and your family."

"I didn't have any family. I grew up in a foster home in Brentwood. There were other children but most didn't stay long before moving on. I guess the people of Brentwood were the closest thing to family for me."

"It's not going to be easy to deal with; any one of us can tell you that. For me personally I found that keeping my mind occupied with what I need to do to help these people works. You will have to decide what's best for you in the long run, but don't be afraid to talk to anyone about it because we are all going through the same thing."

"OK, thanks Doc, I guess I should probably get ready to go now."

"Yes, don't forget the glass."

They walked outside to be met by a group of four people sitting on some logs near the center of the settlement. Everyone else in the settlement stopped what they were doing to watch.

"You already met Valerie and Jill, the other two here are George and Jake, they all work with the major. Everyone, this is Jack, I need you to take him to the major now. I apologize for the rush but he will want to talk with Jack ASAP. I'll pack up some food for you to eat on the walk back."

Jack gave a shy wave to everyone as he sat on one of the logs.

"Sorry about all this attention Jack, but you and your friends were the first people to successfully attack the enemy, all without any of their weapons. We're just excited to meet you," said George, reaching out to shake Jack's hand.

Jack shook his hand and smiled.

Doc walked back to the group with a small sack of fruits and vegetables, "It's not much but it should keep you going until you get to the major. George I want you to keep that sheet of glass Jack has in your pack and make sure nothing happens to it."

"What's so important about a piece of glass?" asked George.

"I'm sure Jack will explain on the way back, but now it is time to go. I am really sorry for rushing you four, but this is extremely important."

"OK Doc, we've been getting pretty restless waiting around here anyway. Time to move out people," said George.

Jack got up, handing the sheet to George, who looked at it with confusion before putting it in his pack, "Well if Doc says it's important, then it's important, even if it just looks like a piece of glass to me."

George led everyone out of the camp towards the remains of the city. He started telling Jack about the group, "As you've probably guessed the four of us work with the armed forces. We're engineers, not soldiers, based out of Ottawa. We all live and work there most of the time. We help with designing everything from arms storage facilities to remote detection stations. We were out here helping to decommission an old armory down by the stadiums so it could be turned into a museum."

"We were on the bottom level examining the vault door for the main storage room. It was never designed to be removed so we were trying to figure out the fastest and cheapest way to dismantle and remove it," said Jake.

"The whole building is... was... like that. Lots of giant blast doors that were never meant to come out," said Valerie.

"The ground started shaking and all the lights went out. We were lucky the major was with us. He knew the place inside out and led us out. The stairs between each floor were on opposite sides of the building, so it would have taken us quite a while without him," said Jill.

"When we got outside the city was in chaos. Car accidents everywhere, people panicking, we didn't see it but there was apparently a blast of light in the mountains that a lot of people thought was a nuke going off," said George.

"Same thing happened in Brentwood, then a wave of light," said Jack.

"Yeah, that happened here too, not good at all, fires broke out all over the place from all the burning electronics. Quite a few people were burnt. Luckily none of the fires got out of control," said George.

"We thought it was all over after nothing else happened during the day, then those damn strings came, three waves over an hour, millions of them, taking everyone away. We were lucky they couldn't get in the armory or we'd be gone too," said Valerie.

"We eventually found a few others who hid in bank vaults or storage vaults under a few of the office buildings, but everyone else was gone. A couple of the older buildings, like the Hotel Vancouver, had not been damaged. Not a single burnt out light or anything. They didn't work though since there was no longer any electricity. The major decided to set up a headquarters in the hotel and keep all the survivors there, but that didn't last long," said George.

"Why not, I thought the hotel is still standing?" asked Jack.

"It is, but the soldiers who took the first lookout watch on the top floor spotted one of those light balls on the south end of the city destroying everything with those strings. The major decided to move all non military people to the park since it had not been attacked," said George.

"Valerie and I went with a few of the soldiers to help them determine if the buildings were safe to use for shelter. At first they were, but at the end of the second day the plants had grown into everything so much they were starting to collapse, so we had to camp outside. By the next day the bamboo in the park had grown and spread so much we could use it to build some better shelter," said Jake.

"The major sent a scouting party out a couple times to see if there was anything to attack, but there was nothing but that light ball and strings destroying everything. Then during the night when they were just outside the downtown area and we were about to evacuate, the shock wave from your attack rumbled through the city," said George.

"We could see the flash of light from the blast off in the distance and thought they were getting ready to attack again. But then all the strings went back to the light ball," said Jill.

"Was that the end of all the attacks?" asked Jack.

"No, but we missed most of what happened after that. We were injured when a building near the hotel collapsed a week later. The major can explain what's been happening... So... how did you do it? We've heard the captain's stories of the attack. Let's hear it from the person who did it," said George.

Jack proceeded to recount all the major events that happened to him up to the attack on the tower, leaving out the details of his dreams since he was still worried how others would react. As he was telling the story they came into view of what was left of the city so he paused to look for a moment. Most of the high rise buildings were still standing, with a few fallen over against the buildings next to them. All the buildings were in a similar condition to the ones he had seen in Chilliwack, but there were also trees growing on most of them. The plants did not appear to be very healthy, with most of them having a brownish yellow tint.

"They did all this in five weeks?" asked Jack.

"No, three days, if you hadn't attacked that tower all this and all of us would be gone now," said George.

"That made them stop?" asked Jack.

"For a while, but what Captain Ellis found in the rubble of the main tower has kept them at bay. We've only heard the story second hand but he apparently discovered the armor has some sort of weapon that can stop the strings. We've never been given the details, but maybe the major will be more willing to tell you about it," said Jill.

"Yeah, he'll probably want you to help them with the fight," said Valerie.

"But I'm not a soldier, what use would I be?" asked Jack.

"You have no military experience and yet you still managed to hit them hard without any fighting," said Valerie.

"I don't know if that was anything more than desperation and luck," said Jack.

"We're sure hoping it was more, or else what's been the point of fighting these past few weeks?" asked Jake.

"I'm sure Jack doesn't need this kind of pressure people, so let's go a little easier on him. Don't let us stress you out Jack. I doubt any of us seriously think one person is going to save the day, but your showing up out of nowhere has given us all a lot more hope," said George.

"But you have their weapons now, why would you need me?" asked Jack confused.

"Well... I was going to let you find out from the major, but since you asked... We are not even close to winning this fight. Every week someone gets taken by the strings because their armor stops working or malfunctions. Most of us had given up hope of living more than a few more weeks, even after you showed up. But the look on Doc's face when she told me to bring you to the major told me she now believes we have a chance because of you," said George.

"Probably more because of the sheet of glass than me," said Jack.

"Doc never did say what it was. Did you figure it out?" asked George.

"Maybe... it's a map and Doc thinks it has their plans on it," said Jack.

"Wow, and you still don't believe you will be helpful. Before you showed up we thought that was a piece of glass. I'd say figuring out it might be the enemies battle plan is pretty damn helpful," said Jake with everyone else agreeing.

The rest of the walk to the hotel was spent mostly in silence as Jack thought about everything that had been said. *If I really am useful then why does everything happening accidentally? After all I was just playing around with the glass when the map showed up. Then again, what made me want to pick up a sheet of glass instead of one of the books? Is someone really communicating with me through the threads and giving me clues on what I need to do to survive? And the voice I heard at the tower telling me to use the sphere, was* that the threads too? Maybe they are talking to me in my dreams too, but if they are why is what they are telling me so confusing? Maybe the person doing this doesn't understand English very well.

As they got closer to the hotel Jack saw the north side of the hotel sticking out from behind the large office building on its west side. The hotel and sidewalks surrounding it had no plants growing out of them, looking completely untouched. A couple more blocks to the east all the buildings were gone.

"When Doc said it wasn't destroyed I thought she meant it wasn't as damaged as the rest of the buildings. How can one building not be affected by any of the plant growth?" asked Jack rhetorically.

"Not just this one, we've seen three more out in the wasteland that are like this. We have no idea how or why they were left alone," said George.

Outside the main entry to the hotel two guards wearing the now familiar body armor were guarding the entrance. One guard signaled to the group to stop as he approached them. "Who is this, friend or enemy?" asked the guard.

"I'm Jack Campbell."

The guard looked at Jack for a moment.

"Yes, that Jack Campbell," said George.

"The major will want to speak with him."

"That's where we are going."

They entered the lobby which was empty. With the exception of a small amount of light coming in from the entry way it was completely dark. They walked up an emergency stairwell to the second floor, entering a meeting room that had been turned into a makeshift command center. Sitting at a large table covered with maps were two scruffy looking soldiers having a conversation.

One of the soldiers stood up as they approached. "Well this is a surprise, glad you're back. I didn't think you four would return for at least another week. I'm still amazed none of you were crushed by all that rubble. So who's this then? I thought I had asked Doc not to send any more people from the park to headquarters unless they were military," said the soldier.

"Good to be back Major Janko. This is Jack Campbell," said George with a smile.

"He is, is he? Remarkably well preserved for a dead man wouldn't you say?"

"No really, I am Jack Campbell."

"I think I'll decide that for myself son. Lift up your pant leg."

"Huh? OH! I see, OK," said Jack as he reveals the wound on his leg.

The Majors face went white as he examined the wound closer. "Good god, it really is you. This is just how Captain Ellis described it, but why hasn't it completely healed? You've been missing for over a month."

"I'm not sure. To me it feels like everything just happened a few hours ago. When I woke up in the park it was like I had just had a short nap."

"Very strange indeed, what did Doc have to say about it?"

"We never had a chance to talk about it. After I figured out what the glass was, she had me rushed here."

"Glass? What glass?"

"Oh right, you'll be wanting this," said George as took the sheet of glass from his pack, handing it to the major.

"You five rushed here to give me a window pane?" asked Major Janko very confused.

"Not quite, Doc thinks it's a battle plan of some sort," said Jack while touching the glass with his palm, causing the holographic map to appear.

"How are you doing that?"

"Doc thinks the threads are powering it."

"Threads? You have some in you? How many?"

"Doc said seven."

"Seven! How the hell did you do that? It took us a week of experimenting with their equipment before we managed to get just one into somebody!" said Major Janko.

Jack once again explained the how the wolf attack transferred the threads to him.

"Bloody amazing! We can talk about the threads some more later. Let's examine this map first"

"Take a look at the cities, see how they have a green glow around them, and the little red glows out here in the valley are where I saw the towers or balls of light."

"Ah yes, and these spots down here are where we have seen the lights. But there are many more red glows where there is apparently nothing, which makes me wonder if they didn't do anything there because of your attack, or are they planning something in the future. Can you view a larger area?"

"Yes, I saw the whole planet when it first turned on but I am not sure how to get it back." Jack moved his fingers and hand around trying to find a way to shrink the globe. He eventually discovered that if he touched a spot then pulled it to the edge of view the globe started shrinking.

"Excellent! Now let's look for the area where the cities have not been marked and that will be where our enemy or their allies are located," said Major Janko sounding both excited and worried.

Jack rotated the globe slowly as they examined every continent but found no unmarked cities. He zoomed into Ottawa, Washington, London, Moscow, Beijing and Tokyo but still found the glow. They spent an hour examining every major city on the planet but they were all marked.

"This doesn't make any sense! If this is a battle plan then why would someone destroy everything including their own cities? Everything is marked on this map," said George.

"It makes sense if you don't want any competition around "said Major Janko.

"What? Somebody wants the world all to themselves? Where are they going to live if they destroy everything? Wouldn't any country that could make these kinds of weapons have them secured to stop someone from doing something like this?" asked George.

"No person or country is doing this. This looks like all trace of the human race are being erased from the planet."

"Wait a minute, are you saying little green men from outer space are doing this?" asked Jack incredulously.

"I doubt they are little, green or men, but other than that, yes."

"So they just show up out of nowhere with no warning and BAM, Goodbye earthlings?" asked Jack.

"If you were going to do something like this would you announce your arrival first?"

"I... I guess not. Do you really think we are being erased, as you put it?" asked Jack, realizing that the major was serious.

"I've had my suspicions for a while, but after seeing this map and the equipment we found, yes. That equipment is far beyond anything I've seen made by the most advanced military. It's the kind of stuff people think we have and we wish we had."

"What chance do we have then? What if Jack is the only one who successfully attacked them?" asked Jill, "The rest of the cities on the planet could be gone now."

"That's why we need to fight harder than ever. We could be the last humans still alive. There were a few pieces of equipment we retrieved that don't seem to do anything, but maybe you can do something with them Jack. After all you turned a chunk of glass into a battle map."

"I can try I guess," said Jack.

"The way they've been cautiously sending out only a handful of strings to attack us every day shows me they are now afraid of what we can do. Every time we use one of their weapons the strings retreat and stay away for a few days. Whatever is using the armor and controlling their wolves are probably nothing more than a security force protecting the equipment. I doubt they were expecting us to attack them let alone destroy a bunch of their towers and take their equipment."

"What do these weapons do, someone said they are in the armor? Maybe if you show me how your men have been using them I will have an easier time figuring out the other equipment."

"Yes, the armor suits are the weapon. Doc accidentally injected one of those threads into her palm while trying to figure out what the body scanner was. The next time she examined one of the suits it partially turned on when she touched it."

"So the guards can use the armor to fight? How do they work?"

"Yes they can, but there is a problem, the armor doesn't seem to be getting enough power. Sometimes it works and sometimes the armor shuts down for a moment."

"You want me to try one on don't you?" asked Jack with a worried tone.

"Yes, but don't worry, you won't be fighting. Even with their weapons we won't stand a chance once they decide to finish their job. I am hoping you can figure out some way to use this stuff to protect us, or even get us away from here, before they realize we aren't really a big threat to them. We have been doing our testing just inside the wasteland after dark in order to minimize any damage if something should go wrong. So until then, take the glass and see if you can find anything else useful that it can do."

Jack nodded, sat at the table and started experimenting with the map. Other than zooming or rotating the map he was not able to do much so he decided to see how far in he could zoom in on the red glows where the large tower had been. Once he expanded it to take up the full field of view he could see a faint outline of a tower with rows of various colored spots inside it. With the majors help they determined that each color represented different equipment that was in the tower. There were thirty six spots representing the armor, but only seventeen pieces were recovered, leaving the major to assume the others were destroyed in the blast.

Jack positioned the map to show the spot where the huge ball of light was located in Chilliwack. Zooming into this area only revealed a single striped white spot at the center of the glow. They did not know what this meant since there were no striped white spots in the tower, and Jack had not been close to the larger ball to see anything special.

Major Janko asked Jack to go to the glowing spot closest to their location where nothing had appeared yet. As he zoomed in, multiple outlines started to appear around the spot. Each outline contained dozens of spots representing the armor. Jack had noticed something appear on the edge of the map at their location as he zoomed in. So he positioned the map over the Hotel, seeing a spot that was cycling through all colors. They concluded that this must be marking the location of the map. In order to verify this, they decide to take the glass with them that night to check if the spot moved to the wasteland or stayed at the hotel.

Major Janko asked Jack to start checking the areas around smaller cities and sparsely populated areas for anything different while he got updates from his lookouts on the top floor. After about half an hour of checking the map the only thing unusual he had found was a large red glowing area in New Zealand along a cliff covered part of the coast on a peninsula far from any city. When he zoomed in he saw thousands of outlines, but had no way of knowing what kind of structures they were supposed to represent. Each one containing various colored spots, but unlike the ones he had seen in the locations of the towers, these had patterned surfaces. He began to get tired after staring at the map for about half an hour and nodded off.

Once again Jack found himself in front of a ball of light with light strings circling him. A now familiar voice boomed out "You are safe. Your time will begin. The others can end your time. Find him."

"I do not understand what you mean. Do you understand me? Is this a dream" asked Jack, again noticing towers appearing in the ball, this time a little clearer.

"He apologizes, minds too primitive. We understand. A dream?" said the voice sounding a little confused.

"Are you not from this planet?"

"Understanding! You are learning. Progress"

"Why are you destroying our world?" asked Jack angrily.

"Not destroying!"

"Is he not one of them?"

"He is them, they are he," said the voice as the dream faded away.

Jack was woken from his short nap by the sound of something being dropped and Jake swearing. He was torn over whether or not to tell the major about his dreams. If he delayed too long the major may not be willing to trust anything he said or did in the future. The major may also think he is being controlled by the Lights. But he had already used the alien technology to help, so there would be no reason to distrust him. He decided he had to tell the major. He walked over to a soldier looking out one of the windows. "How long does Major Janko usually take to return after checking with the lookouts?" asked Jack.

"He usually stays up there until shortly after sunset, studying the landscape and trying to come up with a way out of this. He says it's nice and quiet up there and he can think clearly," said the soldier.

"I need to talk with him about something important, how do I get up there?"

"We use the emergency stairwell, but it is over ten floors up, you think you can handle that?"

"I think so, I do a lot of mountain climbing and hiking," said Jack as he started walking to the stairs. The climb was fairly easy for him since he was used to walking up much steeper and uneven surfaces. He checked a couple rooms before finding the major sitting in a chair looking out a window on the south side of the building.

"Major, I need to talk to you."

"Ah, Jack, find something interesting."

Jack paused for a moment, remembering the map, "Oh, yes, I did, but I wanted to talk about something else too."

"Ok, grab a seat and tell me then. Start with what you found on the map first."

Jack showed him the area he found in New Zealand.

"I'd be tempted to say they are building a base, but this seems too large and in such a strange spot. Other than that you found nothing different or unusual."

"No, but it's a big planet. I'll have to examine everything again zoomed in a bit more, then a bit more and so on. But what I really needed to talk to you about is my dreams."

"I don't know what an old soldier could help you with there, but go ahead anyway."

Jack described what he experienced in each of his dreams before he pushed the sphere down the ramp in the tower. "Fred thought I was just having trouble dealing with what happened, but they no longer feel like dreams. I feel the same way I do talking with you right now. Do you think these threads are screwing with my mind?"

"No, I think you are perfectly sane, and I believe we have a sympathizer in the enemy's ranks. Happened in every war I've known about, someone sympathizes with the other side and tries to help them. Besides, all my men who have had a thread put in them are experiencing strange dreams with light balls in them too. They haven't mentioned anything about it talking though, could be the extra threads in you helping with that."

"So I'm not going insane?"

"No son, you have become even more valuable than we first thought. I don't know if whoever they are can do anything to save this planet, probably not, but maybe they can get us out of here and prevent the human race from being wiped out."

"To where?"

"Some place they are not interested in hopefully, or else their help would be pointless. I suggest asking them where we can go so they can help us next time you have the dream. I doubt they completely understand our language, so don't expect clear answers."

"Shouldn't I just try to sleep all the time in order to talk with them?"

"That would be tempting, but I am not completely convinced just one of them can help us, especially when we are surrounded by hostiles. After we get back from experimenting with the other equipment tonight you can try communicating again."

"OK," said Jack, looking out the window for the first time to see a much clearer view of the destruction, now realized why everyone was calling it the wasteland. Other than the small area they were in, everything was gone. There were no buildings or piles of neatly stacked rubble, just bare rock and dirt as far south as the eye could see. Near the center of the wasteland there was a set of six pillars with a single light ball.

"Unbelievable, isn't it. I've spent every evening for the past four weeks up here looking at it and I still can't accept it has happened"

"Did that one light ball do all this?"

"No... no, there were about a dozen of them, but after you destroyed the towers all but that one out there left. They zipped up in the sky and off to the south west. Every day or two that one sends out some light strings and our men who have armor chase them away. Unless their armor fails... then they get dragged into the ball."

They sat in silence for a while looking out the windows then the major stood up. "Let's get back downstairs and I'll show you some of the equipment while we pack it up to bring out to the test area. Don't touch any of it yet though, wouldn't want to accidentally set off a weapon in the hotel."

Once back in the meeting room the major ordered two soldiers to retrieve the equipment with some crates to move it. They brought in three items: one looked like a small metal pipe, another, a large metal cylinder, the last one Jack recognized.

"That's what destroyed the tower!" said Jack pointing to a large metal sphere being pulled out on a cart. The soldier carrying the sphere stopped dead in his tracks looking at the major.

"No need to worry, just don't get it to close to Jack and we'll be alright. After all, that thing survived through the tower collapsing on it and went through a damn bumpy ride from Abbotsford. Put it in the basement for now and make sure it can't roll around. We'll save it as a last resort," said Major Janko.

"I have not seen the other two items before, but they look like they are made out of the same metal that sphere is made from."

"OK, listen up everyone. Experimenting with these devices could be extremely dangerous. I will not order anyone to assist us tonight, but I will accept volunteers. Anyone willing?"

Everyone immediately raised their hands. "Good, I knew I could count on all of you. I think we would be best suited to have a couple of the engineers come with us since we are just trying to figure out what these things do at the moment. You four will draw a card from this deck after I shuffle it. Suit rank from lowest to highest will be hearts, diamonds, clubs, spades."

Major Janko took a battered deck of cards from his pocket, shuffled it, then had George, Jake, Valerie, and Jill choose a card. "Looks like George and Valerie are going with us. Let's pack up and go. It will be dark enough when we get there if we leave now. Put the glass in the crate too, I want to examine one of the marked spots close to us where they haven't built anything yet."

They met up with a soldier wearing the body armor in the lobby. Everyone except Jack helped carry the crate. The major had Jack walk on his left while he helped carry the crate on his right. Everyone else surrounded the crate, to avoid Jack touching anything until they were ready to start experimenting. They had a short uneventful walk to the wasteland which was four blocks away from the hotel. The area where they would be testing was shielded from the view of the light ball by a partially demolished building.

Far in the distance to the west Jack could see what appeared to be a building, but it was too far away to make out any details, "Did they build that way over there" Jack said pointing west.

"No, that's another one of our buildings they didn't touch," said George.

"We can chat about the scenery later, right now we need to find out what these do," said Major Janko, turning to the soldier in the armor. "Sergeant, you can take off the armor now and watch for any activity from the light ball while we do the tests."

The sergeant nodded as George and Valerie helped him take off the armor. They used the same kind of device that Doc used earlier to examine Jack, but now it was cutting a seam in the back of the armor. There did not appear to be any latches, zippers, or clips to hold the two sides together.

"How does that work? What keeps it together?" asked Jack.

"We think it is a self healing metallic polymer, kind of like the one developed for cars and airplanes twenty years ago. This Aot can be used to cut or seal it," said George, noticing a confused look on Jack's face. "Oh, sorry, Aot is short for all in one tool. This thing seems to do almost everything."

"This stuff can withstand a blast from a grenade without a scratch, but whatever this Aot is generating can cut or seal it," said Valerie.

Once the sergeant was out he walked to the edge of the building where he could watch the ball. The inside of the armor had a flat black finish with no visible life support or monitoring mechanisms. "How do you turn it on? How do I keep from suffocating in there" asked Jack nervously.

"As soon as you have all arms, legs and your head in, everything turns on. Just touching it turns on a small display in the chest area. Probably some sort of diagnostics system but we still haven't figured it out. The face plate will appear to be transparent to you and will have various colored lights moving around it. We don't know what most of them represent, but a large solid white light indicates a light ball and small white spots represent the light strings. They will appear relative to where you are looking. Squeezing both your fists will cause the armor to blast a small shock wave from the chest. It has always scared off any strings that have shown up," said George.

"The first thing we would like you to do once you are inside is to try moving your hands and fingers into various positions. The soldiers have made the display change when they squeeze just their right or left fist. I think there are sensors in the gloves, but one thread in a person isn't always enough to activate them. The armor will let us hear you and vice versa, so don't hesitate ask us anything. Once we see what you can do with this, we will get you to examine the other two objects," said Valerie.

George and Valerie held up the armor, motioning for Jack to get in. "You're sure it is safe in there? How do I get out if something happens to you?" asked Jack nervously.

"Absolutely safe, you will be the only one here that will be able to chase off anything that may attack. With seven of those threads in you, you won't have to worry about the armor sensing your hand movements. I am sure of that. As for getting out, just grab the Aot I was using and run the tip along the side of the armor. It will automatically open it," said George.

"OK, here goes nothing," said Jack as he put his legs in the armor. When he put his arms in he noticed it felt like the inside of a diving suit but was extremely heavy. He was having difficulty standing until the head piece was put on and it turned on. The armor became more rigid and started supporting itself, making him feel as though he was floating. From Jack's perspective, the head piece was completely transparent without any obstructions. He could see hundreds of various colored lights moving around his field of view. When he looked in the direction of the light ball a large white light came into view, even though there was a building between him and it.

"How ya doing in there?" asked George as he finished sealing up the armor.

"This is incredible! It's as light as a feather and the entire helmet is invisible. Some of these lights look like the spots I saw on the map. I can see dozens of the white lights, they are all different sizes. Maybe that indicates how far away they are."

"The entire helmet is invisible?" asked Major Janko, both excited and confused.

"Yes, is that not normal?"

"I not sure, but the soldiers who have used this armor have only had the area in front of their faces go transparent. Be careful Jack, I think the armor is not self powered like we thought, but you have fully powered it with your

92

threads. No telling what you could do with it. Major, I think we should stay behind the rubble back there while he tries to figure out how it works," said Valerie sounding very nervous.

"Right. Jack, I do not want you to try and create a blast, for all we know a fully powered suit may be able to level a mountain. Understood?" asked Major Janko.

"Understood major, please leave that Aot here and if things start getting out of control I will cut myself out in order to turn off the armor."

George left the Aot as everyone took cover behind the rubble. Jack tried making various gestures with his right then left hand, but the only thing he discovered was clenching his right fist cycled what was displayed one direction while clenching his left fist cycled in the opposite direction. When he pointed the index fingers on both his hands forward the armor felt like it rose slightly.

"Jack! You're floating," said George.

Jack attempted to look down by leaning forward, causing him to glide quickly across the ground. He instinctively leaned back causing the armor to stop moving. He turned around, pointed again while leaning forward very slightly, causing the suit to start gliding. He could easily turn by leaning slightly to one side. When he had lined up with the road that they walked up he leaned forward steeply, shooting down the road at high speed. He stopped leaning, quickly decelerated. He spent the next few minutes racing down the road trying different maneuvers, eventually returning to the point where he started.

"I think we need to put more threads in the soldiers. Jack, why don't you examine the other two objects now, the armors display might give you an idea of what they are," said Major Janko.

"OK major, I'll start with the cube," said Jack, opening the crate. He paused, staring at the cube for a moment.

"Is everything alright Jack?"

"Wha... Oh, yes, sorry, got distracted. I can tell you exactly what the cube is because it is now transparent to me. It is filled with threads, probably thousands of them. I'm going to see if I can get them to go in the Aot." Jack held the Aot against the cube. After a few seconds the threads started moving into it. "It's working, they are going inside!"

"George, how many suits do we have left?" asked Major Janko.

"Thirteen, but only eight men have a thread right now. Doc hasn't been able to get threads in anyone else yet."

"I have a feeling Jack will be able to solve that problem. Imagine thirteen men in fully powered armor. We might have a fighting chance at survival now."

"Looks like the Aot is full now, there should be more than enough for everyone in this cube. Major, did you want me to try and get some more of them in the sergeant?"

"Examine the cylinder first. I want Doc to be around when we try to inject more of those into someone in case there are any medical complications."

"OK, I'm going to pick up the cylinder now. It doesn't look any different than when I wasn't in the armor. Just looks like a solid chunk of metal... wait... a small display appeared on the side with a bunch of colored spots in a row... now I can see a glow inside."

"It's not inside, we can see it too. Put it down and get behind the rubble! Everyone take cov..." before the major could finish talking, the top end of the cylinder produced an extremely bright beam of light which lit up the thin clouds in the upper atmosphere. Jack let go of the cylinder, which lit the side of a bare mountain to the east with the beam as it dropped. Out of the corner of his eye he noticed thousands of small white spots in the armors display. "Major! I think the ball has sent out a bunch of strings!"

"Use the armor Jack! It's the only thing they are afraid of!" yelled Major Janko as everyone started running away from the partially collapsed building.

Jack turned to face the building which was between him and the strings, moving closer to avoid hitting anyone with the blast. He squeezed both his fists causing a blindingly bright light to blast out of the armors chest, expanding as it moved towards the strings. The blast vaporized the remains of the building. When the strings noticed it they attempted to retreat. The blast expanded enough to vaporize the side of a few buildings in the distance, while accelerating fast enough to catch up to the strings. When it hit them they exploded in a shower of blinding sparks, producing a very loud high pitched screeching sound. The light ball started accelerating up but was hit by the edge of the blast, causing it to loop wildly while giving off sparks as it moved up towards the east. More light balls could be seen moving up towards the east from the mountains and other areas in the wasteland.

"Holy shit, you just vaporized them all!" yelled George excitedly as everyone else stood in shock, watching pieces of the buildings in front of them fall to the ground.

"Grab the crate, leave the cylinder and everyone get back to the hotel now!" said Major Janko.

"What's wrong, didn't I just chase them off?" asked Jack sounding confused.

"Yes you did, and I cannot thank you enough. But I fear they have just retreated to allow a heavier military force to come in and clean us out," said Major Janko sounding nervous.

"Oh crap. Then I'll carry each of you back to the hotel and then I'll take the crate. This armor will let me get all of you back in half the time it would take on foot"

"Good idea but take the crate first, those threads are more important than us. Everyone double time it back now! We can't assume Jack will be able to get us all, especially if an attack is coming."

Jack picked up the crate, which felt weightless, leaning forward he raced it back to the main entrance of the hotel. When he got back to the group he was able to carry two people at a time. Major Janko insisted he take the two engineers first. He got everyone back in one quarter the time it initially took them to walk to the wasteland. The major explained what happened to the two guards, ordering the sergeant to run upstairs to inform everyone else.

"Major, I think I need to at least try to get more of these strings into these two guards. We may not have time to get Doc here to help us before we are attacked. I am absolutely sure it will work since everything I touch appears to be fully powered. Once they are done, they can load up the other Aots you have and inject everyone else, while I go back to the park and take care of the guards there."

"You may be right. Damn. I was hoping to take this a bit slower and with Doc's help." The major thought for a moment. "OK, do it. We really don't have a choice."

"You said they each only had one thread, correct?"

"Yes, just one"

"OK, I'll add six more so they each have the same amount I do." Jack cut a small opening in the upper arm of each suit while the major explained how Doc used the Aot to inject a thread. As Jack followed the instructions, the threads started leaving the Aot, entering the soldiers arm with roughly a one second pause between each one. After verifying that the soldiers were alright and their armor was now fully powered, Jack took the Aot preparing to leave.

"I am going to the park now to give some more threads to the guards there. These two can help inject others here."

"One last thing Jack, stay in the park. Even if you hear fighting coming from the city, do not come back for us. With my men in fully powered suits they will believe one of us is responsible for the earlier blast and everyone in the park will remain under the radar. I want you and the guards out there to protect the people in the park and try to find a way to get them far away from here."

"Understood and good luck Major."

It took Jack only a few minutes to get to the camp using the armor. He decided to not glide into the camp in order to not startle the guards, maybe causing them to attack. As he approached the unlit camp he could hear many people talking. When the guards saw him they blocked the entrance appearing ready to attack. Before they did anything Jack yelled out, "Wait, it's me, Jack. Major Janko sent me to help."

"What happened out there? We saw bright flashes and that god-awful sound. Were you attacked?" asked one of the guards.

"Yes, but they were driven off, I need to talk to Doc right now."

The guards let Jack pass. The armors display was amplifying the light making it easy for Jack to see Doc in the center of the camp, talking with everyone else. She was a little confused when she realized it was Jack in the suit, but he quickly explained everything that had happened since he left.

"If the major is correct about an impending attack then I agree, we need to put more of these threads in the guards and hope they can hold off whatever comes at us next," said Doc.

"There are enough of these things to give everyone some. Might be the only way to keep us all alive in the long run"

"I'll think about that while you take care of the guards. It's tempting, but I have no idea what, if any, negative effects they are having on your body."

"Fair enough," said Jack as he turned to walk back to the guards at the gate. He explained what could be done with the fully powered armor. They both had no objections to getting more threads since they were eager to have these new abilities. When each guard had seven threads he gave them the Aot to inject the other guards. Doc was in the center of the camp talking with a group of people, so he walked over to find out what how he could help.

"We've been discussing the threads Jack, and everyone agrees that the risk of any long term effects outweighs getting slaughtered by whatever may be coming for us next. I'll start injecting everyone after the guards are done and you can get some rest."

"Are you sure Doc, I am not tired at all and I am more than willing to help."

"Absolutely sure, you are not tired because you are pumped full of adrenalin. I'll wager that if you sit down and rest for a few minutes you will start to feel exhausted. I know you would rather help, but burning yourself out will not help any of us, especially you."

"I'm not going to be able to convince you otherwise, am I?"

Doc shook her head.

"OK. Then I guess I'll lie down for a bit, but I want to stay in the armor. If we are attacked there will be no time to put me back in."

Jack sat on the ground, leaning against one of the walls, watching Doc inject threads into everyone in the camp. He also watched the lights in his display, trying to determine what they meant. After less than one minute he started to feel tired, quickly falling asleep.

Jack was once again in front of a ball of light, only this time he was on the edge of a very tall cliff, next to various sized stone towers and other stone structures. The sky was dark with a storm which was causing massive waves to crash against the cliff. A voice boomed from the ball, "They were not expecting you. He was not expecting you. They are hurt and afraid. You must get away now. If they find you first he will not be able to help."

"Get away to where? There is nowhere left to go!"

"Follow the water it will lead you to safety."

"Wait, I can understand what you are saying a lot better now? Why did you speak so cryptically before?"

"The shell is aiding us. The ones in you are old and do not understand your mind. The shell understands and is teaching"

"Shell? You mean the armor?"

"Inaccurate description, it is much more. Do not do anything to attract their attention; their fear may cause them to destroy you."

"Before you said my time is over, but then you said my time must start. What does that mean?"

"Your known existence is almost over. Your future existence will be to prove humans are deserving."

"Of What? And what's the point if you have wiped them all out?"

"He will explain. Trying to explain now may cause more confusion."

"Who is this he you keep talking about? How do I find him?"

"He is one of our greatest minds. He will find you if you can avoid them."

"I assume they are the ones that attacked us?"

"Yes, he did not want to correct you this way."

"Correct us? How is destroying an entire species correcting anything?" asked Jack angrily.

"Explanations will come when communication is no longer confusing."

Everything disappeared in a flash of light as the sound of the crashing waves faded away slowly.

Chapter 7

Jack was jolted awake from his short nap by the screeching sound he had heard earlier. As he jumped up he saw three light balls in the sky above him zooming towards the city. From the direction of the city he could see flashes of light with more screeching followed by the sound of buildings collapsing. Most of the people in the camp were hiding in the buildings. Doc was talking to a guard on the part of the walkway that faced the city. He could hear the end of their conversation as he ran over to them.

"I've counted fourteen so far Doc, and that's just the ones we can see coming in from the west. No telling how many are coming from the other directions," said the guard on the walkway.

"OK, don't attack anything unless it is obviously coming for us. We don't want them to know we are out here," said Doc.

Jack looked in the direction of the city but in his display he could see nothing but a large undulating white glow. "Doc, I need to talk to you. I had another one of those dreams" yelled Jack over the sounds coming from the city.

"Jack we can talk about your dreams later, we need you up on the wall right now."

"The dream may be more important. I have not had a chance to tell you yet, but the major thinks someone on the enemy's side is trying to help using the threads to communicate with me."

"What makes him think that? It sounds more like he is grasping at straws trying to find a way out of this hopeless situation."

"His men started having strange dreams like mine when they had threads injected. He thinks having more in me is what is letting them talk with me. I just had another dream, if I can call it that, but this time I could understand them better. Apparently the armor is helping."

"Damn the major, he should have told me about this. Well, what did they say?"

"The important part, which was pretty obvious to me, was to stay away from them, the ones who are attacking us. They also said to follow the water to get to someplace safe."

"Sounds more like they are trying to lure us out into the open to capture us. Any water we follow will lead to the edge of the wasteland."

"They might be limited to where they can go without raising the suspicions of the others. The only way for them to help us may be for us to go to them. The major thinks they may be trying to take us some place where no one will care about us."

A bright flash of light came from the city followed by more screeching sounds then silence. A moment later nine light balls zoomed overhead heading west. Jack looked towards the city but the glow was gone." He then scanned all around finding no glow or white lights anywhere.

"Guards! What's happening? Can anyone see anything?" yelled Doc.

"Nothing here!" yelled one guard.

"I think they've gone," yelled another.

"They have all left. My display shows nothing nearby," said Jack.

"You can see them in your display?" asked Doc with confusion.

"Yes, I haven't told you what these things can do yet have I?"

"No one has, but I can't blame any of you. Everything is happening so fast I am just glad you had time to explain it to the guards. I'm going to gather everyone and you can explain the major's idea to them. I will let them decide what we will do, but I suspect you will be going no matter what we decide."

"Yes, I have to. They haven't misled me yet... I have only told the major this, but at the tower they told me what to do to destroy it."

"Oh... I see. I'll just go get everyone," said Doc sounding a little disappointed.

Jack walked over to one of the logs at the center of the camp and sat down. Everyone slowly gathered around him as Doc returned with the people who had tried to hide. After explaining the major's theory to everyone, he asked the guards if they had strange dreams too. They reluctantly admitted that they started having the dreams after they were injected, but the major told them not to tell anyone. Doc was obviously angered but said nothing.

"So you want us to just walk out into the edge of the wasteland where we will have no cover? Sounds like suicide to me," said a man.

Jack explained how the armor let him see where everything was and that he could no longer see anything in the city. The guards confirmed that they also saw nothing.

"Is there nothing else we can do? I don't think it's safe to go out there, but I also don't think it's safe here anymore," said a woman.

"You are right, it is not safe out there and they will eventually find us here. So the choices are really: do we wait here to eventually be killed, or do we risk being killed sooner by going out there and maybe finding whoever is trying to help," said Jack.

"Do you really believe someone is trying to help us?" asked Doc.

"Yes I do, as Captain Ellis said: 'it would not follow the enemy's pattern to toy with a few random people before killing them', and I agree. Someone has been going out of their way to keep me alive, and while I do not know what their true purpose is, I believe it is partly to help keep as many other people alive as I can."

"Why do you think they would care about helping any of us? Maybe they just want you," said another man.

"Because in my last dream they told me 'your future existence will be to prove humans are deserving'. I didn't find out what they meant by that, but to me it sounds like they want me to show them we deserve to exist. In the dream I sensed that they wanted us to survive and were genuinely worried that the ones that attacked us were going to succeed in wiping us out. The major's last request of me was to get everyone as far away from here as possible, but I won't force any of you to come with me. I will be leaving shortly, I want to wait a little while to make sure the attack is over and they are not coming back."

As everyone started discussing what to do, Jack walked over to one of the ladders leading to the walkway, climbing up. He walked to one of the two guards who stayed on the walkway. "Has there been any activity since they left?" asked Jack.

"No, and I no longer see any spots in the city. If they marked the threads in the guards, then it's very probable that everyone at the headquarters is gone. Wait... look to the south east... do you see that."

Jack saw a line of white spots pulsing with a rippling effect that made it look like they were moving away, in the same way a string of decorative chasing lights would look. "I think they are trying to show me which way to go." He quickly climbed back down the ladder then walked over to Doc at the center of the camp, "I've got to go now Doc, I believe they are showing me a path out of here."

"Jack is there no way I convince you to stay. I really don't believe you will be able to get very far without being attacked, even if there is someone out there willing to help," said Doc.

"I have to try. I believe it's the only hope we have to survive. Is there anyone who wants to come with me?"

"Just these five here," said Doc, pointing to five people standing next to her, three men and two women.

"I was hoping more would want to leave. Once I find whoever is trying to help I will do my best to convince them to send help here."

"Good luck to all of you. Please be careful and don't believe everything they tell you just because they seem willing to help."

"Don't worry Doc, I know that even though they may be willing to help me their people have wiped out almost all of us, and probably could not be stopped by one of their own if they found out we were still alive. We should probably move as fast as possible so we are far from what is left of the city when the sun comes up."

Jack and his new travelling companions headed out of the camp towards the line of spots. Once they were out of the woods he could see that the spots were following the shoreline around the bay towards what was once the university grounds. A large number of buildings that were standing the last time he was here were now gone or had collapsed with a large cloud of dust now covering the remains of the city. "The path I see in my display has us walking a few meters into the water."

"Do you think it matters if we are in the water?" asked one of the men.

"Probably, this display is very accurate about where everything is, so there may be something in the water that will help hide us." Jack led them into the water following the path, which at certain points led them into water deep enough that they needed to swim. The landscape around them looked quite surreal, all the beaches had been untouched but the land where the city had been was nothing but bare ground. There were no signs of the light balls or strings anywhere in the wasteland. Other than the noise they were making in the water there was no sound.

After a few hours they came to the end of the beaches at the beginning of the university grounds. Jack could see that the spots ended a short distance away near a steep sloping piece of land covered in trees. When they arrived at the location of the last spot, they saw a spherical stone about one meter in diameter sitting in amongst the trees.

"Is this it? Is this where we are supposed to be?" asked one of the men.

"Yes, the spots stop here. That sphere is about the size of the ones I saw on the towers, only they were metal, not stone," said Jack.

"What are we supposed to do now?" asked one of the women.

"Examine the sphere. If it is something useful the armor will let me know"

102

They walked over to the sphere, which had a surface similar to that of the towers. Jack's display was showing a faint glow in the center of the sphere but nothing else. He was getting a strong feeling that he needed to touch it. As he approached it he was sure he could hear a voice far away telling him to touch it, so he placed both hands on it causing a faint hum to start.

"Should you be doing that? Is it safe?" asked another of the men.

"Yes, I believe this is why we were brought here"

The sphere started glowing faintly with everyone hearing a voice in their minds, "You are safe now. You will be brought to him." A flash of light came from the sphere causing Jack to lose consciousness. He woke for a moment, or was he asleep, it was hard to tell, everything was in a haze. He was surrounded by light strings, there was water moving far below him, nothing but water was visible all around. After a moment everything faded away again.

Jack slowly woke up in total darkness, feeling like he was in a bed, wondering if everything that had happened was just a bad dream. He felt for the lamp on his bedside table, but there was no table. He realized there were also no sheets. As he sat up the ceiling gently lit up revealing he was in a square room. The only objects in the room were the bed he was on and a podium against the wall across from him. The bed was more of a platform with an unknown spongy material laid on top. The walls, platform and podium appeared to be made of the same stone material as the towers, except this material had a sandstone color to it. The wall behind the podium appeared to be a mirror so he decided to give it a closer examination. As he approached the podium he could see the top was hollowed out with a hole in the bottom. The mirror was the same material as the rest of the wall, except it had a polished reflective surface.

For the first time since the invasion started Jack saw his reflection, making him realize why he felt like he had not showered in weeks. He was covered in dirt, his hair was tangled, and his clothes looked like they had been dug up out of the ground. He examined the podium a little closer noticing a deep groove around the top of the carved out area. As he touched the groove, water started pouring out into what he now assumed was a sink, it stopped when he moved his hand away. There were no visible openings in the walls, floor or ceiling, but there were small grooves near the top and bottom of one wall with warm air blowing out of the lower grooves.

"Hello! Can anyone hear me!" yelled Jack. There was no response, so he started tapping on the walls listening for any hollow sounding spots but found none. After pounding on the walls and yelling some more, he concluded that either no one heard him or he was being ignored so he decided to wash himself in the sink. When he cleaned the wound on his leg he wondered again why it only looked a couple days old when it happened so long ago. It was still sore and red. Maybe it was infected. Maybe the threads did not fix infections. After about an hour he had managed to wash a large amount of the dirt out of his clothes, got his hair untangled, but had created a muddy mess around the sink. With nothing else to do he decided to lie on the bed, waiting, but soon fell asleep.

For the first time in a long time Jack was getting some real sleep, but it did not last long. Less than half an hour after falling asleep he was woken by the sound of grinding stone. A section of the wall next to the mirror was slowly rising into the ceiling revealing a passageway beyond. When the wall had finished opening everything was silent again.

"Hello... is anyone out there?" asked Jack. There was no response so he cautiously looked out the opening to see he was in the middle of a narrow passage about fifty meters long, a little more than twice his height, with no other openings along the walls. The section of wall that opened was about half a meter thick. The ceiling in the passage was lit the same way as the ceiling in the room.

He stepped out of the room, deciding to walk to his right. At the end the passage there were stairs on the right side heading downward into darkness, so he decided to go back the other way. As he walked towards the other end he banged the walls with his fist listening for hollow sounding spots, but once again found none. At the other end of the passage there were stairs on the left side, but these led up into a brightly lit area, so he continued on.

The top of the stairs emerged in the center of a large hexagonal room. Each wall of the room had a large opening to a beach with pillars nearby. As Jack looked around he was startled to see a group of people on one side of the room staring at him.

"Looks like another one has woken up. You look like you've had a rough ride here. We thought they had already rounded everyone up," said one of the men as he walked towards Jack.

"Where am I, who are you, how did I get here?" asked Jack.

"Ah, sorry, just excited to see another new face after so many weeks with nothing happening. I'm Harry Benson and you are in Australia."

"Are you the one who has been communicating with me through the threads and armor? Are you working with them?"

"Threads and armor? I'm not sure what that means. Who do you mean by them, the ones who invaded or the ones trying to help? The ones trying to help have left some of us here to reassure everyone coming through that they are safe now. You've been talking with one of them too... how?"

"There is more than one of them helping us? Who are they, where are they from?"

"Ok, since you have been talking with them, you probably know more about what's going on than the others who have been through here. So why don't we tell each other everything we know about the situation, then maybe we'll both be a little less in the dark."

"Alright, but you can start. I am getting tired of explaining everything that has happened to me to everyone I meet."

"Sounds good, I haven't had a chance to tell anyone what I know in a while. About a month and a half ago when this all started I was vacationing in a small fishing resort just down the beach from here. Some of the people sitting over there were at the resort too. At first we had no idea what was happening, just a bunch of lights in the sky then the electricity going out. We weren't hit by the blasts that took out all the gadgets and lights, so we assumed it was some sort of meteor shower that damaged the power grid. One of the resort owners decided to drive to a town about two hours away to find out how long the power was going to be out, but when he didn't come back by nightfall we started to get worried."

"Then the strings came right?"

"No, they never came out here. Guess the resort is too isolated to worry about. That night we did notice the lights running through the sky after they flared up, but that was it. None of us got much sleep, worrying about what was going on and then in the middle of the night a bright glow appeared far down the beach. We couldn't see what was happening, but decided to wait until daylight to investigate. Another owner took a dune buggy, with a few of us tagging along, riding to where we saw the glow only to find this structure being built with a big glowing ball of light hovering above it. As we got closer we saw what appeared to be wolves wandering around the structure, which made no sense because there are no wolves here."

"They are not wolves, they are robots."

"Ah! That explains a lot. Once they saw us they started running towards us, so we turned tail and sped off as fast as we could go. But they actually caught up and dragged us out of the buggy to this place. I remember other smaller lights surrounding me then waking up in one of the room inside this structure. After what seemed like hours one of the walls opened and a man appeared."

"They are men like us?"

"No, no. This man was one of us. He said they were using him as an ambassador of sorts to help communicate with us better. Apparently they don't speak like we do, but they have invented something that can directly communicate with human minds. He told me that we have been invaded by one of their clans who claim this is their planet. The ones he communicates with are trying to help as many of us as they could. He asked me and a few others to stay here and do our best to calm down all the people that would be brought through here."

"Through here? Where are they being taken? Do the ones helping us have names, what should I call them?"

"To some sort of refugee camp apparently. They have names of sorts, but they aren't words or anything we could translate into words. The ambassador has been trying to explain to them that we are more comfortable with names, but so far they have only referred to the two groups as us and them."

"Is he here? When can I speak with him?"

"No not here, but you will be taken to him in a while. So that's pretty much all I know. Where did you come from? What happened there?"

Jack sighed, "Sorry, it's a long story and I don't like reliving it very much." He continued by once again explaining everything that had happened to him so far, only with much less detail, only covering major events.

Harry's face went pale as the story went on. "So they're destroying the cities? I had hoped that the ones helping us were going to be able to stop the invaders and we could eventually go home. Does this mean the people coming through here are the only ones left? And you destroying those towers must have pissed off the invaders, which might not be a good thing for us if they find out their own people are helping."

"I am sure they would not be helping if they did not believe we could be kept safe. How many have come through here so far?"

"My best guess is maybe a few thousand, not much out of ten billion is it? I'm starting to wish I never asked you what you went through."

"You would have found out eventually. The important thing is they have not succeeded in wiping us out."

"Yet... I think I need to sit for a while. I'll tell everyone else what you told me. I understand why you don't like talking about it. If you decide to go outside be careful, there are wolves, or robots I guess, patrolling and they don't like us trying to go past the pillars."

"OK, thanks for the warning." As Jack walked to one of the openings he could now see each pillar was about twenty meters in front an opening, looking the same as the pillars he had seen at other locations. Once outside he could see the structure was actually a tower, but its height was hard to guess because there were no openings in it other than the six at the base. He decided to walk over to a pillar to get a better view of the tower. When he got close to the pillar, three nearby wolves start watching him so he stopped walking any further. He now saw that the sides of the tower sloped inward slightly. There were also openings at the top that lined up with the openings at the base. Holding his fingers at arm's length for a gauge, he guessed that the tower would have twenty floors if they were all the same height as the one at the base. He started examining a pillar which also appeared to slope slightly inward just like the tower but had no openings or markings.

The wolves were still watching, but not moving any closer, so he decided to slowly walk a little further from the tower towards the water. When he was about to pass the pillar, an invisible force threw him back towards the tower. He landed on his back in the sand with a loud thud. The three wolves walked quickly over to him but just watched. "Well, that wasn't a smart thing to do," said Jack wheezing as he looked over at one of the wolves. As he slowly got up, trying to catch his breath, he saw Harry with a couple other people watching him from one of the openings.

"You OK?" asked Harry.

"Yes, I think so. Why did you not tell me what would happen if I tried to go past the pillar?" asked Jack while walking back to the tower.

"Because no one has been out that far before. The wolves never let any of us get more than a couple meters away from the tower before herding us back in. They seem a lot friendlier towards you."

"Huh, maybe they think I'm one of them."

"Why would... Oh you mean because of the threads don't you?"

"Yes, it could be the way they tell who is a friend and who is not. Have you seen any of them go outside the pillars?"

"Now that you mention it, no I haven't. Have any of you?" Harry asked the other people, but no one said anything.

"Hmmm, whatever that was is probably keeping everything from getting in or out of this area. When was the last time anyone came here to take people away?"

"Three days ago, they used to come out every day, but as the number of people that came here went down they came less often. Let's go back inside, it's almost time to eat."

"What exactly do you have to eat if you cannot leave this area?"

"They are providing food, and it's quite nice. A lot of fruits, vegetables, grains, and what I am guessing is some sort of synthetic meat. It tastes good, but the texture takes a bit to get used to."

Walking back into the tower Jack saw that a section of the ceiling had opened and a large stone slab with various kinds of food on it had been lowered into the room. "Is there someone in the tower preparing all this?"

"We're not sure. We haven't heard any noises from up there. Even when this slab is lowered there isn't much of a sound. I think it's probably all automated."

"Has anyone tried climbing up there?"

"Yeah, quite a few of us have, but the only thing up there is a big empty room with no apparent way in or out. One day I decided I was going to wait up there until the slab was raised, to see what was going on. But while I was up there the slab wouldn't raise. I must have waited half a day at least, but came down when everyone else was complaining about getting hungry. As soon as I was clear of the slab it quickly rose up and a few minutes later lowered with more food."

"There must be a hidden door like in the room below."

They started discussing the room above the slab some more, when one of the men who was with Jack at the stone sphere emerged from the stairwell. Jack walked over to greet him, explaining where they were while leading him to the food. Over the next two hours the rest of the people who were at the sphere emerged, being brought up to date by Jack. After the last of them finished eating, when everyone had moved away from the slab, it quickly rose up into the ceiling leaving no sign that there was an opening.

As the day wore on with the sun getting closer to setting Jack noticed a spot appear on the horizon. "Something is out there!" said Jack.

"I guess you are pretty important to them, but you probably already knew that. They are sending the transport early," said Harry with a smile.

"A little part of me has been hoping I was going crazy and they were not really communicating with me. What in the world could they want from me? I am not a soldier or scientist, how could I possibly help them, or us for that matter?"

"Well, it won't be long till you find out now."

As they watched the spot get bigger its shape was hard to make out due to the glare of the sun. When it got close to the beach it slowed down, rotating before landing. The transport was a black cylinder with rounded ends, with no markings or openings on the surface. After a moment the end facing the tower split open, revealing a man using an Aot in the same way it would be used to open the armor.

"Is that one of them?"

"No, he's one of us. They use him as a sort of translator on the trip to their settlement. He has threads in his body like you do, and can communicate with them. His name is Tom James and he was one of the people at the resort."

As the opening got bigger Tom exited the transport followed by two beings in the armor. The two beings moved ahead of him stopping between two of the pillars, causing a flash of light between their armor, opening up a hole in whatever was blocking passage, allowing him to continue to the tower.

"Are those two one of them?"

"No, they are a different species. They are called Juvo. The Juvo work with them doing various jobs. Apparently they are helping to maintain equipment and guard things here."

"Harry! Good news, they said almost everyone has been rounded up so you won't be stuck out here much longer," said Tom.

"Good! The beach is nice, but over a month of it is pretty boring. This is Jack Campbell , apparently they have been talking with him in his dreams," said Harry.

"Good to meet you Jack, you are the reason they sent me out here before the end of the week. They consider you and your friends to be very valuable."

"Good to meet you too. Did they tell you why we are so important?" asked Jack.

"No, I was hoping you had some idea since they've been communicating with you."

"I think they have tried to tell me, but everything they say is very confusing."

"They did mention something about the Draad you have not being correct, but I'm not sure what they meant by correct."

"Draad?" asked Jack sounding confused.

"Oh sorry, I forgot to tell you, that's what the Juvo call the threads," said Harry to Jack, "They were apparently transferred to him when a damaged wolf bit him," said Harry to Tom.

"Then I'm amazed you can make out anything they say to you. The Draad in the wolves were meant to work the computer that runs them, not a human mind. We should get you to the settlement so you can get some made for humans," said Tom.

"OK, I am ready when you are. I have enough questions to keep them talking for years," said Jack.

Tom led Jack and the people who came with him to the transport, which was made from the same material as the armor. The walls had a few displays and maps which blended into the surface. Once everyone was inside, Tom took out the Aot, using it to seal the back of the transport.

"What is this made from?" asked Jack, "It looks like the same stuff as the armor."

"I was told it is some sort of organic metal alloy, whatever that means. They tried to explain it to me, but I'm not a scientist so I didn't understand anything they were talking about. I assume when you mean the suits when you say armor, yes they are made of the same stuff but they are much more than armor I am told," said Tom.

"Where are the seats, do we have to stand during the entire trip?"

"You won't be standing. If you suffer from motion sickness or vertigo you may want to keep your eyes closed, All sealed up, we should be good to go guys," said Tom.

"Do they understand English?"

"No, they can't even hear our voices very well. We all have Draad and they transmit our thoughts to whoever we want to talk with and turn them into something they can understand. It takes a while to learn how to use them, but from what they told me you seem to have a natural ability with them."

The two Juvo made some gestures on the displays causing the ship to turn transparent as everyone started to float weightlessly.

"Hey! Wait! What the heck is happening?" asked Jack in a panic.

110

"No need to worry everyone. The interior of the ship has been shifted out of normal space, so we no longer have any gravity. The walls are still there, they are just letting us see everything outside. Now the fun part starts."

The transport rose above the water a few meters as it accelerated very fast, but no one inside could feel any movement.

"This is incredible, I feel like I am flying. But I don't really feel anything," said Jack with excitement and nervousness.

"That's because the inside of the ship is in a different space than the outside. There is no gravity or inertia here so when we move we feel nothing. That's pretty much all I know about it though, but I am sure they could tell you more."

"Everyone keeps saying 'they', but what are they called?"

"They don't have any name that we could use. They communicate with colors and shapes in their writing and use light for their equivalent of speech. That's why they created the Draad. Otherwise they would have great difficulty communicating with any other species."

A bank of dark clouds could be seen on the horizon moving extremely fast towards them. "How fast are we going, and where are we going anyway?"

"Just a second, let me check," said Tom, looking at one of the displays then thinking for a moment, "We're going about twenty four thousand kilometers per hour. The settlement is in New Zealand so we should be there shortly."

As they approached the clouds, entering the edge of a thunder storm, lights appeared on the dark horizon. The lights slowly grew bigger giving way to the shapes of towers and other buildings stretching for a great distance along tall cliffs.

"I've seen this before, in my last couple of dreams."

"They must have been showing you where they wanted you to go. I see why they say you have a natural ability with the Draad. Took me weeks before I could see images they were trying to communicate, and you did it with some that weren't meant for humans."

The transport slowed down before landing in a small clearing on the edge of the cliffs. The walls changed back to their black opaque color, gravity slowly returned, Jack stumbled nearly falling over.

"Sorry about that, I should have warned you that gravity was coming back. Follow me and I'll show all of you to your rooms," said Tom as he took out the Aot to open the back of the transport.

"How long until we get to talk with them?" asked Jack.

"I'm not sure. You will be meeting with one of our people first. He is some sort of genius scientist who they have been working with. They call him our ambassador and send him to meet with everyone to bring them up to speed. I apologize for the bareness of all the rooms. They only create buildings for shelter, so there is very little in them."

The Juvo stayed behind as everyone left the transport. The buildings once again appeared to be made from the stone material used everywhere else, with openings in the walls revealing the rooms inside. The light in the rooms that were lit was coming from the ceiling as it did in the tower on the beach. Only humans could be seen in the rooms with no sign of any guards. A few people were looking out the openings, watching everyone as they left the transport.

A large opening in the building next to the transport led them into a medium sized room with platforms lining the walls. Each one looked very similar to the bed back at the tower. The rain stopped at the opening even though there was nothing visibly blocking it from entering the building. There was a large spiral walkway at the back of the room leading to the top floor of the building.

"Haven't they ever heard of elevators?" asked Jack.

"They don't need them, the ambassador told me it takes no physical effort for them to move around. The first room over there is yours Jack. You are free to go where you want, but I suggest you get a little rest. It's been a long day but the ambassador still wants to talk to you about everything that has happened before it's over," said Tom.

"Ok, I'll try to rest then," said Jack.

As he entered the room the ceiling lit up, but there was not much to look at. It was much like the room under the tower, but with a large opening in the wall that looked outside. He walked over to the opening noticing the rain was being stopped from coming in the room. He reached out slowly but as his hand got near the point where the rain was blocked, it felt as though it was touching a solid surface. Next to the sink was a slightly indented area in the floor with a small hole in the center. He leaned over the hole to get a better look when a shower of warm water started pouring out of the ceiling, startling him, causing him to jump back, which caused the water to stop. He decided to stand under the shower for a while to try washing out the remaining dirt from his clothes. After a few minutes he realized his clothes were as clean as they were going to get, so he walked over to the large opening to watch the storm for a while. He quickly got bored with it so he decided to lie down on the bed. After a few minutes of staring at the ceiling he heard someone walking down the hallway then stopping outside the opening to his room.

"Jack, are you in there?" asked the person outside his room.

"Yes, come on in. I am just resting on the bed... If that is what it is supposed to be," said Jack.

A scruffy looking man with grey hair and dirt stained clothes entered the room, smiling while extending his hand. "Good to finally have you here Jack."

"Have I met you before? You obviously know me but I don't remember you," said Jack as he sat up.

"No, we haven't met before. I'm Doctor Walter Wright. Other people you have met probably referred to me as the ambassador, but I prefer just plain Walter."

"Ah, good to meet you, I have enough questions to keep you occupied for hours."

"I'm sure you do, and I have many things to tell you. Come with me to my lab, I have a many things to show you also. We can talk along the way. It's just down the hall on the other side of the building," said Walter.

"Did they tell you why they think Earth is theirs and more importantly why they decided to wipe us all out?"

"Wipe us out? No, no, quite the opposite! They've gone out of their way to make sure no human gets hurt during the initial phase of the correction."

"But they have been dragging everyone into those light balls! Stuffing millions of people in something that small would kill them!"

"And yet they are still alive and well, including all your friends. Those balls of light are, among other things, transport points. Go in one, and come out another."

"Fred and Bob are still alive, how?" asked Jack looking confused and excited.

"Yes they are, I can bring you to them later, but we have important things to do first. Maybe I should start by explaining a little about the beings that are doing this. I call them the Lights, mainly because they emit a huge amount of light. Not very creative I know, but what do you expect from an old physicist. They came into existence throughout the galaxy shortly after this universe came into being. Their bodies are made from various flexible crystalline metal alloys. A type of matter I've never seen before or even knew was possible. Their minds are not linked to an organic brain like ours, but linked to the entire structure of their bodies. At first I thought they were just giant metallic brains,

113

but after hours of discussing their physiology with them I still really don't understand how they work."

"They must have spread everywhere by now, since the universe is so old. Why haven't we seen them before?"

"You would think so, but the conditions needed for their bodies to form only existed for a short time in the early universe so there are a limited number of them."

"Wait, how old are they?"

"As old as the universe itself. I know what you're thinking: 'That's impossible. Their bodies should have decayed long ago', which would be true if they existed the same way our bodies do. You see, every atom in our universe exists in four dimensions, the three we can see and time. If you could see an atom four dimensionally it would extend for trillions of years in the time dimension. Your body would be a jumble of matter coming and going throughout the length of your life and would be quite long, four dimensionally speaking. Our minds are bound to our brains at a single three dimensional point and are pushed through time and along our brains by weak waves in the time field. The majority of atoms in this universe are so long and interwoven with billions of other atoms that time waves don't move them very much. But the matter that existed at the beginning of time was made up of atoms that only had a length of a few days. Their bodies are made up of these special atoms and they are pushed along in time with their minds allowing them to exist forever."

"Ok, none of that made any sense to me. How do their minds develop if they have no brains and their bodies don't change?"

"That's the same thing I asked them. It turns out our theories about how minds work is all wrong. A mind exists separately from everything else and doesn't actually need anything else to exist or function. Turns out our brains are just a biological interface between our minds and bodies that allows us to experience the universe in three dimensions. The connection between the two limits what our minds can do, what they can sense, and the memories they can access. When we reach the end of our lives our minds pull themselves back to the beginning to relive everything again when the next time wave comes by."

"But that would mean everything in our life is already laid out and we have no control over what happens. What's the point of even existing if we are just reliving the same story over and over?"

"Ah! But you don't have to relive the same story as you put it. We do have control over what we do, but it is limited. With enough determination our

114

minds can move our bodies to do something different than what is already laid out. Have you ever come to a point in your life where you have two or more choices on how to proceed, and you feel like you have to make a certain choice but you really want to make another. You find it difficult to make the other choice, and even if you do it feels much more difficult than you think it should? That difficult choice may be a different one than you made the last time, forcing you to use all your minds strength to pull your body and all the atoms that make it up on to the new path."

"Hang on! If they are immortal, and their bodies are flowing through time, and they are just showing up now, then this would be my first time through my life. Nothing should be laid out yet! And the next time I go through my life they will be long gone so none of this really matters anyway."

"I understand your confusion, but this isn't your first time through life. We both have lived through this many times. They are not stuck in the flow of time any more than our minds are. They can move to any point in time the same way we can walk to any point in this building. For them this is the fifth time trying to correct us."

"OK, all this stuff about minds is too confusing and hurting mine. It does not sound very realistic to me anyway. Let's talk about something else for a while instead. You say they are correcting us, what exactly does that mean?"

"In the early days of this planet and many others like it, when life was first forming, they settled on them to monitor what was happening. They had never seen organic matter form into such complex forms before and they we curious as to what was going on. Throughout our history they have monitored our progress as a species and tried to push us in a direction that will prevent us from destroying ourselves and allow us to increase our intelligence. The last time they did this was about ten thousand years ago. They left, for a reason they have not told me, and were very unhappy when they came back, seeing what we had become and how we were treating the planet. The majority of them wanted to correct us the same way they always did: gather everyone up, destroy the existing settlements, educate the younger humans to give them more knowledge about how to live in peace and pursue intellectual interests, and keep the older ones in isolated settlements to prevent them from influencing the younger ones."

"But they have wiped out our entire history. Everything that we are and everything that we have created is gone!"

"That is one reason why he did not want to do it this way. He believes, and rightly so I think, that almost no one will accept what they have done and will fight anything they try to do. So far this has been true. Every time they try to correct us it ends with the majority of people trying to fight them and destroying humanity in the process. He believes we have progressed to the point where if they destroy our weapons and reveal themselves to us, offering to help instead of forcing it upon us, that most of us would accept them."

"If they have failed over and over, why do they not believe him? And just who is he anyway."

"He is the one helping us, although he is neither a he nor she. I probably just chose 'he' because I am male. They don't reproduce and they are all that exists or ever will exist of their species. As for why... each time the others believe they have discovered the reason for failure and want to try again. They are stubborn and refuse to believe they are wrong. But this time you shocked them good and maybe they are changing their minds."

Jack got a confused look on his face.

"When you destroyed their settlement... you had never done that before. And then you attacked and injured one of their expedition leaders. No one was expecting any of that and you have frightened them, which is not an easy thing to do. Your brain's exposure to the Draad over so many lifetimes has probably given it the ability to access more memories of what happened previous times from your mind, and is allowing you to change events drastically."

"When did I attack one of them?"

"In Vancouver when you were wearing one of their expedition suits."

"That light ball was one of them? I thought those were for transporting us?" asked Jack sounding worried and confused.

"That light ball was a part of one of them sticking in to our three dimensional space. So were the lights it sent out after you, they can be thought of as fingers."

"They must be really pissed off at me. How badly did I hurt it? It looked like the strings were vaporized."

"They are more afraid then angry. He said it would be the equivalent of some broken fingers to us. It has been a very long time since any of their kind has been hurt... Ah, we are here, please go on in. I need to get those primitive Draad out of you and give you some meant for humans."

The lab looked much the same as Jack's room. The only difference was a second platform that appeared to be used as a table. Walter walked over to the

116

table to pick up a different Aot, "I believe you've seen one of these before, how much do you know about using it?"

"Well, I've used it to open and seal the armor, remove threads from a cube, and put threads into some soldiers."

"Interesting, how did you figure out how to use it?"

"I was shown how to open the armor, but I just knew what to do for everything else. Do you think the threads in me were telling me how to use it?"

"Threads? Oh, you mean the Draad. I guess they do look like threads don't they. They don't actually have any intelligence themselves. They only create a link between minds and heal serious wounds. What I believe is happening is that your brain has learned how to use them to access more memories than you would normally have. Remember, we have all been through this multiple times and the memories of how to use it are in your mind."

"Are you trying to tell me I am remembering how to do something I haven't done yet? How do you know these aliens are telling you the truth? Everything they have told you sounds very unbelievable. I believe the truth is that they are afraid of us now and they have made all this up in order to get us to stop fighting them so they can finish taking over the planet."

"I suppose they could be making it all up, but why? They have already finished taking over. Your military friends from Vancouver were captured by the others shortly before you left, your friends in the park were captured by him shortly after, and the last of the cities has been destroyed. Other than a few architectural monuments they left, everything is gone."

Jack's expression sank a bit. "So everyone is here now?"

"The ones he captured, yes. The ones the others captured are in a kind of suspended animation inside their camps waiting for the construction to be completed."

"Sounds horrible, where are these camps?"

"They are all over the world, where the cities used to be. You saw the beginnings of one where you destroyed the settlement they were building."

"So they're just keeping everyone in fields like livestock?"

"Not quite, they create buildings about the size of this room, with all the same amenities that are in your room down the hall. So they all have food, water and shelter."

"But nothing else right? I can see why their plans fail and always will. Humans are not animals, we need more than that."

"Exactly, and he realizes that, but none of the others are willing to admit they are wrong and he is right. Now let me get these old... threads as you called them... out of you. I think I like that name better... threads... yes, much nicer."

When Walter put the Aot on Jack's arm the seven threads moved into it. After a moment other threads started moving into his arm. Jack counted them in his mind, one, two... seven... ten, "Why are you putting so many in?"

"They are meant to work in groups of thirty six. I'm amazed you could do anything with only seven."

"Major Janko's men managed to get the armor to work with only one."

"Really? That shouldn't have been possible from what I know about them. By the way, it's not meant to be used as armor or a weapon. It's used for transportation, construction, and environmental protection. There, all done, how do you feel."

"Kind of weird, I can hear lots of whispering voices. Is that supposed to happen?"

"At first, yes, you are hearing the Lights thoughts that involve you. Any time you think about one of them, they also hear whispers. With a little practice you can block out any thoughts that aren't directed at you. It's like being in a room with hundreds of people talking, eventually you just learn to block out anyone not talking to you."

"So his enemies can hear my thoughts?"

"No, no, they aren't his enemies they are more like rivals, and they only hear the same thing you are hearing now. Only thoughts directed at someone can be heard clearly. You see in their culture they don't have leaders the same way we do. They all go about their own business and don't interfere with each other. If more than one of them is interested in studying the same thing or something needs to be done, they form a sort of clan then discuss how to do it. Once there is a majority that agrees what to do the one that came up with the idea becomes the leader and they do it. In some cases, like our situation, some of them may be so opposed to the leader's idea they will break away and form a new clan to try and do the task their way. Neither side will interfere with the other. They will just try to prove their way is the right way."

"Do they not get in each other's way trying to do things differently? They must fight over our cities and what to do with them?"

"Both sides can do things their way in the same place but in different runs through the correction. Remember that they are not as locked into time as we are. When both clans want to try something in the same place, the larger clan

118

will get to try their way first, then if that fails the smaller clans will get to try things their way when they start over. But what they do with the cities became a secondary priority for them after the first attempt to correct us."

"Because we fought back, right?"

"Exactly! In the entire history of our species we had never done that before, and the worst part is we ended up destroying the planet and killing everyone in the process of trying to drive them away! But he has apparently seen something in you and your friends that can help prove to the others that his way is the correct way. Before you ask, no, he wouldn't tell me what it is."

"When will I get to talk with him, can I just do it now by directing a thought at him?"

"Maybe, but I think you will want to wait for him to be ready to talk with you. Remember that he communicated with you in your dreams because he knew you would not be doing anything at that time that required your full attention. You probably don't want to disturb him if he's doing something that needs his full concentration. I have usually talked with him in the mornings so I suspect he will have time tomorrow."

"I suspect he has all the time in the universe as many times as he wants it."

"Could be, but in any case we are stuck in time and still have to wait. You are good to go now, so if you don't have any more questions I would be happy to show you to your friends. I think you have a lot to tell them."

"I would definitely like to see Fred and Bob again. I have many questions, but I am still trying to understand a lot of what you have already told me, so I think it would be a good idea to let my mind rest a bit."

"Ah yes, I probably went on a bit didn't I. I apologize, but you are the first person in weeks I have had a chance to sit down and talk with about everything. Your friends are on the other side of the complex. Follow me and I will show you."

The complex was made up of many buildings which were all connected through openings in the walls. Most of the rooms they passed had people in them.

"These rooms aren't very private. Is there no way to block the openings? What about toilets and kitchens? I haven't seen those anywhere"

"Everyone has complained about the lack of privacy and I have told him about it. Apparently they have always used this layout, but I don't know if it is laziness or just not caring that has prevented them from changing it. There are rooms with toilets all throughout the complex, again with no privacy, and the food is served at fixed times in the main hall of each building. He told me they will fix these problems, but considering this is the fifth time they have been through this I doubt it is a very high priority for them."

"This place is more like a zoo than anything else. We are being treated like animals. This is a funny way of helping us."

"I suspect that to them we are no different than animals in a zoo. I believe they genuinely can't see the difference between these shelters and our original homes since they have provided all the same basic amenities. They don't understand things like entertainment or recreation since they have spent their entire existence doing nothing but studying the galaxy. Maybe you will have better luck trying to explain the problems with this place to him than I did."

For the rest of the walk Jack thought about how he could possibly explain the deficiencies of the settlement to a being that obviously doesn't understand a concept like privacy. Most of the people he saw looked either bored or unhappy with very few talking.

As they passed a room with a man standing near the opening, the man jumped out, attacked and knocked over Walter while yelling, "Traitor! You sold us out!"

Jack instinctively pushed his way between them, attempting to grab the man's arms but getting punched a few times in the process. Before he could stop the attack a string emerged from the ceiling, wrapping itself around the man while pulling him back into his room. Jack stood in stunned silence watching the man trying in futility to escape from the string. Distracted by a groan coming from the ground he looked down to see Walter holding his head with blood running down his arm.

"Don't move, I think you're hurt pretty bad."

"Ugh, my head hurts like hell. But there's no need to worry, the Draad will fix it in no time. Help me up won't you?"

"I had almost forgotten about them fixing injuries. Why did that man call you a traitor, is there something you are not telling me?" asked Jack, helping Walter stand up.

"There is a lot I haven't told you, but that's because of a lack of time not because I 'm withholding anything. I'm afraid that the people here may have the same reaction to you after you talk with him. Many people think I was working with him to help with the invasion and refuse to believe some of them want to help. Let's get moving again, Bob's room is just up ahead."

They arrived at Bob's room but there was no one in it. "He might be with Fred, let's go check his room."

As they approached Fred's room they could hear two men talking in low voices. When they got to the doorway they could see Fred and Bob standing by the opening to the outside world watching the storm while discussing something they could not hear clearly.

"Fred! Bob! You really are alive!" said Jack as he walked quickly over to them.

Fred spun around grabbing Jack in a bear hug, "Jack! You lucky bastard! We thought you had been killed in the blast."

Bob smacked Jack on the back, "Great to see you alive and well Jack! We've been told you've had quite the adventure in Vancouver, what happened out there?"

Jack started telling them everything that happened to him since they were separated as Walter quietly left the room to go back to his lab. Jack gave detailed explanations of how all the various technologies functioned, along with everything Walter had told him.

"So let me get this straight: They have been doing this to humanity over and over throughout our history and now that we wise up and fight back they want us to help them? They must think we are insane, why should we help them. You must have scared the shit out of them in Vancouver for them to want our help," said Fred incredulously.

"I think they actually wanted our help before that happened. Apparently he sees something in us that can fix everything. I am not really sure what though," said Jack.

"You said you were going to talk with him tomorrow right. So let's come up with some questions that you can ask that will help us figure out their real intentions," said Bob.

Jack, Fred and Bob spent the next few hours trying to come up with questions, but soon gave into the realization that they would not be able to trick a being that is as old as the universe into revealing anything it does not want to reveal. Jack decided he will just ask what their real intentions are, then decide how to proceed by the reaction.

Jack decided to go back to his rooms to try to get some sleep but first he stopped at the room of the man who attacked Walter. He stood outside the room for a moment then knocked on the wall. "Is anyone in there? Is it alright if I come in?"

"Who's there? Do I know you?" asked the man.

"My name is Jack. I was with the man you attacked earlier"

"Are you one of his friends? Are you working together?"

"I just met him a few hours ago when I was brought here. He brought me to my friends down the hall," said Jack, stepped into the opening.

"Ok, I guess you can come in, but only for a few minutes, what do you want?"

"I was wondering why you attacked him. Did he do something to you?"

"To all of us! He's working with those things that captured us, he's helping rounds us all up!"

"Did he tell any of you what was happening in the rest of the world or why you were brought here?"

"No, but he doesn't have to, I know what happened, I saw it with my own eyes! Those things came out of nowhere and grabbed everyone in the city. They dragged us all away, we passed out, and eventually we woke up here. He showed all of us to these rooms and explained how to use everything. He's the only one who knows anything about this place so he has to be working with them."

"Hmm, he really should have told you what was happening. You've probably already figured out we've been invaded..."

"Yes, yes, it became pretty obvious once we saw that small ship and the aliens inside it. Do you have anything useful to tell me?"

"Sorry, I'll try to make this short. The ones you saw in the ship are not the ones who invaded us; they are just workers. The one who had them bring you here is trying to keep us safe from the others of his kind who invaded. Everyone on the planet has been rounded up, but only a few thousand have made it here. Walter, the man you attacked, has been trying to learn everything he can from the one who is trying to help. It has been difficult for him because they do not communicate the same way we do. That is probably why he has not had any time to talk to any of you."

"You mean they have already won? No one is left out there? What are they going to do with us?" asked the man.

"We are safe here and I intend to find out how just one of them is supposed to help us. Tell you what, when I get more information out of Walter, I will tell you about it as soon as I can. So please, no more attacking him OK? Let's see what he can learn from the one helping us," said Jack.

"Ok, I guess. Thanks you for telling me all this. You are the first person to tell me anything about what is going on. Is it ok if I tell my friends?"

"Of course, I don't want anyone kept in the dark. The more we all know about them, the better our chances of finding a way out of this," said Jack, preparing to leave.

"Thanks again, you have no idea how much it means to us to know what is going on. We all thought for sure that we were going to eventually be killed."

"You're welcome, I am glad I could help."

On the way back to his room Jack contemplated going to the lab to chew out Walter for not telling anyone what was going on, but decided against it. He assumed Walter had been overwhelmed by the number of people showing up, while he trying to learn as much about the aliens as possible. Once back in his room he quickly fell asleep after laying down on the bed. Once again he did not communicate with anyone in his dreams, getting a chance for some real sleep.

Chapter 8

A loud clap of thunder directly over the building woke Jack in the morning. The storm was still raging outside with the rain heavier than last night. The bed was surprisingly comfortable allowing him to stay asleep through the entire night. He sat up, feeling a little groggy but refreshed, while looking over at the sink and shower. Do they really expect us to walk around soaking wet? Why didn't they give us a way to dry off? He walked over to the sink to examine himself in the mirrored wall, seeing he was definitely cleaner than yesterday morning, but still looked pretty rough. After quickly washing his face he decided to go to Walter's lab. Most people were still sleeping, the building was quiet except for the sound of the storm outside.

Jack knocked on the wall outside the lab when he arrived while looking in, but it was empty so he entered. It was an unimpressive room, making him wonder how anyone could do anything with only a few wall displays and the Aots. He watched the displays on the wall for a while but didn't understand what anything on them meant. There were colored and patterned spots, along with various shapes in different colors.

When Jack took the Aot sitting on the slab used as a table, he saw a rectangular area that he had not noticed before. It appeared to be a piece of glass embedded in the table, the same size as the map he had used in Vancouver. He placed his hand on the glass causing a holographic map to appear, showing an outline of part of the settlement with the lab at the center. At the spot where Jack was standing there was a multicolored spot, just outside the opening to the room was a grey spot. His face turned red when he looked over at the opening to see Walter watching him.

"Oh, don't worry my boy, you're not in trouble. In fact I had hoped you would show up when I wasn't here and start looking around."

"You wanted to see how much I could figure out on my own didn't you?"

"Yes, but that's not the only reason," said Walter changing to a whisper, "I don't believe they are telling me everything. I keep getting the feeling he is angered by some of my questions. I was hoping you could find some useful information in all this equipment that I have not been able to."

"What exactly should I be looking for?"

"I don't really know. Anything you can find that seems out of place or unusual would be a good start. I'm expected in here in about an hour, so you can use this equipment until then. Let me explain what all the symbols on the map mean, at least the ones I know about."

Walter used a wall display to help explain the meanings of some of the symbols that could be seen on the map then walked over to it to show some examples. "Well this is interesting to say the least."

"Did I do something to it?"

"No, but the spot that represents you is multicolored, but it was white when he showed me how to find people on the map a few weeks ago."

"What does that mean, did the threads you put in me change it?"

"I don't think so, see, I am still grey and I have them in me also. I've never seen a spot like this before. Let me check something." Walter touched the map and positions it to show Fred and Bob. "Hmm, Fred is now red, orange and yellow stripes, while Bob is blue, green and yellow."

"They weren't like that before?"

"No, they were both white like you. I've never seen anything other than solid colors on a person before. They must be monitoring you three closer now that you are here. I've seen complex coloring like this on objects to describe their functionality, maybe this represents what they want you for but I have no idea what the colors are supposed to represent in people. Here, you can use it some more while I go finish up my morning walk."

Jack zoomed out the map so he could see a larger area of the building, but could find no other spots that were not white or grey. As he zoomed out even further he could see that this settlement was the same one in New Zealand that he had observed on the map in Vancouver. He quickly moved the map to Vancouver seeing it was now covered in a similar but much larger settlement, with densely packed white and grey spots and a couple black ones. As he moved the map to show Abbotsford he could see all the land had been covered with a settlement with only a few small open areas left. The more he looked at it the angrier he got. This is just a giant prison! He decided to zoom out the map until he could see the entire planet.

Once all of Earth was visible Jack noticed there were a few faint lines moving away from it so he continued zooming out to find where they went. Earth was now a tiny blue dot with the lines moving off towards other stars. When Earth was no longer visible the lines became a little less faint allowing him to see thousands connecting stars all throughout the galaxy. He zoomed into one of the stars where some lines converged on a yellow dot near the star. As he zoomed in, the yellow dot appeared to be another planet. The surface was mostly a light yellow color with a few large patches of purple. He could see various settlements all appearing to be like the ones on Earth, also packed with millions of white and grey spots with the occasional black one.

Jack examined more planets discovering they were all the same, covered in settlements packed with dots. He got a sinking feeling in his stomach, the aliens didn't appear to be helping anyone on the planets he had checked, but they appeared to be imprisoning everyone instead. He zoomed out the map again to start examining the galaxy for anything different. The only thing he found was a small area on the outer edge of the opposite side of the galaxy where there were no lines going to the stars and no planets mapped out around them.

"Find anything interesting?" asked Walter as he walked back into the lab.

"A couple things. First, what do the black spots represent? Second, why is this area not mapped out or connected to everything else?"

"Black is sadly a dead person, as for this, I have no idea. I never noticed it before. Looks like you have found something interesting. If they are as old as the universe itself, then why have they not been here?" asked Walter rhetorically, looking at the unmapped area.

"Maybe they have but they found nothing."

"Not likely, they claimed every planet they found for themselves, and I doubt this many stars in one area have no planets. No, something else is going on here and I am extremely curious as to what."

"You said black is dead? I found a couple planets where most of the spots were black, and every planet I looked at appeared to have the same types of settlements as Earth on them."

"What! This is not good, not good at all. He assured me they do not kill anyone and that they only correct races when they are on a course of self destruction. I should have checked some other planets myself."

"Maybe this is just a map of what they have done. Like a kind of historical record."

"No, it is showing us fairly recent activity, at least that's what he told me. They can apparently move from one end of the galaxy to the other in about fifty years. These maps are all interconnected and it takes the same amount of time for the data to make it from a map on one side of the galaxy to a map on the other side. I... I want to ask you to do something... but I don't think..."

"You want me to ask him about what I found, right?"

126

"Yes, I'm not a brave man Jack, and I'm afraid of what he would do if I anger him. I've spent all my life in a lab and had no desire to do anything that could get me hurt." said Walter sheepishly.

"I understand, but you didn't have to ask me since I had already decided to confront him with this. If he really intends to help us we need to know what the others true intensions are towards us."

"Thank you, you are braver than I ever will be."

"Don't put yourself down, bravery comes in many forms. Most people would not be willing to have these thread put in them or to talk with an alien being in their mind. Just because you don't want a fight doesn't make you a coward. If anything it probably makes you smarter than me," said Jack with a laugh.

Walter grinned, "I don't know about you but I am a little hungry. There should be food in the entry halls by now."

"Sounds good to me, this map was starting to depress me. Maybe some food will help take my mind off it for a while."

They walked down to the room where Jack first entered the building to find a large group of people eating food from slabs like the one he saw back at the tower, only these were protruding from the walls.

"How many rooms here are used for eating?"

"I remember counting seventy six. Your friends would have gone to one closer to them."

After everyone had finished eating, the slabs slid back into the walls which then they sealed up.

"I think I am going to go find Fred and Bob and ask them what they think about what's on that map, care to join me or do you still have to be back in the lab?"

"Yes, I would like to come and no I don't have to be in the lab. Shortly before I arrived back I received a thought from him saying I would not be needed this morning."

"That's a bit of a coincidence. Do you think he knew what I was doing?"

"I'm not sure, but it's possible."

They walked to Bob's room but he wasn't there again, so they continued to Fred's room finding them both. They all discussed what Jack found on the map and concluded that there was indeed something being kept from them. Jack heard a voice in his head, "Find me at the landing area, we have much to discuss."

"I think he wants to meet with me, at some place called the landing area," said Jack.

"I know, he just told me too. The landing area is where you arrived here," said Walter.

"I want you two to be there also. We are all supposed to be important to him so we should all find out what he wants at the same time."

"Couldn't keep me away if you tried," said Fred while Bob nodded in agreement.

They made their way back to the landing area but found nothing but thunder and rain from the storm.

"He should be here shortly, be warned, he is very bright, it may take a while for your eyes to adjust. And don't forget you will be communicating with thoughts, so you don't need to speak for him to hear you. You can still speak if you want to, but you will have to remember to direct your thoughts towards him so the threads will translate for you," yelled Walter over the howling wind.

"What about us? How will we hear what it says?" asked Fred.

"You won't, we'll have to fill you in afterwards."

Standing near the edge of the cliff, Jack noticed a light on the horizon which was getting larger and brighter as it moved extremely fast over the ocean, "Is that his transport?"

"No, that's him. They don't need transports, they can move anywhere they want very quickly."

As the Light got closer Jack realized it was about the size of the huge ball of light they saw in Chilliwack. "Do they all look like that? I saw one about that size in Chilliwack."

"Some are bigger, some are smaller. Their bodies all look different, but they are so bright it is hard to see any detail. You say you saw one like that? Strange, Chilliwack is controlled by the others and their leader is about the same size as him. He normally doesn't appear before everyone on the planet has been rounded up."

The Light did not slow down until it was almost at the cliff when it decelerated very quickly. It was extremely bright so Jack had to shield his eyes. Eventually he could make out the shape of a hexagonal lattice in the glow, but could not see any details.

"Do not worry, I am not going to hurt any of you," said a voice in Jack's mind as a group of strings emerged from the Light. Fred and Bob took defensive stances as the strings circled everyone, but Walter reassured them that they were safe.

"Are you the one who has been looking for me? What is your name?" asked Jack in his thoughts, directing them at the Light.

"Yes, it is good to see you again Jack. We do not have names as you do. We identify each other by our thought processes and a series of colored lights."

"Well, I need to call you something, if not for your benefit then for ours so we are not confused as to who we are speaking about. Is it alright if I refer to you as Alpha One, and the leader of the others as Alpha Two?"

"You always have. Has Walter explained our history with this planet to you?"

"He said that this is the fifth time I am living through this and that you are trying to 'correct' us. I'm not sure if I believe that though, it seems a little farfetched to me. I am confused as to how destroying our cities and keeping us prisoners is correcting anything!"

"The others refuse to take my advice to just destroy your weapons. This way has always worked throughout your history and they still believe it will work now, even after many failures. It has unfortunately become the way of my race to not look for different solutions to problems. Our great age along with a long history of success has made us complacent. I have always strived to find new ways to perform tasks, to try and prevent situations like this."

"But why did you ever do it this way? Destroying everything we have created, taking away our freedom, how can you see that as something good?"

"The last time this was done the majority of the humans on this planet were living in very poor conditions, with only a few controlling everyone else's life. Your existence was quite primitive, making these living conditions a luxury for most. We have been correcting the human race every few thousand years since it came into existence. Your young always accepted us and followed our teachings. The older humans were isolated but treated well, and they also, eventually, accepted us. We had considered you to be the equivalent of pets; something that could not survive on its own for long. For a while you would live peacefully with each other but would slowly move back towards violent behavior."

"Couldn't you see what you were doing wasn't working?"

"But it was working. The time it took for you to revert always increased. We had used this method with many other species throughout the galaxy and always had success. We were trying to extend the time it took for your violent

129

tendencies to return to allow you to evolve intellectually to the point where you could control them. This has to happen before you evolve technologically to the point of being able to destroy yourselves or the planet. Many species had done this without our help, but yours was not among them."

"What went wrong with us?"

"We were required to leave for some time. If we had stayed, we would have influenced which humans were allowed to become leaders, eliminating humans who favored violence."

"You mean you would have killed people to stop them from leading us?"

"No, not killed, we would convince them through their dreams and thoughts that they had another purpose in life that did not involve them being in any position to control people. In your recent history you have had an unusually large number of leaders who have favored war to resolve differences. With war there are always giant technological, but limited intellectual, advances. When we left we had expected you to have advanced to the point you were at two thousand years ago, it was further than we wanted but considered acceptable. When we came back we were shocked at how fast you had progressed."

"Why did you leave? Does it have something to do with the empty area we found on your map of the galaxy?" There was silence, Jack got a deep feeling of distress and anger but it was not his own, so he decided to change the subject. "You must realize by now that humans would never accept this way of life. We are no longer a primitive people who only exist to serve a few with all the power. We have complex and varied lives. If those are taken away and we are kept in what is no better than prisons we will always do everything we can to drive away whatever has imprisoned us, even if it could mean our own deaths. Freedom and control over our own lives is what we value the most."

"I do see it. I saw it after the first attempt at correction. But the others do not. Billions of years of correcting many species the same way has made them stubborn and blind."

"Why are you different? What made you see that this would not work?"

"I have always preferred to find new ways to accomplish tasks, I find doing the same thing each time to be tedious. When something that has been done before does not work, I will always try something different the next time. The others always believe that a process that worked once should always work and it must only need to be adjusted to fit the situation. In this case they believe the timing of the various phases of the correction need to be adjusted."

"If you cannot convince them then how are we supposed to help? I doubt they will be interested in the opinions of 'pets'!"

"With my help they will be. I had tried to tell you what your purpose would be in this process, but the primitive Draad made communication very difficult. You and your friends will need to show that humans can live in peace on their own, without our control."

"Exactly how do you expect us to do that when you have destroyed everything?" asked Jack angrily, "None of the people here have shown any interest in anything other than destroying you and the others. So I very much doubt you will find them to be very peaceful!"

"You have all the attributes for a peaceful leader. I want you to be the leader of these people. I will teach you and your friends various ways to live harmoniously with the planet. I will also teach you how we pursue intellectual activities which will open up new ways of thinking for you. You will then teach everyone else and build up a new society. The process will take many years, but should be enough to convince some of the others I am correct."

"I seriously doubt any of that will work. We do not accept leaders that are forced upon us. Besides, I have no interest in being a leader, and neither do my friends. That is why we lived our lives the way we did."

"But you must still try. If your people here cannot show the others that there is another way, they will continue attempting a correction until it succeeds, which I believe can never happen. So you will be trapped in this scenario for the eternity of your existence."

Jack thought for a moment, "That may be true, but I will not even consider helping until you improve the conditions here."

"What is wrong with this place? I have provided you with everything you need to exist"

"Existence is more than just food and shelter. At the very least we need more privacy in the living spaces, soap for cleaning ourselves, a way to clean our clothing, and more clothes to replace the damaged ones."

"Walter has tried to explain privacy to me but it is an unfamiliar concept to my kind. I do not know what soap is, but there is a cleaning area in each room which should be adequate."

"Privacy is a person's ability to isolate themselves from others. It's not hard to understand even if you don't need it. At the very least we need doors that we can control in the entrance to each room. Walter can explain what soap is. Just water is not good enough for us."

"You do not need any of this to survive!" said Alpha One, sounding a little agitated.

"This is not negotiable, if you do not make these changes then we will not help you!" said Jack angrily.

"You will do as I say!" said Alpha One as one of the strings grabbed Jack, throwing him against the wall of the building. He hit the wall with a loud thud and fell to the ground.

Fred looked as though he was going to charge at Alpha One but Walter grabbed his arm. "Don't even think about it. You'd be dead before you got near him."

Bob ran over to Jack who had blood coming out of his nose and mouth. "Don't move Jack, you're hurt pretty badly."

"I'll be ok in a minute," said Jack in agony.

"Why did you do that?" asked Walter angrily, directing his thoughts at Alpha One. "You said you needed him!"

The strings moved back to Alpha One as he accelerated off into the distance. Walter stood stunned watching him leave while Fred ran over to Jack.

"He doesn't look to good. Walter is there any sort of hospital here?" asked Fred, but Walter didn't hear him.

"I will be ok... the threads..." said Jack.

"Do you really think they can fix this?"

"Yes... I can... feel bones... moving..." said Jack as he passed out.

"Walter! Snap out of it. Is there anything like a hospital around here?" yelled Fred.

"Wha... Sorry, he's never done anything like that before. I'm not sure what to make of it," said Walter as he ran over to them.

"Forget him for a minute ok! Jack's hurt pretty bad, is there a hospital here?"

"No, but he won't need one anyway. He has a full set of Draad in him. He probably only has broken bones and internal bleeding. Worst case would be a few damaged organs, something they can fix easily."

"What do we do then, we can't just leave him out here," said Bob.

"We have to. If we move him we could cause more bleeding, possibly killing him before they can repair everything that has already been damaged. I can wait with him if you two want to get back inside away from this storm."

"No way we're leaving him alone with you! You've been working with that thing from the beginning and the first thing it did when meeting Jack for the first time was try to kill him. For all I know it told you to finish the job when we left!" said Fred angrily.

"Please believe me when I say I had no idea he would do this. He wasn't including me in the conversation, so I don't know what they were talking about or why he did this. When he left I tried to talk to him but all I could sense was a strong feeling of shame."

"Let's just wait until Jack wakes up and he'll tell us what happened. Until then I suggest we avoid accusing anyone of anything," said Bob.

"He's pretty smashed up so it will be a while. It took them about half an hour to fix a compound fracture in my leg when someone attacked me a few weeks ago. I'll just wait over there so I don't bother you," said Walter as he walked closer to the cliff, sitting down, putting his head in his hands.

"I really don't think he had anything to do with this. He looks like someone whose best friend just betrayed him," said Bob.

"I still don't trust him. He's been here longer than any of us and seems to have the run of the place while the rest of us are stuck sitting around doing nothing," said Fred.

They waited in the storm for almost two hours before they heard Jack groan and start moving around.

"Jack, buddy, you alright?" asked Fred while helping Jack to sit up.

Walter heard them talking so he walked back to the group.

"Ugh, I feel like I've just woken up after a weekend of drinking and partying. Everything hurts and my head is throbbing," said Jack.

"Let me check if they are finished," said Walter as he took an Aot out of his pocket.

"Just what are you planning on doing?" asked Fred quickly grabbing Walter's arm.

"It's ok Fred, let go of him. That's just a tool. It can scan my body for problems," said Jack.

"Do anything stupid and we'll find out if those threads can fix a snapped neck," said Fred while glaring at Walter.

"Fred! Why are you being so rude? What happened when I was out?" asked Jack.

"I believe he thinks I only brought you to him so he could kill you, and that I was supposed to 'finish the job' after he left," said Walter.

"Jeez Fred, you have to stop jumping to conclusions. All of this is my fault. Walter had nothing to do with it." Fred's face turned slightly red and he avoided eye contact with Walter.

"What happened between you and him? He wouldn't talk to me when he left."

"He told me he wanted me to be the leader of all the people here and he would teach all of us new ways to live. Apparently that would somehow convince the others he is right. I got a strong feeling that I should not choose to help yet, so I gave him a list of demands for changes to this place to make it more comfortable for everyone. I told him I wouldn't help unless he met those demands."

"Ah, now I understand what made him angry. Your feelings may have to do with the fact that each of the previous corrections ended with everyone dead and the planet destroyed. Your mind still has those memories and it is probably trying to avoid getting you killed again. I don't understand what he thought he would accomplish by attacking you though. He has always told me you are the only person who could prove humans have the ability to look after themselves peacefully without leaders. So his statement that he wanted you to be our leader is very confusing to me."

"Maybe he meant I would lead by example, he did say he would teach me and my friends and we would teach the others."

"You aren't starting to believe all this nonsense about living through all this before are you?" asked Fred.

"I think I knew about it long before anyone told me. I've never told anyone, but many times in my life I have remember things that are going to happen before they happen."

"That's just déjà vu, everyone gets it."

"This is different, I've remember days worth of events that are going happen weeks before they happen. The last time it happened was when we rescued that hiker that fell into a ravine. The only information we had as that he had not come back from his trip and no one knew exactly where he went."

"I remember that, I flew the helicopter to the area we were told he usually hiked, but on the way there you saw a glint of light in the ravine he was in as we flew over."

"Do you also remember that I suggested a flight path for you and you were confused as to why I didn't want to go straight to the destination?"

"Yeah, I thought it was strange until you told me you had heard there were high winds through the valley that took the direct path."

"I just made that up to get you to fly over the ravine. I also didn't see any glint. Three weeks earlier the memory of everything we did that day came back to me. I knew everyone would think I was crazy if I ever tried to claim I could see the future, so I never told anyone. It didn't matter anyway since I always remembered what I did to get other people to do what I wanted."

"You really think I'm going to believe that? If you could remember things that were going to happen why would you not have stopped me and Joan from driving into town the day of the crash?" asked Fred slightly angered.

"Because I wasn't there and had no memory of the events that took place in the accident. Everything I have remembered has always been something I have done"

"Makes sense to me. I have many memories of my childhood, but none of yours since I wasn't there," said Bob.

"Bah! We live once and we can't remember something that hasn't happened yet, end of story. Nothing you can say will convince me otherwise," said Fred gruffly.

"I wasn't trying to convince you. I've known you too long to every think I could change your beliefs."

"You said that was the last time, there has been nothing since that rescue?" asked Walter.

"No, nothing, just strong feeling about what to do or not to do."

"Interesting. He did say you never attacked them before. Maybe we are running through a series of events happening for the first time. You may have enough memories of the previous times to prevent yourself, and hopefully the rest of us, from failing this time."

Jack thought for a moment then started frowning. "You know, no matter what choice I think about, if it involves helping Alpha One I get an extremely bad feeling about it." Everyone gave him a confused look.

"Sorry Alpha One is what I decided to call him. I'm calling the other leader Alpha Two. I told him we would use those names to cut down on confusion."

"Ah, good idea... Maybe there is no way for us to prove he is right. That could be why helping him feels wrong to you," said Walter.

"Well if we don't help him, what are the chances he'll do anything to improve things here?"

135

"None I'd say. We need to concentrate on finding a way out of this place and getting our hands on some of their weapons again," said Fred.

"What chance would we have at defeating them when the soldiers who had the suits could not do it?"

"You are assuming that that thing is telling the truth when it says they were captured."

"Well if they were not captured then they are dead. Remember that I didn't see any sign of them in the armors display after the fight."

"Forgot about that, but you guys only had seven of the threads at the time. You're fully loaded now, and if we all had a full load of those threads in us I'll bet we could take out a few of them."

"That's unacceptable! They have never intended to kill us. They only want to stop us from wiping ourselves out. We need to find a way to convince them that we can do that and that no matter how they do the correction it would always fail," said Walter.

"Listen, I know you've bought into all this bullshit about things happening over and over, but I haven't! If we don't stop them now, humans will be their prisoners and slaves for the rest of eternity!" said Fred angrily.

"The important point here is that neither Walter nor I believe we can fight them and win. If we kill a few of them I'm pretty sure their anger will result in the death of the human race and..."

"Good! Better dead than a prisoner or slave!"

"Why should we be allowed to make that choice for everyone on the planet? It might be ok for you but I doubt most people would agree."

"Bah! I'm getting nowhere with you bunch! We've lost everything and you want to help the things that did it to us. Count me out!" yelled Fred angrily as he stormed back into the building.

"Fred wait, don't go," said Bob as he started to walk towards the building.

"Forget it Bob, let him go. He just needs some time to cool off," said Jack.

Bob stopped, "Yeah, you're right. I really don't like it when he gets like that."

"Yeah, me neither. I am just glad he was not in one of those suits or we would have been toast," said Jack with a chuckle.

"He's not going to hurt anyone in that condition is he?" asked Walter nervously.

"No, the worst thing he would do is to yell at someone if they stared at him or got in his way. He's quick to temper and can argue for hours, but I've never seen him start a physical fight with anyone."

A brief memory appeared in Jack's mind. Fred was in one of the suits far above the ground. He was fighting one of the Lights, shooting gigantic blast waves from the suit towards it. Jack was also in a suit, trying desperately to convince him to stop fighting. The Light was able to dodge all the blasts, with many of them hitting Earth, vaporizing large holes through the crust deep in to the mantle.

"Shit! We need to find Fred and keep an eye on him!" said Jack as he jumped up running into the building with Bob and Walter chasing after him.

"Wait Jack! What's wrong?" asked Bob.

"I just remembered him fighting one of the Lights and causing massive damage to Earth in the process."

"But that never happened," said Bob confused.

"Not yet, it is going to happen. This was one of those memories of things that will happen I was telling you about."

"Fred's the reason for the failure?" asked Walter.

"Maybe, I don't know. But we need to make sure he doesn't get his hands on one of the suits just in case. Are there any kept here?"

"No, the Juvo are the only ones using them, and they only keep spares at the demolition and building sites."

"What about the two in the transport, do they stay here? Wait, there he is... Let's keep an eye on him from a distance until he calms down," said Jack returning to a slow walk.

"No they don't stay here. They were called out once a week to bring people here from the tower. They will be making one last trip in a few days to bring the rest of the people here."

"Then that is probably when he got the suit, but how? Even if he has one of the Aots I don't think either of the Juvo would just let him take their suit. Alpha One must have memories of what happened. We should ask him about it."

"Maybe you will remember. All the new threads you have may be letting you access you memories again."

"Maybe, but I didn't need them before the invasion. Maybe events have just fallen back into the same pattern as before and we are heading towards failure again."

"Maybe the attack against you is what triggers Fred to attack them?" asked Bob.

"Speculating about it will just end up making us doubt every action we want to take. Jack's right, we need him to tell us what he knows about what will happen," said Walter.

"Is it possible for you to tell the Juvo to hold off on bringing everyone else here until we know a bit more?" asked Jack.

"No, but I can tell him and he can let them know, assuming he will talk to any of us. He does tell me when they are coming so I can greet the new people, so the next time I can get you two to come with me."

"Good idea, there is a much better chance the two of us could talk some sense into Fred if he does try to get one of their suits."

"Guys, if you want I can keep an eye on Fred. We've spent most of our time the past few weeks talking about how to get out of here, so he won't be suspicious of me. I'll just give him a while to calm down before I try to talk with him," said Bob.

"Ok, but don't hesitate to find us if something doesn't feel right to you. Jack and I will be in my lab," said Walter.

"What are we going to do in the lab?"

"I want you spend more time trying to figure out how to use all the equipment he has provided. I've already experimented with all of it and have run out of ideas. Experiment with everything in the lab and look for any hidden functionality."

"Ok, I'm not sure what I can do that you have not already done but I will give it a shot."

When they arrived at the lab, Walter took two Aots out of his pocket, placing them with one already on the table. He explained what some more of the shapes and colors in the displays meant before letting Jack experiment. The first thing Jack did was to try cutting open the pedestals and walls of the room using an Aot in the same way he cut open the armor. When he got to the area next to the displays on one of the walls a tiny hole appeared as he moved the Aot across the wall.

"Well look at that, I knew you would find something!" said Walter excitedly.

Jack moved the Aot vertically from the hole that appeared causing a paper thin gap to open up in the wall. Once he had made the gap as large as possible

138

the closest display on the wall changed to show two shapes: a solid square and an outlined square.

"Those are the symbols for open and close right?" asked Jack.

"Yes they are! You ready to find out what they've hidden in the wall?"

"As ready as I will ever be. It cannot be anything to big. These walls are only about half a meter thick."

Walter touched the outlined square which made the wall slowly slide open to reveal a completely black void with no walls, floor, or ceiling visible.

"What the hell? Why can't we see anything in there?" asked Jack.

"Must be something blocking the light," said Walter sounding slightly unsure.

Jack moved his Aot in to the opening, but it did not disappear. He then moved it to where the floor should be but was able to keep moving it down. "What the...? There's no floor!" said Jack as he jerked his arm away from the opening.

"Amazing, let me check," said Walter as he tried to touch the walls in the opening with his Aot, getting the same results.

"What's going on? Why is it going through the walls?"

"I don't think there are any walls," said Walter, taking a small apple out of his pocket. "I was keeping this for a snack, but I suppose I don't need the whole thing." He bit a large chunk out of the apple, took it out of his mouth, and threw it in to the opening. The chunk of apple made an arc in the air, but as soon as it entered the black void started moving faster in a straight line downward. It stayed illuminated by the light from the room for a short time before disappearing from sight.

"How? What? It should have...?" said Jack completely confused.

"That is not a space in the wall. I think it's an opening into another three dimension space, an empty space from the appearance of it. Probably the same one the transport and suits shift into."

"Why would they have a door to something like this? If it's empty why isn't all the air being sucked out of the room?"

"There's probably a field keeping the air in here, similar to the ones in all the openings to the outside of these buildings. I suspect that their other settlement have portals like this. They probably use them to transport things between settlements."

"Why not just use a transport and fly from place to place?"

"I suspect the space in there is warped so the distances between these portals would be much shorter in there than out here. All the transports I've seen so far operate while partially in our space and are limited to how fast they can travel just as we are. If all the planets they live on have these, and there are transports operating completely inside there, it would explain how they can move across the galaxy so quickly."

"That opening is making me nervous, could we close it please?"

"Ok, probably a good idea anyway, wouldn't want to fall in there. Why don't you see if you can find any way of showing this opening on the map while I check the displays to see if opening that caused any new information to show up," said Walter.

Jack experimented with the map for a while, but could not find any indication that there was a door in the wall. "I don't think they have every detail on these maps. There is no indication of any opening on any of the walls in the settlement, or the rooms the food comes from. Hmm, I wonder..." said Jack, staring at an Aot for a moment before placing it on the glass.

The surface of the Aot lit up displaying four different colored squares. When Jack touched each square the map changed what was shown. The first square showed the map they were already familiar with, the second showed a web of lines surrounding the planet, the third showed the buildings with more details, and the fourth showed many white dots, some moving, at various places on the planet.

"Ha! You did it again! When I was brought here I found those things sitting on the glass but it was off. I must have unconsciously assumed they do nothing with the map. That web is obviously the web of lights we see in the sky at night. The white dots are probably the transport points, or balls of light as you called them. Let's look at the detailed buildings a little closer."

Jack switched back to the detailed building view. The buildings were all drawn more accurately, with the thickness of the walls being shown as well as all openings and doors they knew about. They both experimented for a while, trying to make the map show more, but were not successful.

"Well, better than nothing I guess. We haven't found any new information in the map, but at least we know there are no other hidden doors," said Walter with a sigh.

"You have discovered the portal much faster this time," said Alpha One's voice in Jack's and Walter's minds.

"Did you hear that?" they said to each other simultaneously.

"I'm confused; you knew we were going to find the door? Why did you not just show it to us?" said Jack directing his thoughts at Alpha One and Walter.

"I needed to find out how much memory of the previous corrections you have access to before I could fully decide how to proceed this time. I have no way to fully apologize for my attack on you earlier Jack, your refusal to cooperate came much sooner than I had hoped. During the previous corrections I was able to work with you for many years before you stopped cooperating," said Alpha One.

"But I don't remember doing any of this before."

"Your mind remembers everything, but unlike your mind, your brain is limited to remembering only your past. While your mind is connected to your brain it is limited by your brain's abilities. In order to overcome that limitation, many minds have learned how to embed small clues in the brain and attach them to objects or events that have not been seen yet. Your mind seems to have embedded the urge to touch and place the objects you find here on other objects."

"That would certainly explain a lot of my more unusual behaviors throughout my life. Why did you attack me earlier? If you need my help then attacking me is a strange way to get it."

"My kind has always avoided violence and only uses it in desperate situations. My erratic behavior has caused my allies to no longer trust my judgment and form a new group. They believe my failures to prove I am correct have made me angry and unstable, which I fear may be partially true. Your defiance and the failure of the correction have come earlier with each correction, Having you reject us before anything has been attempted has altered me. Whether it is for good or bad I have yet to determine. You should be aware that if this correction fails, then my role in the next one will be minimal. Being on my own would only provide me with minimal resources and access to a small number of humans."

"So they are no longer working with you? Are your former allies not going to follow your ideas?"

"They do still believe I am correct, but they no longer want me involved. We will still be working together now, but I will no longer be permitted to meet with any of you alone."

"Ok, but that probably doesn't matter anyway. I seriously doubt anyone here is going to cooperate with any of you until we are treated like more than animals in a zoo... A little while ago I had a memory of one of my friends

141

fighting one of you high above this planet, but all he ended up doing was to blast the planet. Do you remember anything like that?"

"You memory was of the first attempt at correction. We kept the settlements near the Juvo's work sites thinking humans would have no interest in them. Some of your people took equipment from the sites and learned how to use it. Afterwards many of your people took the suits and used them as weapons, destroying the planet while trying to destroy us. As for your demands, my former allies do know of them because you have always, eventually, given them to us. We have always ignored them since we believed that once cooperation had ended there could be no success."

"I think you are confusing cooperation and obedience. Cooperation has benefits for both sides."

"We had always assumed the benefit for humans would be the potential of peaceful living, but I and my former allies have now realized that we don't fully understand the needs and desires of your race. Because of that, a few of them have decided to study your existence in the past five hundred years more closely to help us understand."

"So you expect us to live like this while they spend five hundred years studying us?"

"No, to you they will only appear to be gone for a short time. We are not bound in time as you are; they will only be observing the way humans live at a few specific times and then returning here. They will take what you have told me into account as well as what they observe when they determine what changes need to be made. I realize that you will not be willing to work with us at the moment, but I am no longer going to withhold information from you to test your abilities. It has become obvious that your mind has adapted to this situation and is able to give you the memories you need to proceed. The map does not have all openings marked. The back wall of every entry hall of each building is also a door. I will leave what is behind them for you to discover, but I think your people will be pleased."

"I will withhold my thanks until we see what those doors are hiding. You should also know that even when you do make conditions better here, most of the people will still have great resentment and probably hatred for you and the others. Our lives and culture, for better or worse, greatly involve the material objects we collect and create. You can never replace all the photographs and videos we had created of the events in our lives, or our art and music. Destroying all those things destroyed a large piece of who we are."

"It is a very alien concept to us, the need to create and collect. I think I am starting to understand, but I do not think the others are trying. We have spent the majority of our history trying to make organic life forms more like we are, less chaotic and violent and more intellectual. I fear we may have held back the potential of many races instead of advancing them as we thought we were. The others wish to question me further about what I have done and I must go now. I do not know when we will talk again."

"Wait, I have more questions!"

"No one is listening, when he says he is going he will be gone by the time he finishes his sentence," said Walter.

"It seems to me like they could use a lesson in manners."

"I don't think they normally have conversations with the races they correct. It's more of a 'do what I tell you and don't talk back' kind of relationship. I don't know about you but the doors he mentioned have piqued my curiosity."

"I am curious, but also very wary. I do not know if I can trust what he tells us yet. For all I know they have deemed this round a failure and opening those doors will suck us all into the void we saw behind this door."

"I don't think that's the case. I didn't feel any malice directed towards us, did you?"

"No, is that something I would be able to feel?"

"Yes, the Draad not only translate thoughts between us, but emotions also. If he was intending to hurt us we would know it right away."

"That explains why I was feeling shame and disappointment."

"Yes, I sensed it too. I think something snapped in his mind when you made those demands, sort of like one of us having a breakdown."

"Great, just what we need in this situation: an unstable alien who could crush us all without even trying."

"I hope it's not that bad, but we could speculate all day and in the end his mind is still alien and works differently from ours, so I doubt we know what is really going on. Anyway, I'm more interested in those doors right now."

"Yeah, you are right. Whatever they decide to do, they will do whether we like it or not. Maybe there is something useful behind the doors. He did say we would be pleased."

"Excellent, let's go. Maybe your friend has calmed down now. You think he would want to come along? You could try telling him about what you remembered. Maybe if he knew he was one of the people originally responsible for destroying the planet he would think again about fighting them."

ERIC PAUKER

"I doubt it. Fred has always believed that fighting an oppressor and dying in the process is nobler than living as a prisoner, no matter how good off you are in your prison."

"Ah, I see. Well he may still be interested in what is behind the doors. Might take his mind off wanting to fight."

Jack and Walter walked to Fred's room, noticing that everyone in the hallway was watching them as they passed. They could hear the echoes of Fred and Bob arguing long before they arrived. As they got closer they could hear what was being said.

"That would be suicide and you know it!" said Bob.

"Look, what part of better off dead than a prisoner are you not getting?" shouted Fred.

"So much for calmed down" whispered Walter as they enter the room.

"Oh great! More people to tell me I should be a nice prisoner and cooperate" yelled Fred.

"Not me, as a matter of fact I think you may be partially correct," said Jack.

Everyone stared at Jack in stunned silence.

"Wha... you agree with me now?" asked Fred a little confused.

"Partially. I no longer believe cooperating will get us anywhere. But I also don't think we should be so quick to get ourselves killed. At least not until we have tried to find a way to drive them off Earth."

"What do suggest doing? Maybe throw fruits and vegetables at them until they leave? We have no way to fight," said Bob.

"Not yet, and we may not have to fight if we can show them they cannot ever succeed."

"What makes you think they would leave just because they can't get their way? And what do you mean not yet, did you find some weapons somewhere?" asked Fred.

"No weapons, but we just finished a conversation with Alpha One. To make a long story short: he does not seem to be in charge anymore. Apparently they do not like violence very much and do not trust his judgment anymore. He also mentioned that his former allies are trying to learn more about how we lived before the invasion happened to try and improve conditions here."

"Awe gee, I feel so sorry for him. But we are still prisoners," said Fred.

"The point is that not only are they failing, they seem to have finally realized it. They are starting to realize we will never cooperate and are trying to find a way to fix everything so we don't even think of attacking them. If we

144

can find some more of their armor then we won't need to fight them because they do not want to fight. I think all we need to do is make them believe we are going to try to attack and destroy them in order to get them to leave."

"So how does that get us justice? How do we make them pay for destroying everything?"

"I thought this was all about not being a prisoner, not getting revenge."

"Well... Yes... But we can't just let them get away with this. They destroyed everything!"

"I know, but would you really want to make another species go through what all of us have gone through?"

"Well, I guess not, but they have to be made to pay somehow."

" I truly believe that they did not realize how much damage they did to us by destroying our cities, in much the same way most humans would not understand what kicking over an ant hill does to the ants."

"Hmmm, maybe, but we are still prisoners here. How do you expect to get out? I don't think you would survive jumping off the cliff, even with those threads in you."

"We found a door in one of the lab's walls which apparently leads to some sort of empty universe. Walter thinks they use it to transport things between settlements. The interesting thing though, is Alpha One told us there are also doors in the main entry halls and we would be pleased with what we find behind them."

"You really think you should trust that thing? They might not like violence, but that doesn't mean they wouldn't have something behind the doors that could hurt us."

"One of the nice things about these threads is that they not only let us hear someone else's thought, but we also sense their emotions, and neither of us sensed anything bad. So what do you say? Want to come with us and find out what is behind them?"

"Why not, I'm fairly certain I won't convince you to not open them, so when things go bad I want to be there to say 'I told you so'!"

Jack shook his head while sighing as they left the room, walking to the nearest entry hall. Once again people in the hall were watching them.

"Why is everyone watching us? They we doing it earlier as well," said Jack.

"Many of these rooms have a view of the area where you talked with him, I mean Alpha One, earlier. They are probably wondering why you are still alive after being smashed into the wall out there."

145

"Well I wish they would stop. It's making me uncomfortable."

As they passed the room of the man who attacked Walter they heard a voice. "How did that thing not kill you? You should be dead after what it did!" said the man.

"I'll catch up guys, I promised him I'd keep him up to date with what is happening around here," said Jack, walking into the man's room.

Jack gave a quick explanation of the attack and what had happened since. "I just realized I never introduced myself last time, my name is Jack."

"Mine is Bill, do you mind if I come along to watch you open the doors?"

"Not at all, in fact I was going to ask you to come along. That way if we find something that would be of interest to everyone you could spread the word while we open more doors."

Jack and Bill left the room to meet up with everyone else. When they arrived at the entry hall Walter saw Bill and waved. "Good morning Bill."

"G'mornin' Walter, I hear you all found something interesting."

Walter noticed Jack looking slightly confused. "I forgot to thank you Jack. After you talked to Bill yesterday he tracked me down to talk. I hadn't realized how much I had isolated myself from everyone else, so we spent a long time talking about what I have been doing around here."

"Ah, good. I wanted Bill to be here to see what we find so he could let everyone else know," said Jack as he took the Aot from his pocket. After scanning every part of the wall he could reach he found nothing.

"Nothing, why am I not surprised," said Fred.

"Hang on, just because it doesn't open like the one in the lab doesn't mean there is nothing here," said Jack as he started scanning the underside of the nearby ramp that led to the other floors. When he got to a point slightly above his head a display appeared in the stone when the Aot was near. The display looked like the one in the lab, with one solid square and one outlined square. He touched the outlined square causing the wall at the back to start rumbling and slowly slide open, revealing a large field filled with tall grass, a few large trees, and woods beyond. There was a gravel path leading from the door, through the field into the woods. The storm was still raging outside, but the rain was not falling anywhere in the field or woods.

"This is much nicer than the tiny courtyards in these buildings," said Bob.

"I'll go tell everyone else!" said Bill excitedly as he ran back towards the rooms.

146

"You might want to wait until we check it out first!" said Fred loudly, but Bill didn't hear.

"I don't think we would have any chance of keeping everyone in here after they have been locked up for so long. We better start looking around and make sure there is nothing out there that is going to hurt anyone," said Jack as he walked through the opening.

Chapter 9

"Why did they keep us locked in the buildings when all this is out here? It looks like they've even protected it from bad weather to make it more comfortable for us," said Walter.

"I suspect they were going to use it as a reward for our, or maybe my, cooperation," said Jack.

"Ah, so we do as they say and they'll make life a bit easier for us. I'm liking these guys more every minute," said Fred.

"I wonder why Alpha One told us about this. Is he trying to sabotage his original plans because the others no longer want to work with him, or does he think his plans have completely failed and he is just letting us have access to everything because he has given up?" asked Jack.

"I don't like either choice myself. They would both mean the Lights will be trying another correction, and who knows how the new group would handle us," said Walter.

"Well, if we're lucky none of them will be paying much attention to us now and we might be able to overpower those two aliens that fly the transport the next time they show up and take their armor," said Fred.

"I forgot, you haven't seen what one of those suits can do have you Fred? Even if we managed to get a close enough to try and cut them out, they would just fly us into a wall and splatter us all over it. But I don't think we should ignore them. Maybe they are in a similar situation to us. If I try communicating with them I might be able to convince them to help," said Jack.

"I doubt they would willingly give us the suits they are using since they can't survive in our atmosphere. If you did manage to open one of their suits they would have no problem killing you before they died," said Walter.

"Why, are they stronger than us?" asked Jack.

"Not really. But picture six machetes connected to a large pineapple and you get a rough idea of what you are up against." said Walter.

"Why are they in suits that look like us if they have six arms and legs? Isn't it uncomfortable for them?" asked Jack.

"So we wouldn't be afraid of them. Think of how humans ten thousand years ago would have reacted if the Juvo didn't disguise their appearance. They have more than enough room in the suits and don't need to contort themselves to get in. They would be uncomfortable if they had to support themselves though. You might have noticed a feeling of weightlessness when you were in

148

the suit. That's because the suits operate the same way as the transports, shifting the inside to an empty space where there is no gravity. Since the suits operate and move by thoughts the Juvo don't need to know how to walk or move like us." said Walter.

"I thought they were operated by the hand gestures I made," said Jack.

"Why did you think that?" asked Walter.

"Because I was told to make a fist with both hands to create a blast wave, and then when I was experimenting with the suit I made it move forward by pointing my index fingers forward." said Jack.

"What was going through your mind as you did that?" asked Walter.

"I was wishing the suit could fly, then it started floating... and when I created a blast I was thinking I need to destroy the strings to protect the soldiers! So you are saying I could have gotten the suit to do anything I thought about?" asked Jack.

"Anything they are built to do, your thoughts just turn their different abilities on or off. When you first tried doing things you just happened to think about you wanted them to happen when making the gestures," said Walter.

"I wonder how things would have turned out if we had more time to experiment... Look up ahead! There is a small stone podium at the edge of the path just before the start of the woods," said Jack.

As they approached the podium Jack could see the top had an embedded sheet of glass like the table back in the lab. He placed his palm on the glass, revealing a map of the newly discovered area. The map showed a large number of small buildings scattered throughout the woods over a very large area. It also showed many paths leading through the woods down to the coast line on the other side of the peninsula.

"Well this isn't on the other maps. We should examine some of these buildings to find out what they are for," said Walter.

Jack glanced back at the settlement to see dozens of people at the newly discovered doorway, cautiously walking outside. "We should warn everyone to be careful first," said Jack pointing at the people exiting the building. "Everyone, could I have your attention for a minute?" yelled Jack while running quickly to the group. "Please be cautious about what you do out here. We do not know if there is anything dangerous in this area or in the buildings up ahead. There is a map of the area at the end of the path and I suggest looking at it first before going too far from the buildings."

"Who elected you boss?" asked a man somewhere in the crowd.

"No one, I am not trying to tell you what to do. I am only suggesting how to not get hurt. None of us are familiar with this new area, or what they have put in it. There appears to be many buildings in the woods, so we are going to check them out. Feel free to come along if you are interested." Jack and a few people from the group walked back to his friends, who had now made it half way back to the settlement.

"Made some new friends?" asked Fred.

"I guess so, I invited anyone who is interested in seeing the new buildings to come along," said Jack.

They continued walking along the path into the woods towards the first building shown on the map. The trees were quite tall, but far enough apart to see the sky at certain spots. Other than a few ferns, there was not much growing on the forest floor. In the distance they could see a building which looked like it was made from the same material as the settlement. When they arrived they saw the interior was the same size as the rooms in the settlement, with a bed, sink, shower, toilet in an alcove, and a ceiling that lit up when they walked inside. All the nearby buildings were about five meters away from each other.

"Strange, I wonder why they built one of these rooms out here in the woods?" asked Walter.

"Maybe this is the start of another settlement like the one we just left," said Jack.

"I doubt it, since there are only a few more people scheduled to be shipped here," said Walter.

"Let's check some more of these buildings and see what they contain."

Building after building was the same, just simple living quarters. All of the buildings were placed so that the openings were not in a direct line of sight to the openings of another building.

"Do you think they created this after I made my demands?" asked Jack.

"They are fast, but I don't know if they are that fast. Maybe this is where they were going to put us after we cooperated enough and they thought we were ready to make a new society," said Walter.

"What do you mean? What are they planning to do to us?" asked one of the men in the group that followed them.

"We are supposed to be their Guinea Pigs for some big experiment to make a better human race," said Fred gruffly.

"What? Are you serious?" asked a woman in the crowd.

150

"He's making it sound worse than it is. They want to teach us a different way to live in order to prevent us from destroying ourselves," said Walter.

"If they think destroying our cities, then locking us in that building back there will make us want to listen to them, then they better think again!" said the man as many people voiced their agreement.

"I told them that earlier, and many of you probably saw their reaction," said Jack.

"So what does that mean then? Are they going to kill us now that they know we won't be part of their experiment?" asked the woman.

"No, nothing like that, I think I should tell you everything I was told before more confusion builds up," said Jack who then proceeded to recount everything he was told by Alpha One earlier.

"Have they abandoned us then? Sounds like you think they were saving this area for later so why let us out if they were coming back? It doesn't sound like the two groups are going to be handling people much differently to me anyway. Both sides lock us up then try to force us to act the way they want us to."

"Now that I think about it you could be right. Did Alpha One tell you how his way any different Walter?" asked Jack.

"The only thing I can think of is when he mentioned he wanted you to lead us and your friends to teach us. Could be that the others do the leading and teaching while humans are expected to be obedient students."

"Why should I do what you say? No one elected you as our leader!" said another man.

"You shouldn't, and I don't want to be your leader. I tried to explain that to him, but I do not think he fully understands. I have no intention of being anyone's leader. As for them coming back, I am sure they will, but I do not know when."

"Well I for one am not going to wait for them to come back and try to tell me what to do. I am going to lay claim to one of these buildings and live out here instead of in that cramped stuffy building," said Fred.

"That is a good idea. At the very least we have more privacy in these buildings. There are more than enough for everyone from what I saw on the map. The map also showed some sort of open space not far from here. Let's check that out next since all these buildings appear to be the same."

151

As they walked to where the open area was marked on the map, Jack glanced up when there was a flash of lightning. "Strange the way they keep the weather out. I wonder how the plants stay alive."

"I suspect it is like the field at the building's entrance ways, and is only keeping out violent weather. If this was a light rain storm then the water and wind would probably not be blocked," said Walter.

"Why is it not extended into the landing area? It would have been nice to not get soaked when I was unconscious out there."

"The field apparently interferes with the transports circuitry and the Lights ability to move around."

"Hmmm, sounds like we need to learn more about how these fields work," said Fred.

"I'm not sure if they would be much use since they don't actually stop them from passing through. They kept the area clear mainly for the transports, not themselves."

"Still, it we could figure out why it slows them down it could be of some use."

"Well unless they have accidentally left some sort of intergalactic instruction manual for them lying somewhere around here I think we are out of luck," said Jack.

They continued walking, eventually arriving at a large open area covered in gravel, with three large buildings around the perimeter, and a pedestal in the center. Each of the buildings was identical, all empty with a large opening on each wall. When Jack touched a piece of glass that was embedded in the pedestal s surface, holograms of random objects were displayed including: something similar to a car, one of the buildings, and a tree.

"This doesn't look very useful to me, just a photo album of random stuff. Why would they leave something like this out here?" asked Fred.

"Hang on a minute and let me see what I can do with it," said Jack as he attempted to manipulate the images. When he tried to grab the image of the building he was able to move it and pull it closer to himself. He then tried using the same gestures he used on the map to zoom in, causing the building to be broken into four disconnected walls, a floor and a ceiling. When he grabbed one of the walls making it larger, a faint line appeared running from its side to an image of six pillars surrounding a tower. When he grabbed one of pillars to enlarge, it was broken up into hundreds of pieces with each one of those being made up of multiple pieces having lines connecting to unfamiliar devices.

"Do you know what this is?" asked Walter with amazement.

"It looks like it is showing us how they built everything," said Jack.

"And hopefully somewhere along the line it shows how we can do it, starting with the simplest elements. I think this is what they were going to use to teach you how to do things their way. With any luck there won't be any restrictions on what we can view," said Walter excitedly.

"This doesn't seem right. Why would they just give us access to this without controlling what we could see?" asked Fred.

"I don't think they would. I think he, Alpha One, did. Whether it is because he was worried the others would not follow his plan, or because he is mad at them and trying to ruin the experiment, I don't know," said Walter.

"Either way makes me nervous. How are the others going to react when they find out we have access to this?" asked Jack.

"Well, he did say they avoid violence, so I doubt we are in physical danger. There is the possibility they would just lock us in the buildings for the rest of our lives, but then they would not be able to continue with their experiment. The most likely outcome is they would control what we could view and try to bring everything back under their control to continue on."

"Then we need to study as much of this as we can before they show up. Fred, try grabbing that thing that looks like a car," said Jack.

Fred reached out but was unable to do anything with the image.

"Damn, I was hoping anyone could do this but I guess you need threads in you to use this thing."

"I really don't like the idea of some alien crap in me, but if it lets me use this thing then I think I will be alright with it," said Fred nervously.

Jack, Bob and Walter all look at each other with concern.

"What? What wrong?" asked Fred.

"I have to tell him guys," said Jack.

"Tell me what! Is there something wrong with me?"

"I know you won't believe this, but right after our fight earlier I had a memory of you fighting the Lights in one of those suits and destroying large parts of the planet. Alpha One said it was a memory of the first time they tried this. Without the threads in you, you will not be able to use their equipment but..."

"But with them I can destroy the planet? Do you really think I would do that?"

"Not purposely, no, but in my memory you seemed to be focused only on the Light you were fighting and ignored all the damage you were doing."

"Look, I know you believe all this crap about being able to see the future and living this over and over, but how do you know all that hasn't been planted in your brain by them to prevent you from giving any of us these threads. Maybe they saw me as a threat and decided to make you think I would destroy the planet"

"That is possible I guess. But how do you explain all the times earlier in my life when I knew what was going to happen weeks before it did?"

"Maybe they have been watching us for a lot longer than we thought, and they have ways of accurately predicting what is going to happen in the future. For all we know they have computers that could simulate everything on this planet. If they really have been around for billions of years wouldn't they have made something like that a very long time ago?"

"That does sound plausible, perhaps they have been controlling us with false memories all this time," said Walter.

"I don't like that idea very much. How much of what I remember would be real? I don't know what to think now... do you guys think it is safe to give Fred the threads?"

"I do, sorry Jack, but his explanation makes more sense than yours," said Bob.

"From a scientific point of view, both explanations are possible to me. So we won't really know if it is safe unless we do it. At this point I see no reason to prevent him from gaining access to their equipment as long as one of us is with him at all times to remove them if needed," said Walter.

"Ok then, thread me up!" said Fred.

"Ah, there is one slight problem. I have no more threads. They gave me enough for Jack and that was it."

"Well why the hell didn't you say that before? All this arguing for something you can't do anyway!"

"Have any of you seen a metal cube anywhere, about one meter wide? The soldiers in Vancouver found one at the destroyed tower and it was full of threads," said Jack.

Everyone shook their head, so Jack climbed on top of the pedestal to address everyone in the area. "Hey everyone, when you are exploring these woods and buildings, please keep an eye out for any large metal cubes. If you find one, or anything else we haven't seen before, please inform me or Walter as quickly as possible."

"You really think they are going to just leave them lying around unprotected?" asked Fred.

"No, I doubt it, but giving everyone something to look for might give them some hope that we have an idea how to get out of this," whispered Jack.

"Speaking of looking for something, shouldn't we open the other doors? They may not all be connected to this area. Maybe there is something useful behind some of them as well," said Bob.

"Good idea. The map we were looking at covered most of the area behind the settlement, but not everything," said Walter.

"What about this thing, shouldn't we try to learn as much as possible from it in case we don't have it for very long?" asked Jack.

"Yes you're right, I'll stay here and learn what I can from it and you can go open the doors. Here, take the extra Aot. If you do find one of those cubes you can fill it up too."

"Ok, but don't get your hopes up to high. I am pretty sure if there is a cube somewhere in this settlement it will not be easy to get to."

"Good luck then, let's hope there is..."

Jack felt an intense sensation of pain, causing him to fall against the pedestal, as he heard a voice in his mind calling out. "Help me!"

"What the hell was that? Was that Alpha One?" asked Jack gasping for breath.

"I don't think so," said Walter, helping Jack to steady himself.

They heard more voices in their minds. "Stop them! Help us!"

"I think... not everyone has been captured," said Jack.

"They must be attacking the Lights," said Walter, "This is similar to what I heard and felt when you attacked them."

"Then they may be distracted for a while. We should go open the doors as quickly as possible."

"You won't be much help if you collapse every time one of them is attacked," said Fred.

"I will be ok. I just was not expecting it. I will be able to block most of the pain with a little practice," said Jack as he stood up, starting to walk quickly towards the settlement.

"Hey, wait for us," said Fred.

"Be careful, we don't know how they are going to react to being attacked again," said Walter.

Jack's walk turned to a jog then to a run as they rushed back to the building. "They may have been shocked after my attacks, but I am worried that they are going to see us as a real threat if more happen."

"Right, we need to find a way to defend ourselves before they see humans as out of control and decide to kill everyone but the youngest," said Bob.

"Forget defend, if we can get some of those suits we need to force them off the planet, and if they won't go then kill them!" said Fred angrily. Jack frowned and was about to speak when Fred interrupted, "I know what you're going to say, 'You'll destroy the planet!' But I can guarantee you that will not happen. You've already explained what these suits can do and there is no way I would fly around randomly trying to attack them. We need to be organized and only attack them from the ground."

"We're getting ahead of ourselves guys. Until we actually have some more threads and some suits, arguing is pointless," said Bob.

"Agreed, let's just find out what is behind the rest of the doors first," said Jack.

Arriving back at the settlement they saw thousands of people filling the field, wandering into the woods. The doorway was packed with people leaving the building causing them difficulty getting back in. Once inside they easily moved to the location of the closest door because almost everyone had left.

The first door opened up to a large amphitheater with a pedestal at the center which contained the same holographic images as the one Walter was investigating. The second door opened to another field, but this one was filled with the same kind of platforms used for beds as well as another pedestal. The third door they found opened to a huge room filled with piles of gravel and various metals. The fourth door opened to another huge room filled with stacks of what appeared to be miniature pillars, each about one meter tall, as well as a small stacks of Aots all locked together. After experimenting with his Aot for a few minutes, Jack was able to unlock one from the stack. The fifth door also opened up to a huge room, this one filled with nothing but large stone blocks. Every other door in the settlement opened up to a field with paths running out to woods they first found.

"So I guess all that stuff stored in there was going to be used to show us how to use their technology, but I don't understand what the stone blocks were for when they had a room filled with the raw material we would need to build stuff," said Bob.

"They may be containers of some sort, and not solid blocks," said Jack.

"Well why didn't you say something when we were there? Let's go back and open a few," said Fred.

"Because I wanted to wait to see what Walter learns before we open what might turn out to be something that could kill us."

"I doubt there is anything like that, but I'm willing to risk it. Give me one of those tools you use and I'll try to open some while you go fetch Walter."

"Ok, but don't say I didn't warn you," said Jack as he handed an Aot to a now smiling Fred.

"Let's go get Walter," said Jack to Bob.

"Well that made him happy, but do you think it's safe for him to open those things" asked Bob as they left.

"Maybe, maybe not," said Jack, changing to a whisper, "I don't think anyone without threads can open stuff with those tools." Jack grabbed his head and groaned.

"You ok?"

"Yeah, just more calling for help and slight pain."

"You think Alpha One is helping other people? Maybe he showed someone how to get some suits"

"I hope not, because if he did and the others found out, they would probably assume he gave us access to them also. I don't want to think about how they would treat us if they believed that."

"Me neither. Let's hurry to back to Walter," said Bob.

The trip back was easier than anticipated since everyone had finished leaving the buildings, dispersing throughout the woods. When they arrived back at the clearing Jack explained what they found to everyone near the pedestal.

"So it's looking more and more like they were going to teach us how to use their technology, but why wait so long to start? I know they said you were important to all this, but why keep us all locked up and not even let those of us who could understand this stuff look at it?" asked Walter.

"Maybe they tried it that way last time, who knows. Did you find anything useful while we were gone?" asked Jack.

"I think so. From what we can make out, one of their factories, if you can call them that, is made up of six large pillars arranged around a tower with a transport point above it. We haven't been able to figure out what the tower or pillars actually do yet but I am sure in time someone will. Hmmm, I just noticed Fred's not here, did he have another outburst?"

"No, he wanted to try and open up the stone blocks. I told him we should wait for you but he didn't want to. I gave him one of the Aots, but I doubt he can do much without any threads in him."

Walter took out his Aot and examined it, "Which one did you give him? Can I see the one you still have?" he asked sounding concerned.

"Sure, what's wrong? I didn't think you could do much besides inject threads unless... Oh crap, the old threads are in one of these still aren't they?"

"Yes, but they are in this one you kept. I think I will swap with you for now until I find a way to get rid of them. He might still be able to open the blocks if they don't contain anything dangerous. The threads are meant as a sort of security mechanism and are only needed when opening or using something not everyone is supposed to have access to."

"That was really stupid of me. I should have remembered the old threads were in one of these."

"No, there was no reason for you to think I hadn't got rid of them."

"So could Fred have used them?"

"Yes, but what he could do would have been limited since they were not meant for humans. I am still amazed that you managed to use them to control one of the suits. He may have been able to power up a map or open a secured door. We should..." said Walter stopping abruptly, getting a worried look on his face. "Did you hear that?"

"No, what? Are they calling for help again?"

"No, Alpha One just said he was being attacked but was cut off mid sentence. I also briefly saw a group of suits and three transports flying together."

"Were they the ones attacking him?"

"I'm not sure, it all ended before I could figure out what was happening. This whole situation is getting out of control. We should get back to Fred and help with those blocks. If Alpha One is hurt they may just see us as a failed experiment that can be thrown away. We may not have a lot of time to find a way to defend ourselves."

"What about this thing? Shouldn't you be learning as much as possible from it first?"

"Ah yes, I found a way to allow anyone to use it, so some of the other people here have been helping me go through it. They are more than capable of learning from it so they don't need me here."

"That is good to hear. Time for another workout, I haven't jogged this much in years."

"You two can jog, but I'll have to walk. This old body doesn't like moving very fast. Too many years sitting at a desk or lab bench I think."

"Tell ya what, I'll keep the professor here company and you can jog back to Fred," said Bob with a grin.

"Sounds like you have spent too much time behind a desk too" chuckled Jack as he started to jog back to the buildings.

"You should have just sent your thoughts to me instead of wasting time running around," said Walter.

"Wait, we can do it over long distances too?" asked Jack, stopping, looking confused.

"Yes, the threads do all the translation and transmission so you can communicate with anyone else who has them. There is supposed to be a limit on how far away someone is, but I don't know what it is. The Lights that can communicate with us have threads also, if they didn't they would have to meet us in person and use lights and shapes to try to communicate."

"Hmmm, ok, next time I will try that," said Jack as he started jogging again. I wonder if anyone else from Vancouver still has the threads in them. "Major Janko! Can you hear me?" said Jack while directing his thoughts at the major. He waited a moment but did not get a reply. He tried sending thoughts to the other soldiers but also got no response. Well, I can only hope they are still alive but seeing the aftermath of their fight in the city doesn't give me much hope. Arriving at the room with the blocks he saw many of them missing a side, revealing various unknown devices inside. He walked over to the closest open block, picking up what appeared to be an abstract sculpture of glass. As he examined it he heard someone walk up behind him.

"All these things seem to contain is a bunch of weird sculptures like that thing," said Fred.

"These are probably more than artwork. The maps and that database we found in the clearing all are built from what looks like a sheet of glass," said Jack turning towards Fred.

"So what are these then, more maps?"

"I would guess they are the bits and pieces needed to build some of their more complicated equipment or computers. Walter will be here soon and he will be able to tell us if any of this stuff was in the database."

"Well in that case, let's not waste time with these. Help me open up some more of these things, there are a couple that I can't open, maybe you can figure them out. Try that one over there."

"Sure, but there could be something dangerous inside so stay alert," said Jack, walking over to the block. His attempts to open it were unsuccessful. "It looks like there are two spots the Aot can be placed, but neither one will open it. We should try using both spots at the same time," said Jack.

They tried opening the block with two Aots but nothing happened. "Must be something really important in here," said Fred.

"Important or dangerous, I suspect we need two people with threads to do this. Walter said they are uses as some sort of security to keep people out of things they are not supposed to be in."

"Well I hope so. I really want to see what is in here."

"You may change your mind once it is opened. Let's open more rest of the blocks you have not tried yet."

After opening a few more blocks to find more unusual glass-like objects, Bob and Walter arrived.

"Well this will save us some time," said Walter, picking up the object Jack had been examining earlier.

Hearing Walter's voice, Jack and Fred walked over to them. "Do you know what that is used for?" asked Jack.

"I'm not sure what it does, but I saw it in one of the diagrams that shows the internal workings of a tower. They must have wanted to show us how to build them, but not all the individual parts. Sort of like an automotive class in high school: the students have parts like a muffler, brake pad, or computer control unit to work with, but they don't have to make those parts themselves," said Walter obviously excited.

"Well then, the crates we can't open must contain the key parts since we can't get in them," said Fred.

"Can't get in?" asked Walter.

"They appear to need two people to open them, but I suspect both need threads in them since Fred and I couldn't do it," said Jack.

"There could be something dangerous in them too, I suggest Fred and Bob take cover behind one of the other blocks near the entrance just in case," said Walter.

"If something attacks you I want to be able to help you guys and I can't do that by hiding," said Fred.

"You misunderstand. By dangerous I meant something like radioactive or poisonous materials. If we find something like that you may need to seal this room off quickly, even if it means sealing us in here too."

"No chance I would leave you two in here to die. Besides, if there is something like that won't your threads be able to fix you?"

"Maybe, I'm not sure of the extent of their abilities. But you two don't have any so there would be no hope for you."

"OK, tell ya what, we'll wait by the entrance but if you find something bad we won't close it until you two get out."

"I'm not going to be able to convince you to do anything else am I?"

"Nope," said Fred as Jack and Bob grinned slightly.

"Ok, wait by the entrance and we'll let you know if you should prepare to close it after we leave," said Walter with a sigh.

"Sounds good to me," said Fred as he and Bob walked to the blocks near the entrance.

"Has he always been like that?" asked Walter.

"You have no idea. This is a good day for him," said Jack.

Jack and Walter waited for the others to get to cover then placed their Aots on the block. The surface of the block glowed briefly before a display appeared near each Aot.

"Is it supposed to do that?" asked Jack.

"Not sure, you ready?"

"If you are."

"Ok, let's open it then."

As they pressed the open symbol on the displays the entire block slowly faded away revealing a large block of Aots neatly stacked on each other.

"There looks like enough for everyone. Are you sure they meant to give these to us?" asked Jack.

"Maybe over time but not all at once. I am now sure that Alpha One wasn't supposed to let us have access to all this so soon. I just hope we are able to figure out how to use everything to defend ourselves before the others find out," said Walter sounding concerned.

"Well then we will just have to stay up night and day until we do," said Fred and he and Bob approached.

"You think we should start showing people how to use these things?" Bob asked Walter.

"Maybe, but we shouldn't give them to everyone at once. We don't know all of the abilities these have and I don't want people running around using them like a toy," said Walter.

Fred picked one up comparing it to the one he had.

"Wouldn't it be ok for them to use since no one else has threads? That would stop them from doing anything that could damage something wouldn't it?" asked Jack.

"Possibly, but do we want to take that chance?" asked Walter.

"It looks to me like the locked blocks only contain stuff they probably didn't want to give us right away, so why don't you two open some more of them?" asked Fred.

"It does look that way doesn't it? What do you say Jack, want to open another one?" asked Walter.

"Definitely, there has to be more useful stuff in the other blocks."

They walked over to the next block which also produced a brief glow before opening. As the block disappeared, four unconscious creatures floating inside glowing fields were revealed. They had six large limbs each with one sharp edge, and their bodies were covered in spiky scales.

"What the hell are those?" asked Fred sounding nervous.

"They look like Juvo, but why were they in the block?" asked Walter rhetorically.

"Are they going to be ok? I thought they couldn't live in our environment?" asked Jack.

"I think so. Look, they appear to be breathing. These fields must be holding in an environment they can live in. They also appear to be asleep or in maybe some sort of coma. This doesn't make any sense though, the Lights don't need to transport them like this. They have colonies all over the galaxy and one of them is only a couple months from here. At least that's what the Juvo on the transport told me."

"Even if they did need to move them around like this why would they leave these four here?"

Jack and Walter heard more calls for help in their minds, this time much louder. "Did you hear that? It sounded like someone was standing next to me yelling for help that time," said Jack.

"Oh no, this is not good, not good at all!" said Walter sounding panicked.

"What's wrong? You guys hearing more Lights being attacked?" asked Fred.

"I don't think it's the Lights, I think it's these Juvo we found! Quick, we need to open the rest of the blocks."

"Wait, the Lights aren't being attacked?" asked Jack.

"Yes they are, but they aren't the ones we heard calling for help. As soon as we opened this block the voices got a lot louder. I don't think these Juvo are working with the Lights."

"You mean they aren't the happy little helpers that Alpha One told us they were? Can't say that I'm surprised," said Fred.

"Why would they do this to them, I thought they were allies?" asked Jack as they prepared to open another block.

"I did too, but now I'm getting a bad feeling about everything. I don't think we were ever supposed to be in here and I'm now worried about why Alpha One told us about the doors. He may just be trying to cause problems for his former allies and that wouldn't be good for us at all."

The block faded away to reveal four more Juvo. As they opened more blocks they discovered twenty four more Juvo, as well as sheets of material used for the suits and transports.

"Well great, looks like we have a bunch of alien prisoners that we probably weren't supposed to know about in a room we probably also weren't supposed to know about. What are we supposed to do now? I doubt the other aliens will be too happy when they find out what we have been doing," said Fred.

"We probably have enough materials here to build suits for these Juvo, but trying to figure out what we need to build to create those suits will take quite a while. I am going to contact one of the Juvo from the transport, if they know about what is in this room they may be able to clear up what is going on," said Walter.

"And if they don't know?" asked Jack.

"Then hopefully they will help us determine who these Juvo are, why they are here, and how to get them out. They will definitely be too far away for me to use the threads so I'll have to use the computer in the lab. Why don't you three wait here and keep out anyone who may wander by. I think everyone is outside, but I don't want to take any chances."

"Sure, we can start sorting through everything in the other blocks. Try to hurry since we have no idea how long they will stay alive inside those fields or if the blocks were somehow helping to sustain them."

Walter nodded as he walked briskly out of the room.

"How do we know we can trust these Juvo any more than the Lights? After all, they are working together. This bunch might just be some sort of backup force to use in case we start fighting back," said Fred.

"Well, like Walter said, they don't need to transport them like this, and if they were for backup I think they would be more useful being awake and alert," said Jack.

"Jack and Walter also heard the calls for help get louder once these guys were out of the blocks. Sounds more like they are prisoners to me," said Bob.

"Why would they be keeping their allies as prisoners? It doesn't make sense to me," said Jack.

"It does if they aren't all allies. Maybe this group doesn't like the arrangement the Lights have with their people and they fought back," said Fred.

"If they did then it is pretty obvious how well that went for them. It's pointless speculating anyway. Walter will find out what is going on and then tell us. Let's start sorting through the blocks. Who knows, maybe there is something interesting buried under all the parts. I'll work on the group by the door, they all appears to have the same parts in them. You guys can each take one of the other groups over there," said Jack.

Fred and Bob walked over to two different groups of nearby blocks to start rummaging through the contents. Jack found a few parts that were different from the rest along with a few sheets of glass like the one the map was on, but the sheets did nothing when he tried to turn them on. After a short time Jack heard a voice in his head. "Can you hear me Jack?" asked the voice.

"Yes, who is this? You sound familiar" said Jack directing his thoughts to the voice.

"Right behind you," said the voice.

Jack spun around to see Fred waving an Aot. "Looks like these ones have threads in them!" said Fred with a grin.

"You didn't?" asked Jack.

"You bet I did, no way that I would pass up a chance like this."

164

"Please promise me you won't try to steal one of the suits from the Juvo. They have done nothing to you."

"They helped to wipe out everything on Earth! They are not important to me and they shouldn't be important to you! Our top priority should be to drive them off this planet. But don't worry, I'm not stupid enough to try and take a suit from one of those things. They would probably slice me to shreds before I could pull them out. It's also pretty obvious from your description of the fight in Vancouver that the Lights move too fast for us to have any chance of fighting them with the suits and winning so we will have to find another way to get rid of them."

They heard Walter's voice in the distance yelling something, along with the sound of running footsteps approaching, "We can talk about this later, that sounds like Walter's coming back."

"Don't touch anything else!" yelled Walter as he entered the room gasping for air.

"Why, what's wrong?"

"I contacted them," Walter gasped for air, "They said not to touch anything," he gasped again, "Until they get here," he sat on the floor looking like he was going to pass out.

"Are you going to be OK? You shouldn't have run all the way back."

"I had too... If you had touched those fields... they might have turned off... and the Juvo in them would have died."

"Why would they turn off just by touching them, and why didn't you just talk to me using the threads?"

"Only if you or I touched them... The threads in us might trigger them to turn off," Walter took a few deep breaths, "As for using the threads, I panicked when they told me not to touch the fields and forgot about them."

"Might turn off? Don't they understand how their own equipment works?" asked Fred.

"Yes, they do, but we don't. Just touching and doing nothing else wouldn't be a problem. But if we were to think about wanting the field to turn off, then it would. Where is Bob? He shouldn't be doing anything else until they get here and figure out what to do with the trapped Juvo."

"Bob! Where are you? Get over here!" yelled Jack and Fred simultaneously, but there was no answer.

"He was by those blocks over there the last time I saw him. Let's go see what he's gotten himself into," said Fred.

"I'm just going to sit here for now. Still feeling a little woozy," said Walter.

Jack and Fred walked over to the area where Bob was last seen, but there was no sign of him. They began to search around the other blocks, something caught Jack's eye, "Fred! Over here!"

Fred ran over to Jack who was standing in front of the block that held all the Aots, many of which were now gone.

"Why did he take so many of them?"

"I think he figured out they are loaded with threads the same as I did. He's probably gone back outside to look for volunteers."

"But why sneak out of here with them? We would have eventually done that anyway."

"Eventually being the key word Jack. Not everyone here wants to proceed as slowly as you do. Actually, other than Walter, I don't think anyone wants to go as slow."

"If we rush everything all we will end up with is another failure and them starting the correction all over again."

Fred started to speak but Jack interrupted, "Yes I know you don't believe any of that 'crap', but Walter and I do. You know the Lights are much too powerful to fight off, so if we don't plan out every move carefully we have no chance of getting control of Earth back."

"Yes, I do know that, but I also know that you can sometimes be too cautious. Arguing about this is pointless. Let's go tell Walter that Bob's not here."

They walked back to Walter, who was looking a little less pale, to tell him about the Aots.

"Well, I can't say that I'm surprised. Most people here seem to think I'm being too cooperative with the Lights and many have told me I should be trying to find a way to fight them instead," said Walter sounding dejected.

"How are we ever going to convince anyone to not try and fight now that we have access to all this stuff? It's only a matter of time before someone figures out how to use all this to build something that could be used as a weapon," said Jack.

Before anyone else had a chance to say anything else, one of the Juvo from the transport appeared in the hall gliding extremely fast towards the room. It glided into the room stopping in front of the nearest group of trapped Juvo. After quickly examining them, the Juvo turned to face everyone. "Do you remember them?" it asked.

166

"No. Should we know them?" asked Jack.

"These ones tried to help you and your friends during the first correction. We were told they had been sent back to our home to prevent further interference on their part. I do not understand why they are in these preservation cells. They are meant for those who are seriously injured or in immense pain. They suspend physical sensations and abilities while maintaining minimal mental functions to allow for easier recovery."

"They don't look hurt," said Fred.

"How do you understand me?"

"We found a supply of Aots with threads in them over there. They have been distributed to everyone," said Fred sternly.

Jack frowned at Fred, "Alpha One told us about the doors to these rooms and the areas outside. I think he wanted us to proceed on our own now that he is no longer fully in charge."

"I do not understand. What do you mean not fully in charge?" asked the Juvo.

"After he attacked me, his allies no longer wanted him involved. I get the feeling that he wants to see if we can figure all this out on our own. I also get the feeling he didn't let his former allies know that he told us about the doors," said Jack.

"He attacked you? I do not understand. Why? They have always told us that respecting and caring for other species is their priority."

"Apparently he doesn't have the patience the others do and when Jack refused to cooperate he attacked him," said Fred.

"If we could free the Juvo in here, maybe they could shed some light on what is really going on. We found some material that the suits are made from in a block over there, and what appears to be different parts for larger machines or computers. We also found a sort of database on how various machines are built. Do you know how to use all this stuff to build some suits and get them out?" asked Jack.

"I am what you would consider and archeologist, not an engineer. I do understand the basic idea of how their machinery works. But their more complex equipment, the machines that build other machines or parts, will be inoperable even if all the parts are here."

"Why? What is missing?"

"The larger machines are not controlled by a computer, but by one of their own minds. Without their help a machine that could build a suit would be useless."

"Is that why we always saw a ball of light hovering over their larger towers?"

"Yes, those towers are the machines that dismantled your cities and built the settlements."

"It seems a little strange that they do not have some sort of automated system to do all the work. We always saw light strings moving from the towers to wherever something was being destroyed, and I was told the strings were part of them, similar to our fingers."

"Interesting analogy but not entirely correct, they have attributes similar to your eyes, ears, and fingers and allow the Lights to easily sense things at a great distance. The strings you saw doing work were part of the machine, not the Light who controlled it. The machines are automated, but they need a mind to control what they do."

"So it is similar to the way our computer systems were automated, but still needed a human to tell them what to do."

"Yes, you understand now."

"Couldn't one of us just hook up to one of the machines and operate it? I'm sure I could figure out how to control it with a little experimenting," said Walter.

"That may not be as safe as you believe. These systems have been designed to work as part of a Lights own mind. If any of you did manage to connect your mind, it could become so entangled with the machine that it may never be able to free itself."

"Why would they have provided everything we need to make their machines if we wouldn't actually be able to use them? They must have been planning to help modify them to allow us to control them somehow. Maybe that information is somewhere in the database and we just haven't found it yet," said Walter.

"That is possible. I suggest you try to find that information first Ambassador. You may not be able to control anything without it. There is a spare suit at the tower on the beach. I will retrieve it and we can put the leader of this group in it, then find out why they are here."

"Is there anything Fred or I can do while you are gone?" asked Jack.

"For now, just guard this room and protect my people. If anyone with threads in their body touches the fields they could be accidentally turned off."

"Are you not afraid of what the Lights will do if they find out you freed one of these prisoners?" asked Fred.

"No, because they are our allies and I do not believe these are prisoners. We have worked together for millions of years, accompanying them on their missions and learning all that we can about the histories of the species they are trying to preserve. I am sure the leader will have more knowledge of why they are here instead of on our home world, and why they had to be suspended."

"Well, if you say so, but I have my doubts about them being allies to anyone. Try to be quick about getting that suit. This whole situation feels wrong and I want to know what is really going on," said Fred.

"I will move as fast as I am able," said the Juvo, quickly gliding out of the room.

"I'll go back to the clearing and search the database to see what I can find. If you two need anything, remember that you can communicate with me using the threads," said Walter as he started to leave.

"OK, we will. Good luck in the search," said Jack.

"So what are we supposed to do, just stand around waiting?" asked Fred.

"I am going to try and communicate with the one who is supposed to be the leader. I haven't heard any calls for help in a while. If it was these Juvo they could be aware of what is happening around them," said Jack.

"That's a bit unsettling. If they are aware that means they are not in some sort of suspended animation like they are supposed to be, but only immobilized. Who knows how long they have been trapped in there."

"Well, if it is true they tried to help during the first correction then that would be almost five of our lifetimes at least. I do not like the idea that I may be responsible for them being trapped like this."

"You really believe that this has all happened before don't you? Those other aliens seem to believe it as well. I don't understand how those Lights could have brainwashed so many of you so easily."

"It's more than just them telling us to believe it, at least for me. Remember that I have had memories of things that have not happened yet all my life. They just gave me an explanation for why."

"Don't forget that they could have been responsible for those memories, and they could have been manipulating events all around you for your entire life, and implanting memories of events that they have laid out to happen?"

"I know you believe that, but why would they do that?"

"It's pretty obvious: to get you to believe that if you fail to set us free this time around, you will always have another chance the next time and that you can keep trying as many times as you need. That way you won't bother thinking for yourself and let them control what you do."

"Why would they even bother with something so complicated and elaborate? They don't need our help to take control of this planet. They don't need us for anything."

"Maybe they are just experimenting with us to see if we could be useful to them in any way. Every one of their settlements might have a Jack and Alpha One working together to free the human race, but in reality we are just lab rats. Look at the Juvo, they work as archeologists for them and are convinced they are allies. But these Juvo trapped in here say otherwise."

"I... I don't know... The memories feel real to me... I need to think for a while," said Jack as he wandered to the hall with a lost look on his face.

"Wait Jack, I didn't want to upset you."

Jack ignored Fred while standing in the doorway looking at the trapped Juvo. "Can you hear me?" thought Jack while directing his thoughts at them. "They said I should know you, but I do not remember any of you."

"Help us," said a voice in Jack's mind.

"How can I help you?"

"Stop them!"

"Stop who?"

"Help us"

Jack gave up, realizing that if it was the Juvo calling for help they probably could not hear him. He wandered over to the nearest block, picking up one of the objects that looked like a glass sculpture to examine.

Fred wandered over to the block, "I didn't mean to upset you Jack. I just want you to see how everything looks to the rest of us."

"I know... I know. Everything you said does make sense, but for some reason I still believe what they have told me. I really hope we can get this Juvo here released and he can clear everything up."

"Me too buddy. That other Juvo seem genuinely shocked that these ones were trapped in here. I tried talking to them, but I got nothing."

"I did too, but all I heard were the same calls for help. Whoever is calling doesn't seem to be able to hear me." Jack looked at the glass as he tossed it back into the pile with the others. "I'm getting tired of looking through all this junk. I am just going to sit and rest until someone comes back."

"Good idea, Walter will be able to figure out what to do with all this much easier than we can."

They both sat down in front of the block, waiting.

Chapter 10

After waiting for more than an hour, Jack and Fred were in a semi-awake state. Occasionally one would nod off but be quickly woken when their head flopped to one side. The sound of footsteps in the distance snapped them out of the daze.

"Sounds like somebody's coming this way. Time to go into guard dog mode," said Fred with a chuckle.

"Please don't bite anyone. I would hate for them to catch your grumpiness," said Jack.

Looking down the hall they could see Walter in the distance, walking at a normal pace towards them.

"I wonder if he found something useful. I was expecting him to spend the rest of the day at the clearing."

"Couldn't have been anything too useful or else he would have used the threads to tell us."

"Did you find anything that could help us?" said Jack when Walter got closer.

"Maybe, but I'm not sure if we want to try it," said Walter sounding concerned.

"Why not, what did you find?"

"Well, there are instructions for building a mini tower to go with those mini pillars, as well as instructions for how to connect a human mind to it all."

"Great! So why wouldn't we try it?"

"Because I haven't found any instructions for disconnecting someone after they are connected. From what I can understand of the instructions it may not be possible."

"What! You mean they intended to hook one of us up to it and keep us that way?"

"I don't think so. I think that a Light needs to help disconnect us. I suspect it's like the Juvo said and that we would become so entangled with the machine we could not disconnect ourselves."

"So unless Alpha One comes back or one of his former allies agrees to help us then we're screwed?" asked Fred.

"Not necessarily. If one of us volunteers to be connected, one of the Lights may help to disconnect that person when they found out," said Walter while looking at Jack.

"Oh no, no way I'm going to take a chance that I'll be permanently stuck to one of their machines!" said Jack.

"There's no way I'd let anyone do that unless we could guarantee they could disconnect," said Fred while glaring at Walter.

"No need to get agitated, it was only an idea. I may still find something in the database, or these Juvo may know more about the machines. Don't forget that the other one said this one tried to help us before," said Walter.

"I think you're putting too much hope in their knowledge and abilities. I suspect they're just as much prisoners as we are. They've probably been told very little about how these machines actually work."

Walter got a blank look on his face for a moment. "They are back with the suit... They've also brought the rest of the people from the tower at the beach with them. Hmm, they weren't supposed to be doing that until tomorrow. I need to get to the main entrance to show them where everything is and let them know what is happening here."

"What should we do?" asked Jack.

"Wait here. The Juvo will be here shortly. I'll be back as soon as I can."

As Walter turned to leave, the Juvo from the transport appeared down the hallway. It was carrying an empty suit and moving fast. It glided into the room, stopping in front of the trapped Juvo.

"I will need help from you two," said the Juvo while looking over at Jack and Fred.

"Sure, what do you want us to do?" asked Jack.

"Hold the suit up so the opening is close to the field but not touching it."

"What will you do?"

"I will open a hole in the field and attempt to put the leader in the suit. I will have approximately forty two seconds before this atmosphere starts causing permanent damage. It is extremely important that you hold the suit steady and keep it open."

"Have you ever done this before? Is forty two seconds enough time?"

"Yes I have, in a way. I have twice needed to transfer myself from a damaged suit into a working suit in this environment. Both times took me nine seconds."

"But you have never done it to someone who is unconscious?"

"No, but with your help holding the suit it should not be very difficult."

"Ok, let's get this over with," said Fred, grabbing one side of the suit.

"Ready when you are," said Jack, grabbing the other side.

They maneuvered the suit in front of the field while the Juvo touched the field, causing an opening to appear. He pulled out the unconscious Juvo's lower appendages, guiding them into the suit. As soon as they were exposed to the room's atmosphere they quickly developed spots.

"Is that normal, is he going to be OK?" asked Jack.

"Yes, if I am fast enough," said the Juvo while pulling the upper appendages then body into the suit. "Close it now."

Jack and Fred pulled the sides of the opening together while the Juvo used an Aot to seal it. Once sealed the suit stiffened up and stood.

"Is he awake?"

"Not yet, the suit has activated and is generating an atmosphere he can live in. It will then slowly bring him out of suspension. The process will take a few minutes."

"Walter said you brought everyone from the beach back here, but he wasn't expecting them yet. Why did you bring them early?"

"This area is safer. The coordinator at the tower has received reports that some of the Lights have been attacked."

"Ha! I knew that some of our people would find a way to fight back!" said Fred excitedly.

"I am not sure who it could be. All of the people in your various military organizations have been tracked since the correction started, and they are all still in the camps, as is everyone else."

"Obviously these Lights aren't as good at tracking us as they thought!"

The suit began to move slightly, wobbling a little.

"It moved! Is he awake yet?" asked Jack.

"He is waking up now. He will probably be disoriented," said the Juvo.

"I am awake. I was never fully unconscious, just immobilized. It is good to see you again Jack, and even you Fred," said the Juvo leader.

"What the hell is that supposed to mean, and how do you know our names?" said Fred angrily.

"I meant no insult. It was only a failed attempt at humor. Do either of you remember me?"

"No," said Jack and Fred.

"That is a shame. They must have conditioned your minds to forget me and what we did. You always referred to me as Beta One, Jack. Fred had a less flattering term for me most of the time."

Fred frowned as Jack chuckled, "I have been told you tried to help us the first time. What exactly did you do and how did you end up trapped in the blocks?"

"My friends and I have been marked as traitors and are being punished."

"By who? The Lights would never do this!" said the other Juvo.

"You may have a difficult time believing what I am going to tell you, with the exception of Fred who has never trusted the Lights, but not all of them are what they once were. The first problems started a little over one million years ago when some of the leaders on our home world decided they no longer wanted the Lights to have any influence on our people's lives. They were very open about it and wanted the Lights to leave peacefully. They knew they could not fight them and win."

"Yes, we have all been taught about those events when we were younger. The majority of our people didn't agree with the ones who wanted the Lights to leave, so the Lights agreed to help them build a new home on another planet where they could be left alone."

"They were allowed to live on their own, but forbidden to leave their new home world. The Lights controlled every planet with intelligent life on it and decided where and how all organic life lived. They have always insisted on controlling even the most intelligent and peaceful life forms. The exiles did not like the idea of the Lights interfering with every intelligent race in the galaxy. They believed that if a race cannot overcome its violent tendencies without destroying itself then it had no value and should never have existed in the first place."

"I think I would like these exiled leaders of yours," said Fred.

"You would. You and they think very much alike. The Lights mistake was in trusting them to stay on their new home. Their existence from the day they were transplanted was dedicated to finding a way to travel to other planets and help the beings on those planets become free from the Lights. They had been left with the most advanced living facilities and factories, but no scientific or research facilities. Since none of them were scientists, it took many generations to learn and discover what our scientists already knew."

"So then they built spacecraft and travelled to other systems?" asked Jack.

"They tried, but a field had been placed around their planet which prevented anything from getting out. They eventually developed the ability to built rockets, but each one they tried to launch into orbit was destroyed when it hit the field and they could find no way to counteract it. They did know that the

Lights travelled through an empty compressed space to reduce the time it took to get somewhere, but they had no idea how they entered it. They spent almost ten thousand years developing new ideas and theories to eventually discover how to enter this space. They had great difficulty navigating in it because of the lack of planets and stars. They realized that the Lights must have had the same problem and would have found a way around it. They searched the empty space that aligned with the space in this universe near their planet, slowly searching further out, until they found a beacon. They discovered a way to detect the beacons and over time found billions of others. After hundreds of years of travelling to beacons and surveying the planets near them, they decided to contact the more advanced species they had found to see if they wanted help to drive off the Lights."

"We found a map of this galaxy and examined some of the planets in it. Some of them seem to indicate everyone is dead, and there is a small area that is not mapped out. Are these places where the people tried to drive them off?"

"Yes, the species on many of these planets have been exterminated, deemed uncorrectable by the Lights controlling those planets. The blank area is where it all started. The Lights have been driven out of that area."

"Really! I thought they were too powerful to fight," said Fred excitedly.

"The various species in that area are extremely intelligent and had discovered many things about this galaxy that even the Lights did not know. Once they had discovered some of the Lights were exterminating entire species because they could not be controlled they asked for an explanation of why they were doing this. The Lights said they had no reason to explain themselves to anyone because the entire galaxy belonged to them and they would protect it as they saw fit."

"That must not have gone over well. Is that when they drove them out?" asked Jack.

"No, at that point they had no way to fight the Lights. They avoided aggravating the Lights any further by agreeing that the galaxy was theirs, while trying to convince them to stop giving up on species. But the Lights refused to interfere with the judgment of the leaders of each world. After that they started developing weapons that could be used to drive away the Lights. What they created was a horrific weapon that caused a Lights body to slowly vaporize over a period of two days, leaving their detached minds drifting through the universe."

176

"That does sound horrible. Did the Lights leave when they threatened them with it?"

"No, they used it to destroy three of the Lights then threatened to destroy all the Lights if they did not leave their region of space. The Lights were terrified. Up to that point the only way any of them had been hurt was by getting too close to an exploding star. They retreated and have stayed out of that area for the last ten thousand years. Many of them have since resorted to violence to control the species they had sworn to protect, and most are now preventing them from becoming too technologically advanced. Those of us who they once called allies are now no more than prisoners or slaves."

"Why have I not heard about any of this? Wouldn't our home world have demanded they stop the violence and informed us all of these events?" asked the other Juvo.

"I don't know any easy way of telling you this, but our home no longer exists. They did demand a stop to the violence and that the Lights leave our home. The result was the people of our home being declared uncorrectable and then being exterminated. When Alpha One sent us back he did not know what had happened. On our way back we were first intercepted by some of the Juvo that had been travelling the galaxy looking for species that wanted help. They explained what had been happening and were going to help us go into hiding. But shortly afterwards we were intercepted by Alpha Two who had been waiting for them to contact us. He tortured us, trying to get information about how the other Juvo could be found, but none of us knew. He then declared us traitors and imprisoned us in those fields where we were physically suspended but still aware of everything that was happening. We have been forced to watch him sabotage Alpha One's correction attempts each time."

"Are you telling me you believe all this crap about going through this over and over too?" asked Fred.

"I know it to be true because I have lived through it and have retained all my memories. Normally our minds move from the beginning of our lives to the end, then quickly move back to the beginning with the memories of the previous lives being mostly isolated from our brains. Alpha Two has developed a way to pull our minds to any point in our lives without taking away our brains access to all the memories. We have been trapped in these fields for the equivalent of one hundred fifty eight years."

"That sounds more like torture than punishment to me. Why did he let us free you? Is he planning on doing this to us too?" asked Jack.

"He is unaware of what is happening here, as are most of the Lights. Many of the Juvo on this planet had also been contacted by the Travelers and have been planning an attack for some time. Some of them knew I was imprisoned here. They have been trying to communicate with me, but I could not respond with anything other than calls for help. They attacked all the Lights initially, but after discovering that Alpha One and his allies were not among those using violent methods of control they asked for his help. So far he has not been willing to help either side and has avoided both. They only have the suits and transports to use as weapons, so I fear it will not be long before the Lights overcome the initial shock of being attacked then kill all my people."

"Then we have work to do so we can free your friends. Are you familiar with how to build the machine that makes the suits? We seem to have all the parts. But the instructions Walter has found so far indicate a mind is needed to control them."

"I am somewhat familiar but I am afraid that if you were planning on connecting a human mind to the machine, it would most likely be a permanent connection. Unlike the Lights minds, yours are much weaker than the machines computer."

"In that case, how do we contact Alpha One? We need his help and if he really wants this correction to succeed his way he needs to help us."

"I don't know if it is possible. I have been trying to contact him and others but so far have been unsuccessful. All of the Lights seem to be ignoring us," said the other Juvo.

"Great, we can build everything but can't use it"

"Let's at least start building it. Maybe that will get his attention and he will come back to help us," said Fred.

"Now you want his help?" asked Jack.

"Not really, but he does seem like the only one who can or would help. At the very least he would probably stop the others from killing us."

"Ok, then let's get started. Walter has been going through a database we found and it contains instructions on how to build their machines. But I don't think he has worked out what parts and materials we need to do it. You said you know something about building all this, just how much experience do you have?"

"During the first correction we helped you and your friends build a smaller version of one of the factories. It could create simple things like buildings. If you have the instructions for creating other types of factories then the process

178

would be similar. We would just be using different components to build it," said Beta One.

"Is that why you were sent away? Because you helped us build it?"

"No, that was something we were always meant to do. We thought you were doing so well and learning so quickly that we gave you access to one of our storage facilities to allow you to experiment with their technology. When you discovered the spare suits, Fred and a few others took them and tried attacking the Lights. They had no idea how easily the Lights could evade attacks from someone with so little experience using the suits, and ended up destroying most of the planet while trying to destroy them. Alpha One and Alpha Two decided we were overeager to help you learn and would most likely end up causing the next correction to fail also. So they decided to send us back to our home world where we couldn't interfere. Unfortunately for us, Alpha Two knew our home was gone and had other plans."

"Wait, Jack told you about seeing me destroy the planet, didn't he?" asked Fred.

"No, he didn't have to, I saw it for myself. You remember those events?" Beta One asked Jack.

"Yes, a short time ago the memories came back to me," said Jack.

"Amazing, humans don't normally remember previous existences. Your minds usually block all but tiny pieces of those memories."

"Hang on, you remember that happening? It wasn't some unexplained flash of memory or someone else explaining it to you?" ask Fred.

"I remember it as though it just happened. Those horrific events are burned into my memory and I cannot block them no matter how much I try. This planet being torn to pieces, billions of people slaughtered, and all because we misjudged your readiness."

"This can't be true. There has to be some other explanation," said Fred.

"Ok, let's forget about this for now since there is nothing we can do about it anyway. Is there some place specific we need to build this factory? How do we start?" asked Jack.

"We will need a fairly large open area. Something about ten meters in diameter. After you have decided where to build then we should bring the parts needed to that spot to begin assembling them," said Beta One.

I know the perfect spot," said Jack and Fred simultaneously.

"The clearing by the database?" asked Jack.

"Yes, and stop saying what I say while I am saying it," grumbled Fred.

"Maybe you should contact Bob and ask him to come back and help move some of this stuff to the clearing. He probably wouldn't trust me if I asked."

"He doesn't mistrust you Jack, none of us do. We just think you move too slowly. But I will contact him for you, and you should do the same with Walter."

"Letting a large number of humans in this room may not be the safest thing for my friends who are still trapped in these fields. We will start moving parts into the hall so they can get to them without entering this room," said Beta One.

"We will help after contacting our friends," said Jack.

Fred began to contact Bob while Jack tried Walter. "Walter? Can you hear me? It's Jack."

"Yes my boy, loud and clear. Is everything ok? The Juvo at the transport seemed worried about something but wouldn't say anything."

"Everything is ok for now, but we could use your help. When you were looking through the database, did you find the instructions for a tower that builds the suits?"

"I think so, if I interpreted their symbols correctly."

"Great, the Juvo we freed is apparently the one who helped us build a similar factory during the first correction. He understands how to build it, but we need the instructions for what parts it needs and how they connect."

"Wonderful news! The two of us working together should be able to figure this out in no time. Is it safe to assume he knows how to control it as well?"

"No, he believes a human mind may become permanently entangled if connected to one of their machines. We are hoping that by building this we can get Alpha One's attention and he or one of his former allies will help us use it. There is more to tell you, not all good I am sad to say, but I would rather tell you in person."

"Ok, that isn't the news I was hoping for, but at least we are a step closer to building something. I will be there shortly. I am just finishing showing the new arrivals the complex and our new outdoor areas."

Fred was still communicating with Bob, so Jack walked over to Beta One to help move the parts. "You said humans don't remember what has happened the last time they went through their life. Why is it then that I can remember some things? Fred has a theory that the Lights are just implanting false memories in all of us to make us more cooperative."

"That could be possible, on a small scale. But to coordinate the memories of millions of my people so they all matched perfectly would be impossible, even for beings as powerful as them. Our biological brains would see any inconsistencies or mistakes and reject the full memory that is being implanted. Besides, my friends and I have had the unique experience of living through the previous corrections without living through our entire lives. We all remember the process of having our minds ripped from our brains and forced back to the beginning of the correction each time it failed. The process is terrifying at best and I can only say that I have the greatest empathy for the Lights whose bodies were destroyed and whose minds are now floating aimlessly through the universe."

"Why have the other Lights not tried to help them?"

"Many have been trying, but they have not had any success so far."

"Bob will be here in a little while with a few people to help..." said Fred as he walked over to help. "So, Beta One is it? You said Alpha Two has been sabotaging Alpha One. How could he do that without anyone noticing?"

"He does it by sending subtle thoughts to Jack that manifest themselves as what you call 'gut feelings' about a situation. He uses these thoughts to control how Jack reacts to Alpha Ones requests."

"When I met with Alpha One I had an intense feeling that I shouldn't do anything he asked of me. Was that...?" asked Jack.

"Yes, most likely Alpha Two's influence, since you normally have a natural trust of Alpha One for some reason. That is why he chose to use you for his attempts at correction," said Beta One.

"Why would he do that? If each side is so convinced they are right, why interfere with the other?" asked Fred.

"I suspect it is because Alpha Two is worried that Alpha One could be correct and he does not want him to succeed. He has been the primary leader of the Lights inhabiting this planet since they settled here billions of years ago. If he is proven wrong then many of his allies could side with Alpha One. If enough do this then Alpha One would be the new leader of this group."

"Is there any way we can let Alpha One know about this? Can you contact him?" asked Jack.

"I have been trying, but I think he may be hiding somewhere off this planet to avoid the conflict between my people and Alpha Two."

"Great, so even if we do build this thing he won't be around to see it" grumbled Fred.

"He may not be here, but he is most likely still monitoring this settlement. If we build the machine it will be visible to him, and that may be enough to make him come back."

"I hope you're right," said Jack as they continued moving the parts in silence.

After about half an hour some of the people who were present when the database was found showed up in the hall, so Jack asked them to bring the parts to the clearing. They were followed by a steady stream of people, so he decided to stay in the hall to coordinate all the people coming and going. As the day wore on Bob eventually showed up in the crowd, stopping to talk.

"Hi Jack, I hope you're not to upset with me for what I did. Once I realized you were distracted with watching Fred I had to take the opportunity so I could avoid a fight with you," said Bob.

"I understand why you did it and I am more upset that you thought I would try to force you to not give them out. You should know me better than that, I would never try to force what I want on to everyone else," said Jack.

"The old Jack wouldn't, but you seem different since you arrived here. You seem too willing to help the Lights even after they attacked you."

"That could be because they have been influencing my feeling towards them, at least Alpha Two has been for sure, and I suspect Alpha One has been as well. Did Fred tell you anything that the Juvo told us?"

"Yes, all of it. Sounds like the Lights are not the great protectors of species you made them out to be."

"From what I saw on the map of our galaxy it looks like there are only a small number of planets that have been wiped out by them. But even one is too many. I am hoping that the Lights who have not resorted t violence do not know what is happening and will be able to put an end to it once they find out."

"If they find out. The Juvo can't keep Alpha Two distracted from what is happening here forever. Who knows what he will do once he finds out we have been given control of this place and freed the Juvo."

"That is why we need to move as fast as possible and build something to get Alpha One's attention. We could use more help moving the parts out into the hall if you are willing."

"Sure, I'll be glad to help," said Bob, walking into the room.

Everyone spent the next few hours emptying the room. Once everything was gone, Beta One showed Jack, Fred and Bob how to lock the door to the room while setting how many Aots were needed to open it again. They decided to require four Aots to open the door. During the walk back to the clearing, Beta One explained that the raw materials in the other room would not need to be moved since the strings created by the machines were capable of retrieving it on their own. As they entered the hall where the first door was opened they saw the slabs used to serve food were out with fresh food.

"I just realized I haven't eaten much of anything today. Let's get something before we go outside," said Jack as Beta One walked over to the door. "I just realized you probably can't eat our food can you? How do you eat while you are in that suit anyway?"

"I don't, we have to leave the suit to eat," said Beta One.

"The rooms at the top of the tower contain the same environment as our home, so we do not need to be in the suits. I can take you back so you can eat something," said the other Juvo.

"I am not sure I need any food, the field kept our bodies nourished and we can last for days without eating."

"Yes, but you are no longer in the field. It was giving you the minimum needed to survive. You will start feeling hungry soon."

"How long will it take? They still need my help to build the machine."

"Not long, you will spend more time eating than travelling."

"Go ahead and get some food, we will be alright. It will take some time for us to finish eating anyway so there is no point in you standing around waiting for us," said Jack.

"If you are sure, then I will go. If you finish before I return, do not hesitate to start building. From what I recall you and your friends only needed help with a couple components."

"We will," said Jack as the Juvo walked towards the landing area.

Everyone ate quickly while gathering up food for anyone at the clearing who had not eaten. The sun had set, the storm was still raging, and the gravel on the pathway was glowing with a pale blue light allowing them to easily see where they were going. As they approached the clearing they saw Walter with a few other people near the pedestal, surrounded by small piles of parts, using Aots to connect them together. The three buildings around the clearing were filled with the parts everyone spent the day moving. The pedestal was giving off a gentle white light which was illuminating most of the clearing.

"Looks like you are making some progress," said Jack.

Walter looked up from his work, "Ah Jack, good to see you. Yes, yes we have. We found the instructions for a machine that will embed a computer into the material the suit is made from. That is apparently all that is needed other than cutting and fusing the material into a suit shape, which a few other people are doing right now in the buildings. Where are the Juvo? I thought they would be with you."

"They went back to the tower to eat."

"Ah, good, don't want anyone to be distracted by hunger since we'll be working through the night. Watch how I connect two parts, then you can do the same. We need to build up quite a few different parts out of all these smaller ones. The pedestal is displaying which ones need to be built and how they are connected to each other."

Walter started combining two of the small parts into a larger one with an Aot. As the Aot heated up the edge of the parts it fused them together. He then placed the Aot over a darker section of one, drawing out a string of what looked like molten crystal. He pulled the string on to a darker area of the second part, holding it there for a moment as it fused. He repeated the process for each of the darker sections until they were all connected.

"There, all done. Just a warning, don't get your fingers too close to where the Aot is working unless you want to burn them."

"Ok, looks easy enough," said Jack as he, Fred and Bob examined the hologram.

After studying the diagrams for a while Jack picked up two parts to begin connecting them. The whole process felt familiar, he was unsure if it was because he had done this before or one of the Lights had implanted the feeling. The parts started looking familiar as he began remembering how each one could be connected to another, even though they were not all shown in the hologram. A memory of building a miniature tower, while Alpha One prepared to connect himself to it, returned to Jack.

"Why can one of us not connect to it" asked Jack.

"Your mind would become too entangled with the computer in this machine. I am uncertain if I could free you," said Alpha One.

"Could you just turn it off? Would that not disconnect us?"

"Yes it would, but the shock of being suddenly disconnected would most likely damage your mind."

"We will eventually need to connect ourselves, once the correction is done. You will not be around forever to run this for us."

"Yes, you are correct. But you will need to train your mind in order to learn how to disconnect yourself. The process will take many years. For now we should just see if the machine you have built works."

Jack shook himself out of the memory, "Walter! We can connect ourselves to this thing!"

"What? How do you know that?" asked Walter.

"I just had another memory. It must have been from one of the previous corrections. Alpha One said we could connect our minds after years of training to learn how to disconnect."

"That doesn't really help us right now though, since none of us have has any of this training," said Bob.

"Yes, but now I know it is possible. I wonder if Beta One or his trapped friends know anything about this training."

"Even if they do, I doubt we have will have years before the other Lights decide to come after us," said Fred.

"Come on guys, we will never get through this if we don't stay positive! You are starting to sound like you are giving up."

"Sorry Jack, but after all that has happened I don't see much hope. Even if we do drive off the Lights that leaves us with billions of people with nothing left but their memories and a lot of anger. I see a lot of bad times ahead with or without the Lights here."

"Well, we do have the Juvo to help. I'm sure they could help us to rebuild everything and put our lives back together," said Walter.

"There, that's what I mean. Look for ways to fix everything and don't focus of all the crap that has happened," said Jack.

Fred grumbled while going back to assembling the parts.

"We can try, but don't expect too much from everyone. We don't have the same rosy outlook on life you do," said Bob.

Everyone went back to assembling the parts while Jack thought about everything that had happened. Was his tendency of finding a way to fix a situation why he was chosen by Alpha One? Maybe that tendency was due to interference from the Lights. Was anything he did because he wanted to do it or had he been conditioned by the Lights to act a certain way?

After working for over an hour in a daze, Jack looked around, examined the parts everyone else had made, realizing he had been building something different. "Hey Walter, how long have we been working?"

Walter looked at something in the holographic display, thought for a moment, and then looked over at Jack. "About an hour... what in the world are you making?" Hearing the surprise in Walters voice, everyone looked over at Jack to see he had combined a group of parts into a large cube.

"I'm not sure. While I was working I was thinking about things other than what I was building. Is this anything useful or have I just wasted a bunch of parts."

"It looks familiar. I think I saw it somewhere in the database when we were studying it earlier. Let me quickly scan through it and see if I can find anything."

Fred examined the object for a while, "Looks kind of like a modern art sculpture I once saw in a museum."

"I am not sure what it is, but when I was building it I felt like I knew what I was doing," said Jack, looking around the area, "Have the Juvo come back yet? They have been gone for quite a long time."

"I haven't seen any of them. Hey Walter! You heard anything from the Juvo?"

"Hmm... What? Oh, the Juvo. No, haven't heard a thing from them," said Walter while searching the database.

"If they've run into trouble, we may not have too long before it comes here too."

"I should have never suggested they go back to the tower. For all we know Alpha Two has assumed all the Juvo are going to attack him and he attacked the tower first," said Jack.

"Well, whatever's going on I'm sure we'll find out soon enough."

"There it is, found it! Bring that thing over here and let's find out if it is the same," said Walter.

"So what is it supposed to be?" asked Jack.

"If it is what is in the display, it will be a field generator. Like the ones built into the buildings keeping out the weather."

"Why in the world would I build that?"

"Maybe during one of the previous corrections we didn't already have them," said Walter while comparing the object to the hologram, "Yes, it does look like the same thing. It's not something we were planning on making, but another field generator could come in handy if we decide to expand beyond this peninsula."

"It's still a waste though since we have no need for it now."

186

"We can always add it to the machine we are building. These field generators can be added into any of their machines that need to be protected from the weather. That will allow us to move it anywhere we want, even outside this field, and not have to worry about things like lightning strikes."

"Speaking of protection, isn't this thing going to be a little vulnerable when we get it done? All the towers that the Lights built were stone. A tower of these parts could easily be smashed apart."

"As near as I can tell from the holograms, one of the parts is already loaded with the materials needed to make a single string. Once the machine is turned on, it creates that string which can then be told to bring back raw materials from the storage room for the machine to build more. Once it has built a few, they can be told to bring back raw material and build a stone shell for the tower. Then you are all set to start using the machine for whatever it is designed to do."

"That is assuming we can attract Alpha One's attention and get him or one of his former allies to help us," said Fred.

"How exactly are we going to power this thing when it is built? I didn't see any parts that look like batteries or generators," said Jack.

"I don't understand how these things get their power yet, but according to the holograms we use an Aot to jump start a certain part which then starts drawing power from... somewhere. Not sure where though. We should probably get back to building. Do me a favor Jack. Try to not think about what you are doing again, I am curious as to what else you remember how to build. We have more than enough parts to build this machine, so don't worry about possibly wasting a few," said Walter.

"Ok, but don't expect any miracles."

They all went back to building parts, while Jack tried to think about something other than what he was doing. As the hours passed, the smaller parts were slowly assembled into larger parts with the miniature tower started taking shape. The base was a large disc roughly twice as wide as the tower which sat on it, with the cube fitting on the disc next to the tower. As morning approached everything was almost complete.

"Ok, now hand me those two pyramid shaped parts. They should go right in here... There, now to fuse them... that's one... that's two, now to connect them... one... and two! Well, for what it's worth, I think we have done it," said Walter.

"I still have a bunch of parts. Did I make too many?" asked Jack.

"I'm not sure what these are supposed to be but I haven't seen anything like them in the database. I think your mind may have wandered again, but this time nothing useful came out of it. I'll see if I can disassemble these later since there are only three of them," said Walter while examining the parts.

"Ok, well I tried anyway I guess. Can we put the tower upright and turn it on now? I don't think the Juvo are coming back so there is no point waiting for them."

"Yes, they should have been back long ago... Let me double check the instructions before we move it into a clear area and I attempt to power it up." Walter examined the holographic diagrams for a while and then thought for a moment. "Ok, the tower needs to have a fairly large clear circular area around it. I think it needs to roughly ten meters in diameter."

"You think? What if that's too small?" asked Fred.

"If it's too small the machine will not power up properly, but nothing bad will happen. If we put it between those two buildings over there we will have much more space than that. Everyone grab part of it and we can carry it over. I'm not sure how fragile it is, so I would like as many of you to support it as possible while it is being moved."

About two dozen people helped move the tower, carefully supporting it with the palms of both hands in order to not put too much stress on any of the individual parts. Despite its size, the tower was quite light and very solid, even though it looked fragile enough to shatter with a light punch. Once the tower was standing up, it was roughly twice Jack's height, looking like a cedar hedge made from glass. Walter marked six spots around the tower where the pillars needed to be, while others retrieved them from one of the buildings.

"Now before I turn it on everyone should move away. I have no idea if anything is going to happen in the area surrounded by the pillars," said Walter. As Everyone walked away he began looking around the base for something. "Ah! There it is." Walter placed his Aot slightly inside the edge of the towers base, pressing various symbols which appeared on the tool.

"Is it doing anything?" asked Jack.

"It seems to be doing something, but I am not sure what? I thought it would have started creating the first string by now. I only have a few more steps before I am done... there... why isn't it building the string? It looks like there is power running through it. Look, there are little lights moving around the crystals. I'm not sure what I missed, let me check the holograms again," said Walter, walking back to the pedestal. As he exited the area surrounded by the pillars the machine let out a loud crackling noise while giving off an extremely bright light.

"Holy crap! Is it supposed to do that?" asked Fred.

"Yes! Yes! I guess it was waiting for the area around it to be completely clear!" said Walter.

"Look, there is a string coming out of the side!" said Jack.

Through the glare, everyone could barely see a string slowly emerging from the center of the tower. Once the string was completed it rushed away towards the settlement.

"Ha! It's working! It's gone to get some raw materials!" said Walter.

Jack's eyes were starting to hurt from the bright light, so to get some relief he looked up to the darkened sky to see three balls of light dispersing the clouds. "Hey Walter, look up there! Is the machine doing that?"

"I don't think so, those balls look more like what we saw the day all this started. Did you see where they came from?"

"It looks like they came from the direction where the beach and tower are located."

"You think we got Alpha One's attention? Maybe he's doing that?" asked Fred.

"Maybe, but I don't think so. Look, there are some black dots following behind. I can't make out what they are."

As they watched the sky, the balls of light circled back, small spots of light left them heading towards the black dots. A bright flash of light was given off by each of the black dots, heading towards the spots which disappeared.

"This is not good. That looks like what happened in Vancouver when I shot a blast wave at one of the light balls," said Jack.

"You think that's the Juvo and the Lights fighting?" asked Fred as a loud screeching sound came from the sky. "What the hell was that!"

"I am absolutely sure now. That's exactly what I heard in Vancouver."

The balls of light reversed direction, accelerating away from the dots which continued to follow them. They split up, moving in three different directions, while the dots split into groups following each one. A loud explosion came from the direction of the settlement as smoke could be seen rising from behind the trees.

"Aw crap, they are attacking us now!" said Fred.

"I don't think so. Everyone is out here working on this tower or exploring, they would have attacked here. Something may have happened to the string that the tower made," said Walter.

"You stay here and watch over the tower, we can go back and check it out," said Jack.

"Let me know what you find as soon as you get there. If the string has been damaged I'm going to have to figure out how to turn off this tower and reset it so it will make a new string."

"Will do, let's go guys," said Jack as he, Fred, Bob and a few others started running towards the settlement.

As they approached the clearing outside the settlement they saw the entry hall building had collapsed, with smoke rising from the rubble. The smoke was coming from under the rubble along with the sound of something moving. The rubble near the hallway that led to the storage rooms was thrown up in the air as the string that the tower created flew out, heading towards the tower.

"Did that thing cause all this?" asked Bob.

"I don't think so. It was too close to the hall. I think it just got here and started digging through the rubble. Whatever did this is probably whatever is making all that smoke over there," said Fred.

"I sure hope no one was in here when it collapsed. Ok everyone, we need to start clearing the area in case anyone is buried. Break into groups and start moving everything out into the field," said Jack to everyone.

"This is going to take quite a while. Some of these chunks look too big for even a large group to move."

"We will just have to dig around them for now. Once Walter figures out how to get the tower to start building suits we can ask the other Juvo to move them for us... Did you hear that?"

"Hear what?"

"I could have sworn I heard a very faint voice near the edge of all this rubble. There must be someone under here."

"Well let's get digging then. No time to lose if someone is trapped."

"Ok, I'll just let Walter know what has happened," said Jack as he paused to send the message.

Everyone started moving rubble away, but progress was slow because of the size of the pieces. They paused once in a while to listen, with everyone eventually hearing a faint voice but not being able to make out what it was saying. After an hour of moving rubble they were nearing the bottom but there was no sign of anyone trapped.

"What's going on, there should be someone under here, I can hear them talking. I still can't make it out, but it is louder," said Jack in confusion.

"Maybe we're in the wrong spot. I'll go over to the other side of the rubble and listen," said Fred as he moved away. "I can hear someone over here too!"

Jack and Bob walked over to listen.

"I can hear them too. It sounds the same as it did over there," said Jack.

"Me too, what the heck is going on," said Bob.

"There must be enough airspace under all this for their voice to travel quite a distance. We should spread out and see where it sounds the loudest," said Fred.

"Jack! Fred! Bob! Can anyone hear me yet?" said the voice very faintly.

"Did you..." said Jack.

"Yes," said Fred and Bob.

"I can hear you. Where are you? What part of the building were you in when it collapsed!" yelled Jack.

"This is Beta One. I'm not in a building. What has happened?"

"Beta One? Where are you? We thought there was someone trapped in the main building. Something caused it to collapse."

"I am travelling back to you along the ocean floor with the survivors. The tower was attacked. Many of my people have been killed. We are trying to keep out of sight while the fighting continues."

"Are we in danger? We saw three lights fighting with something in the sky earlier. Could they have done this?"

"I don't think so, since just one building has been damaged."

"We also got the tower built and started up. Is it possible the string it created did this? We saw it move out of the rubble when we got here."

"That is unlikely, unless it is malfunctioning. They have to be specifically told by whoever is controlling the tower to demolish something. Your people should leave the settlement and stay in the smaller structures in case there is something wrong with the infrastructure of the buildings."

"We need to finish looking through the rubble for anyone who may have still been in the building first. There also seems to be something burning under the rubble."

"That could be the organic matter that is stored in the machines that create your food. One or more of the cylinders it is stored in may have been ruptured in the collapse. We are still quite far away but will help when we arrive. We need to take cover, I see a Light in the distance."

"Ok, if we are not at the rubble when you get here we will be in the clearing where we built the tower."

"Well that explains the voices... I hope. Let's clear the area where the smoke is coming out. Maybe whatever caused this is what is burning," said Fred.

"Ok, but we need to be careful. We don't know if those containers will explode or not when heated up by a fire. We should start clearing a few meters away from the smoke and work our way inwards," said Jack.

Everyone started moving rubble again, avoiding standing near the smoking area as much as possible. Every once in a while the rubble could be heard shifting slightly somewhere under them. After an hour of digging, Jack climbed back up to the top of the rubble and realized they should have found the floor.

"Hey Fred, can you see the floor anywhere yet?" asked Jack.

Fred kicked some of the smaller pieces while looking around, "Nope, looks like we still have a ways to go."

"That's strange, because you guys are at the same level as the ground outside now. You should be standing on the floor"

"Hmm, do you know if there were any rooms under this building?"

"No, none that I know of and nothing showed up on the map in the lab either."

"Well, I guess we keep digging. We'll eventually find something."

"We should probably take a break first. No one has had anything to eat for quite a while and I think it is around the time the food comes out. I'll let Walter know where we will be," said Jack as he started communicating with Walter.

"Good idea. I think we can squeeze through the rubble by the opening to the hallway, that string has moved quite a lot of it out of the way. It's not too far to the next entry hall."

"Ok, I let him know what is happening. He said the machine created a few dozen strings in total, and that they have almost completed the stone shell for the tower, but there is still no sign of Alpha One."

"Maybe he's given up on us. None of us with the exception of Walter were too keen to help him."

After everyone squeezed through the opening created by the strings, they walked to the next entry hall to find a few people who had volunteered to bring food back to the clearing for everyone else. After waiting for a while and answering many questions about what happened to the main building, the slabs emerged from the walls allowing everyone to eat. Before anyone had a chance to finish, a screeching sound came echoing down the hallway leading to the collapsed building followed by the ground shaking slightly.

"What the hell, are they fighting in here now?" asked Fred.

"No, that sound was too quite. Remember how loud it was from the fight earlier? I think something else has collapsed back by the rubble. We should take the long way back through the woods in case another building collapsed and blocked the way," said Jack.

"Ok, let head out. Everyone grab some food and we can finish eating on the way back."

"Jack, what happened? We heard a sound echoing through the woods similar to what we heard when they were fighting. Is everyone alright?" asked Walter.

"We are ok. It sounded like something happened where the main building was. We are going back to check it out. I'll let you know what we find."

They stuffed some food into their pockets before leaving, noticing that fewer people decided to come with them this time. They decided to walk this time since they were still very tired from moving rubble. Arriving they saw there was no longer any smoke. They climbed to the edge of the area they were clearing to see a deep pit in the center with the rubble around the edges slowly dropping in.

"Can anyone see what's in there or how deep it is?" asked Fred.

"Not me. We could really use a rope right now," said Jack as the side of rubble pile across from them started to slide into the pit, "Everyone move out of the area now, it's too unstable!"

They quickly moved off of the rubble back on to the field then turned to watch everything slowly fall into the pit which had now tripled in width.

"Crap! How many floors did this building have under it!" said Bob as they carefully approached where the building had been, trying to see inside the pit.

"Look at the other side of the pit. It's not the stone the building was made from, but just the dirt and rock from the ground around us," said Jack.

"Maybe all the rain from the last week seeped under the building from the landing area out front and made a sinkhole," said Fred.

"What is happening in the settlement? We are almost there and I am seeing some disturbing readings in my suits display," said Beta One to Jack.

"The entire main building has collapsed into a sinkhole. We think that maybe the rain from the storm seeped under it during the last week."

"Did you hear anything before this happened?"

"Yes, a high pitched noise similar but quieter to the one we heard when the Lights and Juvo were fighting above us."

"Get away from the sinkhole now! Go to the clearing and we will join you there and explain after inspecting the pit," said Beta One in a panicked tone to Jack, Fred and Bob.

"Ok everyone, we need to get back to the clearing now!" said Jack.

"Why, what's happened?" asked one of the people in the group.

"I don't know yet, but the Juvo that are coming back said we need to get away from the pit now," said Jack as he started to leave the area.

"Is there something down there that's going to blow up" asked another person.

"I have no idea, and I wouldn't want to be standing around here if there is!"

As everyone entered the woods the ground rumbled slightly, the trees swayed a little, and the animals in the woods started making noise.

"Was that an earthquake? That's all we need now," said Bob.

"I don't think so, look!" said Jack, looking back at the settlement to see that a part of the field had fallen into the pit. Everyone started running back to the clearing while the ground rumbled slightly.

"I am glad you guys are back. Everyone is panicking with all these tremors and I don't seem to be able to calm them down! What's happened back there? Did more of the settlement collapse?" asked Walter when everyone arrived back at the clearing.

"No, a large pit has opened up where the main building was standing. The building and part of the field have been swallowed up by it. Beta One contacted us and said to wait for him here while he checks it out. He seemed extremely worried about something he saw in his display," said Jack.

"Sinkholes can be common after heavy rain like we had for the past week, but the land under those buildings is almost solid rock. I don't understand how a pit just appeared in it. And you say the Juvo are coming back, what took them so long?"

"He said they were attacked at the tower, didn't give any details though. Did you find anything useful in the database while we were gone?"

The ground shook again, a little more violently this time, causing some people to lose their balance.

194

"I did find... something..." said Walter.

"Well, what is it? You don't sound like it's something good," said Fred.

"Well... Jack was right... a human can be connected to the machine to control it. But... oh just look at it and you'll see," said Walter, bringing up a hologram that clearly shows a specific human, Jack, doing something to the machine with an Aot to connect his mind to it.

"Is that me?" asked Jack cautiously.

"Yes, it looks like this machine has been designed to work with a specific human mind, in this case... yours."

"You gotta be joking! I'm not going to let Jack connect himself to that thing when we have no way of disconnecting him!" said Fred.

"Don't worry, I wasn't suggesting that. I just thought you should know what I found. I am hoping now that I have these instructions, the Juvo can help figure out a way to manually control it."

"Or maybe plug one of them into it."

"I doubt they would be able to easily disconnect any more than I could, and judging by this hologram it was designed for me so it probably wouldn't work for them, would it?" asked Jack.

"That is correct. From what I can tell, each tower is built for a specific mind. Look at these others I found in here. They are the full sized towers and each one has instructions for attaching a specific light to it... Look, here is the one for Alpha One."

"Are we supposed to have access to those instructions?"

"Probably not, it took five of us using Aots to unlock these holograms, and there are thousands more we still can't get to."

"I wonder if Alpha One knew we would have access to this. If he did, then everything we are doing could be what he wanted us to do..."

"And if he didn't then the other Lights aren't going to be too thrilled with him or us," said Fred.

The Juvo appeared down the path to the settlement, quickly gliding into the clearing, stopping near Jack. "We have inspected the pit and you must prepare to evacuate this peninsula now. Fred told me earlier that he believes everyone now has threads, can this be verified?" said Beta One directing his thoughts at everyone he could see.

"Did everyone hear him? Bob, did you get everyone?" asked Jack as everyone confirmed they heard Beta One.

"Everyone I could find. The only way someone would have been missed would be if they were hiding or had gone outside the area under the protective field. Why do we need to leave?" asked Bob.

"The pit was caused by a piece of one of the Lights that was attacked earlier. I have seen this many times but in every other case a Light had come back to retrieve it before any significant damage was done," said Beta One.

"How the hell can a piece of them do that?" asked Fred, "Their whole body doesn't look like it has the weight to do something like that."

"If they were made from normal matter it would not be. But they are made from very unique matter that was formed in the early universe."

"Yes, Walter told me about that. But why would that make them heavier" asked Jack.

"They are not heavier, but the matter they are made from reacts very violently with many of the atoms that make up the rest of the universe, most metals and some gasses like oxygen for example. The sounds you heard are just a byproduct of that reaction. When you saw them being attacked earlier they were not injured by the blast, but by all the oxygen being pushed into them. Before they developed a device to generate a protective field around their bodies, they could not enter the atmosphere of this planet without being seriously injured."

"The rocks in those cliff have a lot of metal in them don't they? How long will it take for that piece of them to be used up by the reaction?" asked Walter .

"It will never be used up because it is not a normal chemical reaction as you know it. When it comes in contact with normal atoms they are torn into their component parts and release a large amount of energy."

"Sounds like how a nuclear weapon works," said Jack.

"Not quite, your nuclear weapons actually annihilate the atoms and create huge amounts of radiation and energy. This reaction rips apart all the protons, neutrons, and electrons so you no longer have the original atoms. It is happening slowly right now because the rock is not pure metal, but there is a huge magma tube thirteen kilometers below us and it is mostly pure molten iron and nickel. As it gets deeper and the temperature increases, so will the speed of the reaction. The magma isn't under enough pressure to get to the surface right now, but when that small piece hits it the reaction will create extreme pressure and forced everything to the surface."

"There must be some way to stop it. Leaving this peninsula won't help. Can you contact Alpha One? Is there anything the machine we made can do to stop it? Jack built something that is supposed to generate a field like the one around this area," said Walter.

"No one knows where Alpha One has gone. Show me the generator," said Beta One curiously as Walter displayed the hologram.

"Interesting, this is a common field generator. Why did you build it?"

"I did not plan on building it. But when I was working on the parts for the tower I was distracted by my thoughts and built it without realizing what I was doing."

"That is unusual. But I don't see any way it could help us. The other Juvo that came with me are in the storage room preparing to move the imprisoned Juvo, we should prepare to leave also."

"But how will we survive without any shelter or food? We need to find a way to divert any magma that comes out of the pit into the ocean instead. Could this machine demolish the cliff on the side of the pit next to the ocean? Then the magma would empty out into the ocean." asked Walter.

"It is possible if someone is controlling the machine, but right now we don't have Alpha One to help."

"Ok, what about manually controlling it. I have been trying to find a way to connect it to this pedestal so I can control it from here."

"I do not know of a way, but I can check the database to see if I can find one." Beta One examined the hologram of the tower and a few of its parts. "There doesn't appear to be any components here other than the ones designed to allow Jack's or the Light's mind to control a tower. The information in this system appears to be quite limited and without the help of an engineer who understands the Lights technology we will not be able to modify it to work with the pedestal. Unfortunately all my friends are either archeologists or guards and understand no more than I do."

"There must be something we can do other than abandon this place."

The ground started violently shaking, a blast was heard coming from the settlement as rubble could be seen shooting above the tree tops. Beta One turned and looked at the ground in the direction of the settlement. "It has broken through to the magma tube, and the reaction is much more violent than I had hoped. Everyone needs to get to the coast on the other side of the peninsula as fast as possible!"

Rubble started raining down on the woods, breaking tree branches and smashing buildings. Almost everyone started running in a panic as the ground started cracking with ash pouring out.

"How the hell are we supposed to get out of here with the ground crumbling beneath us?" asked Fred.

"Could you blast the cliff face away using your suit to redirect the magma?" asked Walter frantically.

"Not without destroying most of the cliff and the settlement in the process. I doubt it would help at this point anyway, the pressure buildup is causing fissures all over the peninsula and the magma is going to be coming out of them soon."

"We can't outrun this! You have to do something! Blast a hole in the ground to relieve the pressure!" yelled Bob.

"That wouldn't help. It would just create another exit point for the magma. The pressure is rising far beyond what I thought possible."

As everyone argued with Beta One, trying to convince him to do something, Jack looked over at the tower then all the people trying to run away, many of them dead and injured from the falling rubble or hot ash. He decided that the tower was the only thing that could help them and he was the only one who was going to be able to control it. He pulled the Aot out of his pocket, looked at it briefly, ran over to the tower, and started the procedure shown in the holograms that would connect his mind to it. As he started, a field turned on between the pillars giving off a flash of light, which caused everyone to look towards the tower.

"Jack! What the hell are you doing!" yelled Fred.

"I have to do this, there is no other way we will get out of this!" yelled Jack as Fred and the others tried unsuccessfully to break through the field.

"Jack! You can't do this. We have no way of disconnecting you. We don't even know if this will work. You could end up scrambling your mind!" said Walter.

"It doesn't matter, if I do nothing we are all dead anyway," said Jack as he pressed the final symbol on the Aot to start the connection process. The strings left the tower with some surrounded and moving him into a horizontal position next to it. The rest moved back and forth between the tower and pillars bringing material to construct a slab beneath him.

"We have to get him out of there! Do something!" yelled Fred.

"There is nothing any of us can do now. The connection has already been started," said Beta One.

Chapter 11

While the strings were building the platform beneath him, everything around Jack began to fade away as a pale blue light faded in. After a few seconds various shapes and colors used by the Lights for communicating began appearing. Jack could no longer see or feel any part of his body or the world around it, but he had a sensation of being off balance and about to fall. The pale light pulsated a few times as the falling sensation stopped. Various memories of his life started appearing, intermingled with the symbols. He could see events from his life in Brentwood, such as the day he was old enough to leave the foster home to live on his own and buying the house next to Fred's. As he reflected on various events, they played out before him as real as the day they happened. But no matter how hard he tried, he could not remember the day he was left with the monks, or anything that happened before then, except for a brief glimpse of a small ball of light hovering over him when he was a baby. There was another pulsing in the light as the whispering voices came back to him.

"Can anyone hear me? Is anyone there?" said Jack.

"I'm here Jack, are you alright?" asked Bob.

"Jack! You ok buddy?" asked Fred

"I think so, it is very strange here. All I see is a lot of the Lights symbols and memories of my life."

"What kind of symbols are you seeing? I understand Lights language quite well and should be able to tell you what they mean," said Beta One.

Jack describes the symbols that were closest to him.

"The symbols seem to be random. They don't make any sense any way I try to group them together. You may not be fully connected yet."

"It is a strange sensation. I feel like I am in another universe and I should be able to just reach out and grab them"

"You are in another universe in a way. Your mind is no longer attached to or restricted by your brain, so you can do whatever you want with it, even see all of your memories from the past corrections with a little practice."

"How can I do that if I don't know what to remember?"

"I may be able to help you remember. My people have the same relationship between or brains and minds, but Alpha One trained many of us in ways to bypass these restrictions and find any memory we want. But this is not the time for that, the peninsula is rapidly crumbling. I do not think many of your people can get away in time. The Lights use the strings in the machines to see and hear everything when they are attached and you will need to do the same. But first you need to communicate with the machines computer, get it to understand you, and then it can connect you to the strings."

The light started pulsing again while the symbols began swirling around Jack at an ever increasing speed. "Something's happening! I feel... I'm not sure what I feel... it seems familiar and unfamiliar at the same time." The spinning continued as he started moving through the symbols in random directions. "Can anyone hear me?" There was no response. Jack started to panic a little. "Hello! What's happening? Is everyone ok?" The symbols started to thin out letting Jack see what looked like a human in the distance approaching very quickly. As he got closer he could see the human was him, attached to a machine similar to the one he was attached to. He realized that this was another memory being played out so it must be from a previous correction. As he wished he could remember how to use the machine, the memory engulfed him, caused him to start remembering the meanings of the symbols and how to communicate with the machine. As he thought about which symbols he wanted they rushed towards him. When he thought about the order they need to be place in, they moved into that order. It soon started becoming second nature, he no longer needed to concentrate on each step in the process, but only what he wanted as the outcome. The first thing he did was command the machine to give him control of the strings. Once he had control, he could sense everything around them. He was no longer bound to two small eyes looking in one direction, but instead could see in all directions around each of the strings. He was also no longer limited to normal human vision, instead seeing all forms of electromagnetic radiation. Though he recognized everything, the world now looked alien to him.

"Jack! What's happening?" asked Fred.

"Are you alright Jack?" asked Beta One.

"I'm ok guys. I believe I just went through the last stages of being connected," said Jack as he made a few strings circle around everyone.

"Are making them do that?" asked Fred.

"Yes, I now have control of the machine," said Jack as he sent three other strings to retrieve the parts he built that were not in the database.

"What are you doing with those?" asked Beta One.

"I remember what they do. They allow the field generator to create a field that blocks everything. I will be able to protect a small area around this tower then I can attempt to retrieve the piece of the Light," said Jack as a string bored a large hole in the stone surrounding the field generator with three others putting the parts inside and connecting them.

"We need to get everyone back here right now, before he turns on that..." said Fred as a wall of complete blackness appeared around them about ten meters away from the pillars. It stretched from the ground to roughly twenty meters in the air in a slight arc with small openings in line with each of the pillars. The ground beneath them stopped shaking as the ash stopped pouring out of the cracks. "Jack! Everyone's still outside this area. You have to get them in here."

"There is not enough time. The peninsula is going to collapse in the next few minutes if I can't stop this," said Jack. Most of the strings left the area, moving over the black wall towards the pit.

Jack could see where the piece of the Light was located far underground because of the massive amount of energy being given off as it destroyed the magma. He guided the strings towards the pit, into the magma that was being forced out. The heat was damaging the strings, which were translating the damage into a burning sensation. Realizing they would probably only last a few minutes, he pushed them to move as fast as possible. When they reached the location of the reaction, Jack formed them into a small sphere, capturing the piece of Light and some of the magma. As the reaction continued heating up the magma, he opened a small hole in the sphere allowing the gas to be forced out like a rocket engine, pushing the sphere up to the surface. As it flew out of the pit, the sphere quickly broke the sound barrier, shooting into the sky out of the atmosphere at an incredible speed. He managed to steer the sphere into orbit around Earth before the heat destroyed the strings.

"What the hell is that?" said Fred, pointing to the brightly glowing sphere in the distance as it rose into the sky.

"Did you do that Jack?" asked Bob.

"Yes, that piece of the Light is no longer a problem, for now. We need to get everyone back here now as fast as possible. I am contacting them all, but there are hundreds of injured out there, so I will need all your help to get them back."

"Ok, but why the rush if that thing is gone?" asked Fred.

"Parts of the peninsula under the magma tube still have a high probability of collapse as all the gas in it is vented through the cracks in the ground. The magma will not have time to solidify and support the ground under us."

"How are we going to fit thousands of people in this small area around the tower?" asked Bob.

"We can't. But I can quickly move the field under any area within a few hundred meters of the tower when I sense the ground collapsing. Then everyone in that area can safely move away."

"Aren't we still going to end up with everyone crammed into this small area once everything cools down and collapses?" asked Fred.

"No, I will use the remaining strings to siphon sea water into the cracks and pits and cool the magma faster, and also fill in any areas that do collapse with rubble. It will take a day or two, and then this area will be safe again."

"How are you going to stay awake for a couple days? After a few hours you aren't going to be able to concentrate on anything."

"My body and brain need sleep, but my mind does not. While I am attached to this machine I am always awake and always one hundred percent alert."

"So... you aren't attached to you anymore? Is your body dead then?"

"No, far from it. Our bodies are just another 'machine' for our minds to attach themselves to. They can function normally without our minds, but they would be more like a robot than a person."

"Won't you... your body I mean, starve and deteriorate if it just lies there doing nothing? After all, you're going to want it back eventually... right?"

"I'm not sure... After seeing things through this machine, and knowing what I can now do, and thinking about what I still have to learn... I do not know if I want to return to it. But the machine will keep it alive and healthy in case I do."

"You can't be serious, how can being trapped in that thing be better?"

"You would have to experience it for yourself. I am not trapped anywhere. With this machine I have more freedom than I ever did in my body. We can talk about this more later, right now I need everyone to start helping the people who are still being healed by their threads and are too injured to move."

"Maybe this is what Alpha One meant when he said he may not be able to free Jack from the machine. It might be because he doesn't want to leave it," whispered Walter to Fred and Bob, not realizing that Jack could hear him.

"He'll get tired of it eventually. I think it's just another high tech toy to him," whispered Fred.

The wall of darkness disappeared revealing the destruction that happened during the short time it was up. All the woods between the tower and settlement had been flattened, with many of the settlements buildings crumbled from when the ground beneath them sank. There were cracks in the ground with large areas already starting to sink. Many people who were trying to flee the area were now coming back to the tower, some of them carrying the injured or dead, with people lying unconscious everywhere.

"Damn! This doesn't look very good. Even if Jack can keep us from getting killed using that machine, it doesn't look like any of the buildings are going to be safe to use," said Fred as everyone moved out to retrieve the injured people.

"Once the peninsula has stabilized, we must leave and head to one of the other settlements. I am not detecting any working machines in the remains of this settlement, which means your people will not have any food or fresh water here," said Alpha Two.

"Neither will you and the rest of the Juvo, but at least you can last a long time without anything," said Bob, examining the first person they approach for a pulse, "Not getting anything, will the threads help him?"

"It all depends on the extent of his injuries and whether the threads have been damaged. Just bring back everyone who is still breathing and I will attempt to revive the dead," said Jack.

"How did you hear me? I wasn't directing any thoughts to you?"

"Sorry guys, I should have told you I can hear everyone near me, even if they are not trying to communicate with me. The threads we were given must have been limited to what they can do, but the ones used by the Lights and strings do not have these limits"

"You mean they could listen in on us any time they wanted?" asked Fred incredulously.

"Yes, when they or their strings are nearby. The threads in these strings can sense everything for hundreds of kilometers."

"That's considered nearby?" said Bob as he helped carry someone with a broken leg.

"To them it is. Don't forget that they travel throughout the galaxy and a few hundred kilometers to them is like a single step to us."

"Speaking of the Lights, have you heard anything from Alpha One? Even if everything you have been doing hasn't caught his attention, the crumbling settlement should have," said Fred .

"No I haven't. I cannot see any Lights anywhere."

"Ha! Maybe the Juvo still have them on the run!"

"That won't last long. They will eventually decide to fight back, and when they do... there won't be any Juvo left."

"Jack is correct. They will eventually tire of trying to get my people to cooperate and decide we are no longer worth keeping around. I fear that has already happened and the Lights are luring them off the planet into one spot before they attack, in order to not destroy the planet," said Beta One.

"Why would they do that? They killed a bunch of your people when they attacked the tower. Why wouldn't they just attack the rest here?" asked Fred .

"Yes they did, but they also left a ten kilometer wide crater where the tower stood. Remember that they consider this planet to be theirs and they do not want to destroy it."

"Oh... Then why did they attack it?"

"They had not planned on a fight at the tower since only the Juvo who work with Alpha One were supposed to be there. They had gone there hoping my friends could convince the others to stop attacking. Unfortunately the Travelers who had convinced the others to attack were at the tower trying one last time to convince my friends to join the fight. The Travelers assumed we were going to be attacked so they attacked first. Now the Lights believe that all the Juvo are working against them. Everyone who came back here with me is all that is left of Alpha One's Juvo allies on Earth."

"You still trust him?" asked Fred with confusion.

"Yes, we still consider ourselves his allies. We believe that his obsession with proving himself correct blinded him from seeing anything else that was happening."

"So you don't think he had any idea other Lights have started to wipe out entire species?" asked Fred while helping someone with a broken arm.

"No, he did know about the few on the other side of the galaxy. He had mentioned that he wanted to try and stop them once your people were proven capable of correcting themselves. But he had stopped monitoring what was happening on other planets. Even after my people suspected something was wrong and tried to get him to investigate he brushed them aside and said there would be time after we were done here."

"Sounds a little to self absorbed to be leading anyone, even if his intentions are good," said Bob.

"You will find that all Lights are like that. They value intellect and knowledge above everything else, and if they can do something to prove themselves smarter than the others they will gain status and eventually a leadership role."

"Do they not value anything else? What about making music or art, or just having some fun?" asked Jack.

"No, they do not. Unless something can be used to help gain knowledge, they don't put any value in it. They do consider protecting other species to be their purpose for existence, but they also believe that those species true purposes are to help them gain knowledge. They do understand other species value different things. That is why they always preserve what are considered the greatest creations of a species when they start a correction," said Beta One as the ground started rumbling then dropped about a meter.

"Jack what's happening? Is it still safe to be out here?" asked Bob as he steadied himself.

"Yes it is. I apologize for not being quicker in moving the field under you. I am still getting used to using this machine to do everything. I have tried reviving a few of the dead, but without any success. The minds of every one of them had already started moving back to the start of their lives," said Jack.

"You are able to see that happening?" asked Beta One.

"In a way, I can sense them leaving but I am not sure how to explain what I am sensing. The strings allow me to see more than just the three dimensional space I lived in before. I tried to contact a few to convince them that their bodies could be fixed. But they all ignored me except for one, who just told me 'too much pain' as it continued on its journey."

"Can you really see that or are you just being tricked again?" asked Fred.

"I know you do not want to believe this Fred, but I can see it. For the first time in a long time I have full control of my mind and nothing is interfering with it. I can even see your mind and I know what makes you not willing to believe."

"What do you see?" asked Fred nervously, unsure if he really wanted to know.

"You don't want to live through the accident again. The thought of..."

"OK! That's enough! I don't want to hear anymore of this crap, OK!" said Fred angrily.

"I'm sorry. I didn't mean to upset you. I shouldn't have told you what I saw," said Jack but Fred ignored him.

"Don't get too mad at Jack. Who knows what that machine is doing to him or making him see," said Bob as they went back to helping people.

Jack decided to stop listening in on their conversation as he decided to learn what else he could do with the machine. The first thing he told the machine to do was to build the computers needed for the suits. His first attempts failed when the machine did not understand what he was asking it to do. He quickly realized that he was using the symbols that represented a suit as a piece of clothing and a human designed computer. After examining the instructions for creating the suits he quickly found the correct symbols enabling him to tell the machine what to do. "I have set the machine to finishing the suits for the rest of the Juvo. They will be ready shortly," said Jack.

"Thank you, the retrieval of the rest of your injured people will proceed much faster with more of my people helping," said Beta One.

Jack then started asking the machine questions, "What can you do? Do you have an operational guide?" But it did not understand what he was asking. He asked to communicate with the Lights, causing streams of faint light to shoot from the top of the tower into the sky, meeting up with the streams already there. Once they were connected he was able to sense all the towers the streams were connected to, but he could not sense any Lights. He was able to travel to the towers through the streams, sending out thoughts to anyone or anything in the settlements nearby at each one he visited. He repeatedly received no response, until he visited a tower near the former city of Portland, Oregon. "Can anyone hear me?" asked Jack not expecting any response.

"Yes, I can hear you! Where have you been? We thought you abandoned us!" said a voice.

"I am not one of the Lights, I can't find them anywhere. My name is Jack Campbell. I am in New Zealand at one of their settlements."

"Jack? Are you the one I met in Abbotsford? This is Eddie Vern."

"Yes! Eddie, it is good to know you are alright. Is the Captain with you?"

"Yes he is. We were both captured shortly after we crossed the border. We've been stuck in this dreary settlement ever since. You said you are looking for the Lights? Where did they go? We've been alone here for a couple days."

"There is a lot to explain, but the important thing to know is that many of their allies, the ones in the suits we saw in Abbotsford, have turned on them."

"What! Why would they do that?"

"Not all the Lights are the protectors they make themselves out to be. I can see that you have a pedestal at your settlement. I will send you the information we have in ours. Do you or anyone else there know how to use it?"

"Yes, a few of us have been learning how to build their simpler computers. They put those Draad things in me because they think I have the potential to be some sort of leader and they needed a way to easily communicate to teach me stuff."

"Good. Have any of you had your minds connected to one of their computers? Anyone who has would be able to help me search for them."

"No, none of us are connected. We have been told that it is not possible for us to connect."

"I am connected, that is how I am able to communicate with you. I am using the link between the towers to find where the Lights went."

"You? How? They said it would kill us!"

"I will have to explain later, the survival of the people here may depend on me finding help. The peninsula we are on is breaking apart and I don't know how long I can keep them protected. Examine the map of this galaxy I am sending and you will begin to understand why we cannot trust the Lights. There are also instructions for building many of their machines which you will not have seen yet. I will contact you again when I have more time to talk."

"Ok, take care of yourself, especially since you are hooked up to one of their machines. They may not be too happy when they find out."

"I hope they are not happy. Then they may come here to try and disconnect me."

"Why would you want that? I'm sure they wouldn't bother to worry about hurting you in the process."

"My plan involves having the Light who made this settlement here when that happens, but I need to find him first."

"Well, good luck with that. I would try and hide myself, but you sound like you're pretty sure of your plan."

"Yes, but only if I can find the one I am looking for. I am going to go now, there are tens of thousands of places I still have to look," said Jack as he moved on to another tower.

In the next settlement Jack discovered everyone was dead, at least ten thousand people in all. They appeared to have died recently and quickly, many still having food they were eating in their mouths or hands. He searched through the settlements database for any indication of what happened, but only found instructions for building simple components of the Lights computers so he decided to move on.

The next three settlements were severely damaged in the same way Jack's settlement was when the piece of Light crashed into it. But in these settlements the pieces of Light had been retrieved by someone or something before any major damage was done. There were many injured and dead at all three settlements, but no signs of the Lights or Juvo.

Jack grew weary of searching the settlements, so he decided to check the holographic map at his tower for any indication of larger or special settlements. Examining the map using the machines computer revealed much more information than he had seen before. He zoomed into the peninsula, which still appeared as it did before the disaster. He quickly found his marker, which now had basic information about who he was, as well as a few short descriptions: Nexus, extreme loyalty, and memory keeper were a few. He checked the marker for Fred and it also had the description of extreme loyalty along with Nexus Arm, but there was also a slightly disturbing one: broken mind. Bob's marker also had the descriptions: extreme loyalty and Nexus Arm.

Jack zoomed out so he could see the entire planet. Looking for anything unusual, he immediately noticed six unique markers. Four equally spaced along the equator and one on each pole. He zoomed to the marker in the Pacific Ocean, finding a short description of 'interplanetary link node'. He decided to leave the map to find whatever was at that location using the streams linking the towers. As he approached he saw an enormous tower protruding from the ocean. When he reached it, he was repeatedly asked the same questions by the towers computer: Who are you? You are not scheduled, why are you here?

"I am Jack Campbell"

"Jack Campbell unknown. Who are you? You are not scheduled, why are you here?"

"I am looking for the Lights"

"Lights unknown. Who are you? You are not scheduled, why are you here?"

"We need help, the peninsula is crumbling!"

"Peninsula Unknown. Who are you? You are not scheduled, why are you here?"

Jack thought for a minute as the tower continued repeating the questions, when he remembered what he saw in the map, "I am Nexus, I authorized myself."

"Mind scan confirmation complete. Welcome Nexus. Full control granted to Waypoint Delta."

Jack was in a now familiar environment similar to the one at his tower. This one was slightly different, since there were no longer just symbols and shapes floating around him, but also map and database interfaces as they would appear in the physical world. He started by examining one of the databases, looking for information about what the Lights had been doing and where they might have gone. He quickly realized that this was not just a simple database like the one at the settlement. This database had access to much more of the Lights knowledge.

The last entries about Earth were progress reports on the settlements created by Alpha Two, one of them was a little disturbing to Jack, "I have terminated settlement six five seven again. They not only refused to cooperate, but also attacked the Juvo. The humans in this settlement are uncorrectable and will not be included in any replay corrections that may occur." Was this the settlement where I saw all the dead? What did Alpha Two mean by not be included?

When Jack decided to start looking for information about himself, he was a little shocked to find that both Alpha One and Alpha Two had created large amounts of data associated with him, with the last data entry being created by Alpha Two. "Alpha One's experiment with finding a Nexus among the Humans has failed again, as I told him it would. If he would stop this nonsense of trying to find a human capable of correcting Humans without our help we could end these tedious corrections and proceed with rebuilding the race. I have repeatedly shown him that planting doubt in their minds will cause them to falter, but he insists that he can find a way to negate my implanting." Alpha One knew I was being manipulated? Were they working together?

The second to last entry was from Alpha One, "Jack refused to cooperate with any of my plans at our first meeting. He has never done this before, but I do not believe it has anything to do with Alpha Two's work, but instead my over eagerness to accelerate his training. I am ashamed to report that I lashed out and nearly killed Jack when he refused. Could Alpha Two be correct? Are we all going to eventually resort to violent methods when our old ways fail. I am fearful we will end up destroying all the biological life in this universe if that happens."

Jack started to feel a combination of sick, terrified, and disgust mixed together. They had been working together, each manipulating him to do what they wanted. He decided to go to the very first entry about himself in the database which was created by a Light who he was unfamiliar with, "I have found a Human with mind tendrils that appear to be connecting to every mind near it. This is fascinating! I did not believe that Human minds were capable of this. I will be informing Alpha Two when we discuss how to start the correction. This human may be very useful in controlling the rest."

I can't look at this anymore. They don't want to help us. They just want an easy way to control us. I need to find something that can protect us from them. As Jack paused for a minute to think about what to do next, he started seeing more memories from the end each of his lives. They all end a few months after the festival when a world war obliterated the planet's surface with a type of bomb he had never seen before. He saw one of the bombs explode over Chilliwack, producing a ball of plasma and lightning which destroyed everything for hundreds of kilometers around it. I know what Fred would say, "Better that than being a slave or prisoner. But there has to be a way out of this.

"Are there any Lights here?" Jack asked the towers computer.

"Define the proximity."

"Here... Anywhere on the planet."

"None detected."

"Are there any Lights in this solar system?"

"Unknown."

"Where did the Lights go?"

"Unknown. Communications with other systems were disrupted shortly before they departed."

Jack wondered how he could help anyone on the peninsula if he could not contact Alpha One or his former allies, when he remembered the three field generator parts he built without thinking. He started searching the database for the parts, but could not find them in any of the schematics for any of the machines. "Does this database contain everything known by the Lights?" asked Jack.

"No."

"Where can I find everything the Lights know?"

"No single database contains that information."

"Where can I find information about field generators or weapons?"

"Unknown."

"Does each Waypoint have different databases?"

"Yes."

"Can you connect me to their databases from here?"

"Yes, connections will be complete in twenty one seconds."

Jack could sense massive amounts of information becoming available to the towers computer, flowing into his mind as it appeared. He immediately searched for the parts again, finding they were pieces of a much more complicated machine which was unfamiliar to him. He looked for any mention of the machine in the database, finding one entry from Alpha One. "It is a dark time for my people. Three have been destroyed by cruel weapon created by the Dren. We have been forced to enveloping their solar system in a blocking field. The energy from their star will have nowhere to go and will eventually destroy everything in the system. I am unsure if we can still be considered protectors if we are willing to destroy an entire species in order to protect ourselves."

Jack was confused so he looked at the map of the galaxy once more. The blacked out area only took up a small area on the opposite side of the galaxy, but it was still much larger than a single solar system. Have the Lights blocked out a larger area than mentioned, or did they just abandon everything around it? He examined the machine again, realizing he was starting to understand not only how the parts worked together, but what each one was for. He could now see a way to modify his tower to generate a much larger blocking field. "Is there a way for me to transfer information from these databases to the one in the computer where I came from?" asked Jack.

"No, the computer you came from cannot process any more data."

"Can I access these databases from my computer?"

"Yes, your computer can link to any other."

"Great! But what if I lose the ability to access these databases? How do I stop the Lights from blocking my access?"

"Nexus has been created to control these databases. Access cannot be taken away."

"Ok... what do you mean by Nexus has been created?"

"You are merging with us. You are Nexus, the one meant to oversee this world."

Jack began to panic. Merging with it? What have I done to myself! I am going to end up just another piece of this computer system. I've got to get out of here. He traveled back to the tower on the peninsula as quickly as possible, realizing as he arrived that everyone had been trying to get his attention.

"Jack! Snap out of it! We need your help!" yelled Fred.

"Sorry guys, I was out looking for help. What's wrong?"

"We have observed cracks between the magma tube and ocean floor. This peninsula is exerting enough pressure to force the magma out of those cracks and allow the land to continue sinking. We have calculated all the land within fifty kilometers of this area is going to drop approximately fifty meters over the next two hours," said Beta One.

"This whole area is going to be under water when it's over. The Juvo can carry some of us out, but with thousands of people they can't get everyone, and there's no way we can get away on foot in time," said Bob.

"How far can you move that field you've been using to shield us when the ground drops? Could you use it to get everyone out of here" asked Fred.

"It is already extended as far as it can go. But I think I have found a way to modify it. Beta One, please continue taking people away from this area in case my plan doesn't work. Walter, I want you to go with them."

"I can't! There are the injured as well as much younger people who should go first!" said Walter.

"They will go, but I want you with them. They will need someone with your intelligence to survive if something happens to the rest of us."

"No! I can't leave you here without help!"

"We don't have time for arguing. Beta One, please get him and the younger people out of here now."

"He is correct Walter. The younger humans will need you if this cannot be stopped," said Beta One, picking up Walter, who gave him an angry look.

"I hope you are right about making him leave. He knows more about this alien stuff than any of us," said Fred.

"Not anymore. I'll explain later, this should take about half an hour," said Jack while getting a confused look from Fred and Bob.

Jack used all the strings to start building new parts for the tower while unconsciously monitoring the ground. Since he no longer had a way to fill in the collapsing areas, he used the fields to slowly lower the people to the ground after it settled. After about fifteen minutes, everyone saw the new parts were three rings, each a diameter a little wider than that of the towers base. As the strings put the first into place, a bright spot of light appeared in the sky above them. "Beta One! I need your help. The Lights area back! I'm almost done. Can you keep them away for a few more minutes?"

"We will try, but I don't know how long we will last. I think they have probably come back to kill all of us," said Beta One. The Juvo placed the humans they were carrying on the ground before racing back to Jack. Three more Lights appeared in the sky as dozens of strings shot from the first one towards the tower.

"Everyone get as close to the tower as you can and steady yourselves. The ground is probably going to drop a little," said Jack. He turned off the field under the tower, creating a new dome shaped field over a large area around the

212

tower, leaving a small gap around the edge for people to pass under. The ground shook a bit, a few areas sank a little causing people to trip and stumble. Fred and Bob ran out to help the slower people get under the field.

The strings released by the Light rammed into the field, producing a deafening screeching sound as they were thrown back in the air in random directions. The Light appeared to lose control of where it was going, spiraling towards the ocean. The Juvo arrived before the other Lights, so they started shooting blast waves at the Lights. Easily dodging the blasts the Lights sent a large group of strings towards the Juvo. One of the Juvo was quickly enveloped by some strings which crushed his suit.

"Beta One, don't fight them, just try to avoid them and draw their attention away for a few minutes," said Jack.

"We can try, but they are too fast. I don't think we will last much longer," said Beta One as a string closed in on him.

"Jack, you better do something fast! There's more strings coming in from the woods!" yelled Fred upon seeing a few strings wobbling slowly through the woods towards them.

"Just a bit longer guys, the first part is almost done," said Jack as the connection between the tower and the first ring was completed. The ring began to hum while lighting up. After a few seconds he was able to move the field towards the Lights. The field moved much faster than the Lights so he attempted to surround them with it. Realizing what he was trying to do they split up, two of them moving towards the tower. He moved the field quickly towards the two Lights attempting to swat them with it, but they anticipated his moves, easily avoided it.

The towers strings finished connecting the second ring, which also started to hum while lighting up. Now Jack was able to expand the field to ten times its diameter, engulfing a large area of the sky, easily trapping the three Lights and pulling them towards space. As the Lights were dragged away, the strings they created were dragged along with them. He accelerated the field away from Earth opening it up, shooting the Lights away from the planet.

"Jack, there are still strings in the woods!" yelled Bob.

"I see them. They are from the Light that went flying into the ocean. It was injured when those strings hit the field. I will try to guide them back to the Light," said Jack, shrinking the field, attempting to corral the strings in the woods.

"Injured? How? It didn't run into the field, those strings did," said Fred.

"Those strings are part of it. The strings the towers use are designed to mimic them so the Lights can still perceive the universe in the same way when connected."

"Why are you helping it? Those bastards weren't here to help us. They came here to kill us!"

"We lived through the Lights attack this time, but we would not survive a full attack, at least not yet. After I shot those Lights away from the planet one of them told me I would not be able to repel the thousands of Lights that they will be gathering. If I can show one of them we aren't a threat then maybe the rest can be convinced also," said Jack. The final ring was connected to the tower, enabling him to break the single field into many smaller fields, making the corralling of the strings easier.

"We would be of no use to you in any battle with the Lights. They are no longer holding back their abilities and their only intent appears to be to destroy us," said Beta One.

"Wait a minute, what did you mean by 'at least not yet' Jack? What are you planning to do?" asked Fred.

"At the very least, now that the rings are complete I can protect a large enough area to keep everyone here safe. But I doubt the Lights will leave just because we are in a protective field, and we won't survive for long in it. When I was searching the other towers I discovered that I have been merged with their network of computers. They contain huge amounts of information and I was able to design these rings from it." said Jack.

"So you think you can come up with a way to protect the entire planet using this information then?" asked Bob.

"Maybe, or convince them to leave us alone. But I will probably still need Alpha One's help. Even though I don't think he can be completely trusted, I believe he doesn't want us to be killed."

"Why can you not trust him, is he not trying to help your people?" asked Beta One.

"He and Alpha Two have been working together trying to prove their theories using us as their lab rats. He even knows about the Lights turning to violence, but from what I gather from his notes in the database he is not going to interfere even though he is worried about it."

"Sorry for saying this, but I told you so Jack. And just what do you mean by merged?" asked Fred.

"Don't apologize, if they had not been interfering with my thoughts and emotions I would never have brushed off your opinions so quickly. As for being merged, I think it means my mind is now part of their computer system. This is probably why Alpha One wasn't sure I could be disconnected. I am also sure that I wasn't supposed to be merged until I was completely under their control."

"Does this mean you're stuck in there?" asked Fred.

"Maybe, but I am not really stuck. I would feel more stuck in my body if I was disconnected now. I can sense more now than I ever could using my body."

"But you're no longer human. Do you really want to spend the rest of your life as a machine?"

"Why would I no longer be human, because I don't have a flesh and blood body to live in? I am still as human as I was before, only in a different shell. Our humanity is not in our bodies, but in our minds."

"But how long will you stay this way, how long until you become just another cog in their machine?"

"I think it will end up going the other way. I am slowly gaining the knowledge from and control over every machine of theirs on Earth. Eventually they will all be part of me and I will control who I am, not them."

"I hope you're right about that," said Fred pessimistically.

"I am, but we need to worry about stopping the next attack first. We still need to get everyone off this peninsula before it completely sinks. These new generators will allow me to protect everyone here until they can be moved to safety. Beta One, I know you and your people are not safe here and if you want to leave I will understand."

"If it were not for you, we would have all been trapped in those blocks, buried under the collapsed settlement right now. The least we can do is to help move your people to a safer place," said Beta One.

"Thank you. If the Lights do return before everyone is moved I will do my best to block them from attacking you. But right now I need to talk with the injured Light and get him out of the ocean."

"I still think you are wasting your time with it. They see us a nothing more than lab rats, you said so yourself," said Fred.

"That may be, but I have to at least try to convince them we are not a threat. Don't forget that they can go back to the start of the correction and do whatever they want and we are powerless to stop them."

215

Fred scowled while getting a slightly upset look on his face, but said nothing as Jack sent most of his strings to the Light that fell into the ocean. When he found the Light it was slightly embedded in the ocean floor, not as bright as before.

"How seriously are you hurt" asked Jack, getting no response. He picked up the Light, slowly bringing it to the surface. Setting it on a nearby beach, he could now see the lattice structure of its body much clearer. There were a few spots that were cracked or broken, with threads running around those spots repairing the damage. After a few minutes the fields corralling the Lights strings arrived, releasing the strings which started circling around the Light.

"Please don't destroy my body. Let me go and I will never bother you again. I do not want to be lost in the void like the others," said the Light.

"I have no intention of hurting you or any of the Lights. What do you mean lost in the void?"

"I don't want to be like the ones who were destroyed by the Dren."

"How are they lost? I thought their minds were floating around the universe unattached to a body. Don't you know where they are?"

"No. The Dren's weapon destroys our bodies then hurls the mind into the void space. None of them have been found."

"That's horrific! Are you saying they have been stuck in the empty space you use to travel around all this time, and completely alone?"

"Yes, we searched, all of us searched, for thousands of years. But we have found none of them."

"I can assure you I would never do anything like that to anyone. All I want is to help you so you can leave and go back to Alpha Two."

"Why would I go to him? Did something happen to Alpha One?"

"No, not as far as I know. I just assumed you worked with Alpha Two since you attacked us."

"No, we were not attacking your people. We had travelled to your past to research your people's cultures. When we returned our tower and everything around it had been destroyed. We went to Alpha One's dwelling where he explained that the Juvo had rebelled. We came back here to check the settlement only to find the Juvo with you. The settlement was partially destroyed, so we assumed they were attempting to destroy our work and attacked them."

"Well you attacked us too. There were no Juvo around when you came after me and my people."

"I don't understand. We did not attack any humans. We only attacked the Juvo and their tower."

"The tower is ours, we built it and I am controlling it."

"How is that possible? You would have to merge with it first."

"I did merge. When we were building the tower we found the instruction that allowed me to do it."

"I am very confused. Where did you find these instructions, and how did you build a tower without help from us?"

"Before Alpha One left, he told us about the hidden areas in the settlement. After we found them we figured out everything else on our own. We also freed the Juvo that were imprisoned and found out from them how your people wiped out their home."

"That's not true! We would never do such a thing. They have lied to you!"

"I am afraid it is true, I have accessed the databases in your systems on this planet and have seen the records for myself. A large number of Lights have turned to destroying species that don't fully cooperate. Alpha One and Alpha Two both know about it and I suspect Alpha Two is fully involved in it."

"This can't be possible. Why would Alpha One have kept this information from us? We are supposed to protect species, not destroy them!"

"You mentioned that you went to Alpha One's dwelling. Where is that exactly? I have been trying to find him for a while now."

"It is on Mars. He likes the solitude on that planet and spends much of his time there."

"How can I contact him? Even though I am supposed to be something called Nexus and have access to everything, I can't access anything off this planet because all communications with outside systems was cut off."

"Nexus? How? Alpha One and Alpha Two told us they were needed to create Nexus... None of this makes any sense... Communication may have been disrupted by the Juvo to prevent anyone from requesting help."

"Well I guess they were wrong. How long will it take your threads to repair you? Alpha One needs to know what is happening and get back here before Alpha Two comes back and starts killing everyone."

"At least another four hours, but I should be able to move again shortly. What happened to my friends? Were they hurt also?"

"No, I threw them off the planet."

"It seems you really are Nexus then. We did not think you could achieve this without our help and many years of training."

"Well it isn't just me. My friends are pretty smart people, and I had a lot of memories come back to me about what happened during the last corrections."

"It is still impressive. I will go to Alpha One as soon as I am able. He will come back here. I will not give him any choice in the matter, especially with our experiment progressing so rapidly."

"You still only see us as an experiment don't you?"

"No, that was just a poor choice of words. You have move beyond what our experiment intended, although I think he was hoping for something like this all along. I can move a little now. Will you allow me to leave?"

"Of course you can leave, you were never being held here. We don't want a fight. We just want control of our lives back."

"Thank you, I will do my best to convince Alpha One to come back here."

"When you come back, please contact us before you get here so there won't be any more misunderstandings," said Jack as the Light slowly rose off the ground to begin the journey to Alpha One.

Jack moved his strings back to the tower, but instead of taking a direct route he moved them through the heavily damaged settlement to look for anyone who may have stayed behind. Half of the buildings had collapsed while the rest were cracking or crumbling. The storage rooms were nothing but rubble with anything left inside destroyed or heavily damaged. The entire area the settlement was built on had sunk about twenty meters with large parts of the cliff near the pit fallen into the ocean. He found no signs of anything living so decided to move back to the tower. He realized that the strings now felt as much a part of him as his body did. He wondered if he could ever be satisfied living in a human body again with all its restrictions, hindrances, and weaknesses. Arriving at the tower he could see that most of the people had left with the few that remained watching over the inured.

"So did you find it?" asked Fred, noticing the strings coming back.

"Yes, he was damaged, but his threads will be able to fix everything."

"Strange choice of word, why do you say damaged instead of injured?" asked Bob.

"Their bodies aren't alive like ours. I am not sure exactly how they work, but from what I could see they are just a lattice of that weird matter, with no organs or anything else like we have."

"Doesn't sound like a very useful body to me," said Fred.

"That's probably why they have the strings. They did not look like they were connected to the body at all, so I am not sure if they are part of it or something totally separate."

"How do the ones you are using work? Maybe theirs work the same way."

"I don't know. I haven't had time to look up that information in their systems. They don't appear to be connected to anything, but they feel like a part of me."

"Well that's a little creepy. It's bad enough having these threads in me. I couldn't imagine having a bunch of strings invisibly connected to me too."

"It's not that bad. I don't notice the threads, and they have kept most of us from being killed today," said Bob.

Fred made a disapproving grunt, "We've brought all the injured we could find back to the tower and almost everyone else is moved out. If it weren't for the Juvo and their suits we would have missed quite a few under the rubble. Now we need to get them out of here."

"I will let Beta One know you are ready to go and ask him to come back to guide us to where they brought everyone else."

"Us? You're coming with us? I thought you couldn't be disconnected from the tower?"

"I am fairly sure I can be disconnected, but I don't know how yet. I am going to take all of us, the three buildings, and everything around here to the new area. We will need them and the supplies in them to start a new settlement."

"How exactly are you going to move all this?" asked Bob.

"With the fields I used to block their attacks. The transports operate with similar fields, but they do not block sound or light, just objects. They move around when the fields around them are moved. All I have to do is create a large field under all this then when I move it we will move too."

"Are you sure that will work? Can it actually support everything in this area?" asked Fred.

"Absolutely, the Lights used the same kind of field to block off an entire solar system so it shouldn't have any problems with a few people and three buildings."

Beta One arrived as they were discussing the move so Jack explained his plan.

"So do you think this will actually work?" asked Fred.

"I have seen the Lights move an entire settlement with the fields used by the transports, so it is possible, but also dangerous with this type of field."

"Why, what could go wrong?" asked Jack.

"The field you will be generating has the properties of deflecting anything that hits it. So what you will essentially be doing is pushing the field into the ground around us causing it to be deflected. If you push quickly enough you could potentially throw us into space. I recommend accelerating the field extremely slowly and only raising us high enough to clear what is left of the woods."

"How slow do you think I should go?"

"You will have to worry about how fast you accelerate and decelerate since that is when everything can become unstable. If you are accelerating too fast the ground around us will most likely start bouncing up and down on the field."

"I don't know Jack, this sounds pretty unsafe. You sure I can't convince you to let the Juvo move everything?" asked Fred.

"They can move the people, but the buildings are too heavy. I am currently supporting this area with the field anyway so I need to at least try," said Jack.

"My people will take all of you and the injured, and I will stay here to guide Jack," said Beta One.

"No way I'm leaving Jack alone while he tries this. If everything starts jumping around here the tower could topple over. I'm staying," said Fred as he stepped forward.

"Me too," said Bob also stepping forward.

"Us too!" said a group of uninjured people who had stayed behind to help.

"It settled then. The Juvo can take the injured away, and the rest of us will keep the tower and pillars from falling over," said Fred.

"I won't argue with you. I learned a long time ago that is a waste of time when you have your mind set on something," said Jack as Fred smiled smugly.

The other Juvo arrived after a short time to begin carrying the injured people away. Once they had all been moved, Jack prepared to move everything near the tower, expanding the field under the area into a bowl shape which extended a few meters above the ground at the edges. "Everybody steady yourselves, I have no idea how rough this will get," said Jack. At first he moved the field extremely slow with everything lifting up only a few centimeters in about a minute.

"It would be faster for us to carry all this back at this rate Jack. Everything is rock solid where I am standing. Try moving a bit faster," said Fred.

"I will soon enough. I was sensing some instability near one of the buildings, but is seems to have settled down," said Jack as he started to slowly increase the fields acceleration. Once they had cleared the trees Beta One flew ahead to guide them to the new settlement. When Jack moved the field to follow Beta One, the ground started to shake violently as the buildings began sinking into it.

"Slow down Jack! Everything is shaking apart!" yelled Fred.

"Sorry about that. I got a little over enthusiastic and didn't change direction slowly," said Jack as he slowed down the acceleration of the field until the shaking stopped.

"Much better! I thought I was going to be swallowed up by the ground for a second there," said Bob.

"Do you have any idea how long it will take to get there?" asked Fred.

"Beta One said it is about ten kilometers away, so it will be a little under two hours. I am only going to bring us up to a speed of ten kilometers per hour, but at such a slow acceleration it will take a while. I don't want to go too fast in case I need to stop quickly." The trip was uneventful with Jack managing to slow down and land everything without any more shaking. The new location was on the edge of an extremely large beach around a bay which was surrounded by large mountains, some covered in trees and others bare. The land near the base of the mountains looked as if it was once used for farmland, but it was now overgrown. "Ok guys, the Juvo will take you out of here and then I will start moving the buildings"

"What about you... and the tower... and pillars?" asked Fred.

"I will move all that in one go after everything else is out. I will use the strings to steady everything when I find a spot to put it all."

"What about everything that's going to be left in here? What are you going to do with that?" asked Bob.

"I'll dump it at the end of the beach where there is nothing but rock and sand."

While the Juvo started taking people out to the beach, Jack created a field under one of the buildings. He slowly moved it out to the edge of the beach, lowering it to the ground. He turned off the field causing the building to shift slightly as the ground under it was compressed by its weight. He did the same with the other two buildings then the tower and pillars. They wobbled slightly when he turned off the field, but their weight was not great enough to compress the ground very much. He then moved the field with the remaining ground far down the beach to a barren area. Deciding to experiment a little, he accelerated the field up as fast as he could for a fraction of a second then stopped it, throwing the ground out of the field into the air. As it fell back into the field, the impact shot most of it hundreds of meters into the air with anything that fell back into the field being repeatedly deflected back up.

"What the heck are you doing?" asked Fred.

"I want to see the field can do, but don't worry, if I accidentally throw anything over this way I can easily block it with another field," said Jack as the ground slowly stopped being thrown into the air. He accelerated and stopped the field again, but this time when everything has been thrown in the air he accelerated the field again. This time much of the ground was reflected far into the sky out of sight.

"Holy crap, that thing can really pack a punch!"

"Yes, and now I can see why the Light was so badly hurt"

"I still don't understand how it was hurt. It didn't hit the field, the strings hit it," said Bob.

"I suspect that their minds are somehow physically bound to their strings as well as their bodies, so when either is hit by something the force of the impact is transmitted through their minds to the other parts."

"That couldn't happen to you could it?" asked Fred.

"Yes it could. In order for me to sense anything through the strings I am sure my mind has to be connected to them. I can tell them to go off and do something on their own, but then they would only capable of gathering stuff or building something that is in the database."

"So you're connected to all of these then?" asked Bob, gesturing to the strings.

"No, just these four near you, right now I feel overloaded if I try to connect to any more than that. Beta One, you and your friends should probably get off this planet before the Lights come back. The Light I helped earlier said Alpha One was at his home on Mars, so you may be safe if you can get there," said Jack.

"Are you sure you don't want our help anymore? You can't win a fight with the Lights on your own," said Beta One.

"I don't want you risking your lives to help us. I can shield us from their attacks and hopefully they will eventually get tired of trying to kill us. You should be safe with Alpha One, and if he decides to come back, then it would probably be safe for you here again."

"If you are sure, then we will go. I do not feel right leaving, but maybe we can help convince Alpha One to help."

"I hope so. Good luck," said Jack as the Juvo began to leave.

Walter arrived at the tower after a long walk from the other end of the beach, "Why did you throw all that ground up into the sky?"

"He was playing around," said Fred wryly.

"Just doing some testing," said Jack.

"Oh, ok. I've been trying to figure out what we are going to do for food, but there just doesn't seem to be enough around here. The fields over there have a lot of edible berries, but they won't keep thousands of people going for very long. A few parties have gone out looking for wildlife, but other than a few rabbits and a couple deer there doesn't seem to be much," said Walter worryingly.

"I can take care of that, in the short term anyway. This bay and the waters beyond are home to a lot of fish," said Jack as he prepared to communicate with everyone, "Hello again everybody, I understand that many of you may be worried about food since the old settlement no longer exists. I just want to let you know that we do have everything we need here to survive. First, we need to gather up firewood from the woods on the other side of the fields. So if everyone could go out and bring back as much as you can carry we will have enough for a few days. Second, I will build some fire pits for cooking and then gather up some fish from the bay for everyone."

"You really think there are enough fish out there for all these people?" asked Fred.

"For a couple days anyway, but Alpha Two and his friends will be back before then so I will either convince them to help us or..."

"I would rather not think about the or part. There must be some way you can scare them off now that you have control over all their machines."

"Unfortunately, this is the only tower that has the ability to generate these fields. I have already calculated it would take me three days to modify the rest of them and that's assuming I can find other storage facilities with their computer parts. I am still going through their databases looking for anything that can help, but there is a huge amount of information."

"A lot of us could help with that if you want," said Walter.

"Yes, I would appreciate that. The pedestal is able to access everything they know now, so you can start any time you are ready."

Walter looked at the holographic display on the pedestal, stopping with a confused look on his face.

"What's wrong Walter?" asked Bob.

"I don't recognize most of these symbols, and it doesn't seem to be laid out the way it was before. Jack can you explain how this thing works now?"

"Damn, I didn't realize it changed the way the pedestal worked. When I connected it to their systems it must have switched back to the way it is normally set up. It's easy enough to figure out if you understand their language and let your mind flow through the system."

"I thought I did understand, you mean there is more to it? How did you learn it so fast? How exactly do I flow through the system?"

"There's a lot more to it than what we were initially taught. When I merged with their systems the knowledge of their language just became part of my memory. I also just realized you probably wouldn't be able to use it anymore because your mind is not connected to the system."

"Well that's disappointing to say the least."

"Let me try to figure out how to put the pedestal back to the way it was before. There will be something somewhere in here that will show me how it was set up."

"Don't spend all your time trying to fix it. I suspect you can do a lot more on your own than all the rest of us combined."

"I won't, I can get the system to do the searching for me since I have a rough idea of what I need. But first I need to get some fish for everyone. Fred, Bob, I hate to do this to you, but someone is going to have to help prepare the fish for cooking. I just don't have enough strings to do it all by myself. Gather up a large group of people to help out. I can get the strings to make some stone knives from the rocks on the beach."

"What are we going to do with all the fish guts? There is going to be a pretty big stink when they start to rot," said Fred.

"I can take care of that. If we make it through the next couple days they will make good start to the material needed for the organic storage cylinders the food generators use."

As Fred and Bob went off to look for helpers, Jack scanned the bay for fish, finding several large groups. He created large bowl shaped fields in the water around two groups of fish, slowly lifted them out, bringing them to the beach.

"You aren't going to dump all that on the beach are you?" asked Walter.

"No, they'll all just wash back out to the bay. When everyone is ready I will tilt the fields and allow some of the fish and water to get out."

Over the next couple hours as Jack continued searching for something to help protect them from the Lights, the fish were prepared as the cooking pits were built. Only about half the fish were needed so he returned the remaining to the bay. He sent some of his strings to the barren end of the beach to break up the rock into materials that could be used for new buildings. The remaining strings were sent to gather materials for the tower to build more strings. By sunset they had started hundreds of shelters, which were nothing more than shells compared to the ones that were at the settlement, but they would provide cover from the weather. Fortunately the weather was clear, although very cold, so no one needed the shelter to keep dry yet. He used a few strings to create a large pit in the field near the mountains, to store the remains of the fish. Once night set in, everyone huddled close to the fires to keep warm. As everyone started to sleep, Jack was reminded that he no longer need any sleep. Watching everyone sleep, he could sense their minds gathering up memories from their brains, with a few sending tiny pieces of memories to their brains. Realizing he was not the only one who had the ability to remember what could happen in the future, he wondered if anyone else knew they had this ability. Looking over at his friends, he noticed that though Fred was snoring, his brain was doing nothing. Upon closer inspection he could sense that Fred's mind was not gathering up memories, leaving his brain in a comatose state. As he concentrated on Fred's mind he could feel his own mind trying to connect to it, so he let it make the connection.

Jack found himself surrounded by a white glow with someone sitting in the distance. As he approached the sitting person he realized it was Fred, who was muttering to himself, looking down, repeating the words "there has to be a way" over and over. "Fred? Are you ok?"

Fred looked up but did not appear to recognize Jack at first. "Do I... I do know you... Jack, Right? Why am I thinking about you?"

"Yes, I am Jack. You are not thinking about me, I have connected my mind to yours. Do you know where you are?"

"What does it matter? I only have one purpose, and that is not it."

"Why have you stopped communicating with your brain? Don't you want all the memories of what is happening to you?"

"Memories are irrelevant. My life after is irrelevant. I only have one purpose," said Fred who looked down again.

"What is your purpose? Is there something I could help you do?"

"I must stop this!" said Fred as a pickup truck crushed under a logging truck abruptly appeared in front of them.

Jack was shocked by the unexpected appearance, quickly realizing what he was looking at. "This is the day of the accident, isn't it?"

"Yes, yes! You know about it? How can I stop it? Nothing I have tried works. Hundreds of lifetimes, all ending in failure!" said Fred.

"How have you tried to stop it from happening?"

"I have tried everything, making myself leave earlier, or later, or on a different day, or taking a different vehicle. The truck is always there! It always kills her!"

"Maybe you can't stop it."

"Anything can be changed. Anything! Why can't I change this one damn event!" yelled Fred angrily.

"Then you might not have the knowledge you need to prevent it from happening."

"What do you mean?"

"Maybe something that happens to you after this will give you the insight you need to stop it from happening?"

"But I have done everything possible, in every way possible. The first time she is anywhere near a road after the day it usually happens, that damn truck kills her! It even drove through our damn house once!"

"I don't know what to say. I can think about this for a while. Maybe the Light's computers will allow me to figure something out."

"You can try, but I doubt someone's computer will help you."

"You haven't connected to your brain since the accident, have you?"

"No, of course not, everything after is irrelevant worthless memories of pain."

"The Lights are a group of extremely powerful aliens that destroyed all our cities and put everyone in settlements. You don't know about any of that?"

"If everything is gone, then there is nothing I could possibly learn now that would help me."

"I will be back when I figure something out. I doubt I can convince you to connect back to your brain unless I can help you."

"That's the first smart thing you've said since you started talking. I don't believe you will find anything to help me in some alien's computer. I know your intentions are good though, I remember you always trying to help, so I thank you for wanting to help me."

"I won't give up on you Fred. You've thrown away too many memories and I will not give up until I find a way to help you," said Jack as he disconnected from Fred's mind. The beach faded back into view, most people were now asleep with the fires slowly burning out. Jack wondered how he was going to help Fred, now realizing what the Lights description of broken mind meant. He sent one of the strings out to keep the fires going while searching the Lights databases for instructions to build the machines that created food. After a short time he found a database that had the instructions for the majority of the machines used by the lights, but was disappointed to discover that it would take up to a week to create the various parts. He decided to send a few strings back to the old settlement to salvage some of the machines from the rubble. He noticed Bob had woken and was poking at one of the fires with a stick. "Can't sleep Bob?"

"Oh, hi Jack, yeah, I'm too preoccupied with everything that has happened over the last couple of days I guess. I don't see any way for you to fight off the Lights and keep us alive. Even with all the abilities of the tower there is going to be too many of them."

"You are right, there is no way I could fight them and win. Even the Juvo couldn't do it and they have been using the Lights technology for who knows how long. I am still hoping that Alpha One or one of his former allies will come back and be willing to help us."

"Other than their attack yesterday we haven't seen much of them, so I wouldn't get my hopes up."

"I may still find something in their databases, so don't give up hope yet."

"Oh I won't, I'm just making sure you realize we are probably on our own for this."

"I do... This is probably going to sound a little ... creepy, to you, but I could sense what everyone's mind was doing when they were sleeping. I noticed something disturbing about Fred and I am worried about him, or I should say his mind."

"It is a little unsettling. Exactly how much do you see? Were you watching our dreams? Sounds a little like an invasion of our privacy to me."

"No, it's nothing like that. I can sense memories moving between your brain and mind, but I can't see what they are. I noticed Fred's mind wasn't doing anything though and I managed to connect to it and talk with him. Well, not him, but his mind."

"I don't understand. Who exactly did you talk to?"

"It's a little complicated, but I think Fred's mind has isolated itself from his brain. It has not gathered up the memories of everything that has happened to him for a long time. I know the reason, but it I'm not sure if I feel comfortable talking about what we discussed since he most likely assumed our conversation was just between us."

"I can make a pretty good guess as to what caused it, but I won't say anything since you are right about him not wanting you to tell me anything. We have both looked out for Fred for many years, so if there is anything you need me to do, just let me know."

"Thanks, I'm still not sure how I can ask for help without telling you more. I just needed to tell someone. Fred won't know anything about our conversation either since his brain and mind are completely disconnected, so I can't talk to him about it."

"I don't envy you with all these new abilities the Lights machines have given you. You can see much more than the rest of us, and I don't think I would want to see most of it."

"You are right about that. A couple days ago I thought my life was over complicated and out of control. Now that seem like paradise to me. Some of the stuff I am finding in their systems is unsettling and I would rather not know about it. But I can't stop looking, partially because of curiosity, but mostly because I am desperate to find a way out of this for us."

"Maybe there is no way out. Could be that we are just a blip in the life of the universe and our time is up."

"I would rather believe that we can control that. Just because the Lights are more powerful and could destroy us without much effort, why should we just lie back and let them. Every other species that has, has been wiped out, but at some point one of them has to be able to be able to convince the Lights that they shouldn't be interfering with our existence."

"Well, I hope we are the ones to do that, but as long as they see us as a threat we haven't got a chance."

"Maybe I just need to convince them to talk to us so we can work out a way to co-exist."

"Ah! There's the challenge, getting them to talk before they stomp us out of existence."

228

"You know, when I first connected to the tower I felt like I had the power to do anything. Now with everything I have learned I feel like a little kid trying to get the playground bully to stop beating up his friends."

"I will assume you are speaking from experience. How did you handle the bully?"

"He beat the crap out of me, but my friends got away."

"Hmm... don't think that's going to work here. I'm starting to feel sleepy again, do you mind if I try and get some sleep?"

"Of course not, thank you for staying up and talking with me."

"Anytime, I know if I were in your place I would be feeling a little overwhelmed, so I'm available any time."

"Thanks Bob. Get some sleep, who knows what waits for us tomorrow?"

As Bob went back to sleep, Jack decided to look to his own memories for something that could help. He was unsure of how to remember specific events from previous lives without knowing what they were. He likened it to a situation where someone has suffered from a blow to the head, forgetting everything about their life. Deciding to start with the piece of a memory he had already experienced, he thought about the correction where he was first connected to the Lights computer. He remembered having fewer abilities, only two strings to use, and very little to do. When Alpha One tried to help disconnect his mind from the computer, something caused the reconnection to his brain to fail and Jack started to die. As Jack was dying, Fred vowed to make the Lights pay for everything they had done. The last thing Jack did was to plead with him not to do anything stupid, but Fred told him he was going to destroy all the Lights or die trying.

After that disturbing memory, Jack decided to try remembering his life before the Lights started their corrections. He remembered back to the time when the festival occurred, but in the first few lifetimes he just remembered a normal day relaxing around his home. His idea for the festival did not occur until he has lived through his life a few dozen times. He tried remembering events after the festival but in every lifetime a war broke out between the various superpowers, quickly enveloping the entire planet. After a week of fighting, the bombs he remembered earlier were used, causing everything on the planet to be destroyed fairly quickly.

Jack started to think that his life was filled with nothing but disturbing memories, so he thought back to being a baby, trying to remember his parents. Unfortunately the only memory he had was of being on a table with a bright light above him. Someone was telling him "There there, everything is alright, all done now." He concluded it must be taking place in the hospital shortly after he was born. He realized that he could spend an entire lifetime just remembering events from previous lives but finding nothing useful, so he decided to go back to looking through the databases.

Before Jack could do anything else a message appeared from each of the waypoint towers, "Interplanetary communications reestablished, incoming warning." This can't be good news. A Light appeared in front of him, "The Juvo on hundreds of our worlds have begun attacking us. We have not ascertained a motivation for their behavior, but it cannot be allowed to continue. All Lights are advised to use extreme caution when interacting with any Juvo until we are able to determine why they are turning on us. If your world is under attack we advise leaving it and gathering at Core until enough Lights can be organized to capture the Juvo without hurting them or any other life forms on your home." As the message ended Jack was left more confused than ever about what was happening. If the Lights do not interfere with each other's planets then why are they being told not to hurt the Juvo or anyone else and leave? What and where is this Core they are going to gather at?

Jack realized that if other worlds can communicate with Earth, maybe he can communicate with them. "Open a communications link to Alpha One on Mars" said Jack.

"No waypoints or settlements exist on Mars."

Jack started to realize that when the Light he helped said Alpha One liked solitude, he meant total isolation from everyone else. Was he really so different from the other Lights that he did not even like being around them or do they all like to be isolated from others? "Where are Alpha One and Alpha Two?" asked Jack.

"Unknown. Neither being is on Earth any longer nor left any notification of their new location."

Jack decided to stop his wild goose chase to concentrate on protecting as many people as possible. The first thing he did was to tell the waypoints to command any strings they control to start building the parts to create blocking field generators. The system indicated that only four of the waypoints had strings, only two of those had the materials needed to build the parts, and they would take nearly five hours to build.

The strings Jack sent out earlier started returning with pieces of the damaged food generators from the old settlement, as well as one completely

230

intact system but without any storage tanks. As he examined the parts, trying to determine what was usable, he saw a bright flash of light in the sky near the moon. A few seconds later three more flashes appeared as he realized it was probably the Lights and Juvo fighting. He watched for a while longer but saw no more flashes nor could not sense any of the Lights. As he wondered if they were now on their way to kill everyone, he started to feel overwhelmed with everything that had happened, so he decided to rest his mind by thinking about nothing for a little while as the strings continued building.

Chapter 12

Jack's rest didn't last long. He sensed a few dozen Lights speeding towards Earth. "Everyone wake up!"

"Huh? What's the matter Jack?" asked Fred as he and everyone else groggily woke up.

"The Lights are back, and I don't know if they are friendly or hostile! Everyone needs to get as close to the tower as possible so I can shield you."

"I don't see them anywhere, are you sure they're back?" asked Bob.

"Yes, they are still outside the atmosphere and moving fast. They probably don't realize I am in their systems and can see them," said Jack, noticing hundreds more Lights approaching.

"What can we do to help?" asked Fred.

"Just stay close so I can shield you. There is no way you can survive a fight with them, I'm not even sure I can do it. We can only hope that Alpha One will be convinced to come back to help."

"How are you going to know if he does come back if we are all inside the field? Doesn't it block everything?" asked Walter.

"Yes it does. I am going to have to keep a few small openings in the field so I can sense what is happening, and more importantly to allow fresh air and water in. I only hope I am fast enough to keep them out because we won't last long if I have to seal us off from everything. When they are close enough I will try communicating to let them know we are not a threat to them."

Everyone started moving closer to the tower while Jack worried he would not be able to generate a field large enough to shield them. He created fields as large as possible over and under the area but could only cover about three quarters of the people.

"What's wrong Jack? Why did you stop?" asked Fred.

"The tower can't make a field large enough to shield everyone from above and below. I only hope it takes them a while to figure that out and start digging under it," said Jack, turning off the field under the area to expand the one above, while bending it towards and into the ground.

"I doubt it will take them long to figure that out. Maybe you could use the fields to block each of them instead of protecting us," said Walter.

"That won't be possible, there are thousands of them now and they are all heading here. But I have an idea how I can distract them from all of you. Could everyone please move just outside of the pillars?" asked Jack. As soon as the

232

last person was outside, he moved the field so it no longer covered the tower or pillars.

"What are you doing? You're going to be a sitting duck out there!" yelled Fred.

"Giving them something easy to attack. If I stay under the field with you they will just dig under it and slowly wipe us out. With the tower out in the open they will go for it first and I can concentrate on protecting a much smaller area."

"There's got to be another way. This is suicide!"

"No, he's right. If he's under here they will go after everyone and he won't have much of a chance to defend any of us. If he only has to defend the tower he won't have to guess where they will attack," said Walter.

"How long do you think you can hold them off? If there are thousands of them, then there will be tens of thousands of strings! You can't keep that many off of the tower!" said Fred.

"I plan on a more offensive defense than what you are thinking. They should be close enough now, I am going to try and get them to talk."

"I sure hope you know what you're doing."

"Hello, is Alpha One or Alpha Two among the Lights coming towards this settlement? We do not want a fight. We are not a threat to any of you," said Jack, directing his thoughts towards the Lights.

"What you want is irrelevant," said one of the Lights.

"You have no reason to hurt these people. They have done nothing to you! I will not allow you to harm them!" said Jack angrily. Getting no response, he commanded all of his strings to move towards the closest group of lights while attempting to connect his mind to each string. He was able to create a connection with eighty four before he felt like he was going to lose control. He commanded each of the strings he did not have a connection with to each attack a different Light and keep it distracted. He then used the strings he was connected with to attempt to lure some of the Lights into a collision course, but they easily avoid each other.

A group of strings managed to grab two of Jack's strings, trying to tear them apart, causing him to sense the damage as pain. The pain induced anger, causing him to stop holding back on his attack. He started whipping the two captured strings around until they were freed while setting the others on a collision course with the Lights and their strings. He sent half of the strings he was controlling to the largest of the Lights, which he assumed to be the leader of the group, while sending the others in small groups towards various Lights. He attempted ramming each of them, successfully knocking a few of the smaller ones around a little, but without much affect.

Jack sensed a few dozen Lights coming from the old settlement, moving along the surface of the planet towards the tower, so he accelerated his strings back to the ground preparing to defend the tower. As he approached the tower he noticed something familiar about the Lights travelling along the surface.

"Jack! You should move the strings back to the tower as fast as possible. They will not attack them there," said the largest Light near the surface, who Jack now recognized as Alpha One.

"After our last meeting I didn't think I would be this happy to ever see you again," said Jack.

The large Light stopped following Jack, sending its strings towards Alpha One. "Your experiment has failed again and you have abandoned it. Leave now!" said the Light as its strings started attacking Alpha One.

"What are you doing? This is not our way!" said Alpha One as the strings wrapped around his lattice.

"Stop it! Why are you attacking your own people?" asked Jack getting no response from the Light.

"You're damaging me! Stop it!" said Alpha One.

"Stop hurting him!" said Jack as a loud cracking noise came from Alpha One's body. Jack sent all of his strings towards the attacking Light, "Let go of him now or I will rip you apart!" yelled Jack as his string wrapped around the Lights lattice, pulling, creating loud cracking noises.

"No Jack! Don't hurt him!" said Alpha One.

"You cannot hurt me. You are insignificant and overconfident," said the large Light as one of its strings collided with the field protecting everyone, causing it to disappear. His allies started attacking the tower and everyone that had been under the field while Alpha One's allies attempted to block their attacks.

"I am not as insignificant as you believe!" said Jack as he created small fields that ran through the middle of the strings that were attacking everyone on the beach trapping them in mid air, and then pushed the rest of his strings to the limit of their strength causing a piece of the large Lights lattice to snap.

"Ah! Stop! I will release him!" said the Light as it moved its strings away from Alpha One. They both fell slowly to the ground while the other Lights started attacking Alpha One.

"Stop the attack now! You are supposed to be protectors, not killers. You were order back to Core and told not to hurt anyone!" said Jack as his strings continued pulling.

"Do as he asks. Stop the attack," said the Light, sounding weakened and defeated.

"Why? They cannot win!" said one of the attacking Lights.

"Neither can we. The human has control of our systems. If we destroy the tower it will just move to another... we should have returned to Core," said the larger Light as the other Lights stopped attacking while Jack released his strings.

"Now do you understand what we are becoming Alpha Two?" asked Alpha One as Jack realized who he was fighting. "You are not only willing to destroy the humans but your own people. We no longer care about anything if it won't do as we want or would cause us to change. We used to relish change and look for new things to discover. Now all we do is destroy anything that is different or frightening."

"I have always known, and I do not care. Our existence is pointless. Ever since these biological life forms appeared, all we do is try to stop them from destroying everything they touch. It is pointless. Biological life thrives on destruction and nothing we do will ever change that. As long as it exists it will destroy," said Alpha Two.

"Is what we are doing any different? You didn't always feel this way, none of you did. Before the Dren attacked you were always the one who wanted to discover something new or help other beings advance. The galaxy is slowly turning on us and we will not be able to stop it. Jack is proof that Nexus do exist, and they will not allow us to continue. Even without our technology they will eventually become powerful enough to destroy us all. The Dren were the first, now the Humans. If we do not adapt and learn to live with them, we will either be destroyed or driven out of this galaxy."

"How do we know any of them will be willing to exist with us? Our only choice is to destroy all biological life before it destroys us. You should have never given them access to our systems."

"As I have already said, the galaxy is not allowing us to do this. Our actions are the reason the Nexus have come into existence. We are not going to be permitted to continue destroying their societies and forcing our ways on them. I did not give Jack access to anything except our stores of supplies and a training pedestal. He and the other humans built everything on their own."

"How is that possible? Human! How did you gain access to our systems? Who helped you?"

"You can call me Jack. No one helped me, when we started building the tower that was shown in the pedestals database I unconsciously built the parts needed for generating the field. When I connected myself to the tower, I just started remembering everything about how to use it and took control of your systems," said Jack, trying his best to remain calm.

"That is not possible! You would need years of training before you could be connected!" said Alpha Two skeptically.

"It is possible for Nexus. You know as well as I that our systems could never be controlled by a normal human mind. There is no other way that Jack could have gained control other than being Nexus," said Alpha One.

"Human! How did you gain control?" asked Alpha Two.

"Please call me Jack. We all have names and prefer them to be used. Your system at the waypoint asked me who I was. It didn't recognize my name so I told it I was Nexus because I saw that description of me in your maps. I was scanned by something and it confirmed who I was and gave me control."

"Our own systems recognized you? That would mean I was wrong. That is not possible, I am never wrong! Someone must have given him access!" said Alpha Two defiantly.

"I have known for many thousands of years that your theories about what was happening in this galaxy were incorrect. My few allies could also see this, and now I can see that many of yours are also seeing it now. If you would stop fearing everything and bring back your sense of curiosity and desire to help less developed life forms we could stop these pointless corrections and help stop these Humans from destroying themselves and our home," said Alpha One as a few of Alpha Two's allies move away from him.

"No, we should stop the corrections and let them destroy themselves. Then this planet would be ours again."

"Do you not remember what this planet was like after their war? Even our shielding could not provide enough protection for us to exist here. There is nothing we can do to change what is happening, it is the will of this galaxy. You seem to have forgotten that it controls its own destiny and we will never be allowed to change it. But if what happened with the Dren could not show you that, then I doubt anything I say can make you see," said Alpha One as more of Alpha Two's allies moved away from him.

"He is correct Alpha Two. We have all deluded ourselves into believing we could control everything that exists. We have been told to return to Core and we should all go before we do any more damage," said one of the Lights still with Alpha Two.

"Have you all lost your senses? We are Lights! We control everything! The galaxy does what we want, not the other way around!" yelled Alpha Two defiantly.

"We need to leave now, or do you also believe you are now wiser than Core?" asked another Light.

"No, of course not. Core understands and sees more than any of us," said Alpha Two sounding defeated again.

"You can't all leave! I can't take care of the entire Human race all by myself. There is too much to do and too many people that need help," said Jack desperately.

"We cannot stay here. If the Juvo return they will attack us and while we would certainly not be hurt, the same could not be said for this planet or the life forms on it," said one of Alpha Two's allies.

"I would not allow them to fight here. The only reason they attacked you was to stop your people from controlling us. Now that I am in control they have no reason to fight. If they do come back they will only be allowed to stay if they vow not to start fighting with you," said Jack.

"While I was returning from Mars I encountered my Juvo friends and requested that they track down and inform the rest of their people of what Jack has accomplished here. If they are successful I do not believe the Juvo will cause problems here. Some of them also informed me of what you had done to them Alpha Two. If they had not shared their memories with me I would not have believed it. Torture and imprisonment are the tools of primitive beings. But I will not judge your actions. That is for Core to do. Jack, I am willing to stay for a short time to help, and I suspect a few of my allies will also, but we will also need to return eventually to impart our memories to Core," said Alpha One.

"I may have made some mistakes, but Core will understand why I did what I did," said Alpha Two. Jack sensed a feeling of embarrassment from him, although he could not determine whether this was due to his actions or because they were discovered by someone.

"We will leave now and make sure Alpha Two finds his way back to Core. Do not remain here too long Alpha One. If you are correct and the galaxy is what is causing Nexus to appear, then you need to communicate your theories to Core so our new path can be determined," said one of Alpha Two's allies as they began to leave.

"I will only remain long enough to show them that we are no longer needed. Jack is still learning and adapting to our systems and has yet to realize he does not need help," said Alpha One.

As the majority of the Lights departed, Fred, Bob, and Walter started examining the pillars and tower for damage. "Jack! You better look at this," said Walter as he walked around the tower.

As Jack moved some of his strings to Walter he saw the platform that was supporting his body had been damaged. Getting closer, he could see that his body had been cut in two from its right shoulder to left hip. "Oh no! Can the threads fix it?" asked Jack.

"This is far beyond their ability to repair," said Alpha One.

"Am I stuck in your system now? Will I spend the rest of my life trapped in a machine?" asked Jack sounding worried.

"Yes, your mind no longer has a brain to go back to. Do you really feel trapped? You can move almost anywhere on this planet instantaneously through the system, and the strings allow you to sense everything for great distances around them."

"No, it is and incredible experience using all this, but how could I ever convince anyone else they should listen to me if I no longer am one of them?"

"What happened to all you talk about you still being a human even though you're in that machine?" asked Fred.

"I am still human! But if I couldn't convince my friends, then how could I convince anyone else?"

"By letting other connect with the system and experience what you have. They will see that your humanity is not lost just because you are no longer in an organic body," said Alpha One.

"I thought this tower was only designed to allow me to connect. How can anyone else do it?"

"It is, but you can design the systems that will allow others to connect. You may not realize this yet, but you know how all our technology works and have the ability to design and build anything using it. But there is now the unforeseen problem of the loss of your body."

"Why is that a problem? I feel alright, although I will admit I am slightly frightened."

"Your mind is unharmed, and that is good. But it no longer has any way to connect to your brain. You no longer have a way to return to the beginning of our life. This confuses me greatly, because if you are Nexus, you must return. If you don't then your brain will not have a mind connected to it and will just wander through life without any purpose. Everything you have done will not happen again. I do not yet understand why this has happened but I know we will eventually discover the reason."

"Exactly how long are your computers and machines designed to last? If I am going to be in here for the rest of my life, how long is that going to be? And what will happen to my mind after the system stops working?"

"I was hoping you would not ask that question..."

"Why not? Are your machines not designed to last a long time?" asked Fred.

"No, quite the opposite. Everything we build contains components that allow for self repair. As long as there is material available and nothing severely damages the system it will continue to exist."

"So it will outlast everything? Everyone I know will be long gone and eventually there won't be any more humans around, but I will still be here."

"Yes, we will also be here. But remember that what you perceive as time is nothing more than another physical dimension in space. So even though it will seem as though everyone else has gone, they will still be here, just in another location in time. You do have the ability to disconnect your mind from the system whenever you want, although I do not know what will happen to it if you have no brain to reconnect to."

"Wouldn't I end up lost, just floating around if I'm not attached to anything, just like those Lights the Dren vaporized?" asked Jack, becoming increasingly worried.

"I cannot say with any certainty what would happen since no one has tried doing that. We have yet to experience the outer reaches of time. We have many theories about what the universe is like there, but until we arrive we will not know. But there is no need to worry about any of that now. From what we have observed, most of the matter in this universe should extend for trillions of years in the time dimension."

"You did this to him! If you hadn't let him hook himself up to this thing his body still might be in one piece!" yelled Fred.

"You know none of that is true Fred, I chose to connect myself. If I had not then all of us would be dead right now. Even knowing this outcome would not have changed my mind to connect."

"He is right, aside from you Fred, Jack is the most stubborn person I have ever met and nothing would have stopped him from connecting once he made up his mind," said Bob.

"Who are you calling stubborn?" demanded Jack and Fred simultaneously.

Jack was certain he heard a chuckle from Alpha One. "Did you just laugh?" asked Jack.

"We do not laugh. We have a difficult time understanding the concept of humor," said Alpha One.

"Hmm... no matter, Bob is right. I am the cause of my situation and there is no way any other outcome was possible. The question is what can we do about it?"

"I am unsure. This sort of situation has never occurred before. For now I will assume that the galaxy has some other purpose for you that none of us are aware of yet."

"You've and the other Lights keep talking about the galaxy like it is alive."

"Yes, many of us believe this and other galaxies have an extremely powerful mind guiding many of the events that happen. We first realized something much more powerful than us was at work when our more destructive actions started to be counteracted throughout the galaxy all near the same area of time."

"Can we talk to it and find out what it wants with me?"

"We would be extremely happy if we could do that, but so far we have not found a way to locate or communicate with this mind if it does exist. For all we know it may be something we will never be able to do unless it wants us to. It may not consider us a significant enough intelligence to communicate with."

"Why not? You have gathered up a huge amount of knowledge and created a lot of impressive technology," said Walter.

"Would you be interested in having a conversation with an ant? For their size they have an impressive amount of knowledge and build fantastic structures."

"Ah, I see your point."

"So if we piss off the galaxy it will just knock over our ant hills and stomp on us?"

"In its own way, yes, but I don't believe its purpose is to harm any of us but to guide us in the direction it wants us to go. Most of my people still believe our purpose is to protect and guide the intelligent organic life of the galaxy, but somewhere in the process we started destroying their civilizations when we believed they we advancing to quickly. Many of us believe the galaxy wants us to use protective interference instead. Stopping a species when they are about to destroy themselves and then offer our help to overcome the destructive behavior. I want this planet to be the first place where that is tried, and we will see how the galaxy reacts."

"How the hell can you try that now? You've already destroyed everything!" said Fred.

"You forget that we are not bound to the flow of time as you are. Before this unfortunate conflict with the Juvo started I had sent some of my allies to your past to research your ways of life. We have come to the conclusion that you would never accept us if we try to correct you the way we have in the past."

"Damn right! But it's a bit late to realize that now isn't it?" interrupted Fred.

"No, not at all. If we help you to restore your world now and return it to the way it was before the correction started, but without your governments, militaries, and weapons, many of you will more receptive of us when we return to the point the correction was started, and we will have a much better chance of preventing the destruction of this planet and everything on it. The process may take more than one lifetime to perfect, but eventually it will be at a point that is acceptable."

"There is no way that can be true! We can't be stuck living this life over and over, so just drop it already!" yelled Fred angrily as he stormed away.

"Why does he react so angrily any time any of us bring that up? He usually doesn't get angry when someone has a different idea of how everything works than he does," said Bob.

"I think we all know why. Remember when I told you about connecting to his mind," said Jack, communicating with only Bob and Alpha One.

"That was a very dangerous thing to do, and impressive that you could disconnect. Many of us had done the same to try and help him. We always required help disconnecting when we became entangled in his obsessive delusion," said Alpha One.

"I've known him for a long time, most of it from before Joan died. I understand what makes him tick and I also know that his mind will never give up in its search for a way to stop that from happening. I promised to help him find a solution and that seemed to calm him down and I disconnected."

"Interesting, we spent our time trying to convince him to give up," said Alpha One.

"I'm not sure if I should be listening to this. It still feels like I'm invading Fred's privacy," said Bob.

"In this case I think your friend would forgive you, but we should talk about this later. There is much to do in order to get this planet back to a more acceptable state for your people."

"How can we rebuild everything the way it was when your machines work with crystalline circuits and stone buildings? We build with all sorts of things: wood, metal, fabric. I've never seen any of your machines work with those materials. Why not just go back to the start of the correction right now and do it differently?" asked Jack, no longer communicating with just Bob and Alpha One.

"You will design new machines that work with those materials. You have already done something similar when you designed the field generator for your tower. As for travelling back now, we do not know if it is the correct path without first giving our knowledge of everything that has happened to Core. After that a new path will be determined."

"What is this Core thing anyway? You speak about it like it's some sort of super intelligent leader."

"In a way it is, but that is another thing we should talk about later."

"How am I supposed to do all this by myself?"

"You will not be alone. Did you see the description of Nexus Arm that was associated with Fred and Bob in the map?"

"Yes, I assumed it meant they were meant to help me with something."

"Correct, and more than just help. Their minds have the ability to control some of our machines. There are thousands of humans who can do this and they have all been marked."

"I'm not exactly keen to be hooked up to one of these things. After all, look at what happened to Jack" asked Bob.

"Your particular minds do not need to be connected to the machines to control them. They only need to be able to communicate with the computers in

242

them. Connection is only need to absorb knowledge and gain total control over a system."

"Ok, what about Fred's mind not talking with his brain then?"

"That is not an accurate description. If his mind had completely disconnected from his brain, his personality would have changed drastically since it is made up of components in his mind. His mind may no longer be accepting memories from his brain, but it is still connected. Because of its current instability, I would not allow him to try and connect his mind to our technology. The results would be unpredictable and could cause permanent damage to his mind. For now only allow him to communicate with the machine to use them."

"So all these people can help me build things using the machine I am supposed to design?" asked Jack.

"Yes, the first step will be for you to study the designs for all our machines in the database at Waypoint Delta. We only have the designs for what is used on this planet, but studying them should be enough to trigger ideas in you."

"I already started that a few hours ago when I was looking for a way to protect everyone here."

"Very good, continue studying them. Ideas for the new machines will begin to come to you. My allies and I will start building a new settlement here for you to use until the cities have been rebuilt."

"I thought I locked you out of everything. How are you going to build it?"

"No, you only locked us out of our main control and knowledge systems. We still have access to the towers that build the settlements since each of them are independent of everything else. They cannot be used for anything else on their own, but it is enough for our task."

"So what's stopping any of you from building everything again and then just destroying the system I have?"

"You would not allow that to happen. The towers may be independent, but you could still connect to one that is in use and force out the mind controlling it."

"I doubt I would be able to keep all of you out for long, especially if you took control of all the towers at the same time."

"Interesting, you still don't realize how powerful you really are as Nexus. Alpha Two almost realized what you had become too late. A few more seconds and you would have shattered his body."

"I was only trying to stop him from hurting you. I wasn't trying to destroy him."

"That is why you need to learn what you can do as Nexus. Without this knowledge, you could destroy something or someone you are trying to help. Studying our machine designs will trigger some memories and transfer related knowledge into your mind."

"What if my mind runs out of space?"

"That is not possible. A mind grows as it needs more space for knowledge. There is no limit to what you or any other mind can learn or how big it can grow."

"Huh, interesting. I'll start studying the designs then," said Jack as he began studying information in the database. Over the next few hours he studied the designs for machines that built everything from simple computer circuits to the machines that created food. He felt familiar with the machines as he studied them, but was unsure if this was because he already had the knowledge or his mind was absorbing the information before he studied it. When he came to the design for the machine that triggered him to design the blocking field for the tower, he was prepared to skip it but decided to studied it again. Studying the machine, he learned it generated a field which reflects all wavelengths of light, with the designer being Alpha One.

Jack decided to take a break to check what the Lights had been doing. Reconnecting to his strings he was surprised to see the fields between the beach and mountains were filled with the beginnings of hundreds of shelters, with a few dozen larger buildings started along the edge of the beach. There was also a new tower with six pedestals nearby just outside the settlement. He flew his strings over to the tower to find his friends standing by one of the new pedestals. "Looks like the Lights have been busy."

"Yes, they do tend to work fast," said Walter.

"I'm even starting to believe they are going to help us now. I must be going insane," said Fred wryly.

"They've even set up a new pedestal for us to use to talk with other settlements, but they have to get them all set up first," said Bob.

"Have they told any of the other settlements about what is happening?" asked Jack.

"Some of them, apparently they all have at least one of the Nexus Arm type people and they are just waiting for each one to wake before they talk with them. Alpha One did seem a little upset when I asked him about how the other settlements are doing, so that worried me a little," said Walter.

"I know what upset him. Alpha Two has killed all the people in some of the settlements because they wouldn't cooperate," said Jack.

"What! Why the hell didn't you tell us? They better not let that bastard back here!" said Fred angrily.

"You should have said something about what he did," said Bob sounding disappointed.

"I'm sorry guys. I just didn't know when it would have been a good time. I knew you would not be happy with the news and I didn't want any of you to be distracted from everything we needed to do to survive an attack when they came back."

"Well, in this case you were probably right. If I had known what he had done I would have tried to go after him myself!" said Fred.

"I know, and then you would be dead, I probably would have destroyed Alpha Two, and this planet would be a wasteland right now."

"How many other things are you keeping from us?" asked Bob.

"I really don't know. The amount of information that has been dumped in my mind is overwhelming. I try to remember to let you know what I have found, but I keep getting distracted by new stuff. I mostly have been studying the designs for their machines. Every once in a while a piece of knowledge about the history of the design shows up, but nothing that... Wait, one thing was interesting. Apparently Alpha One designed the machine that inspired me to design the blocking field. His only reflects light though."

"I wonder what he designed that for. Maybe it's a flawless mirror for a telescope? I'll have to ask him next time we talk," said Walter.

"I thought you would be interested in that. Most of their designs are fairly simple and boring, but I hope they will trigger some ideas like Alpha One thinks they will."

"Simple and boring? You have changed Jack. Didn't you once tell me you almost failed algebra in high school, and now you find these plans simple?" asked Fred.

"Yes I did, but I haven't changed, I am just no longer restricted by my brains abilities. I am starting to miss being in my body though. With the amount of information being fed into my mind I have a constant feeling like when I am about to fall off a ladder."

"Sounds like a typical Monday morning when I was in college," said Fred.

"Except in my case I do not get to enjoy a night of partying before. Where are all the Lights? I don't see any near us?"

"They've all gone to other settlements to talk to everyone when they wake up, and build them a new pedestal, Oh, and Alpha One's Juvo allies have started returning. They are going to be assigned to help each of the settlements when the Lights are gone," said Walter.

"What about the other Juvo, do they know what is happening?"

"Some of them do and unfortunately so do the Travelers, the Juvo who started all this."

"Why is that not good? They should be happy we have control of this planet again"

"They consider anyone who is working with any of the Lights to be their enemy. They gave up on co-existing with the Lights a long time ago. They've been mainly making attacks in the empty space when someone is using it to travel somewhere fast, so we might be safe from an attack for now," said Fred.

"I'm not sure if I should be using all my time to rebuild our cities then. We need to have a way to defend everyone on this planet from a potential attack."

"Exactly what Bob and I were thinking, but we also didn't want everyone to be stuck living in these cement bunkers for a long time."

"Yes, I was thinking maybe these other people who can control the machine will be able to do the rebuilding, leaving you free to build more of these blocking field generators," said Walter.

"I hope that is possible. It all depends on how quickly everyone can learn how to use these machines without being directly connected to the system. I had the advantage of not really needing to learn anything since it just sort of gets absorbed into my mind. I am going to contact one of the settlements I visited yesterday... I just realized I haven't told any of you about that have I."

"No you haven't. What happened to the people there?" asked Fred.

"Nothing bad, it's a settlement near Portland. I found Eddie Vern there and I think he may be one of the Nexus Arms since they were already teaching him how to use these systems."

"The corporal we met in Abbotsford? What about the captain?"

"He's there too, but I didn't speak with him."

"They taught me too, but I'm not one of them, so I wouldn't get my hopes up. What does the map say about him?"

"Ugh, I never thought of checking that. I keep forgetting what information I have available to me. I'm not sure I should be absorbing all this knowledge so quickly. Every time something new comes in I get distracted by it and forget about what I was doing... The map does have him marked as Nexus Arm, but not the captain."

"You need to take a break from all this learning. Go talk with Eddie and see what he can do to help. Maybe check the map for other people that can help and talk with them," said Fred.

"Before you go I want you to try something with the map. I discovered that the symbol that represented our old settlement could be expanded. It contained a list of every other settlement on the planet and I could select each one and the map would move to it. I'll bet you can do the same with the symbol they used for Nexus Arm," said Walter.

"I just did it as you were talking and it does show me a list... Wow, there really are thousands of Nexus Arms. Huh, Doc, Valerie, Jill, George, and Jake are all on the list," said Jack.

"The names sound familiar, who are they again?" asked Bob.

"Some of the people I met in Vancouver. I didn't have a lot of time to talk with them, except for Doc, but they seemed nice enough. Ok, looks like I have a few people to talk to now. There's no way I'll be able to go through this entire list but I will talk with the people I know. I guess that's why we need the new pedestals, so messages can be passed along from settlement to settlement."

"Makes sense, I don't think they expected you to be constantly travelling everywhere passing on messages," said Walter.

"Well, the sun is coming up here so everyone in Portland will have been awake for a while now. I should go and try to contact Eddie," said Jack as he began traveling to the tower at the Portland settlement. He was moving faster this time, with less effort, causing him to realize that his mind was actually moving through the system, not just making some sort of remote connection to the tower. He also realized that even though his mind was not at his tower, or any of the other towers he had visited, a piece of it was still somehow connected to each one. This time when he arrived at the tower he could see that Eddie was using the pedestal. He was unsure how he could see everything until he realized that Eddie's tower had also created some strings which he had unconsciously connected to. "Hi Eddie! I see you've learned how to get the tower to make strings."

"Wha...? Oh, is that you Jack? Is everything alright in New Zealand? We saw some flashes of light in the sky shortly after you contacted me and got worried that the fighting was going to come here. We've been doing nothing but study these schematics, but most of the stuff we need to build them isn't here. We did manage to get the tower to spit out a few strings, but that's all. These plans use a lot more symbols than the ones we have been taught, but I think we have the basic idea of how we could build everything if we had the parts."

"I'm sorry, I forgot that you wouldn't have had the same access to stuff we did and I should have talked to you about that before I left. In our old settlement there were doors hidden on the back walls of the large halls where the food was served. They could be opened with an Aot, the handheld tools they gave us. Most of them gave us access to storage rooms, and a couple let us out into a new area. Did you have time to look at the map?"

"Yes, we did, and it has a lot of people around here extremely worried. Do the symbols mean the same thing at each location? One of the older people here died a week ago and they were marked with a black spot..."

"Yes, the meaning doesn't change. You saw the settlements with nothing but black spot didn't you. Did you look at any other planets?"

"Yes to both questions. Why are they killing everyone? How are we going to defend ourselves against something so powerful?"

"The simple answer is they have been changing for the worse for quite a long time. But many of them have realized they are on the wrong track and are trying to change the ones that have lost their way. As for defending ourselves, they won't be a problem since I have taken control of their systems and have convinced them to leave for now, but we all still have a lot of work to do in order to make sure this planet is permanently protected."

"That's unbelievable! How did you take control? Why wouldn't they just kill you and take back their systems?"

"It's complicated. If you have some time I can explain everything. Does anyone else there have threads, and are they nearby?"

"Yes, a few of us do now. I injected what was left in my Aot into the captain and a few others. Everyone here going over the holograms has them. They all know about what you did in Abbotsford and really want to talk to you."

"Good, I can talk to all of you at the same time," said Jack, preparing to address everyone around the pedestal. "Hello everyone, my name is Jack Campbell. I want to let all of you know what has been happening over the last few days, and I will also need your help. I will start with the day I met the

Light named Alpha One". He proceeded to explain all the major events that had happened to him along with everything he had discovered.

"This is all a bit much to take in, especially that bit about being stuck reliving our lives over and over. I think I liked it better when I was in the dark not knowing what was happening," said Eddie.

"Yes, that does seem a little unbelievable to me. But you said you remember things that happened during the previous invasions. How can you be sure they are real memories? We should be rebuilding our armies now that you have control," said Captain Ellis.

"When I was still connected to my brain I couldn't be sure, but once I was detached the way I perceived everything changed. I don't know how to explain it if you haven't experienced it for yourself. As for rebuilding the armies, they are part of the reason the Lights decided to do what they did and are not part of any solution to helping us. If we ever want our lives to return to the way they were, or at least close to it, then I know we need to at least try to make Alpha One's plan work. We are no longer divided up into a bunch of countries trying to control as much of the planet as possible, and we need to focus on rebuilding our cities."

"But it hasn't even told you how they are going to avoid destroying everything next time around, assuming there really will be a next time like they say."

"If you don't believe them, then believe me. I know my memories are real, I know they are willing to help us, and I know this has happened many times. I may have been lucky enough to be one step ahead of them at every point this time, but the next time this happens they will know what to expect. Even now I don't doubt they could annihilate everything on this planet if they really want to, but Alpha One has finally convinced the others to leave for a while. The Lights want to help us live our lives without constant conflict, do you really want to turn down a chance to do that?"

"Of course not, but I have no reason to trust them after they have destroyed everything and killed so many people."

"If we can make this work then eventually none of that will happen. I know it's very hard to believe a lot of what they have told us, but once the new machines are built and the Nexus Arms have learned how to use them, I plan on building towers for each of them so they can connect their minds to this system and see what I can see."

"Is that part of their plan, to connect us all to these machines?"

"Not all of us, and it's my plan not theirs. Don't think for a second that I completely trust them, because I do not. I know they are truthful when they say they want to stop us from destroying ourselves, but I know that if their plans don't go the way they want, they could decide to wipe us out in a blink of an eye. With thousand of us connected to their systems there will be little chance of them being able to take control of them or successfully attacking us."

"Well, I am happy that you don't trust them, but we should be connecting soldiers to these systems not..."

"No! The last thing we need is someone who wants to fight controlling the system. From what I can see, the Nexus Arms are all people that will use violence as a last resort. I believe they were created so we could find ways to defend this planet without killing or destroying anything."

"Wishful thinking I say... I can see I am not going to change your mind. You're just like everyone else here, not willing to fight and hoping for a miracle to save us."

"We will save ourselves, no miracles needed. I have many more people to talk to so I need to go now. Eddie, keep studying their machines and let your mind wander as you do it. Every time I have done that I remembered something important from a previous correction, like how to build the parts that generate a blocking field. I will contact you again soon," said Jack as he began traveling to another tower.

The next tower Jack decided to go to was located in a familiar place, Abbotsford, at the same location of the tower he destroyed. This settlement was different from the ones he had seen before. There were no large blocky buildings with hundreds of identical rooms, but individual single room buildings like the ones found in the woods outside the New Zealand settlement. The settlement stretched far off in the distance in every direction with the buildings very close together, occasionally broken up by small park like areas. There was no one at the tower, but there were a few strings floating idly near it, one of which he had already taken control of, so he moved to a nearby building that was marked as containing a food generator. He found it filled with people gathered around food slabs, and noticed a familiar face nearby. "Doc! Good to see you again!"

"Well it's about time you came back! Leaving us here alone without telling us where you were going or when you would be back! What if something broke? We have no way of fixing it!" said Doc sternly.

"I think you have me confused with the Lights Doc. It's me, Jack, we met in Vancouver."

"Jack? How are you controlling that string? Are you in this settlement somewhere? What happened to you and the others after you left? Where are the Lights?"

"Slow down Doc, I'll explain everything. Does anyone else here have threads? I would like to pass on what I know to as many people as possible."

"Yes, these three here with me have them. What's going on?"

"This will take a little while," said Jack as he began retelling everything that had happened to him since he last saw Doc. He wondered how he was going to have enough time to tell every one of the thousands of Nexus Arms about what had happened. Even if he cut back to a quick five minute recap of everything it was going to take him months to tell everyone. But he didn't want to ask people to start relaying his message in order to avoid any misinterpretations from being passed on.

"Well that certainly makes a lot of things that have happened in my life make a lot more sense," said Doc.

"You've had memories of things that haven't happened yet too?"

"Yes, that would explain it. I thought I must have been having some sort of memory problems after the events happened. For years I have been worrying that my mind was starting to go."

"Quite the opposite, if you are a Nexus Arm your mind is one of the strongest around."

"You have no idea how relieved this makes me. The last couple year I was thinking of giving up being a doctor for fear of hurting one of my patients, thank you for this news."

"I'm glad you now know there's nothing wrong. I hate to drop all this news on you then leave, but there are thousands more Nexus Arms I need to talk to, so I have to go."

"Before you go Jack, do you know the fates of anyone else you met in Vancouver? I haven't had any contact with any of them since I was brought here."

"I've tracked down a few of them. You may be interested to know that almost everyone who was in the park is a Nexus Arm."

"Very interesting, I am guessing that our ability to remember important events is what allowed us to avoid being captured for so long."

"Most likely, yes... I am sensing a Light approaching the building."

"Is it friendly? Are we in any danger?"

"All the Lights left on Earth right now are friendly to Alpha One, so we are safe. Let's go outside and meet it."

Exiting the building they could see a small Light, about half the size of Alpha One, approaching. "Greetings, I have been sent here to build your people a new communications pedestal, but I believe you already know that. Hello Jack, we have not met yet, I am..." said the Light followed by a series of colored symbols and shapes.

"It is good to meet you. I have been travelling to each tower to let everyone know what is happening. No point in waiting until every pedestal is done, since this will take a long time."

"Ah, I understand, but you do not need to communicate with each settlement individually. With the pedestals you will be able to communicate with them all at the same time."

"Well that's a relief. I wasn't looking forward to retelling everything thousands of times. How long will it take to finish all the pedestals?"

"We will be finished in three more hours, and the replacement settlement will be finished in five more hours."

"I guess I will just visit a few more where I know the Nexus Arms since there is no need to rush. Thanks for letting me know about the pedestals. I will talk to you again later Doc."

"Take care Jack. I know if I were in your shoes I would feel a little overwhelmed," said Doc.

"Thanks Doc," said Jack as he left for another tower. He spent the next couple hours visiting the towers where Valerie, Jill, George, and Jake were sent. He asked each of them if they knew what happened to the soldiers who stayed at the hotel to fight, but no one had heard from them. When Jack checked the Lights map he could find no sign of them. The last thing anyone remembered before waking up in the settlements was the hotel collapsing.

Jack was becoming tired of retelling the events over and over, so he returned to his tower. He saw the new settlement was at least half finished, with the larger buildings being the locations of the new food generation machines. He was also happily surprised to discover the new dwellings were being built with what looked more like a toilet instead of a hole in a bench, along with the shower in a separate room without windows. As he moved through the new settlement checking each building, he noticed his friends at the end of the beach standing near the top of the rubble pile he created, so he traveled over to them. "Hi guys, what are you doing all the way over here?"

"Feeling damn useless, that's what," said Fred.

"There just isn't anything for us to do right now while the strings build the new settlement," said Bob.

"We can't even use the old pedestal because they are doing something to hook it into the new settlement," said Walter.

"What have you been up to? Out having fun exploring their other settlements?" asked Fred sarcastically.

"All I can say about their settlements is that their idea of creativity seems to be to change the spacing and placement of the rooms and buildings and that's about it. They all look the same, dull, grey, and lifeless. I thought talking to the people at the settlements would be more invigorating, but the main result seemed to be a lot more worried people wondering how they are supposed to be able to help me rebuild everything. On top of all that, retelling the events of the past few days has made me feel like I am just a recording put on permanent repeat."

"Good to see you're having as much fun as us," said Fred.

"I suspect that soon we will all be wishing for nothing to do. Once the rebuilding starts everyone is going to have to try to start up their lives again."

"What use are any of us going to be with all the Lights technology being able to provide us with food, shelter, and healing injuries?" asked Fred.

"Yeah, and there won't be anything for entertainment since that's all been destroyed," said Bob.

"More importantly, what about learning? There are no longer any schools or the things needed for them to operate," said Walter.

"I know there are still a lot of problems to overcome, but over time our way of life will slowly be restored, minus the governments and military."

"So you and the others who can use the machines just going to control the planet without any say from us?" asked Fred.

"That's just isn't right," said Bob.

"No, of course not. You don't need to worry about any of us trying to control your lives. My purpose is to reconfigure the Lights systems to protect this planet from them and anyone else that would harm us, and to help design new machines to rebuild everything. The Nexus Arms purpose is to help with the rebuild, learn how to use the Lights systems, and pass on that knowledge to everyone else."

"Most people like power, so what happens when someone decides they should have more power and they decide to become some sort of supreme leader and make up a new country, maybe even forcing people to do what they want?" asked Fred.

"The strings won't allow that kind of behavior. Remember when Walter was attacked by Bill and those strings dragged him back to his room? Those are fairly simple strings that do one thing: stop people from hurting each other. When they sense someone is hurting another person, they drag the violent person away and hold them until they calm down. If someone keeps up the behavior then a warning is passed throughout the systems on the planet so someone can be sent to look into why the person is being violent. If people want to peacefully make up a new country, then nothing will stop them, but they won't be allowed to create weapons, or a military, or force people to stay or leave. Our lives will be a lot different with all these machines providing everything for us. Human will no longer be able to control each other by withholding basic needs, or threatening to take away something. I know there will be quite a few who will try, but it won't take long for everyone to see it won't work. A lot of people will be bored or feel useless at first, since they have become used to working for others in order to survive. But we will all eventually find our places in the rebuilt world."

"But what's going to happen when you get tired of taking care of all these systems? Are you really going to want to spend the rest of time hooked up to them?" asked Fred.

"In time I won't be needed... as more and more people learn how to use these systems. I'm not sure what I will do though. Being stuck for eternity in this system, while the rest of the human race eventually moves out and explores the galaxy, is not something I look forward to. But with my body gone I have no way of going back to my old life. I really have no idea what I am going to end up doing."

"I have been thinking, and if you and the Lights are right about us being stuck reliving our lives, what's going to happen when we all start over and your old brain has no mind to connect to it? Isn't that going to screw up everything we are doing here now? If you aren't connected to your brain, how can it do what you are supposed to do? Will it even be you anymore without your mind?" asked Fred sounding worried.

"I'm not sure. It definitely wouldn't foresee the various events that are going to happen, and since our personalities come from our minds I have no idea if it would make the same choices I did in life. I'll have to talk to Alpha One about this again. He might be able to figure out what is going to happen. Maybe one of the Nexus Arms has the ability to take my place... This is the first time you've willingly talk about reliving our lives, and without us bringing it up. What's changed?"

"I don't want to believe it, but when you said Bob and I are these Nexus Arm things we started talking about it and he told me about some things he remembered long before they happened."

"And that convinced you it might be real?"

"No... I've had... I have memories like that too damn it! I don't want it to be real! I don't want to have to live through that, that..." said Fred.

"That's ok Fred I understand what you are trying to say. We don't have to talk about it anymore."

"Thanks buddy. Maybe sometime later I'll be ok to talk. I need to think about something else instead... What are we going to do after the Lights leave. We may have more freedom in this new settlement, but that will probably mean more restlessness too, so we can expect the same once we start rebuilding and people move out of the settlements."

They spent the next few hours discussing how they could keep everyone from getting restless during the rebuild. They soon realized that if the rebuild was going to work that Jack and the Nexus Arms could not be making the decisions for how ten billion people would be living their lives. But they had no way to get everyone's opinion on how to rebuild, or any idea of how they would resolve conflicting opinions when they arose. Jack decided that after the new pedestals were completed, letting him inform the Nexus Arms what was happening, the first thing they would need to do is find a solution to these problems before proceeding.

After talking for a while longer, they noticed most of the dwellings were finished at the new settlement, so people had begun choosing buildings to live in. There were a few scuffles when two groups wanted the same dwellings near the beach, but the strings held them apart until they calmed down enough to discuss who would get it. For the most part everyone was calm, simply wanting to have some place to lie down for a while. As they wandered through the pathways in the settlement, they noticed that there were thin stone shutters and doors on the dwellings, allowing people more privacy. There were also no longer single slabs with a cushioned surface as the only place to rest or sleep, but in their place a thin moveable slab on legs with a cushioned surface.

"Looks like they are finally trying to make us more comfortable," said Bob.

"About damn time," said Fred as they approached the new pedestal.

"This must be it. Not too much different from the other one, except for the multiple glass slabs in the surface," said Walter.

"I can see Alpha One and two other Lights coming back," said Jack.

"It must be wonderful having the ability to sense so much with those strings" sighed Walter as the Lights arrived.

"Yes and no. Imagine being in an overcrowded and noisy shopping mall for the rest of your life."

"You can control what you sense through the strings Jack. I will leave that to you to figure out though, as we need to be leaving," said Alpha One as he arrived.

"But I haven't even had a chance to finish studying all your machines let alone start designing ones to rebuild our cities! I thought you were going to help," said Jack anxiously.

"No, this is something you and your people are destined to do on your own. It will be further proof you do not need us to interfere with your existence any longer."

"But I... we don't even know where to start?"

"You already have started. I can see ideas rushing around all of your minds. Once you have the help of the Nexus Arms you will feel must less overwhelmed. They have been told you will contact them soon now that all the pedestals are all finished. You will have no difficulty using the new pedestal since it works the same way as the others. The main difference being that we have included holographic interfaces that will automatically configure themselves for the person or mind using it."

"I really wish you would stay a bit longer."

"I know, but at some point the bird must be thrown from the tree to fly on its own. We will be back, but when, I cannot say. The journey to Core will take many months. Then there will be debates and discussions once we arrive. I am excited to see what your people can accomplish on your own in that time."

"This is strange. We've wanted you gone for so long, but now that you're leaving I'm feeling a little nervous and want you to stay."

"Having the freedom to choose your future and not having anyone else to blame for mistakes can do that to a mind. But I know that you and the others have strong minds that will allow you to make the correct decisions. We must leave now. We will see you all again soon. Before we leave, I would like you to keep this in mind Fred: You have always worked best with your friends help," said Alpha One as he and the other Light prepared to leave.

"What do you think he meant by that?" asked Fred.

"No idea," said Bob.

"I really thought he was going to stay and help for a little while," said Jack.

"Just think of this as another one of our rescue missions. Forget about everything except what needs to be done, and concentrate on finding a way to do it," said Fred.

"You're right! This is no time to feel lost! Let's get going!" said Jack as he took control of the new pedestal, commanding it to connect to the others. After a moment he sensed the other pedestals with the Nexus Arms near them. "Hello everyone, my name is Jack Campbell. I have many things to tell you about what has happened to our planet, much of it you may find hard to believe. But I can assure you everything I am about to say is true. We have a long road ahead in rebuilding our world, and I will need help from all of you. But once we are finished it will be a far safer and more peaceful place than any of us could have imagined."

Jack continued once again to retell his story. Something he hoped he would never have to do again, but realized he would be retelling it to countless numbers of people throughout the eternity of his existence. His mind switched to a kind of auto play, part of it continuing the story without thinking about what he was saying, another drifting to the memory of Brentwood as he realized how much he missed the smell of a barbeque.

www.ingramcontent.com/pod-product-compliance
Lightning Source LLC
Chambersburg PA
CBHW060908250626
47159CB00008B/2920